THE BILLION DOLLAR CATCH

Also by John J. McNamara, Jr.

WHITE SAILS, BLACK CLOUDS
THE MONEY MAKER

THE BILLION DOLLAR CATCH

John J.
McNamara, Jr.

DODD, MEAD & COMPANY
NEW YORK

1 2 3 4 5 6 7 8 9 10

Library of Congress Cataloging-in-Publication Data

*McNamara, John J.
The billion dollar catch.*

I. Title.
PS3563.C3882B5   1987   813'.54   86–29112
ISBN 0-396-08938-0

With love
For Lisa, Emily, Sarah and Joan
And admiration
For those who work to defeat
chemical addiction

Part One

Villa Barerra, Nahant, Massachusetts

Giovanni Barerra was a cautious man, so cautious he conducted his business in his sauna. This snug, wood-lined room was located off the glassed atrium of Villa Barerra, a stone mansion set on a lonely cliff in Nahant, a peninsular town on Massachusetts Bay.

Giovanni Barerra was an old man, seventy-eight years old. He had attained his years by being cautious, for over those years, many law-enforcement agencies had evinced continuing interest in the affairs of Barerra, all without success. The investigating officers and, from time to time, the press, would refer with some familiarity to the old man as "Father Joe." This familiarity by reference was about as close as they ever came to an actual knowledge of the man and his many interests. In search of something provable, there had been many attempts to tap the phones or plant transmitters within Villa Barerra—all unsuccessful. Barerra put nothing in writing, discussed nothing beyond meeting arrangements on the phone, and always chose a site he controlled for his meetings.

Now, in the recent years of advanced micro-transmitters, Barerra had taken to his sauna and had further gone to the trouble of having installed a "white-sound" sonic wash and a sheet-lead lining within the insulation of the sauna. If a visitor were to wear a "wire," it would have to be internal if it were to remain concealed, and even then, it would not have worked. And to assure his privacy further, while the naked visitor was with Barerra in his sauna, household routine called for a thorough search of the visitor's clothing and luggage by the ubiquitous housemen in close attendance. Giovanni Barerra was indeed a cautious man.

On this bitter January morning, Barerra sat in his atrium while his sauna warmed. Near him, the steam from a heated pool rose in the great room and froze to an opaque sheet on the glass panes high overhead. A winter sun fell on these panes, giving a shadowless glare to the room. Barerra liked this light, for it helped his reading. In recent years, his eyes had dimmed, yet he still read avidly. On this morning, he was already through *The Boston Globe,* the *Boston Herald,* and *The New York Times,* and now neared the end of the *Providence Journal.* Barerra read all the daily papers of the areas in which he had interests, and as he had many diverse enterprises scattered all along the Atlantic seaboard, his reading was extensive.

Despite the rising steam, the old man huddled in a heavy cloth robe. He detested the cold New England winters. He was a Sicilian by birth and longed through the winters for the bone-warming heat of the summer sun. At a table close by him, a dark-haired girl attended her nails as the temperature controls by the sauna door gave a soft buzz.

"Ready, Mr. Barerra?" the girl asked in the slightest accent as she came over to the old man's chair.

"Ah yes, Gina," he replied, setting down his reading glasses, getting to his feet. As Barerra turned to the girl while she took off his robe, his bronzed face crinkled into a smile and happiness came into his eyes. They were dark brown eyes, deep set under heavy lids, separated in a narrow face by a long nose that once had been broken. These eyes now held the warmth of a benign uncle, but at other times, the girl had seen them take on the glint of the granite cliffs beyond the windows. They were knowing eyes that seemed to see through her, the girl felt.

Now naked, Barerra walked to the sauna door with certainty in his step, a man of middle height, his body spare, still muscled, with few wattles of age. "I am expecting a guest quite soon, Gina," he said and entered the hot wooden room.

A short time later, the wooden door again clicked open and a middle-aged bear of a man, corpulent beneath a thick mat of black body hair, stepped naked into the close space. Without rising, Barerra extended a welcoming hand, his manner somewhat princely. "Ah,

4

Anthony, you've made it. Good. Welcome—please have a seat," he said, pointing to the slatted bench opposite his.

"Mr. Barerra, good morning," the visitor said somewhat gravely.

"And how was the flight from Miami?"

"Bumpy as hell—half the cabin pukin'—we rode the edge of a front most of the way. Couldn't get above it." The tone was gruff, unpolished.

"I am sorry, Anthony," the old man said solicitously. "And how is your uncle?"

"So, so. The heart and now emphysema. He sends his respects."

"As do I. Please tell him so. For years, I warned him of his weight and those wretched caparillos."

"He hasn't listened. He still tends to business—but he's slipping. Not like you, Mr. Barerra."

"Ah well, he's had his eighty years. Now, why have you come, and at such a miserable time of the year?"

"You know of the committee meeting last week in the Bahamas off Lucaya?"

"Of course. I was invited. I did not think it wise to go. So many, so much power, all in one place."

"It was something. You've never seen so many jets and yachts." Anthony chuckled.

"That's my point. Too much potential for trouble, too many eggs in one basket, if you will."

"Anyway, it went off O.K. Far as I know, finally they agreed on somethin'. They want to try somethin' new on a national level—organize the white stuff and grass on a national basis—orderly, organized, controlled. We take the business right out from under the blacks, the Miami Cubans, even some of Castro's guys. We do it once and for all."

"So, now national narcotics." The old man sighed. "There will be blood."

"You mentioned eggs, Mr. B. Ya gotta break eggs to make omelettes. There'll always be breakage in our business."

"Ah, Anthony, when will we learn? Most of the people have little tolerance for narcotics. There's too much lasting harm. Our other things, numbers, casinos, small loans, women, they will look the other way—they enjoy them."

"With respect, Mr. Barerra, you should have come to Lucaya. They would have listened to you."

5

"Perhaps . . . I didn't know this was coming up. But they should have remembered, there has been good reason we have always left this business with the blacks."

"Oh?"

"Narcotics was always a business for pimps and whores—people beyond the pale—scum. We let them have it. It kept the police busy and that was good. And it was small, too small. Too much hatred. Too much harm—not worth the risk. We always stayed with things people wanted, accepted—things that did them no lasting harm. Narcotics are different, Anthony, very different."

"Times change, Mr. Barerra. A lot of our people are already in it. We've got to keep up. The market says there's a hell of a lot of users. It's not small, not anymore."

"Perhaps not. I don't know." The old man shook his head. "I've stayed with what I do know: numbers, loans, parking lots, labor relations, real estate, some trucking. Narcotics—that is something I have avoided. I'm sure some of my people are in it. Side enterprises are to be expected in our thing, but, if I have people involved, I have not wanted to know. I suppose, Anthony, I should have seen this would come."

"What happened to numbers, Mr. Barerra, is a point for the new play. A lot of places in the country, the numbers are way off. These state lotteries have hurt. But somehow, your game seems to hold up, Mr. B."

"Yes, Anthony, it does." Barerra smiled a small, shrewd smile. "Greed—the greed of the Massachusetts politician. In their lottery, they take too much off the top. All the advertising, the people know that costs. They know if they play our game, they have the better chance. Quick pay, cash, no taxes. There are still the old loyalties." The old man shook his head. "It is ironic—we give the people a better play, but what is illegal for us is legal for the state. A strange world."

In the close sauna, Anthony now puffed heavily and poured sweat, his black mat soaked. "Mr. Barerra, you handle the heat better than me."

"Yes, I do it every day, all winter. Take a cold shower," the old man advised solicitously. "That will fix you up."

Anthony left the sauna to shower, giving Barerra time to think. Long ago, he had read the wisdom of Niccolo Machiavelli, a sixteenth-century political adviser of the Medicis. For Giovanni Barerra, there was good reason to his reading, for in many ways, he saw himself as a man with the responsibilities, privileges, and power of a Renaissance prince. His vision was by no means the delusion of an aged egomaniac. To the contrary, in the day-to-day operation of his organization, he made princely decisions and took princely actions. He had to, for in his principality of shadows, Barerra was the ultimate judge in a judicial system that gave short shrift to elaborate pleadings, a world where disputes, if not swiftly and firmly adjudicated, were settled with bullets and blood.

But there were also obligations that attended his power. The old man saw to the education and ongoing welfare of the families of the convicted and of the casualties that came from time to time within his "family." He could be hard, holding his army to a steely discipline, yet was fair in his promotion of lieutenants from within, and evenhanded in the division of booty. Above all, within his organization, Giovanni Barerra commanded and was accorded the respect due a prince.

Yet the old man did not live in an ivory tower of a remote castle. Through his own communication channels and from his daily reading, Barerra was well aware what an awesome industry narcotics had become. Despite his protestations to Anthony of things he did not want to see or know, he was well aware that some of his people were involved in narcotics with supply sources outside his organization. Until now, for reasons of his own, he had chosen to turn a blind eye on this involvement. Now, with Anthony's arrival, it would appear narcotics distribution within the Barerra organization could no longer be avoided.

When Anthony returned, he exclaimed, "Say, Mr. Barerra, that's some chick you've got out there. Surprised the shit outta me in the shower."

"Ah, so you've met Gina. Yes, she is quite lovely." That it be known nationally he still had women about would do no harm.

"Didn't say her name. Gave me a towel—offered to dry me." Anthony chuckled. "Wow! Does she talk, too?"

"Oh yes, she talks, mostly Italian. *Cara mia* Gina, young, a bit shy. She's here as a student. I have arranged osteopathic lessons in Boston. When she turns twenty, she will go back to Palermo with a dowry."

"Good for you, Mr. Barerra. I hope I do so good."

"You won't, unless you watch your weight, my friend. You must take care, constant daily care," Barerra advised, then switched back to business. "Now, on this new move, Anthony, why have you come to me? I am old. This is a young man's thing."

Taking his bench, Anthony looked squarely at the old man. "There was a lot of talk. There were objections, Mr. B., that I've gotta say. The young ones, they had all kinds of ideas, lots of talk. Finally, the old ones had their way. If they were to bankroll the play, it would be with you—only you. They have not forgotten the old days, the way you handled the booze. My uncle says you were the biggest bootlegger in the States." Never taking his eyes off the old man, he paused for a moment. "That—and trust. They all trust you, Mr. Barerra."

"Ah . . . trust." The old man seemed to savor the word for a time, but his thoughts were of countervailing forces, of greed, distrust, fear, and ambition, of maintaining the delicate balance of "muscled" lieutenants that uneasily supported his throne. Barerra knew he must adjust to the prevailing forces of his time or be toppled, crushed.

Were he not to go along with the times, Barerra knew, he might well foster his own palace revolt. Machiavelli had written as much, in 1513, in his advice to "The Prince." Barerra knew that advice still held, in the now of his own time. He also knew his power rested on hungry young gunmen, ruthless, ambitious, thoughtless, and greedy. Were he to block them any longer from such a promising business, and do so against the will of the national organization, he would soon lose power, if not be killed—that was a certainty. Barerra knew that long ago, he had sold his soul for the power he now had, that there was no buying it back. Being well read, he once had been amused by the words of Henry Kissinger: "Power is the ultimate aphrodisiac." The words came back to him now. And perhaps he is right, Barerra thought. If it truly is an aphrodisiac, I am an addict. The brown eyes drifted away, the narrow face fell long and somber, and then he sighed. He knew what he must say. "I do not like this business, Anthony. I tell you that now, and you are to repeat my words." He paused as his eyes swiveled back on the younger man. "But, yes—I will do it. I will do what has been decided. I have been in this far too long."

"Good. They said you would."

"Yes . . . Well, Anthony, and now to business. You know far more about drugs than I. How do you see it?"

8

"I see it in a couple of parts, Mr. Barerra. The white stuff and the grass—separate. The white stuff is where the real bucks are, but you gotta service the grass trade if you're goin' to own the market."

"You have much to tell me."

The corpulent Anthony sweltered worse than ever. "That will take some tellin', Mr. B. Any chance we can get outta this goddamn heat first?"

"Oh, forgive me, Anthony. I forget, I am so used to it. Of course. We shower and then we lunch."

Over a light meal of baked scrod and green salad, washed down with white wine, a luncheon attentively served by two housemen, Anthony continued. "Let's start with grass. The best is Jamaican, so I'm told. But when the government changed down there, the supply's not so good, not with any volume. What's comin' outta there is amateur stuff—sailboats—one-shotters. Now Colombia, that's the biggest, both product and volume. But their government's controlled by a couple of families and they're tight, too tight, with the Miami Cubans. They got Florida by the balls. To move on that, we'll need an edge. . . . My thought is we poke our government somehow, make it a big political thing. We poke 'em hard enough, they put the heat to the Florida waterfront. When things get screwed up bad enough, we go to the Colombian families, tell 'em there's a better way—our way or no way."

"So, in effect, you propose to use the U.S. government to hijack the business—and the Miami Cubans for bait."

"That's my first thought, Mr. Barerra. 'Course, I want you to know, it was made clear, very clear in Lucaya, we go the way you want to go."

"But I like your idea, Anthony. Go on."

"I think we got a much better handle on the northern docks. So, we leave the heat on down south, move the action north. Maybe Jersey, Brooklyn, Boston, you call it, we got a hand on it."

"No question about the docks. . . . Been so since I was a boy. Now, what about cocaine and heroin?"

"There's a couple of sides to that market, Mr. B. Coke, cocaine, that's the big seller now. But there's awful big bucks in heroin, too."

"Where do they come from?"

"The coke comes outta the Andes. Peru and Bolivia. It's dried

9

leaves then. They grind it into a paste. There are labs that specialize. Colombia's big on the labs. Argentina's growin'. These labs refine the paste, comes out cocaine hydrochloride, a white crystaly powder—kinda reminds you of that sugar for cakes." Anthony paused for a sip of wine. " 'Course, that's not what goes down on the street. You'd blow the customer's head off. It's gotta be cut—which is good for business, too."

"Of course, I read how the drug business has grown. Just how big has it become, Anthony?"

"Big, Mr. B.," he said reverently. "Just how big, no one has a hard handle, but it's big, Mr. B., the biggest business in America."

"Hmm." Barerra pondered and then asked, "What about weights, volumes? What can we move? How is it best packaged?"

"I've got people lookin' into that already. I'll be back when I've got it together. So anyway, on heroin, the same kind of refined product, different sources. Poppies. Turkey mostly, some Laos. The big labs were Beirut and Marseilles. When the Jews and our Marines got through with Beirut, that changed. Sicily, Palermo, that's the comer."

"My family came from Palermo," The old man said.

"That so, Mr. Barerra," Anthony replied politely. "Now, the way things are, the white stuff, most of that comes in by air. Small planes hop up to Mexico, then in low, over the border. Some amateurs have tried parachutes. Then there's the airline way. Customs has gotten pretty good at the airports. There's been all kinds of tries. Diplomats with their pouches. There's been idiots who stuffed condoms up their asses. The rubber pops, they're gonzo. Some of our New York guys tried the frames of cars from France. They made a movie about that, *The French Connection*. The problem with all that is it's too scattered on how it gets here, too small, there's no reliability of supply. For a business, we need volume. And it needs organization, too. Real bad."

"So, let me see. I am asked to see that it comes into America in a good organized way, in volume. Once in, what happens?"

" 'Course it's all up to you, Mr. Barerra. Maybe we go like the Japanese with their cars. Set up regional distributors, retailers, keep a piece of the play right down to the street."

"And who would do this street marketing?"

"That's not set, Mr. B. Again, it's up to you. I would guess it goes best on family lines. That's the usual, but, the first thing was to see if you would take it on. The details come later."

"Well, I've said that I would. And for now, I'll think about your family-line approach. But if I do go that way, it must be agreed, there will be peace. If a play of this size is to work, territories, markets, they must be respected. And later, if I see a safer, better way, something away from the family approach, if I want to change, then it is my say. When squabbles come, and they will, Anthony, it must be my say. . . . No divided command."

"That's why you were asked, Mr. Barerra. No one else could pull them together. Now, you want me to check around one more time, I will."

"Yes, I would like you to do that," the old man said. "My authority must be clear, absolutely clear—no misunderstandings."

"Will do, Mr. B. So, what's next?"

"Well, I need time to think this through—it is all so new to me." He paused for a time. "Well, perhaps not. It's really the same problem of getting by the government agents . . . a different commodity. My first thought is we go right back to where we were with booze, the way we used to do it, with a few changes. We keep each step in a separate box—independent—that was the way we did things in Sicily with the O.S.S. on a need-to-know basis—so if one part gets knocked over, the rest stands—there's no other way."

"Gee, Mr. B. Did you go into Sicily? With Patton?"

"Ahead of him." Barerra laughed. "And onto the mainland, too. And I learned quick, the Gestapo were good. That's why each step of our play stays separate. So, only I know the man in each box. But, Anthony, that brings another problem. We must consider my age. When you get old, Anthony, you learn to take the days one at a time. We must plan for when my day comes . . . and it will, Anthony, and I must think about that. In all events, Anthony, the man for each box will be a man of silence, that I assure you. They may not all be inside, we'll see about that."

"Makes sense to me, Mr. Barerra. So, where do you want me?"

"I think you should settle to one job and keep it that way. . . . You're still on the Atlantic City casinos?"

"Yes."

"I think you should give that over. Become less visible. We'll put you to the purchase of raw product. Yes, I think that will be best.

You tell me the who for payment and the where for product. While you're out buying, you ought to keep track of our competition. That would be helpful. We will work out some codes. I will see to the money and movement of what you buy."

"That's all?" Anthony asked, not hiding his disappointment.

"There will be plenty for you to do, Anthony. Yours will be the major responsibility. Without the commodity, we are nowhere. Yes, I know you will do it well."

While the housemen served sherbert, one of Barerra's few indulgences, the old man reviewed their conversation. "So, Anthony, you go back and be certain that all is agreed on authority. If there are any questions, any problems, you come back immediately, in person. Nothing by phone, only what plane you're on. No more. Like today, we will meet you. Now, if there are no problems, then get on with the supply answers we need. I will expect you back here within the month. I will see to the other pieces of the puzzle."

Villa Barerra, Nahant, Massachusetts

Several mornings later, the second day of a nor'east storm, a bleak, cold day, a whining wind threw white spume onto the causeway of Nahant as a panel truck drove across to the island village. The truck's lower panels were rusted, its signs badly faded. GLOUCESTER MARINE ELECTRONICS, they read.

The truck pulled to a halt before the wrought-iron gates of an estate that sat alone on the south cliff. A granite gatepost bore a small bronze plaque. VILLA BARERRA. After three bleeps on his horn, the truck driver watched the roving television cameras unobtrusively fitted into the coppered ornamentations of the stone villa's chimneys. The center camera swiveled to a stop on the gate. In another moment, there came from the gatepost speaker a polite "Who's calling, please?"

You know goddamn well who's calling, the driver muttered to himself, mildly annoyed, yet knowing the villa staff had a routine, and knowing also that routine varied for no one. "Mike Flaherty, Guido," he shouted.

From the gatepost, "Ah yes, Mr. Michael. You are expected."

Silently, the heavy gates slid open. As he drove through, Flaherty took in the wide shrubless lawns. Their pastoral innocence hid a sensor system so sensitive, it was often set off by sea gulls sheltering down from a winter storm. Nothing, be it by land or sea, could approach within one hundred yards of Villa Barerra with the inhabitants unknowing. Flaherty should know. He had designed and supervised installation of the system.

Climbing out of the panel truck into the icy wind, Flaherty quickly stuffed the keys in his pullover, took test equipment and tools from the back, and hustled up the broad steps. The heavy wooden door was opened by a small swarthy man neatly uniformed in the black pants, black tie, and tan jacket of a houseman. "Good morning, Mr. Michael," the man greeted cheerily.

"Good morning, Guido," Flaherty replied as he strode into the foyer and set down his equipment. He saw Guido's near clone alertly standing on the stairs at the far end of the long hall. At that moment, the foyer filled with a shrill siren screech. Instantly, the clone's hand disappeared into his jacket, while Guido turned off the alarm, then firmly pressed Flaherty against the wall. As the houseman deftly fished Flaherty in a full body search, he asked gravely, "With respect, Mr. Michael, when will you ever learn?"

"Just seeing if you guys were on the ball," Flaherty laughed, for he had also overseen the installation of metal detectors buried in the walls whose sensitivity would have brought an airport passenger checkpoint to a standstill.

Guido dropped Flaherty's nail clippers and truck keys on to the foyer table and stepped into the hall. The irony in his "Thank you, Mr. Michael" amused Flaherty that much more. "Now, shall we start in the basement?" Guido went on.

Flaherty agreed with a nod as he hefted his gear. He was by now well used to the odd ways of this villa, these abrupt and random calls. Most often, he was called for electronic sweeps, to check the mansion for "bugs." Sometimes a glitch arose in the exterior systems, most often in ice storms. Whatever the cause, Flaherty was the only technician entrusted with the task of maintenance, as he was married to Barerra's only grandchild.

"After your tests, he wants to see you, Mr. Michael," Guido said as they went down the basement stairs.

"Mr. B. wants to see me?" Flaherty asked, a bit surprised, for beyond family occasions, he seldom saw the old man. Over the next hour, with the houseman in constant attendance, Flaherty tested the resistance of the telephone circuits, then put on a headset, plugged into his testing gear, and started to sweep the opulent rooms for hidden transmitters. This debugging process was a mind-numbing task, so mind numbing Flaherty could think of other things, and today, he thought, as he often did, about the owner of the villa. For Flaherty, the mystique of Giovanni Barerra was a constant fascination. He perceived the man as something of a Boston folk hero, right up there with James Michael Curley, but more successful, for unlike Curley, who was elected as Boston's mayor while serving a federal prison term, no one had yet laid a glove on Giovanni Barerra. No matter what the papers printed about the man, no one had yet sent Barerra to the slammer.

Although Flaherty knew, of course, that Barerra's organization had to be the sum of muscle and fear, that there had to be blood behind all those bucks, it didn't concern him. It wasn't his worry. Besides, if Barerra was all that bad, he rationalized, why hadn't the guys who were paid to, put him away?

When all his tests proved negative, Flaherty took off his headphones.

"Clean?" Guido asked.

"Clean."

"Then, if you will follow me, please. You are expected out by the pool." The houseman led Flaherty through a library of leather-bound histories and classics, impressive in their ranks. Flaherty knew the books were not the window dressing of new wealth, that their owner, while self-educated, could quote many passages verbatim, readily reaching for his source. He also had a penchant for proverbs, a quote or a saying for almost any situation. For Mike Flaherty, Giovanni Barerra was an enigma, a man who seemed to run his affairs remotely yet, seemingly, very well. He gave the appearance of remoteness, yet stayed on top of the smallest details. His preoccupation with state-of-the-art security systems was but one indication of how sharp he was.

Flaherty's train of thought was broken when Guido opened the library door and guided him onto a patio and into the steamy heat of a Romanesque atrium. The columned expanse centered on a mosaic pool, its water an aquamarine crystal. In the pool, a leather-tanned man churned away laps at a sure, steady pace.

Knowing the regimen, but not knowing the swimmer's count on his daily 200 laps, Flaherty flopped down on a canvas lounge and looked about him. On the far side, bronze dolphins softly spewed rippling water over a rocky cascade that fell to the pool, while by the far corner, the pretty girl in a robe looked up from a magazine. Flaherty exchanged smiles with her, then went back to his thoughts. He found the aura of the atrium tranquil, so tranquil, he soon dozed off.

When the steady slosh of the swimmer ceased, Flaherty came awake to find Giovanni Barerra vigorously toweling himself, his girl in close attendance. "Ah, Michael, you are awake," Barerra said, his tone hearty and warm. "I am glad to see you. How are you?"

Flaherty sprang up to shake the old man's hand. "Very well, thank you, Gabbo. And you?"

"I cannot complain. Would you like a little vino as we talk?" Barerra smiled hospitably, indicating a carafe of wine chilling on a nearby table. "It's a chablis, quite good, I think."

"Why, thank you, I would. And some for you?" Flaherty asked as he started to pour.

"Yes, but small."

Flaherty poured the second glass, then went back to his lounge to watch the old man finish his toweling. Had Flaherty not attended the man's seventy-eighth birthday the month past, he would have put Barerra down as a man in his early sixties. For his years, he sure is in shape, Flaherty thought, knowing Barerra's body was the sum of decades of discipline and restraint, that his brain was even better conditioned.

"Have you done your check?" Barerra asked.

"Yes. The house is clean as a whistle, Gabbo."

"Good—then we'll go talk in the library. Gina, my robe," he ordered, then quickly slipped it on.

As the girl turned away with the towels, Barerra led Flaherty back to the library, where they sat before a warming fire. The old man took a slow sip of the golden wine. "Ah, that is good," he said and then asked, "And how is Rosalie?" His tone was friendly, but there was an appraising hardness in his dark brown eyes.

"She's just fine," Flaherty replied, hopeful of getting past family pleasantries as quickly as possible. Reminders of his wife were not his favorite thoughts. Theirs was an actively hostile marriage with constant shelling across a no-man's-land of a farm in Wenham— the farm, a wedding gift from Barerra.

Flaherty's only joy of that necessary marriage was two rambunctious young sons, Barerra's only great-grandchildren. While miscast as a husband, Michael Flaherty was a close and committed father. He frequently took his sons off to watch the Celtics, Bruins, or Red Sox. The boys attended private schools (with Barerra's financial assistance) where Flaherty was the parent in attendance at all teacher-review conferences. He never missed a home game of Mick's at St. John's Prep or of Patrick's at Shore Country Day. He loved his sons, and they adored him. His unhappiness centered on the boys' mother.

A divorce of the unhappy pair had never been discussed. Flaherty knew he couldn't just decide to divorce "Father Joe's" only grand-child and go to the courts as others might. There were too many blood and business ties between the two families. As with any domestic dispute, there were at least two extreme views and a middle ground. In Flaherty's view, Rosalie had a deservedly empty bed, having driven him from it with her constant carping. And on Rosalie's side, the cause of her carping was her awareness that Michael had for years been playing around with other women. Most likely, Barerra knew of their unhappiness, for his only child, Rosalie's mother, lived at the villa, but if he did, he chose never to discuss the estrangement. Flaherty answered further, "She's got the farm all buttoned up for the winter . . . expecting two foal, come spring. And the kids, they sure keep her busy."

"Ah, the kids, that is good," Barerra said, then lapsed into silence.

Contemplating his near-empty goblet, Flaherty wondered what was on the old man's mind. Would it be a lengthy lecture on the responsibilities within a family? If so, most often, the opening salvo was "One should wash one's dirty linen at home." Barerra attributed this wisdom to Napoleon Bonaparte, a Corsican, and thus of some respect for a Sicilian. In his own defense, the quick-witted Flaherty had assembled a more limited collection of sayings. For Barerra's granddaughter, his preference was Noël Coward's "Certain women should be struck regularly, like gongs." While often tempted, Flaherty had never voiced this thought to Barerra, nor put the words to action.

A movement by the library door caught Flaherty's eye, and in an instant, his thoughts raced back thirteen years to his first meeting with Giovanni Barerra. That summer, Flaherty returned from Vietnam to skipper a family trawler out of Gloucester. He was then twenty-seven, felt lucky to be alive, and was hell-bent to catch up on the living he had missed. At a weekend beach party, he first met the brown-eyed, voluptuous Rosalie. Theirs was lust at first sight. Soon, Rosalie was in Michael's Gloucester pad whenever he was not fishing. She was twenty-three and clerking for a real estate firm in Revere. In not many months, Rosalie rather embarrassedly announced her period was late.

Michael had to admit to himself he had become somewhat careless in his use of condoms, gave her a reassuring hug, and announced that if matters were not right on his return in another week, he would pay for the abortion. Thereafter, a rather teary Rosalie returned to Nahant as her lover went to sea.

A week later, Flaherty stood at the rail of his trawler supervising the stevedores as they off-loaded his catch, when a black limousine came down the dock. All work stopped as a liveried chauffeur got out and asked the workmen, "Where can I find Michael Flaherty?"

"Right here," Flaherty said.

"Mr. Barerra would like to see you," the chauffeur said politely, pointing to the limousine.

Knowing of Barerra, Michael walked down the gangplank with a certain hollowness in his stomach. His grandfather had often talked of the man, and more recently, Rosalie had mentioned her relationship. When Flaherty got into the limousine, he was first struck by the man's hard eyes, but his greeting was most affable. "Michael Flaherty, I've heard a lot about you," Barerra said.

"Yes, sir," Flaherty said, noting the firm handshake.

"Your grandfather and I were partners once."

"Yes, sir, he's mentioned it."

"And now my granddaughter—Rosalie has told me you like each other."

"She's quite a girl," Flaherty replied.

"Well, good." Barerra's tone turned flat. "I'm glad that's settled."

"What's settled?" Flaherty asked, perplexed.

"That a week from Saturday is a fine day for a wedding in Nahant," Barerra said.

"But Mr. Barerra," Flaherty protested. "I'm just back from Nam, just getting started. I'm not sure I can swing a wife and a bigger place."

"I'll help with that," Barerra said evenly. "And I'll see you in Nahant." And so was concluded Flaherty's first meeting with Giovanni Barerra.

Flaherty never had any doubt who engineered his marriage. It was the woman behind the library door, Rosalie's obese mother, Ginny. The widowed Ginny ran the domestic side of Villa Barerra but was seldom seen. Ginny also ran Rosalie's life, her constant coaching rendered in endless hours of telephone conversations, conversations so interminable, Flaherty had a second phone put in at the Wenham farm for his sons and himself. Flaherty knew his mother-in-law thought he was a no-good Irish bastard who knocked up her innocent daughter, a selfish, unfaithful ingrate. For his part, Flaherty had a comparable dislike of Ginny, often wondering if the old man's daughter's corrosion would eventually rust his relationship with Barerra. Beyond occasional lectures on family, there was no sign of Barerra's taking sides. And so, Flaherty waited and wondered where the old man was headed. What came next?

Finally, Barerra looked up from the fire, across at his visitor, and said, "You know, Michael, I have many business interests."

"I would guess, Gabbo. You don't run an operation like this on air." Flaherty laughed as he looked about his sumptuous surroundings.

"No, you don't," the old man replied soberly. "And also, Michael, there are matters we have never discussed, not even in family. You have never been involved in my affairs, beyond my need of your electronic skills."

"That's so, Gabbo. I do know, though, you've done a lot for Rosalie and for me and the kids—the gifts, the boat mortgages, the farm."

"Yes . . . What else can a prosperous old man do with his money. 'There are no pockets in shrouds,' Michael."

"Forget the shrouds, Gabbo. Looking at you, you could be out on the fast track, the wine-women circuit," Flaherty teased.

"Thank you, Michael. Perhaps I look as I do precisely because I am not out on your fast track," the old man said a bit dryly. "But to my point of this morning, I have come upon a particular problem that may well suit your talents. It is not legal, that you should understand from the beginning." As he paused, the old man still stared at Flaherty.

He certainly doesn't pull his punches, Flaherty thought, wondering with increasing interest where this conversation could be going. Flaherty worked hard at several jobs, the principal being the management of Flaherty Fisheries of Gloucester. In that endeavor, he was frustrated for several reasons. The ownership rested with his grandfather, an alcoholic octogenarian, and his widowed mother, a very cautious pair. Flaherty had ideas and plans for more modern boats, better gear, but with such cautious ownership, his hands were tied. Further to his frustration, Flaherty worked in an industry beset by economic forces beyond his control. There was little he could do about a marketplace where the brokers and shippers got such a big cut, a marketplace controlled by a few major buyers whose pricing made no allowance for soaring insurance and fuel costs. And matched against subsidized Canadian and Icelandic imports, it was difficult to meet the demands of the men who fished his boats. As a result, Mike Flaherty was bored and restless, he and his Flaherty Fisheries barely making ends meet. To have any loose money to play the smallest part of the fast track, Flaherty had to hustle hard. New sources of money were welcome words, words to be explored, especially when the words came from Giovanni Barerra and carried the potential of being inside a deal with the man himself. And so the younger man attempted to hide his excitement as he answered, "I understand, Gabbo."

"And further, it could be dangerous, but first, before we even get to my problem, I must have your word on one thing—that what we discuss will never go beyond the two of us."

As Michael opened his mouth to reply, Giovanni Barerra held up his hand, silencing him. "No, Michael, let me be clear with you, very clear, before you say anything. I have said that my need is illegal, that it may be dangerous, but, no matter what happens, you will never talk. No matter what, Michael. Your life will depend on your silence." The old man's eyes had narrowed to shards of glinting brown glass, shards of a sharpness that cut to the very soul of Michael Flaherty.

"I hear you, Gabbo. I understand. You have my word." It was a decision made quickly, a decision based simply on greed with no thought of consequence.

"Very well. You know your grandfather and I were partners, boot-legging back in the old days."

"Yes, he has told me," Flaherty said. "Sometimes, when he has a few extra pops, he talks about it. Guess he liked the action more than fishing."

"It had its moments." Barerra smiled. "Well, what I am interested in, I think, is somewhat similar to the old days—running contraband by Customs into the country. I don't know if I will go into the business yet, and so, I don't know what course I may take, if any. I do know that if I go, and if you go with me, and if we succeed, you will be an extremely wealthy young man."

"That's O.K. with me." Flaherty grinned as he spoke.

The old man took a long sip of his wine. "I want you to find a safe system for bringing narcotics into the country. Heroin, cocaine, marijuana. I want you to turn your entire attention to this project. Look for reliability—simplicity—the best way at the least risk."

Flaherty's first response was a long, low whistle. He anticipated the magnitude of the project, were Barerra to become involved. His ongoing thoughts were both swift and simple. If Barerra was to make the play, Flaherty wanted a part. He had no qualms about smuggling drugs, no consideration for the social consequences. The play held the promise of money and action, the kind of action Flaherty had not seen since his days with the Navy's SEALs in Nam. And further, there was the zest of a challenge by Giovanni Barerra. Yes, he wanted in very badly, but there were family considerations. "What about the business? Who runs Flaherty Fisheries?" he asked.

"I would see to that, Michael. I have some very capable people, bookkeeper types. They would do for awhile. As for you, Michael, I want your full-time attention. I would start you at two thousand a week. You will work for one of my real estate firms. Will that be enough?"

"Hey, Gabbo, that's more than enough." Flaherty laughed, but then the cold reality of Barerra's request, the responsibility of the assignment, struck home. Flaherty realized the system would have to be right and how little he knew of what he was asked. "Gabbo, I don't know my ass from first base on how this stuff gets in. Oh, I read about it here and there, the *Herald,* in the *National Fisherman,* where they grab a yacht or a fishing boat. I don't have any hard handle where the stuff comes from."

"And that's why I asked you. You come at the problem with an open mind. I don't want to know how it has been done. I want to know how it should be done."

"That's just fine, Gabbo, but you gotta start somewhere. Take grass. I'd guess it mostly moves out of the Carib. In Nam, some of the grass was home grown. The other stuff, the hard stuff, I'd guess it was scattered all over."

"With marijuana, that is so, Michael—at least for now. And I understand what you are saying about the hard stuff, that the product could come from many directions. Well, as a starting point, and for the sake of simplifying your problem, let's assume we concentrate the several sources in one place for shipment to America. I have nothing definite in mind, but I have thought about Sicily as a starter. I have friends there, good friends, so let's use Sicily as a shipping point. What I first need is a reliable system of entry. We'll start with that."

"Understood, Gabbo. Now, you want to come in by water? By air?"

"Whichever way works, Michael."

"When do you need answers?"

"When you have them, Michael," Barerra said.

Over the next three months, Flaherty combed the airports and waterfronts of the Northeast. It was a mission just like the old days, scouting a raid in Nam. When he was with the SEALs, the Navy's elite sea, air, and land commandos, Flaherty became an expert in several fields, deadly in hand to hand or with small arms, his specialty was underwater demolition by remote-controlled electronics. He had served his country well, invalided out with a shot-up left shoulder, a Navy Cross, and a short-term outlook. Flaherty lived for the here and now—tomorrow was not today.

And so, scouting holes in the federal Customs screen at the Atlantic entry ports fell readily in line with Flaherty's previous employment. He went at it with a will, his own way. Barerra had offered him discreet introductions in any port where he might hit a blank wall. Flaherty never took up the offer. He did the job his way, by himself.

Within three months, Flaherty made himself an expert on the drug-interception procedures of the Bureau of Customs, the Drug Enforcement Administration, and the United States Coast Guard. He also developed a profile of the Coast Guard's patrol patterns along the northeastern coast. When satisfied he had some answers, he returned in May to Villa Barerra and made his report.

After greetings and an offer of coffee, the old man quickly turned the conversation to business. "Well, Michael, what have you come up with?"

"Gabbo, what I've come up with—why it's so obvious, you're going to think I pissed away your money, that I'm crazy."

"I have never thought you crazy, Michael. If I did, you can be sure I would not have had you look into this."

"I've looked at the airports, I've looked at the docks—Philly, Newark, Brooklyn—all the way up to Gloucester. I think we should go marine. I think we should use what's already there. Why reinvent the wheel? You can't beat the present system for the handling of cargo—the shipping container. It's the best way, and all behind sealed doors—truck, to ship, to truck. The cranes are already on the docks. It's certainly the fastest way of handling any volume."

"Hmm." The old man pondered. "But where?"

"The New York and New Jersey docks are tough. Customs still have pretty active port patrols. They're still doing random strip and search. Now up here, right here in Boston, you could put a nuclear bomb across the docks, they'd never know."

"But you read of their dogs and you see all their people at the airports. Why, when I came back from Italy last fall, I remember how thoroughly they went through my things."

"Maybe they'd heard of Giovanni Barerra." Flaherty laughed. "Maybe they gave you an extra hard look, Gabbo. Immigration does keep big black books on people." Flaherty's gray eyes twinkled as he teased. "But as far as I can figure, it's all a big smoke screen. Reads good, the dogs, the uniforms, the big guys with the big pistols. Sure, it looks good. Makes people think old Uncle's really on the ball. But when you give it a hard look, it's all bullshit.

"Right here in Boston, they've taken the best of their patrol and enforcement people, trained specialists. What have they got 'em doing? They're collecting your declaration when you come out through Customs. Their best people doing clerk's work. Maybe it looks good, but as far as finding the shit, it's nowhere. Take their dogs. There's only one dog in this port—at the airport. Crazy, but true. And that dog's ten years old. They tell me the smell starts to go at seven."

"So how would you work it?"

"I worked up a theoretical—a container of baled marijuana, a forty-foot box." Flaherty's voice bounced along with his enthusiasm. "I made certain assumptions. I figure to get maybe ten or eleven tons of grass in that box."

"But what happens if they open it?"

"That's my point, they don't." Flaherty chortled.

"The Customs don't open these containers?" the old man asked, incredulous.

"Nope, not the way things are goin' down at the container terminal, not nowadays. It's all screwed up. The Feds have budgeted only a few hundred thou for enforcement in the whole port of Boston. They spend most of that at the airport. Now, the State Port Authority runs the container terminal. And you've read how screwed up they are. The longshoremen, they fit pretty good with the governor. One hand washes the other. The guv sees they get theirs. The longshoremen, through the State Authority, they tell the Feds they want almost four hundred bucks just to open the door of a box for a look-see by Customs. The guy with whiskers in Washington, he says screw off, too much. So—no boxes get opened."

"Unbelievable, if true." Barerra made no effort to hide his skepticism.

"It's true, Gabbo. So, here are my thoughts. One way or another, we get hold of a couple of going importers, guys in the business. Buy 'em out, set 'em up—whatever. That's up to you. If we buy 'em, we make sure they're not on the Customs House shit list. The only boxes they ever open are importers that tried stiffin' old Uncle on the duty, phony declarations of value. Once the Feds got a hard-on for you, that's different, they do look, but even then, it's kind of random. If you got a reputation that's clean, they never look."

Flaherty stopped for some coffee. "So we get into importing—legitimate importing. You mentioned Italy, so I looked into what comes out of Italy, regular-like. Tomato paste, shoes, ski boots, wine—they ship a lot of Chianti. So we stuff the deep end of the box, the end away from the door. We put in there whatever we want, grass, white stuff. Now the door end, that gets filled right to the top with legit stuff, whatever the manifest says. Even if they ever get their act together down on the dock, say the Customs do open a box, they'll never go more than a foot or two into the cargo. Too much work on the restow. Too expensive and maybe a lot of heat from the insurance on any breakage or theft."

"Well, that kind of heat could certainly be arranged," Barerra interjected thoughtfully.

"Then there's the trucking companies that lift those boxes out of the terminal for delivery," Flaherty went on. "They'll scream bloody murder to Washington with any delay. The collector doesn't like pressure from Washington."

"And we could also help there," Barerra added. "But Michael, it seems so obvious, so simple."

"Well, that's what you asked for, Gabbo, and that's what you paid me for. The simplest is sometimes the best. Now, the one thing you really gotta watch is that Uncle thinks he's getting his. There's never any heat till Uncle thinks he's getting screwed. Customs by computer—everybody honest. So we get a good Customs House broker—one who really knows the paperwork. We play it the Feds' way. Pay ahead on the duty. No Mickey Mouse on what we declare. That way, the box gets cleared before it's even off the ship. And we make sure it gets empty that night—just in case. Then we fill it with whatever the manifest says, send it along to the customer."

Barerra looked into the fire for a long time before speaking softly. "Well, we'll try it. We'll start in Boston," he said, then added, "But Michael, I want you to give thought to fallbacks. Something will always go wrong. We need a second way, maybe a third, a fourth. Many options, just in case."

Flaherty Fisheries, Gloucester, Massachusetts

On a midweek afternoon the following October, Mike Flaherty drove his panel truck along the western edge of Gloucester Harbor. From afar, he saw the drawbridge over the cut into the Annisquam River had opened, for the spars of a small yawl slid across the roadway. As he slowed to a stop at the end of a long line of cars, he laughed to himself, thinking maybe somebody just doesn't want him to get to work today. The stop gave him the opportunity to look out over the great fishing harbor. His eyes first went to the Flaherty Fisheries sign on top of a sprawled cluster of buildings at the head of the inner harbor. They next swept the Neck, Ten Pound Island, the buoy by Norman's Woe of *Hesperus* fame, finally to fall on a 210 Class sloop hoisting sail in the far distance by the yacht club on Eastern Point. A good day for it, he thought, as he flicked on a weather radio in the dashboard and heard "A large ridge of high pressure will move over the New England region by tomorrow morning, clearing fog from the coastal waters, bringing with it a warming trend. For the next three days, we can expect a return to an Indian Summer pattern with cloudless skies, light on-shore winds, warm days and cold nights. . . ." Flaherty's attention came back to the truck when the road ahead cleared, and he moved along with the traffic.

Driving through the gates of his plant, Flaherty had a friendly wave for the old guard and, on parking in his slot, he took the steps to his second-floor office two at a clip. Mrs. Jessie Grassie sat at her desk by his door, sorting the mail. She had worked there for thirty years, a cheerful galleon of an Italian woman, married to a dour little Portuguese, a skipper of one of the Flaherty trawlers, a good fish finder. There were five younger Grassies of their marriage, now all grown, two of whom worked in the Flaherty fishmeal plant. Family tendrils twined all through the Flaherty enterprises. "Good afternoon, Mrs. Grassie," Flaherty boomed.

"Oh, Mr. Michael, good afternoon." The secretary struggled to her feet and waddled behind him into his office. "There's your mail, Mr. Michael," she said, setting envelopes into a long neat rank on his desk. "Now I'll get you some coffee," she added.

"Thank you," Flaherty said reflexively, standing by the window, looking down on his docks. There were three vessels berthed alongside. Up at the head of the dock, by the repair shop, the bluish glare of a welder repairing a trawl-board caught his eye, the old *Florence T. Flaherty,* named for his grandmother. Looking the vessel over, he thought she looked sound, a spruce seventy-five footer, well coated in the Flaherty fleet colors of dark green with cream trim. Maybe getting a little tired, mostly in the engine space, he mused. His eyes moved on to the middle vessel, an eighty-five footer, the *Kathleen M. Flaherty,* named for his mother. A dock worker was securing her cargo boom while a truck drove off down the dock. The truck's bulging tires indicated a full box of iced fish heading for the Gorton plant on the hill. By the south end of the dock, on the *Agnes T. Flaherty,* named for an aunt, a clanking cargo belt automatically spat a silver-pink stream of trash fish onto the meal plant conveyor. The fish-meal plant was a recent acquisition, purchased in June, right after Flaherty bought complete control from his family. Thereafter, the trawlers and their gear had undergone major overhauls. They now looked and worked far better than they had in many years. Satisfied with what he saw on his docks, Flaherty adjusted the window shades to the glare, then turned to his desk.

He had started in on the waiting rank of correspondence and production reports when Mrs. Grassie came in with his coffee. It did not take long to assure himself that the recent upturn for Flaherty Fisheries continued. Ground fish prices were moving up, his landed catch tonnage had climbed, thanks to new gear, and a letter from a reputable poultry producer offered a firm contract at a fair price for the unsold balance of the year's fish-meal production.

Later that afternoon, Mrs. Grassie again came into his office. "I have a telex, Mr. Michael—the new plywood prices at St. John," she said, setting the cable on his desk.

Flaherty made every effort to contain his excitement as he picked up the cable. Tonight would be the first trial of his second method of beating the U.S. Customs Service at their own game. His first method, containers of marijuana shipped right across the Boston docks in broad daylight, worked so well, Flaherty was now just a bit bored with the routine of it. He loved a challenge, and this night marked a new one. If it worked, the profits would be awesome.

As he read the cable, he said to himself that she must have made a good passage, half a day early on arrival. This newest Flaherty venture was the operation of two chartered vessels, small container ships. Flaherty would employ them on monthly round trips, trading plywood and other forest products of the Canadian Maritimes out of St. John, New Brunswick, across to the Mediterranean. The ships would return with varied cargos, mostly wine, beer, and olive oil. On its own, the venture looked marginally profitable. That didn't matter. What did matter was that the ships were a commercially plausible venture on an established trade route, an operation not likely to draw any governmental interest.

Flaherty got up from his desk, went to the outer office door, and threw the bolt. In turn, the bolt activated a small red light on Mrs.

Grassie's desk, telling her he wanted no calls or visitors. He then went to the pine paneling of the back wall in his office. In the lower far corner, he pushed a pine knot and then swiveled out a hinged section of paneling, revealing a small steel door, barely four feet high. He drew from his wallet two plastic cards, the latest in electronic keys, keys that he alone had encoded. On inserting the cards, the steel door silently slid aside. Flaherty next checked on the back side of the door, opening an unobtrusive lid under the manufacturer's plate. In a small window, there was a digital record of time and day of last opening. Satisfied his singular door had not been touched since he last had been there, Flaherty turned to other equipment in the windowless room.

It was fitted with a vast array of electronic communications and monitoring equipment—a compact assortment that would have drawn a whistle of envy from the communications officer on the Navy's latest frigate. The biggest furnishing in the room was a steel drafting table on which was taped a N.O.A.A. chart covering the Gulf of Maine from Cape Cod across to Nova Scotia's Cape Sable. Flaherty took up a *Coast and Geodetic Current Prediction* book and flipped to the day's date. Based on the predicted "Boston Max. Flood," he now had the number key to decode the plywood pricing cable. As he worked at decoding, Flaherty was interrupted by a buzz of the intercom on his own desk. He went out to his desk and pressed down the intercom. "I'm sorry Mr. Michael, it's your Aunt Agnes on oh-one. Said it was important."

That's always trouble, he thought. Aggie was married to Michael's Uncle Eddie, another of his trawler captains. "Hi Aunt Aggie," he said on picking up the phone.

"Michael, we've got problems," she said abruptly.

And that's not new to you, he thought, but he answered courteously, "Oh, what's up?"

"Eddie and I just came back from the doc."

"The booze or the ulcer?" Flaherty asked, feeling, knowing what was coming.

"The ulcer—he's pukin' blood. Doc wants him back in the hospital this afternoon. Looks like they operate this time."

"I'm sorry to hear it, Aunt Aggie. Tell him to take it easy. We need him back. Thank you for telling me. Bye."

He returned to his decoding and soon had the telex translated to three loran lines back-checked by a latitude and longitude position. He laid the position out on the N.O.A.A. chart. Right on the money, he mused.

The decoded location was in twenty-nine fathoms of water on the northern nose of Browns Bank—215 miles east of Gloucester. The location was in Canadian waters, clearly outside the Fishery Conservation Zone as claimed by the United States, a position where the Coast Guard could find little pretext for boarding. Flaherty had carefully chosen the site, a patch of bottom strewn with jagged boulders, a place notorious in the fishing trade for tearing up gear. The site was swept by the swift tidal currents of the Gulf of Maine and the Bay of Fundy beyond—a very lonely patch of the Atlantic.

Flaherty went back to his intercom. "Mrs. Grassie, want to ask your old man if he'll take the *Florence T.* out tomorrow? Eddie's out sick. The ulcers again. Oh, and have Jack check the fuel, food, and ice on the *Kathleen M.* Tell him we sail at nine."

On returning to the inner room, Flaherty went to a console of specialized electronic equipment. He flicked a series of switches, activating two radio direction finders with tape-deck memories for recording transmission bearings. The first of these direction-finder antennae was built into the Flaherty Fisheries sign on the roof in Gloucester. The second was perched high on a flagpole in a friendly shipyard in Boothbay, Maine. Both were set to scan, record, and take bearings on all communications between the U.S. Coast Guard base in Boston and their patrol vessels at sea. By telephonic signal, Flaherty could transfer the Boothbay recording onto a tape in Gloucester and with the two bearings, crossplot the positions of the Coast Guard vessels originating the transmissions. With this data, Flaherty soon created current locations and past track of the patrols by time and place of their transmissions. Mike Flaherty considered the government of the United States a worthy opponent in a business he perceived as a game, and so far, from what Barerra had deposited to his bank accounts in Zurich and Grand Cayman, it was an extremely profitable game. For Flaherty, the challenge and the money were of equal import.

The Trawler Kathleen M. Flaherty *At Sea*

That night, as he locked his Gloucester office, Mike Flaherty glanced at the digital clock on Mrs. Grassie's desk. 20:53, he noted, and then went down the back stairs that led onto the harborside dock. After carefully locking the building, he again picked up his sea bag and strode across the dock to the gangway of his trawler. The *Kathleen M. Flaherty* was bathed in the harsh glare of her mercury vapor deck lights. The rumble of her warming diesels reverberated off the building's brick walls and down along the dock.

By the upper end of the gangway, a fireplug of a curly-haired man stood waiting, a glowing butt cupped in his hand. The waiting smoker was Jake O'Brien, Michael's first cousin, son of Agnes V. and the ailing skipper, Eddie. Jake's responsibility within Flaherty Fisheries was the maintenance and repair of machinery, most particularly the diesels and hydraulic gear of the fishing vessels. Like Michael, his contemporary in years, he was a Navy veteran of Vietnam, with a solid expertise in diesels.

"Buttoned up?" Flaherty asked.

"Yup," Jake said.

"How's your old man?"

"Operation's in the mornin'. Looks like they gotta cut a foot or more out of his gut."

"Shit, that's tough."

"Yup."

"Let's go," Flaherty ordered brusquely as he stepped onto the gangway. "Single up to the forward spring, I'll back down on that. Get her head off." The skipper clomped on down to the trawler's deck and in turning forward to the wheelhouse, brushed past three crewmen walking aft toward Jake. Flaherty greeted the first with a friendly "Hi," for he was Jake's younger brother Billy. Flaherty acknowledged the other two men with a curt nod, for this was their first trip on a Flaherty vessel. They were older men, in their fifties, with dark weathered faces, wide shoulders, burly chests, and long arms that had hauled nets for a lifetime, taciturn fishermen from East Boston, delegates of Giovanni Barerra. Mike Flaherty gave no thought to their taciturnity. What he did care about was that they did their jobs well. Flaherty climbed the back ladder of the wheelhouse and went in.

The *Kathleen M. Flaherty* was clear of the dock as the bells of the town tolled nine. She sailed for the fisheries with a crew of five—too many, as far as Flaherty was concerned from a view of security, but a bare minimum from a view of fishing credibility in the unlikely event they were boarded by Coast Guard.

Flaherty helmed the trawler through the confined inner harbor at a very slow throttle. Once into the broader channel of the outer harbor, he kicked her ahead to three-quarter throttle, setting her bow for the bell buoy by the breakwater, checking his course in the sweeping green glow of the radar. The *Kathleen M. Flaherty* sailed into an eerie night, windless and heavily overcast, the low cloud softly underlit by the skyline glow of the fishing town. At first, Flaherty could make out the major landmarks of the outer harbor; on his starboard hand, the high battlements of Hammond Castle hovering over the Norman's Woe gong, and to port, the white tower of the Eastern Point Light.

The skipper sensed this visibility would not hold. "Thick-a-fog for sure outside," he muttered, happy with the thought.

The trawler's bluff bow plowed the black harbor waters to a tumbling cascade of phosphorescence and halfway across the outer harbor, nosed into the first wisps of fog. Her skipper's sea sense was right. In little time, the red-and-white warning flash of the Eastern Point Light was obscured by the thickening wisps. By the great granite breakwater at the harbor mouth, the trawler was enveloped by a slate wall of sea fog, the wall so thick, all Flaherty could see through the wheelhouse windows was the trawler's navigation lights softly refracted by the all-encompassing mist.

As his vessel cleared the breakwater, Flaherty flicked on the automatic foghorn and the stillness of the eerie night was pierced by its measured funereal moans. Meanwhile, Flaherty stared at the radar screen as he guided the trawler by the autopilot controls in his hand. The skipper had the radar reflection of the Gloucester sea buoy a shade off the starboard bow at a range of two hundred yards when Jake O'Brien stepped into the wheelhouse.

"Thick enough?" the skipper asked happily.

"Yup," his cousin agreed. "All squared away."

"Good," Flaherty grunted, watching the bright blip of the sea buoy close on the fifty-yard inner circle of the radar. He then put the trawler into a sweeping port turn, out to the east'ard. "Got that buoy along the starboard side?" he asked his cousin.

"Nope," O'Brien said, peering through the glass into the fleeting mist, seeing nothing.

Clang, clang, clang. Their bow wave had tilted the gong; close, very close aboard, yet they never saw the buoy.

When the vessel settled to her new course, the skipper locked in the autopilot and went over to the loran. The *Kathleen M. Flaherty* was outfitted with an impressive array of electronic positioning equipment that included two lorans and a system that gave satellite bearings, all on the leading edge of the navigator's art. Flaherty took a slip of paper from his wool shirt, glanced at it, then punched a series of numbers onto the loran read-out. He rechecked his entry, and when satisfied, set the loran in a mode that controlled the steering of the autopilot. The trawler would now cleave the blind night guided by an unerring electronic helmsman, plowing outbound on an electronic path, a path of safe navigation maintained by Coast Guard and provided to the navigating world by the taxpayers of the United States.

Barring electronic breakdown, the *Kathleen M. Flaherty* would cut a swath through the Atlantic to a trackless patch of ocean more than two hundred miles to sea from Gloucester. She would sail to his unmarked point with an accuracy of course and position of a hundred yards or less in error. Under the guidance of the loran, her electronic helmsman would adjust course for the several tidal currents she would cross on her outbound voyage and attentively

31

attend any set of sea or wind. Her human watch-standers had little to do beyond monitoring the radar screen for the avoidance of other vessels.

Flaherty next set the throttle to full ahead and the pitch of the big diesel soared to a whine. He watched the loran autopilot performance for a good five minutes and then went to the second loran. He back-checked their course made good on this loran and then queried the instrument as to speed over-the-bottom. "11 Knots," it read. *Right on the money,* he mumbled to himself and then spoke to his cousin. "O.K., Jake, you've got her. She's locked on and tracking. Course zero-eight-fiver true." He pointed to a bright blip now square astern on the radar screen. "That's the sea buoy. Hold a departure bearing on it, two-six-fiver, just as long as she comes up on the screen. I want to be sure we're trackin' right. At eleven knots, we got a twenty-hour run."

The quiet cousin acknowledged his instructions with a nod.

The skipper turned to a single-side-band radio, adjusted the channel settings, and then linked it to an automatic direction finder that had been modified to his purposes. When satisfied this equipment was functioning properly, he again spoke. "Now, for watches, why don't you guys do two on, six off. That gives everybody a good sack. You tell 'em what to watch on the engine settings. Unless something screws up, let me sleep through. I'm bushed," and he went down through the companionway to the skipper's quarters.

Late in the next afternoon, after ten hours of solid sleep and a big lunch, Mike Flaherty returned to the wheelhouse. He first saw the day's heat had somewhat thinned the all-encompassing fog, lifting their visibility to five hundred yards or more. *Must be running out ahead of that warm front—it's not clear yet, not out here, but that's O.K.,* Flaherty thought. He then nodded at his younger cousin, Billy O'Brien, who had the watch. "How's it going?" Flaherty asked.

"No problems, Mike," the younger man said cheerily. "Got a clear screen now." He nodded toward the radar. " 'Bout an hour ago, had one blip, twenty miles out to the south. I plotted her track long as we had her. She was headin' west, 'bout ten knots, best I could figure. Probably a fisherman goin' in from Georges."

Flaherty grunted, switched the radar up to the forty-mile range, and noted a clean sweep on all bearings. He then went to the stand-by loran, shifted to the interrogation mode, and read that they were within fifteen miles of the position set out in his decoded telex. With the push of a second button, the instrument estimated an arrival in an hour and twenty-one minutes. Flaherty then went to another electronic console that stood beside the radar and flicked on some switches. This instrument was a bottom-profiling sonar of Norwegian manufacture with a sensitivity that could readily detect the intervening presence of shoals of fish. Flaherty had expanded the capabilities of this instrument with modifications of his own design. He turned the instrument on well in advance of their estimated arrival, wanting assurance the sonar would be well warmed and ready when needed. He took the high helmsman's seat and watched as the passing bottom profile came into focus on the sonar's screen.

The monotony of the featureless bottom led Flaherty to other thoughts and he found himself musing on the original requirements of his grandfather-in-law, Giovanni Barerra. The old man had wanted a second fail-safe system for smuggling his white stuff. *Well, I've sure found him one,* Flaherty thought to himself with satisfaction. Not that there had been any problems with Flaherty's first proposal to move marijuana across the Boston docks. That proposal had been in operation for better than four months without a hitch, four boxes a week, ten tons per box, forty tons a week for unwitting importers who never saw the real consignment.

One facet of Flaherty's container-smuggling plan involved duplication of legitimate consignments by importers. Should a firm order two containers of tomato paste, they would get two containers of tomato paste, a few hours late. Over the interim, Barerra's people would remove the marijuana at a controlled warehouse and replace it with tomato paste bought on the open market. The Customs declarations and accompanying paperwork were always in good order when the container was delivered to the consignee.

Back in May, when Flaherty first proposed his second method of smuggling, it was Giovanni Barerra who decided to restrict the container method solely to the movement of marijuana. Barerra reasoned that were they to lose a marijuana cargo to Customs, it would be an affordable loss. He told Flaherty that using the big container method across the Port Authority docks in the white side of the trade put too much value at risk, a hundred million and more at one move, a sum Barerra was not willing to risk on the random whim of the U.S. Customs Service. And so Flaherty's second approach, one he perceived as far safer, without Customs involvement, was devised and set up solely for the smuggling of two tons a month of white narcotics.

That thought snapped Flaherty back from his musing. He hopped down from the high seat and went over to the single-side-band radio console. He took a tape from the recording unit that was connected to the integrated receiver and radio direction-bearing monitor and went over to the navigation table at the back of the wheelhouse.

Before leaving his office the previous night, Flaherty had gone through a similar operation. By plotting the bearings of Coast Guard cutters in radio communication with their Boston base, he had learned with certainty that there was only one patrol vessel off the New England coast that could pose any problem for the *Kathleen M. Flaherty.* That vessel was one of the "Cape Class" cutters, a ninety-five footer. The taped record of her chatter indicated she had some National Fisheries inspectors on board. They were inspecting trawlers fishing the northern ridge of George's Bank, checking their compliance with net sizes and international quotas. That piece of intelligence set fine with Flaherty; the more boardings the better—keep 'em busy seventy miles or more sou'west of where he intended to trawl.

At the *Kathleen M. Flaherty's* navigation table, her skipper ran his tape through a special transcriber, noting time and bearings of the transmissions of the Coast Guard cutter *Cape Fairweather.* As he knew, with the taped data, where his own vessel had been at any moment of the past day, he was able to lay off a series of bearings on the chart from his known position to the transmitting cutter. A single bearing would only give Flaherty the direction of the cutter. But, as his own vessel's track from west to east had crossed the northern nose of George's Bank on an easterly course, with a series of bearings, Flaherty was able to triangulate tightly the location of the Coast Guard boardings. This afternoon's bearings placed the cutter on the nor'west shoulder of George's Bank, a full seventy-five miles from Flaherty's intended target. He went on with his calculations, planning for the unforseen. He concluded that were the cutter to break off her current operations, an unlikely event, and were she to run immediately to the northard at her full-service speed of twenty-one knots, Flaherty still had almost four hours to get done with his own work. When finished with his plotting, Flaherty happily put his dividers back in their rack.

In the last of the twilight, the fog again closed down on the trawler, limiting the visibility from the wheelhouse to less than a hundred yards. When the loran showed less than a mile remained to his target, Mike Flaherty took the trawler off autopilot and had Jake O'Brien take over the wheel. He rechecked his position with the second loran and the satellite-bearing system and found the three instruments came to a concurrence on position, differing by less than one hundred yards.

He went to the sonar and switched from stand-by to full-sweep mode. The sonar's transducer, mounted below the trawler's bottom plating, emitting and receiving the searching pings below, had also been modified by Flaherty. Not only was it capable of receiving workaday bottom- and fish-finding echos, but it was also capable of emitting command signals for other more specialized equipment.

"Put her in neutral, Jake," Flaherty ordered when the loran indicated they were on their intended position. He then opened the front cover of the sonar, reached in, and pushed one of two unobtrusive buttons fitted along the inside. He held the button down for ten seconds or more, filling the wheelhouse with the warbling shrill of an electronic signal. In another few moments, a bright blip started to paint on the sonar's profiler, a target-type blip on a port bow bearing less than a hundred yards ahead.

"We're almost on it. Kick her ahead, 'bout ninety yards," the skipper ordered his cousin.

A few moments later, the sonar placed the trawler directly over the bright blip on the bottom, an indicated 286 feet beneath the transducer. "Neutral, Jake. Let's see what it takes to hold right over her," the skipper said. He was hopeful of having timed their arrival to the time of slack water on Brown's Bank. Flaherty based his hope on the Current Prediction Tables, but it came as no great surprise to him to soon see the forces of nature were not heeding the predictions of the U.S. government. The steady drift of the blip on the sonar indicated the wallowing trawler was being slightly set to the sou'east by a still active ebbing current. "Give her a nudge. Bring her back on nor'west, then hold her, Jake. Dead slow," Flaherty said.

This new heading and speed adjustment soon negated the current's set and showed the trawler holding steady directly over the sonar's target. Flaherty opened the window on the back bulkhead of the wheelhouse and shouted down to his three other crewmen on the work deck, "Hey, you guys, spread out and keep your eyes open." As he spoke, he turned on the trawler's mercury vapor deck lights, flooding the ocean around the trawler in a silver circle of icy light for fifty yards or more. He then went back to the sonar and pushed the second hidden button. A second, higher-pitched warble filled the wheelhouse. With the end of the warble, the skipper spoke to his cousin. "Now neutral, Jake. I want the prop dead. Nothin' to foul. You look starboard." Flaherty went to the port wheelhouse window and lowered it.

Amongst the boulder and kelp strewn foothills of Brown's Bank, 286 feet under the trawler, Flaherty's first sonar signal had been received by an electronic monitoring unit attached to the casing of a small steel container. The signal had activated a submarine transponder that emitted an electronic pulse of its own, a pulse that painted the bright positioning blip on Flaherty's sonar, enabling him to position his trawler directly over the container on the bottom.

In devising this system for smuggling, Mike Flaherty had simply combined several uses of existing commercial equipment. The major users of such equipment were the airtraffic controllers. In keeping circling aircraft vertically separated, upon the signaled command from the controller on the ground, the transponder of the receiving aircraft automatically transmitted its altitude. This data would show up digitally on the controller's radar screen. The second commercial use of standard equipment that Flaherty had ingeniously diverted to his own ends were the submarine systems developed by the oil-exploration industry. In their need to hold a drill ship over an exploratory hole in very deep water, the drillers had modified the aircraft-type transponders to submarine use and therewith, positioned their rigs.

The marine-exploration industry had also developed submarine-signal means of remotely opening and closing valves on production piping along the bottom. Mike Flaherty had cleverly applied what existed to what he needed.

Once the trawler was directly over the submerged container, Flaherty's second, higher-pitched signal triggered a float release mechanism that automatically inflated and released a bright orange ball, a sturdy neoprene ball, three feet in diameter, that had sufficient buoyancy to drag 300 feet of three-eighths of an inch Kevlar line to the surface. This Kevlar was stronger than comparable steel cable.

"Got it," Jake O'Brien shouted excitedly, jumping back to the wheel. The bright orange ball bobbed in the halo of deck light, not thirty yards off the starboard bow. Jake gave the throttle a jab ahead and then eased back into neutral.

The skipper shouted down to his crew, "Starboard side, you guys." In another few moments, Billy O'Brien snared the bobbing ball with a long boat hook, and the two brawny fishermen brought in the trailing line hand over hand. Once they had brought up the line as taut as they could, one of them shouted, "That's-a-it, Mr. Mike."

"Good," Flaherty shouted. "Now, let's work the line aft to the A-frame. Get a clean lead up through the snatch block, then, some turns on the winch." Billy O'Brien quickly clambered up the large A-shaped crane on the stern and led the now slackened Kevlar line through a snatch block. Flaherty and Jake hustled out of the wheel-house down to the trawler's open stern ramp, directly under the A-frame.

The skipper took the dangling, slack Kevlar from the snatch block to the wide drum of a powerful Hathaway hydraulic winch. "Jake, you run it," he ordered. "I'll hold the turns. Let's get at it." While the winch reeled in the line, Billy O'Brien came back down on deck and moved a second set of controls for hydraulic rams that lowered the tall frame out over the stern. Moments later, the yellowish line came straight up from the sea some fifteen feet astern of the trawler.

"Here she comes," one of the fishermen shouted as a large gray shadow came into the lit water under the extended A-frame.

Flaherty also saw the shadow. "Easy now, Jake," he cautioned. His cousin immediately slowed the winch. A few seconds later, a square steel box came out of the sea, gray in color, about four feet by four feet in size. It hung under a web of stout pipes that housed and protected the Kevlar release reel and the positioning transponder. When his dripping catch dangled ten feet clear of the sea, Flaherty spoke sharply. "Way enough, Jake." As the winch stopped, he spoke to the second brother. "O.K., Billy, now swing her in over the hold."

The two fishermen dropped a ladder onto the deck of the fish hold below as the steel box was swung in and over the open hatch.

The brothers O'Brien reached up and checked the swaying container as Flaherty again spoke. "Good. Now, I'm going to give it to you slow and easy." He steadily paid off against the Kevlar turns on the winch drum, neatly dropping the steel container down through the fish hatch into a waiting sub-hold, a newly contrived false bottom. With the container secure, one of the fishermen cast loose the Kevlar line while the other swung down a section of deck plate and bolted it over the container. Billy O'Brien hand-coiled the last of the line while Flaherty watched the securing of the bolts.

Around the now closed maw of the sub-hold, where the fishermen worked at their bolting, stout wooden pens held back three or more feet of chopped ice. When the covering plate was secure, Flaherty spoke. "O.K., now pull away the pens, we'll button her up."

Using a tackle from the A-frame to the hydraulic winch, they pulled the pen boards up and clear, burying their catch under tons of ice. With the hold hatch cover again in place, Flaherty spoke to his crew. "Good job. . . . Now we run up on Brown's Bank, do a few sets . . . catch enough that we look O.K. Then in." Their entire operation, from positioning, through retrieval, to hatch replacement, had taken less than twenty minutes.

The Trawler Kathleen M. Flaherty *Inbound for Gloucester*

The *Kathleen M. Flaherty* plowed on through the clammy fog to the south'ard, toward the fishing grounds on Brown's Bank, while her crew rigged up her trawl boards and nets. By midnight, they made their first set and trawled through the night, prosaic fishermen working their trade. This voyage of the trawler was indeed a lucky one. Every few hours, they hauled back their great nets to find them bulging with ten thousand and more pounds of pollock and cod. Perhaps more than luck, their good fortune was in having a wide sector of Brown's Bank to themselves. They fished the entire second day without sighting another vessel.

For the trawler's skipper, the mounting catch posed a problem. Flaherty planned to make his landfall at Gloucester in the first hours of darkness just after nine on the third night of their voyage. He wanted the anonymity of night for their discharge of cargo in Gloucester, but because of the catch, he was slightly torn, for Flaherty was not a man to turn readily away from such a great run of fish. As their catch of pollock continued through the second afternoon, the skipper went back to his navigation table and recalculated his return voyage. With the catch now nearing fifty tons, the trawler's draft had deepened considerably, and that would slow their return. Flaherty figured they would be hard-pressed to make a good ten knots. If they were to have any reserve for breakdown or the unforeseen, the skipper's calculations indicated they should turn back at sunset. This would allow seven hours of the next night for unobserved discharge of their catch alongside the docks of Flaherty Fisheries. With the size of their catch, it would be tight, very tight, but possible, using two belt conveyors for lifting out the fish. And so, with the sunset, the fishermen made their last haulback and sailed for Gloucester, the steel container now buried under eight feet of iced fish.

Noon of their third day at sea found the deep-laden trawler eighty miles east of Gloucester, plodding homeward. It was crystal clear with bright sunlight and unlimited visibility. A nor'westerly front had come through in the night, lifting the last of the fog. Through the aft windows of the wheelhouse, her skipper steadily swept the horizon with powerful binoculars.

From his monitoring of transmissions and plotting of bearings, Mike Flaherty was aware the Coast Guard cutter *Cape Fairweather* would also be steaming for Boston that afternoon. His awareness had caused Flaherty little concern, for he had figured the cutter on a direct course from George's Bank to Boston would pass well over the horizon, to the south of his own vessel's Gloucester-bound track.

Around ten that morning, a blip came up on the thirty-mile radar range off the trawler's port quarter. Thereafter, Flaherty plotted the blip's track and learned the overtaking vessel was making good near on twenty knots, far too fast for a fisherman, on an arrow-straight course for the Boston approaches. And that didn't bother Flaherty one whit.

Over his next hour of radar tracking, Flaherty observed the blip had made a small alteration of course to starboard, and after a quick calculation, he figured that if both vessels held present course, they would converge within two hours. The trawler's skipper considered turning off to the north'ard, but then decided against it, reasoning such an odd course alteration might draw attention. The Coast Guardsmen were most certainly keeping their own radar plot. Of his several considerations, Flaherty was least concerned with discovery of his cargo in the event of a boarding. He was most concerned with the delay of a boarding, for he was well aware they had to discharge their cargo in the dark hours of the October night.

With the blip's course change, Mike Flaherty was a bit bothered, for the prudent side of his mind was not about to invite a Coast Guard boarding openly. On the other hand, with his confidence in the undetectability of his system, he somewhat looked forward to the challenge of an inspection. Therefore, he held his course. What would happen would happen. When the radar indicated the overtaking vessel was within the ten-mile circle, Flaherty went to the wheelhouse windows with his binoculars. Around 12:30, he spotted a thin white spar sprouting from the horizon astern. "It's the Coasties all right," he grunted to one of the Italian fishermen who had the bridge watch.

Within the next hour, the white cutter rapidly overtook the plodding trawler. As the range drew down to a half mile, Flaherty, through his binoculars, found himself in an eyeball-to-eyeball confrontation with a young officer on the bridge wing of the cutter. The officer soon left the wing, entered his bridge, and in a few moments, the VHF Channel 16 radio monitor in the trawler's wheelhouse crackled to life. "Coast Guard cutter *Cape Fairweather* to the *Kathleen M. Flaherty*—come back please." Flaherty returned the call, and after a change of channels was politely instructed to come to a stop, that the Coast Guard intended boarding for a safety check.

The fisherman on watch was far more anxious than Flaherty. "Those fuckers, they gotta little to do—musta have a quota—justa like traffic cops," he spouted.

"Relax, Gennaro, it'll be O.K.," Flaherty said, giving the man a reassuring smile as he drew back the throttle. When both vessels lay dead in the water two hundred yards apart, the cutter launched a large gray inflatable. Five men, wearing bright orange life jackets, climbed down over the side into their launch. As the inflatable motored across to the trawler, Flaherty went down onto the boat deck and threw over a Jacob's ladder. When the launch came alongside, one of her boarders threw a line up to Flaherty. With the bowline secured, a young ensign in crisp khakis and a bulky life jacket climbed clumsily upon the trawler. After a brisk handshake, the ensign spoke. "Well skipper, I guess we should start with your documentation papers."

"Got 'em up in the house," Flaherty replied in a tone of resigned tolerance.

"While we're doing that, could you have your men open your hatch?" the ensign went on, politely. "These gentlemen are with National Fisheries." He pointed at two serious young men with carefully barbered beards waiting in the inflatable. "They're monitoring the international quotas."

"O.K.," Flaherty grunted grudgingly, his face a mask of put-upon patience. He saw Jake O'Brien looking out from the crew quarters, obviously awakened by the cutback of the diesel. "Hey Jake, get Billy. Open up the hatch. These guy's want a look-see at our catch. Maybe we sell 'em some," he shouted with an air of cooperation.

Flaherty led the Coast Guard officer up to the wheelhouse. While the youngman took information off the vessel's document, Flaherty watched the two Fisheries inspectors spear some pollock and cod out of the hold and put them in a satchel, ostensibly for measurement. He also saw the other two Coast Guardsmen saunter forward to the crew's quarters with elaborate casualness. They were legally aboard the *Kathleen M. Flaherty* for a document check and a safety inspection of an American vessel in American waters, clearly within the Coast Guard's mandate from Congress. As to what they might find, once aboard, that was another matter. Mike Flaherty knew their game.

In the wheelhouse, the young officer worked along at a form on his clipboard with studied slowness. After the document inspection, he asked for a crew roster and slowly copied that list. Flaherty knew the officer was stalling for time so that his boarding crew could have a good look around the vessel. An unofficial look, of course, so that if any contraband were discovered, the apprehended could not raise the constitutional defense of unreasonable search and seizure. Thus, after the crew roster, the boarding officer next wanted to see and count the life jackets and then check the lifesaving gear.

At that point, Flaherty put aside his pretence of patience. "Hey look buddy, can ya hustle this up? We got to get those fish in and sell 'em sometime," he snapped. "Like tomorrow's auction, maybe."

41

The boarding officer studiously ignored Flaherty's mounting impatience. Unhurriedly, he checked the stitching of the life jackets, noting the number and manufacturer on his form. Finally, a petty officer came out of the crew quarters down on the fish deck and gave the inspecting officer a shake of his head. Flaherty caught the shake and was secretly amused to see how quickly the elaborate safety inspection came to an end. With a hasty shake of Flaherty's hand, the young Coast Guard officer expressed his thanks for the cooperation and waved his boarders back into their launch.

Flaherty accompanied them to the rail to cast loose their bowline. In going over the side, one of the Fisheries inspectors spoke admiringly. "Gee, Skipper, that's sure one hell of a catch you got."

"Yup," Flaherty agreed woodenly, dropping the line down into the launch. "And ya can keep what ya grabbed, no charge."

Flaherty went back to his wheelhouse and whacked the anxious fisherman hard on his back. "See, Gennaro, I told you it would go O.K." He chuckled. He then edged the throttle ahead and put the *Kathleen M. Flaherty* back on course for Gloucester. With the autopilot engaged, he turned to look out astern over the widening gap at the diverging cutter. Flaherty's hands were on his hips and his rugged face had broken into a broad, feisty grin. His world went well, very well indeed, he thought.

Part Two

The Osborne Apartment, Charlestown, Massachusetts

'Twas the night before Christmas in a third-floor walk-up on the east side of Charlestown, and also the third Christmas since Michael Flaherty first went smuggling on Brown's Bank. In the Charlestown apartment, the light of a television screen shimmered across the room, casting silver shadows on an oblivious occupant slumped in a reclining chair. The occupant was a middle-aged man, snoring heavily, completely at ease in a T-shirt, belt slack, shoes off. He was a big man, a six-two frame carrying two hundred and fifty pounds. Thirty years earlier, and forty pounds lighter, the man had been a stalwart guard on the Coast Guard Academy eleven, but for this night, he had done all his guarding, as a trace of bourbon in a large tumbler by his elbow would indicate. That, and the deep resonance of his snores, said a long sleep well underway.

A telephone rang on the nearby table, once, twice, five and six times. With the seventh ring, the sleeper shook himself awake, reflexively reached for the phone, but then paused. The man was wary of phone calls in the night. He had just been through a divorce from a hard-drinking wife, a twenty-two-year marriage that ended in flames. His former wife had a tendency to forget the divorce and when the spirit moved her, frequently picked up the phone, called him at his office, and hurled what molten lead she still had

45

at hand. To prevent these unwanted calls, the sleeper had not listed his number, and thus, he hesitated, wondering who could be calling.

The phone rings persisted, and on the eleventh, the man lifted the receiver. "Hello," he said somewhat groggily.

"Captain Osborne?" The caller's voice was raspy, like pebbles on a steep stone beach.

"Yes. Who's this?"

"That don't matter."

Osborne looked at his watch, then said angrily, "Oh yeah! Look pal, it's almost one o'clock. Now who in hell are you?"

"That don't matter. What does is you, you and your job with the Coasties."

"What about it?" Osborne asked, now fully awake.

"Tonight, at eleven, a grass deal goes down off P-town."

"Sure pal, and you're the sugar plum fairy, and this is my Christmas present. Right?" Osborne said sarcastically.

"Just listen, Cap. Then you can do whatever the fuck you want," the caller retorted.

An alarm bell went off in Osborne's head. Only the district duty desk had this phone number—and now this nut. So maybe he's not a nut. "O.K. I'm listening," Osborne said.

"Eleven tonight. Just inside the hook, Provincetown Harbor, a Panamanian freighter, *La Duquesa*—she's peddlin' four tons of grass to a Plymouth dragger, the *Louise and Ann.*" With a loud click, the line went dead.

U.S. Coast Guard Headquarters, Boston, Massachusetts

Otie Osborne liked to drink. Most often, he did it well, with a capacity and endurance now legendary in Coast Guard wardrooms. Osborne had been at his drinking so many years, his system so inured, he seldom paid a painful price for his indulgence. This

Christmas morning was different. As he shaved, he could not ignore his gaseous stomach, his ashen cheeks, or the quiver in his hands when he picked up the razor. "And you did it all by yourself, you asshole," he growled at his image in the mirror.

When finished with shaving, Osborne went to his fridge and took out a can of tomato juice. He half-filled a large glass, added some ice cubes, and topped off with a generous slug of vodka. After a dash of spice and the briefest stir, he downed his drink with a great gulp. *That should do it,* he said to himself, and he was partially right. The alcohol soon dulled, but by no means deadened, Osborne's hangover. His temples still throbbed, his eyelids were leaden. When sober, Captain Osborne knew he had a problem with alcohol. He chose to ignore it.

What you need, you asshole, is some air—a good long walk, he decided. Osborne dressed warmly for his walk, then went down and out of his building. His street was narrow, steeply sloped, and filled with three-story buildings. Most were of weather-beaten brick, with bay windows, typical of this old section north of Boston. Osborne turned up the hill to a wide square on the crest. The hill was capped with a great granite spike, a monument that marked a distant day and another climb, Britain's bloody climb, in the Battle of Bunker Hill.

This slate-gray morning, the crest of Bunker Hill was swept by a biting wind off Boston Harbor. As Captain Osborne walked the southern slope toward the connecting bridge and downtown Boston, he hunched into his hooded duffle coat and thought back to the call in the night.

He suspected the call was a joke, most probably by one of his classmates, but he was in no way certain. And so, he asked himself what he was going to do about the information. He could sit on it or send out a cutter to check it out. If he sent out a cutter and the call proved out a joke, he'd really look stupid. They'd call it Osborne's Christmas goose chase. On the other hand, if he sat on the call and it turned out for real and somehow, later, the brass learned he had the tip, they'd really hang his ass. With this for a quandary, Captain Osborne did not like his alternatives, not at all.

As the captain crossed the Boston bridge on this cold Christmas morning, his eye caught a white Coast Guard cutter tied up alongside an East Boston pier. It was his old girlfriend, the *Bibb.* He'd heard she was coming in. Also heard they might scrap her. Kind of sad to see the old *Bibb* go to razor blades, he thought. She was a good sea boat. Long buried memories returned with a rush. It was aboard the *Bibb* Osborne learned a painful lesson about government service.

Twenty-six years earlier, Osborne had served as a young lieutenant aboard *Bibb,* a cutter based in the Boston district. It was then that Osborne got himself caught in political coils by a circumstance far beyond his control. *Bibb* was coming in off a North Atlantic patrol when ordered to assist a Russian trawler with engine problems. The Russian had sought shelter in the lee of Martha's Vineyard in American territorial waters. *Bibb* was ordered to check the vessel and render what assistance she could. When she went alongside the trawler, a Russian seaman jumped ship and after a translator was found, asked for political asylum. Several days of radio bickering between *Bibb*, Boston, Washington, and Moscow then followed. Finally, the district commander ordered *Bibb*'s skipper to return the seaman to his trawler. The skipper protested but was overruled by direct order. He ordered the massive Osborne and several brawny bo'suns to force the defecting Russian back aboard his boat. They did as ordered, but then the Boston press got wind of what had happened. In the ensuing congressional investigation, Osborne got his ass singed. The district commander, an admiral, and his assistant were allowed to retire. Despite testimony that the *Bibb*'s skipper and Lieutenant Osborne did as directly ordered, letters of reprimand were placed in their files.

And therewith, Osborne's Coast Guard career went into partial eclipse. After the *Bibb* incident, his early ambition and youthful zeal came adrift. Osborne put in his time, did as ordered, and gave the least possible thought to any alternative actions that might take him outside the regulations. You play it by their book or they hang your ass, that Otie Osborne had learned the hard way.

In a service as small as Coast Guard, there are unofficial ways of dealing with injustice. Osborne's classmates knew he had gotten screwed. They had always considered him a good guy, a suitable officer. And so they loyally dragged him up the ladder of rank to captain's eagles, albeit slowly; as long as he put in his time, stayed out of trouble, and didn't mess up, his pension was there. Do as ordered and don't rock the boat. But what to do when the book doesn't cover a tipster phone call in the dead of night, a call that would cost the service both time and money to check out?

And it was with this background and outlook that Captain Osborne wondered what he should do as he walked the waterfront. His outlook had not changed for many months. It was the same as when he had first reported to the Boston district the September past, resigned to the Boston billet as the last rung of his ladder before retirement. Anticipating a short tour, Osborne rented a furnished flat in Charlestown, a short walk to Headquarters. Thereafter, Otie Osborne firmly established himself as a fixture of the wardroom bar, 16:45 hours onward to close. His postwork imbibing had in no way impacted the hale-fellow regard the other officers had for him. They all knew Otie had personal problems and made allowances, but were he now to send a cutter out on a Christmas Day goose chase, a voyage based on a midnight tip from an unknown source, the question of his drinking might come up officially, a possibility Osborne had to consider.

Not that Osborne was in disfavor and vulnerable, not at all. He had strong friends in high places. The commander of the First District, Rear Admiral Harry Haggerty, was an Academy classmate who had quarterbacked the Academy team on which Osborne had played a guard. They were school friends, old friends, good friends. Haggerty had represented Osborne at the congressional investigation of the Russian seaman incident. With Haggerty in command, and barring a major foul-up, Osborne was assured a smooth tour of duty to early retirement.

The thought of Haggerty brought Osborne back to the here and now of where he had walked, to Atlantic Avenue and Coast Guard Headquarters. Despite the holiday and his casual dress, Captain Osborne decided to go in.

The lieutenant on duty was indeed surprised to see a now pink-cheeked Captain Osborne come down the hall. He jumped to his feet and snapped off a smart salute despite the captain's civilian dress. "Good morning, sir," he said.

"Morning, Lieutenant," Osborne replied. "How long you been on?"

"Since midnight, sir."

"Oh. Did I get any calls?"

"No, sir. Not that I remember."

"Want to check the log to be sure? You might have been in the can or something."

"Yes, sir." The lieutenant checked the communications log sheet. "No, sir. There's been nothing. Everybody's come in for Christmas, the fishermen, our patrols, all the commercial traffic. It's been real dead, sir."

"And no one called, asking for my home phone?"

"No, sir."

"O.K. Say, could you pass over that *Lloyd's Register of Shipping* on the shelf behind you? Yeah, the red book right behind you. Good, thanks." Osborne quickly opened the *Register* to the Ls and soon found a *La Duquesa* that seemed to fit the bill. Roughly translating meters to feet in his head, Osborne saw she was a little ship, a three-hatch 150-foot motor ship registered out of Panama.

Osborne returned the book to the duty officer and went down the hall to his office. From a rack by his desk, he took out the *Coast Guard Register of American Shipping.* It listed a *Louise and Anne,* a seventy-five footer documented out of Plymouth, Massachusetts. Captain Osborne took off his duffle coat and dropped into his chair. *So,* he thought, *no one got my number from district, not last night at least. And the two boats are in the books. There just could be something to this. Maybe—just maybe.*

There were other factors coming to play on Osborne's thoughts. When he had been transferred up from Norfolk to the district intelligence billet in Boston, Osborne knew it was at best a horizontal move on a tranquil millway to early retirement. The prime operating responsibility of the new job was the coordination of coastal patrols for the interception of drugs in concert with other enforcement agencies.

In late summer, when Osborne had reported to the First District, the New England coast was a quiet backwater in the drug wars. Two years earlier, however, the President had turned the full force of the United States against the Caribbean drug trade. The President's resolve had been triggered by his anger when, on seeking the cooperation of several Central American governments in suppressing drug exportation, he had been told, off the record, to mind his own business. The President was not of a make-up to accept, readily, such "fuck-off" advice. Put bluntly, he was pissed—so pissed, he launched his own undeclared war.

In little time, the President received support from legislative quarters he least expected. Congressmen from certain of the seedier constituencies along the East Coast waterfront joined the undeclared war with drum-thumping vigor. While surprised at the source of this support, the President welcomed all the help he could lay hand to. He realized the drawbacks and international implications of a San Juan Hill, Great White Fleet, Marines-on-the-beach approach. Grenada had worked, but not wanting to push his luck, the President assigned the Vice President to head a special task force with orders to stop the Caribbean drug trade. Quietly, but promptly, the full military might of the United States was brought to bear, the sole restriction in their mandate was direct invasion of the exporting countries.

The Vice President promptly reassigned Drug Enforcement agents and Customs officers from all over the country to the Gulf Coast. By coordinating the data of Navy hydrophonic grids, Air Force radar trackings, NASA satellite photographs, and Coast Guard patrols, and after scattering a small army of agents along the waterfront and at remote airports, the special task force soon had the copious drug trade through the Straits of Florida staunched to a trickle.

The families that controlled the juntas that controlled the governments of Central America and their partners in the American drug smuggling industry soon felt the constriction. Being of a free enterprise mind-set, and having established extremely lucrative channels to an insatiable market, they decided to serve their trade by means other than the Straits of Florida. They ordered the vessels with cargos in their control out into the Atlantic for extended ocean voyages to the fog-bound bays of New England.

Several of these cargos had been intercepted in past months by Coast Guard or other narcotics agencies in the Northeast. *So just maybe there's something going on out there we don't know about,* Osborne now thought. *And on Christmas Day—not a bad play— just like the Japanese at Pearl. Hit America on a Sunday or holiday, you can't miss. So, let's take the shot.* With that decided, Osborne reached for his phone and dialed the duty desk.

"Lieutenant, Captain Osborne. Say, what have we got down Cape Cod way or out on the islands? The *Point Gammon*, New Bedford, huh. Good, and her status? Full readiness. And Commander Hollingsworth, is he the relief ops officer? Good. You got his home phone handy?"

U.S. Coast Guard Headquarters, Boston, Massachusetts

On Christmas night, the *Point Gammon*, a ninety-five-foot patrol craft, sailed from New Bedford through the Cape Cod Canal for Provincetown. Prior to sailing, her skipper was briefed by Captain Osborne on what he might expect. He was told to approach the indicated rendezvous at high speed, all lights out, his crew fully armed, to be prepared for any eventuality. While the information might prove out, it might not. The credibility of the source was unknown, but be ready, Osborne warned.

Late that night, Osborne returned to District Headquarters and was stunned to find the tipster's information had proven out. By radio-phone, he congratulated the elated skipper of the *Point Gammon* and learned they had nailed *La Duquesa* with several hundred pounds of baled marijuana still in her holds. The dragger *Louise and Anne* was lashed alongside, her decks laden with bales when the Coast Guard came on the scene. It was the biggest drug bust the First District had yet made.

Over the next five months, Osborne received an average of two tips per month, the source always the same, the information always accurate. And with that, Osborne's career came out from eclipse. The district commander, Admiral Haggerty, took Osborne with him to any and all functions, for he had become a celebrity in the drug-interception world. There was now talk in the district wardroom of Osborne's prospects for an Admiral's star.

Several times, in private conversation, Admiral Haggerty touched on the source of Osborne's uncanny information. Each time, Osborne turned him aside with a booming "Hey, Harry, what you don't know can't hurt you" and a conspiratorial wink. For reasons of his own, the admiral accepted this diversion and went on to other matters.

And yet, despite his success and beneath his hearty facade, Captain Osborne was bothered, deeply bothered. The gravel-voiced tipster had certainly given his career a needed boost, that Osborne knew. *But why?* he asked himself. *There's nothing for nothing, no way, not in this world. So, what was in it for "Old Pebbles"?* The question gnawed upon Osborne and the gnawing grew worse when he returned to his office from a long liquid lunch in May.

As the Coast Guard's intelligence officer, Captain Osborne sat on a coordinating committee for the New England area. The committee was comprised of all agencies involved with narcotics enforcement. It was chaired by Edmund Fitzgerald, the Boston bureau chief of the Drug Enforcement Administration. He was a rooster of a man, nearing sixty, silver-haired, red-faced, unpolished, and abrupt. "Fitzy" liked to drink, and in little time discovered a kindred spirit in Otie Osborne. They soon became fast friends, and thereafter met several times a week.

After their committee meeting, this first morning in May, the bantam Fitzgerald and the hulking Osborne were indeed an odd pair as they walked down State Street for their lunch. They had agreed on Lechners, a small restaurant on a courtyard off the beaten path. In a quiet corner of the restaurant, they discussed the volume of narcotics intercepted by Customs onshore and Coast Guard offshore. The graph of this volume was markedly rising with Coast Guard's record by far the more impressive. On that point, Captain Osborne needled his friend unmercifully.

By their third round of drinks, Fitzy grew morose. "I don't give a damn what the numbers say, Otie," Fitzgerald protested. "There's more shit on the streets of Boston today than ever there was. My guys should know. Christ. They're makin' busts down in the high schools, no less. Can you imagine peddlin' skag in the high schools? That's got to tell ya somethin'. They'll hook a whole generation of kids . . . good business. Yep, I don't care what the numbers say, there's more shit around than ever." The Drug Enforcement chief's silver head nodded knowingly.

Over their luncheon, Fitzgerald's remark seemed to slide by Osborne, but that was not so. The district intelligence officer heard the words, saw the words, again and again. Fitzy's remark would gnaw upon Osborne for a considerable time to come.

A week later, Captain Osborne concluded he was getting played for a patsy, that somehow Old Pebbles and his pals had some kind of a shell game going, the "now-ya-see-it, now-ya-don't" kind of carny game, where the patsy never picks the shell. It had to be. Pebbles wasn't feeding the government grass for nothing. Probably wasn't his grass in the first place. So, somehow, he and his phone calls must be tied to some kind of fight for a market. No one would set up that much grass as a decoy. Or would they? And with that, the Coast Guard's once stalwart guard decided he would play a less passive role.

Osborne planned to create a network of undercover agents, so one way or another, he would find out what was behind Old Pebbles's calls. The district commander approved the idea and in less than three weeks, the first of the potential agents came to Boston and reported to Osborne. He would always remember that May morning when his chief bo'sun entered his office and said, "Sir, there's a Lieutenant Quinn outside, reporting."

"Good, send him in," Osborne replied.

"It's not a him, sir."

"Oh, gawd!" Osborne exclaimed. "Not a female?"

"You better believe it, sir." the chief grinned.

A moment later, a rosy-cheeked, redheaded young woman, natty in her blues, came to attention before Osborne. "Lieutenant Quinn reporting for duty as ordered, sir," she said, saluting smartly.

"Ah yes, Lieutenant," Osborne harumphed. "I'll be a moment. Please be seated." He pushed his intercom button and said, "Chief, bring in our TWX log with headquarters personnel." He turned back to his visitor and noted she was quite pretty, well figured, and all of this bothered him further. "Well, Lieutenant, tell me a bit about yourself."

"Yes, sir," she said. "I've been running one of the forty-footers in the Santa Barbara channel, pollution patrols around the drill rigs, some tanker boardings, a lot of small-craft marine safety inspections."

"Your first assignment?"

"Yes, sir."

The chief entered with the TWX log. Osborne flipped back to his mid-March request of Washington personnel and quickly scanned it. "Five young officers—temporary assignment (up to six months) . . . As soon as available . . . Knowledgeable of small craft and their handling . . . of a judgment and education that would lend itself to independent waterfront undercover roles in the interception of narcotics." When Osborne had drafted his TWX, he had considered it explicit as to his needs, but now realized it lacked specificity as to sex. He muttered to himself, *Who in hell would have ever thought they'd come up with a woman?* Resignedly, he handed the log back to his chief and dismissed him with a wave as he asked Lieutenant Quinn, "And before that, Lieutenant?"

"The Academy, sir. Graduated two years ago."

"How did that go?"

"Fourth in my class, sir."

"Very good. Congratulations. Anything else?"

"Captain of the sailing team, sir. We won the Eastern Intercollegiates that spring. I was also on the pistol team."

"Quite impressive," Osborne said smoothly as he thought, *Oh shit, Otie. You've really screwed yourself this time. She fits what you asked to a T. It's what you didn't say to that fucking computer! In all events, it's not this girl's fault.* And so he asked more cordially, "Did you bring your file, Lieutenant?"

"No, sir. I was told to report to Boston fastest means possible; that my district was sending the paperwork separate cover, sir."

The girl's manner was matter of fact, businesslike, yet carried a certain respect for his rank that Osborne rather liked. Beneath his cordiality, Captain Osborne was of the old school. He had not yet adjusted to the role of women in his service. He again pushed his intercom. "Hey chief, see if personnel has a new file in yet on Lieutenant Quinn. If so, pull it for me."

The captain swiveled away from his visitor to look over the harbor. His dilemma was of his own making and he knew it. When he had come up with the idea of a network of undercover agents, his thoughts had been of five or more rough-and-tumble young men who would readily fit the waterfront scene, be it jobs in shipyards, fish boats, cargo docks, or bars; lads that if worse came worst, could work their way out of it. That maybe, somehow, they'd get lucky, stumble on the deal behind Pebbles. In drafting his idea as a personnel request, Osborne had never envisioned a woman who would fit his words. Yet he now sensed, without even reading her file, that Lieutenant Quinn's record would perfectly fit his request.

With his star on the rise in Washington, Captain Osborne's request had been filled in a remarkable three weeks. Were he now to send this girl back to California, he would have to explain to Washington his reasons and could, thereby, look like an idiot. What to do? If he bluntly came out and told this young lady that she was unsuitable for his mission as she was female, he ran the risk of an unholy stink within a government that was extremely sensitive to female rights and equal opportunity. With his own career now back on track, that was for Captain Osborne a risk not worth taking. He decided to try a mix of forthrightness and fear in hopes this pretty young lieutenant would get the message; that her head could be at hazard. "Well, Lieutenant, I've got to say you come as a surprise," he said, smiling.

"How's that, sir?" she asked, returning his smile.

"Oh, I knew you were coming all right," he said affably. "The name Jamie, it just didn't register as that of a woman."

"It was my grandmother's, sir." The girl looked at Osborne with level green eyes. "Does it make a difference?"

Osborne understood both the look and the question. "Yes, well it might," he temporized. "As I said, frankly, that you are a woman was a surprise. Perhaps we should discuss the mission I have in mind, in general terms. You might not think it a suitable assignment. If so, I certainly will understand. You would of course return to your duties at Santa Barbara."

"Yes, sir," she said, evenly, patiently, noncommittaly.

"Well, the narcotics trade has recently moved up onto this coast full scale. We're catching our share. I have an idea we could do better. I plan to place a few young—ah—people in undercover jobs along the coast. See what they come up with. Find out where the gaps are that need filling. Now mind you, these druggies play for keeps."

"I understand, sir."

"You would be out on your own. If you got in a jam, you'd have to take care of yourself." Osborne looked grave and chose his most ominous tone.

"I can do that, sir," she said confidently. "It should be a very challenging assignment, and I think I can help, sir."

Osborne realized he was not about to run this redhead off his play. For that matter, he was no longer certain he wanted to. He now had the feeling this young lady had come to Boston determined to do a job, that she was strong-minded and eager to get on with it. Captain Osborne liked that kind of spirit. After all, the undercover agent idea was his, an idea he also liked and wanted to see work. That someone shared his enthusiasm for the play was just fine with him—even a female.

As he studied the girl, he decided that beyond spirit, she also had an air of quiet confidence and competence. *What the hell,* he thought, *I'll try and shake her one more time.* "Hey, Lieutenant, this is no laugher. People are going to get hurt. You're out on your own. Completely. No buddies you can trust. No pay, no nothing till you get off the mission. Only one person in the service to talk with—me—and I'll be all business." He paused, looking the girl square in the eye. "Still want to do it?"

"Yes, sir," she said firmly.

"Good, but don't ever say I didn't warn you." He laughed, and there was a heartiness in the way he spoke. "Now, got any ideas on where you might best start?"

"Well, sir, you certainly know more about this district than I do. I do have some training in naval architecture, drafting, outfitting yachts, boats in general. Perhaps that might be a start."

Hmm—yachts—that might keep her out of harm's way, Osborne thought. "Yes, yachts, I think that could be a good start," he said. "Think you could find a job on that scene?"

"I think I could, sir."

And thereafter, Lieutenant J. G. Jamie R. Quinn went out on her own to the yachting town of Marblehead, and with womanly enterprise, soon wangled a job on a racing yacht.

The Yacht Gull off Tinker's Island, Near Marblehead, Massachusetts

A year after Jamie Quinn first went yachting for her country, and four years after Michael Flaherty turned to smuggling, in the late afternoon of a hot June day, a large sloop lay at mooring in Marblehead Harbor. A strong sun had hammered the harbor to rippled bronze plate, old bronze that lazily mirrored the golden gleam of the sloop's varnished topsides. Her slender spar soared high over the eighty-foot hull, far and away the tallest spar in a restless thicket of hundreds of yachts. The yacht's name was *Shillelagh*; she hailed out of Gloucester.

Earlier that morning, *Shillelagh* had finished first in a two-hundred-mile race on Massachusetts Bay. On mooring at Marblehead, her sails and deck had been neatly secured and the sloop hastily deserted by a young crew anxious for the post-race party. Below deck, in the navigation cabin bunk, there remained but one crewman, the owner, Michael Flaherty. He was now stirred from a sound sleep by the soft buzz of his wrist alarm. Flaherty had steered his sloop through most of the night, and, on finish, took a day-long snooze. The wrist alarm was a reminder to get ashore in time for the prize-giving. With a great yawn and a satisfying stretch of his well-muscled back, Flaherty got out of his bunk and flicked on the VHF radio scanner so he could call a launch after shaving.

Out on the bay, well to the south of the moored *Shillelagh*, a small yawl lay becalmed two miles shy of the finish-line buoy off Tinker's Gong. The June sea breeze had gone with the sun, leaving the sea to settle to slow-rolling gloss. The lowering sun cast an apricot glow on the yawl's mahogany topsides and windless sails. Around her, the tranquility of the twilight was broken by the fitful clang of the distant gong.

On the yawl's foredeck, under the drape of a listless spinnaker, two young crewmen dejectedly sat, chins on the lifelines, legs over the rail. The taller was racing his first race as a paid hand on this yawl named *Gull*. As he stiffly got to his feet, he grunted, "Well, Bobby, this is a pretty shitty way to start the season."

"Yup," the other crewman agreed. "Hey, where you going?"

"Below. Gotta take a leak."

"Use the rail."

"The rail? No class to that."

"Then go read the owner's bulletin on the head door. On this bucket, you gotta sit to piss. There'll be no stains on the teak."

"You're shittin' me!"

"Nope. There's only one way on *Gull*. His way." The young man nodded aft toward a tall spare man by the tiller.

After a long, loud piss overside, the new man retook his perch. "Guess we'll miss the prize party," he said.

"Sure will. It started a half hour ago."

"We could always power in. We'd catch the last of it."

"Power in! Commodore Raimond quit a race! Forget it."

Back aft, David Raimond grimly squinted through round steel-rimmed glasses at the buoy of a nearby lobster pot. He was a lanky man in his early fifties, with a long horselike face. His tattered shirt and wrinkled denims were by choice, giving no clue to his shore-side wealth and position. Raimond was a respected Boston trustee, a careful man, not a man for decisions made in haste. It was only after carefully observing the bobbing lobster buoy slide forward the full length of *Gull* that he concluded they were not stemming the ebb tide. He took the pipe from his mouth and spoke down the companionway. "Richard, what time is max ebb?"

Below, the dozing navigator nodded to wakefulness. "One second, skipper. Let me check the tide tables." After a few moments of page leafing, he answered, "Ten-eighteen at Boston, skipper. Maybe five minutes earlier out here."

So we're just seeing the first of it, Raimond thought, as he stiffly got up from the tiller. "Robert, John," he called to the young crewmen off the foredeck. "We're going to go to the hook. I'd like the light anchor, the Danforth."

As they passed the anchor gear up through the forward hatch, the new hand spoke quietly, "You sure called it, Bob baby."

Not long after the anchor splash, the soft slatting of the windless sails was overridden by the harsh crackle of the VHF radio. "Race Committee to the yacht *Gull*, Race Committee to the yacht *Gull*. Over."

The navigator flicked on the transceiver. "*Gull* to Race Committee. Go ahead. Over."

"Is the commodore close by? Over."

"Stand by one," the navigator said and called Raimond below. A few moments later, the transmission continued. "Commodore, we're thinking of calling it a day, or a night, or whatever. Over."

"Transmission understood," Raimond replied. "We're still a couple of miles off. We've had to anchor against the ebbing current. There's no wind here. Over." Raimond's pattern of speech was cultured and proper, very Bostonian.

"It's the same in here, Commodore. Not a breath. And with this full moon, the current's really running." After a pause, "Commodore, we've been checking over the list of finishers. Your handicap has run out on all of them. Over."

"Understood, Race Committee. Over."

After another lengthy pause, "Commodore, we could take your finish as of now, if you'd like. It's not going to make any difference on the finishes. . . . It would get you in for some of the prize party. Over."

Raimond paused to consider. Were he, the commodore, and his *Gull* to be credited with completing the MacKay Cup course by the race committee of his own club, it would not be right, not even for last place. It was a matter of principle. He replied, "Thanks very much, Race Committee, but no . . . We'll stick it out. We'll take our own time when we get to the Gong. I'll leave a note for you at the club desk. Over."

"Understood. Well, have a nice night, Commodore. Race Committee off and clear with the yacht *Gull*."

But Raimond was not through. "*Gull* to Race Committee. Who won the MacKay Cup? Over."

"That new maxi-sloop out of Gloucester. *Shillelagh*. She finished at eight-oh-five this morning."

Back in Marblehead harbor, aboard *Shillelagh*, her owner had finished his shave and was sloshing on lotion when he overheard this transmission and laughed aloud. *Stuffy old buzzard*, Mike Flaherty thought, then strode to the radio, switched to transmit, and called for a launch.

The MacKay Cup Presentation, Marblehead Neck, Massachusetts

The yacht club was an old, shingled Victorian ark with a wide veranda that overhung Marblehead Harbor. The veranda was crammed with a chattering horde of sunburned sailors, their press so tight, movement was nigh impossible.

As the sea breeze faded with the twilight, its gentle cooling was supplanted by an oppressive blanket of moist, hot air, the summer's first heat wave. The reveling yachtsmen countered the heat with a freshet of gins, rums, cokes and tonics, their parched demand so strong, the bars at the veranda ends could barely cope.

On the steps below the veranda, Amos Clark, the new Race Committee chairman, looked up from his watch to again study the closely moored yachts that lay under Lighthouse Point at the mouth of the harbor. The earlier nattiness of his black uniform coat and the crease of his white flannels had long gone to rumple in the press of heat and concern that this, the MacKay Cup, his first major event as chairman, went off just right. He was hopeful the committee boat would soon turn Lighthouse Point with the final results. Clark had preliminary results in hand by radio. He would have preferred the worksheets from the men out on the line, and so, he spoke to the deep tanned woman by his side. "I thought they would have been in by now, Ann."

"Hasn't everybody finished by now?" She laughed. She was a lithe woman gaily turned out in a light blue dress.

"All but your husband."

"Typical," Ann Raimond said, shaking her head, the soft light catching the chestnut tones of her hair. There was a patrician handsomeness to the woman's face as she spoke. Her cheekbones were high and fine, but then, as she smiled, a wide white smile, she became a striking, if not beautiful woman. "I'll never understand why David insists on entering that old *Gull* of his in this kind of competition." The slight slur in her speech gave indication the cocktail hour had indeed been protracted.

"Family tradition, I'd guess," The chairman said absently, again glancing at his watch and then at the milling crowd. "If we don't get on with the prizes, these guys will float home. We'll start right after colors."

A moment later, the party din was stunned to silence by the shattering boom of the sunset cannon near the veranda steps. The boom was closely echoed by the thud of other clubs' cannons down harbor. The reveling sailors turned toward the flagpole in varied semblance of giggling attention as two launchmen lowered the club burgee and national ensign. The last creak of flag halyard sheave retriggered the staccato chatter of the party.

The chairman worked through the throng to a prize-laden table. "Quiet, quiet please. May I have your attention," he shouted. Slowly, the word passed down the veranda and the chatter fell away. "Ladies and gentlemen, it's been a long day. Let's get to the winners. I will start with Class C." He launched into a chant of yachts, their corrected times, and fleet positions. One by one, to bursts of raucous applause, the skippers came forward for the lesser trophies. The chairman continued, "And at last, we come to the winner in Class A, also first to finish and first in fleet—a clean sweep. Our prize," indicating a massive sterling Revere bowl, "is the Commodore Lawton MacKay Memorial Cup. I have asked Mrs. Ann MacKay Raimond," nodding to his companion, "the donor and the daughter of our late commodore—and the wife of our becalmed current commodore," he added dryly, drawing a burst of guffaws and catcalls, "to make this presentation." Referring to his clipboard, the race chairman said, "This year, the MacKay Cup is awarded to the yacht *Shillelagh* with an elapsed and corrected time of twenty-two hours and five minutes. Considering the light winds we have had this weekend, this is indeed a remarkable performance. Will Captain Michael Flaherty come forward?"

Ann Raimond watched the throng give way for a powerfully built man, a tall man in his early forties by her guess—her basis, the slightest steel glint in his curly black hair. She was surprised by his dress, for Ann Raimond had certain expectations of proper dress for a captain, owner of a yacht in Marblehead, especially one who had just won her father's cup. The dress of this Michael Flaherty did not meet them. He wore a green polo shirt embroidered in gold with SHILLELAGH over tight white jeans and open sandals. Perhaps his dress might be appropriate for a prize-giving in Miami, certainly not for one in Marblehead, not in Ann Raimond's view. She next noted, amid a black crop of chest curls, a heavy gold cross. Hiding her distaste in a polite smile, she said, "Congratulations, Mr. Flaherty," shaking his hand, and handing him the heavy bowl from the table. The race chairman could call him a "captain"; Ann Raimond decided "Mister" would do.

While accepting the bowl, Flaherty's bronzed face wore a wide grin. His "Thank you, thank you very much" was level and gracious.

The chairman went on. "And that concludes the day's events. We thank you all for participating. Look forward to seeing you all back next year."

A tight huddle of young people, trim and tanned, all in kelly green polo shirts embroidered with the same golden SHILLELAGH, gathered about the prize table. Michael Flaherty passed the bowl to the brawniest of them, a blond young man. "Here you go, Freddy, fill it," he said. Flaherty turned back to Ann Raimond as his huddled crew broke into a rolling ditty, "'Tis the same old shillelagh me father bro't from Ireland, and divil the man . . .'" *Pop. Pop!* Freddy had his champagne close at hand.

"Exhuberant, aren't they?" Ann Raimond laughed.

"Yeah, they're O.K.," Flaherty allowed, studying the woman. "And they'll get better."

"Oh, and how's that?"

"Drill, and more sail drill. A lot of sail recutting, a lot of practice, some gear changes here and there. We're right out of the box. This was our third race." His manner was analytical and matter of fact.

"And how have they gone?"

"Three races, three aces." Flaherty grinned.

"Pretty hard to beat." Two young men, slight and wiry, wearing gold earrings and red bandannas, their long hair tied off in pigtails, next caught Ann's eye. "Who are they?" she asked.

"Oh, they're some of our foredeck gang—small, fast, and light. The best hook-up guys in the trade—jib changing, chute setting, that sort of thing."

"Rather piratical, I think."

"Perhaps. I hadn't noticed that before. So maybe we're even ready for close combat." Flaherty laughed.

Ann Raimond took the last swallow of her drink and decided she had judged the man too quickly. Despite his inappropriate dress, Michael Flaherty seemed a new, perhaps welcome force on the oft-stodgy Marblehead sailing scene. On closer inspection, she now thought he was very male and somewhat attractive. "And how did you win the MacKay Cup?" she asked.

Flaherty spoke in the gruff tones of his waterfront youth. "Part luck, a lot the boat. I'm beginning to think *Shillelagh*'s pretty fast. But who knows? She's a lot bigger than anything else in the race. We got in before the morning sun rolled up the night wind. That sort of closed the door on the guys behind us. That's luck. Best wait till we get alongside some boats our own size. Then we'll know."

"Ah! In victory, magnanimity," Mrs. Raimond teased, "and with a soupçon of modesty."

"A Winston Churchill fan." Flaherty's gray eyes lit with amusement.

"You know the quote." Ann Raimond was surprised. "And yes, I am a Churchill fan. Aren't you?"

"In some ways, considering I'm Irish. Churchill did fine by the Brits," Flaherty replied guardedly.

"And the rest of the free world, too, I think," she said assertively.

"Maybe," he allowed.

"Oh, come on, Mr. Flaherty, you must think so, too or you would never have remembered his words."

"I have a funny memory." Flaherty directed his full attention to the prize donor. He had not planned his evening the way it was going. Flaherty had made a date for the post-race party with a steward-ess from Aer Lingus. The girl had warned him she was on weekend standby. When he called his answering service after the finish, Flaherty learned he was dateless, his stewardess now in Dublin, and so he found himself at the prize-giving unattached and on the hunt. During the preprize drinking, Flaherty had looked over the women and girls at the party and seen that the hunting was sparse, so now he considered making a pass at Ann Raimond. It was by no means a weighty decision, more a bird-at-hand, why-not kind of whim, the kind of thought that best floats on a fair cargo of rum. Flaherty had first written off Mrs. Raimond as a high-society type but now, at closer range, she somewhat intrigued him. Mike Flaherty was an acquisitive hunter, a connoisseur of what he considered challenging women. He now had the time and means to pursue his sport and consciously strove to acquire the most beautiful women, the most challenging, with the least commitment. He took pride in not making promises, a sporting quirk that led to sunburst relationships, "One-of-those-things" type affairs, fun while they lasted, soon sent astern with a shrug and an eye to the available horizon ahead. With that as a general outlook, how Flaherty set his course on Ann MacKay Raimond, even if she seemed older than he was and definitely on the prim side. "Want a refill?" he asked hospitably.

"I really shouldn't," she said, but she was smiling, and then, indicating the crowd about the bar, "And you'll never get through that—not tonight."

"Oh yeah, we'll see," Flaherty said, struck by her attractiveness when she smiled. He called out, "Jamie," crooking a finger at his huddled crew. A redheaded girl came forward, her green SHILLELAGH shirt sorely stressed by a braless bosom.

"And what would you like, Mrs. Raimond?" Flaherty asked.

"A light Bacardi and tonic, if you please."

"Jamie, could you please get Mrs. Raimond a light Bacardi and tonic, and another Mount Gay on the rocks for me."

"And who's that?" Ann Raimond asked, her eyes trailing the girl, carefully assessing the departing blue jeans.

"That's our cook." Flaherty chuckled as first he watched Ann Raimond and then Jamie as she smiled and effortlessly elbowed her way to the front rank of the all-male press about the bar.

"You seem to have specialists for everything. Can she really cook, too?" Ann Raimond teased.

"Damn right. Wouldn't be aboard if she couldn't," Flaherty replied, but his thoughts were no longer on his cook; they were very much on Mrs. Raimond. In her, he sensed the slightest touch of Yankee patronizing behind a facade of reserved friendliness. It was a first impression, but a strong one, and the possibility bothered him. Perhaps it was but a defensive reaction, the psychic scars of his up-from-the-docks background. Flaherty had not met many attractive Brahmin matrons. The woman's manner and style were far different than Flaherty's Rosalie or regular run of female companions. He suspected, were he allowed through the outer defenses she put up, he would come on a cold, uptight WASP, but that possibility did not discourage him. To the contrary, and to be fair, she seemed to have a certain warmth. So he decided he'd give it a shot. If he was wrong, and she was all right, it might be a memorable trophy, maybe even fun. If not, it was a lost night anyway.

Jamie returned with their drinks.

"Here's to your old man's cup," Flaherty toasted, clinking Ann's glass. His eyes met hers and held them and they laughed.

The MacKay Mansion, Marblehead Neck, Massachusetts

Not long after sunset, a lemon moon floated out of the sea into a starlit sky. Now a bright silver ball high overhead, the moon lit the way while David Raimond slowly drove from the harbor to his home on the ocean side of Marblehead Neck. The road was his, all his. It was well past one of this warm summer night, the respectable citizens long abed, for dawn brought a workday. Raimond was tired, so deeply tired he took small note of the night's silver ambiance. To sleep was his sole thought.

To remain awake as he drove, Raimond reviewed *Gull*'s performance in the MacKay Cup. To have caught two belts of calm in one weekend race had indeed been trying. They had encountered the first calm at dawn the day before, under the crook of Cape Cod. *That's where the leaders must have really rolled away on us,* Raimond speculated. And then, there was the second calm coming up on the Tinker's Gong finish in the twilight. That led to a long night where *Gull* went nowhere until after the turn of tide. Finally, with slack water and fitful cat's-paws of night wind, *Gull* fetched the finish buoy near midnight, then motored to her harbor mooring while her crew furled and covered her sails.

Friends often kidded Raimond on the futility of racing his old Concordia yawl in modern competition. Wooden-sparred, small of canvas, teak-decked, heavy mahogany topsides—Raimond knew all their taunts; too much weight, too little sail to keep up with the newer glass or aluminum yachts. These taunts didn't matter to David Raimond. He loved his old boat for all her shortcomings. He took her to sea as often as he could, and would turn his friends' kidding aside with a "harumph," then growl, "At least I have a proper deep-water yacht." And therefore, there were those in his club who referred to him as "Deep-Water David." These remarks were always made behind his back, for the Raimonds subscribed to a generous share of the club's operating deficit.

Ann had given David the *Gull* twenty-two years earlier as a present upon his graduation from Harvard Law School and his passing the Massachusetts Bar examination. As he drove home this night, he fleetingly wondered what his life might be, had he pursued the practice of the law. The thought brought memories of younger, happier days with Ann on *Gull,* when they had raced and cruised and loved and laughed, days together, now long gone. These were mournful memories that Raimond speedily set aside in search of more positive, more pleasant thoughts. He went back to his review of the race and drew some satisfaction from *Gull* having properly finished the MacKay Cup under sail, even if no one was there to see it. It was done as it should be done, and so, to bed.

As he turned into the hedge-lined drive of the old MacKay place, Raimond considerately lowered his lights, for the household had long been asleep. He pulled up gently, got out quietly, and was surprised to see a third car, a low sports car, on the far side of Ann's station wagon. *Perhaps young David is down from college with a friend,* he thought. Raimond had reached his front steps when the moon gleam on the black air fins of the sports car caught his eye and drew him back for a closer look. He could not recall having ever seen a car like it. Why, it was no higher than his thigh. *What kind of an idiot would waste good money on this?* he asked himself. *You'd have to drive the thing virtually lying down!* On close inspection, Raimond found small markings on the wide truncated rear. LAMBORGHINI—COUNTACH 5000s. Never heard of it, he harumphed, then noted the license plate, SHARK. Definitely some showy fast friend of David's, some young man with too much money for his own good.

Raimond had turned back to his door when he was distracted by splashings from the swimming pool on the ocean side of the house. *Probably David and his flashy friend, and not a bad night for it,* Raimond thought. It was rather late for swimming, but then again, it was awfully hot. Why, though, did he assume it was David? Neighbors' children often dropped in for skinny dips, uninvited. It might be trouble. Best have a look, just to be sure.

As David Raimond walked around the big house, his steps made thin squeaks on the lawn's thick turf. He was about to step through the gap in the hedged windbreak when he stopped short. By the ocean end of the pool, starkly silhouetted in the silver stripe of moonlight, there was a naked couple, kissing. Raimond's eyesight was not the best, but even he soon saw there was more to it than kissing. The man stood waist deep in the shallows, the woman seemed to be sitting on the pool ledge, her legs entwined about his buttocks, softly splashing.

My lord, they can't be copulating, not that way, Raimond first thought, somewhat clinically. *It just won't work very well.* But then, his clinical detachment was supplanted with righteous anger. *Just who in hell are they to be fooling around in our pool?* He brushed through the windbreak, about to shout, when he stepped on a woman's dress, strewn on the lawn—a pale blue dress—Ann's new dress.

Instantly, Raimond retreated into the shadows by the windbreak, first stunned, then angry, but then he caught hold of his anger. *If I break this up,* he thought, *there will most likely be a fight, something I have never done.* Eyeing the muscular back of this stranger, Raimond decided this was not the place to start. It would lead to more than one fight; there would be Ann to deal with. That will put the unsaid out in the open, no longer to be ignored. Was he ready for that—Yet? After all, she was the mother of their children. And if there was noise, and the police came? What then? There's the family name. What of the scandal? She's probably had too much to drink. He must consider all the ramifications. Raimond's temples, which had first throbbed with anger, now pounded with unresolved tension, as he watched his wife make love to another man.

Just minutes before her husband's return, Ann Raimond reached into the pool. "Come here, you mad Irishman." She giggled thickly, the rum having taken its toll. She tugged Flaherty up the shallow steps, and in one swift motion, she had spread her legs, placed him within her, then clenched him to her as hard as she could.

There were droplets of moonlight on the man's shoulders as he moved, slowly, with certainty, deep.

Sadly for David, the moon was bright, too bright, casting the maddening detail of their mating in unmistakeable silver. After a time, he could neither listen nor watch anymore. He turned away, drove back to *Gull* and tried to sleep, numbed by the reality of the night.

The Offices of Pedrick and Oliver, Private Trustees, Boston, Massachusetts

The next morning, David Raimond stood before the tinted window in his office on the forty-sixth floor of a downtown tower. Hands clenched behind his back, he stared blankly down on the vast harbor sweep below him. Raimond had just come from the Monday morning trustee's meeting, a two-hour portfolio review and investment discussion. He had attended, unhearing, uncaring, his mind obsessed by his discovery in the night.

After rowing back out to *Gull,* he had paced the confined cabin all of that night. The searing image of his wife lustfully copulating with a stranger on the edge of their pool could not be walked away or easily dimmed. With first light, Raimond returned to their home, showered, shaved, and changed. On coming from his rooms, Raimond glanced down the long hall at Ann's closed door. There were no sounds of her rising. *Just as well,* he thought, *I need time to think this through.*

The downstairs maid was coming in to the lower hall as Raimond came down the stairs. "Your usual breakfast, Mr. David?" she asked.

"None this morning, Kate," he replied brusquely, brushing by her and out the door.

The old retainer trailed his seersuckered back with arched eyebrows. Mr. David had never passed up a sensible breakfast, not that Kate could remember, and she had been with the MacKay's

70

for twenty-nine years. "Something is awfully wrong this day," she muttered.

The gnawing emptiness in Raimond's belly had turned to sharp pain during the trustee's meeting, a pain that he tried to ignore as he now stared blankly into space. Curiously, Raimond gave little thought to the why of Ann's actions. He was a cold realist. What was, was, and about the past, he could do nothing. Raimond was more concerned with the ongoing implications for his firm, Pedrick and Oliver, Private Trustees, who had been about the business of managing money for a century and a quarter. By far, the largest single account in the firm was the Lawton MacKay Trust. David Raimond was both cold and objective, a mind-set that was of great assistance in selecting investments if not wives or lovers, for he never fell in love with investments. They were bought to be sold, it was hoped at a profit. Ann was, of course, a different matter. Raimond had once loved her deeply and probably still did, although grievously hurt by her. In all events, she was still his wife. He next considered the consequences were he to take legal action against her. He picked up the phone to seek the advice of his lawyer. The man was not in. Raimond left word of his call and returned to his pondering.

The trust instrument of Ann's father, the late Lawton MacKay, whom Raimond had never met, clearly gave Pedrick and Oliver control of the principal until the demise of the last of the second generation to be born beyond Ann—a classic Massachusetts "spendthrift trust." There were not, however, any provisions for the current circumstance. Should he sue Ann for divorce, Raimond was not sure what she would do. Legally, there might be little she could do with any success in moving the MacKay Trust out from under management by Pedrick and Oliver. He did know with certainty that legalities and realities could be far apart where his strong-willed wife was concerned, that when she had decided on something, Ann MacKay Raimond always got her way—one way or another, no matter what it cost.

The pain in Raimond's stomach now matched the sharp fragments of uncertainty that rattled around in his head. *If I do nothing, this farce of a marriage continues with me the cuckold. . . . If I take legal action, Lord knows where it leads.* Strangely, as he stood before his window, Raimond lacked any firey passionate reaction to his wife's adultery. He was far more concerned with how things might appear, what people might think.

His thoughts led to a tortuous review of the successive retrenchments that had marked their marriage. The most singular event had happened six years back, when David had gone off on an extended inspection of western oil and mining properties in which Pedrick and Oliver had chosen to invest. On his return to Marblehead Neck, Ann had gaily led him up to the second floor to show him her latest redecoration. Indulgently, he had followed, for interior decoration was one of her great pastimes, one she had a good eye for. Ann did things well, when she did them, that David knew, but on reaching their second floor that night, Raimond was stunned to find a totally new suite, completely carpentered, carpeted, and decorated in what had been the former guest wing. It was handsomely done with gum wood panelings, rich leathers, and deep tan curtains. On entering the stand-up closets, he saw the ordered ranks of his many pressed suits and shined shoes—but nothing of Ann's. "But where are your things?" he had asked.

"Down the hall, where they always were, in my place. We have far more room to move about that way." And she smiled.

"What about us? Aren't we going to sleep together? In the same bed?" he protested.

"Oh, David, that's getting less important." By then, she was walking down the hall and spoke over her shoulder. "We are getting older—and you snore worse than ever."

And therewith, without discussion, his wife had rendered David Raimond's already sparse sexual existence to the solitary memories of a Yankee monk, cloistered in the most pampered monastic cell on Marblehead Neck.

Should have fought it out then, asserted myself, he now muttered. *But you didn't, you damn fool, you let her have her way. You've let her run things on her terms, ever since her mother died, when she came into her inheritance. You've never stood on your own.*

Despite his education and business acumen, David Raimond had been slow to recognize the widening communications gap and the waning of affection that marked the denouement of their marriage. Bound by his armor of reserved propriety, he was incapable of reaching across the gap and drawing back his wife to him with a gentle touch or light banter. Instead, he made matters worse with his innate stiffness and so, with the redecoration, he had resignedly accepted the separate suite. Thereafter, with time, the reoccurrence of aching loins went away, replaced by a smouldering hurt and a stoic acceptance of what was.

Over the more recent years, the years of his married monkhood, Raimond had never considered an affair, perhaps realizing he could never bring one off with any promise of success. On their constant rounds of parties, Raimond neither drew nor was drawn to women. Chit-chat was not his forte, nor was his dour buttoned-up appearance of any aid in social ice-breaking. The thought of paying for a woman, a trivial expense for a man of his affluence, was simply not within his thought process.

His mind returned to what he had seen by the pool. His reaction was now a glacial anger, an ice-fire, that called for vengeance, a very special vengeance, one that would have to be planned, controlled, thought through, and appropriate. In Raimond's now twisting mind, financial ties, family relationships, social implications, and outward images were all intertwined.

Raimond's bleak reverie was interrupted by the beep of the intercom on his desk. He returned to the massive mahogany rolltop, a desk that had once been Lawton MacKay's, and pressed the intercom. "Yes, Mrs. Evans," he said.

"Thornton Loring is returning your call on oh-three, Mr. Raimond."

"Thank you," he said, closing the intercom and pausing for a moment of consideration. Thornton Loring was one of David Raimond's few close friends, a roommate in both prep school and law school, a frequent cruising companion on *Gull*, now a senior partner of Baxter, Blair and Burnham, the attorneys for Raimond's firm. He picked up his phone and said somewhat stiffly, "Thornton, thank you for returning my call so promptly."

"Not at all, Skipper." The lawyer's opening was far more hearty. "That's what we're here for. Say, reading on the train this morning, I saw the *Gull* didn't fly very high this weekend."

"No," Raimond cut in tersely. "Nor is that why I called."

"To business, David."

Raimond drew breath, organizing his thoughts before speaking. "Thornton, we might have a very awkward situation brewing over here . . . a matter of a client's potential divorce. I've been asked to look into the mess. . . . Quite frankly, it must be a matter for the utmost discretion."

"Of course, and understood, David," Loring replied. "As you know, it's not in our regular line, but we do handle . . ."

"No. No. That's not what I want," Raimond interrupted testily. "I do not want one of your corporate litigators turned loose in the divorce courts for the day. From what little I know, divorce law is a game by itself. For that matter, I am not certain our client will decide to go on with this. What I am doing is exploring the options, finding out what is involved. For that, I want a specialist. Someone who knows how things work in the courts, not in the law books. I would like the name of the man you, or your people, would recommend as the divorce specialist in the commonwealth."

"Very well, David," Loring replied. "I'll be back as quickly as I can. It may be a while. I know my partner, the person I will first ask, is in court this morning."

"I understand, and thank you, Thornton." Raimond paused and then went on. "And one more thing. I'd also like your person's thoughts on an investigator, a discreet private investigator, the best he knows."

"Understood. I'll be back. Have a good morning."

Raimond put down his phone and returned to the window, where, beyond the near expanse of the airport and Winthrop, the green thumbs of Nahant and Marblehead Neck jutted into the shimmering sea.

The Samoset Club, Boston, Massachusetts

As he walked the edge of the pond in Boston's Public Gardens, the man casually watched the tourist-filled swan boats. For the many strollers that he passed, there was nothing singular about him, an ordinary man, slightly over middling height, slightly paunchy, probably in his late fifties from the slight shuffle of his pace. He wore an inconspicuous tan cotton suit and a simple straw hat. For the passerby, he was nondescript, a man out of mind on the instant of passing.

As the walker waited for the Charles Street traffic light, the blanket of heat weighed heavily on him. He drew a handkerchief from his pocket, mopped his forehead, and when the light turned, he crossed over into the Common, walking on toward Beacon Hill. Climbing the Common steps to cross Beacon Street, he had to again wait for traffic, and as he did, he glanced across at the stolid expanse of the Samoset Club, unimpressed by the balanced Bulfinch facade, unknowing that it was an architectural gem of historic significance. The man was preoccupied by the circumstance of his visit, somewhat amused thereby. In all his years about Boston, there was a threshold he never expected to cross. He looked at his watch. Five of five, he noted. Good—never hurts to get off on the right foot with a new client.

On entering the visitor's hallway, he was met by an attentive sparrow of an elderly maid in the uniform of the old days, black with a white lace apron. "Good afternoon, sir," she greeted him chirpily. There was a slight touch of the brogue in her chirp.

The man was about to tease her on it when he thought better of it. "Good afternoon," he said. "Kevin Shaughnessey to see Mr. David Raimond."

"Oh yes, Mr. Shaughnessey," she said hospitably. "Mr. Raimond is expecting you in the garden. He's already signed you in. May I please take your hat?" After setting his hat on the cloakroom table beside the visitor's book, the maid led Shaughnessey through the tall rooms toward the back of the club. She led him into a surprising urban oasis, an open garden, tree-lined, the walls a lush tapestry of swaying ivy. By the back wall, a tall spare man in a seersucker suit solitarily gazed into the pond of a burbling fountain, his hands clasped behind his back. "Mr. Raimond, Mr. Shaughnessey is here," the maid announced and started back into the club.

"Good! You're right on time." Raimond turned and came to meet Shaughnessey, his hand extended. "David Raimond," he said, shaking hands. "Why don't we sit over there," indicating a cluster of metal tables in a shaded corner of the garden.

While walking to his chair, Shaughnessey noted the Yankee rasp in Raimond's voice and his brusque manner. On sitting down, he eyed his host, taking in the blue button-down shirt that matched some kind of yacht club tie. Shaughnessey was immediately struck by Raimond's resemblance to the now departed Leverett Saltonstall, once a governor, later a senator of the Commonwealth, one of the last of the Republican Yankees to be elected to major office in the Democratic fiefdom that Massachusetts had become. In his days on the State Police detail in the governor's office, Shaughnessey had come to know the late senator, a lanky horse-faced man. He had even grown to respect and admire the man. That had not been easy, for Shaughnessey was the son of a Boston longshoreman, reared in a family where voting Republican was more than a mortal sin. Now, recalling the late senator, Shaughnessey chose to set aside his tribal prejudice. He would not prejudge this man Raimond, even if he did come on as a dried-out stick of a proper Brahmin with his steel-rimmed button glasses. *This might even get interesting,* Shaughnessey said to himself.

"Damned hot for early June," Raimond grumped. "Would you like a drink?"

"Sure is," Shaughnessey agreed, "and yes, a gin and tonic would suit me just fine." *At least he takes a drink, I'll give him that much,* he thought.

Raimond punched the bell on the table as he said, "Well, Shaughnessey, you certainly come well recommended by the people at Baxter, Blair." He had barely finished when a black-jacketed steward was by his elbow. "A gin and tonic and a Perrier with a twist of lemon," he ordered briskly. As the steward went away, Raimond returned his attention to Shaughnessey, stared at the man through his small round glasses for a long moment, and then spoke again. "Maybe it would be best if we start with you. Tell me about yourself."

"Private investigator, that you know. Shaughnessey and McDonough's the firm. Harry McDonough and I, we've been out on our own almost five years. A lot of our work's for the large law firms. Whatever they want looked into, we do—as long as it's straight. Mac, he's out of Customs. I'm an ex–State Trooper, retired as a lieutenant, twenty years on the investigation side. Then I did four more in charge of the governor's bodyguard. Before that, I was a Marine in Korea, got hit in the leg at Inchon—not bad, but it gave me vet's preference when I went up for the State Police exam. That was my edge getting on."

"Really," Raimond interjected. "That's a coincidence. I was a gunnery officer on a destroyer off Inchon. Came back from that to the law school." He broke off as the steward returned and quietly set down their drinks.

Shaughnessey poured tonic over his gin, lightly. No sense drowning good gin. He took a long strong pull on his glass, all the while eyeing Raimond, dubious of an ex-Navy officer who drank Perrier with lemon.

"And how did you become involved with Baxter, Blair and Burnham?" Raimond asked.

The investigator went off on a detailed description of a long-forgotten Cambridge murder where at trial, his evidence prevailed over the defense efforts of a then young but now senior partner of Baxter, Blair.

When Shaughnessey paused, Raimond asked, "What's required to become a private investigator?"

"Not much. You need a license from the Department of Public Safety—they supposedly run a background check—see if you're clean. They really don't go very deep."

"Do you go armed?"

"In this trade! You think I'd go naked?" Shaughnessey laughed as he patted a slight bulge on his waist. "Yes, a Smith and Wesson, stainless Model 60."

"Don't you have to have a permit to carry a weapon now, here in Massachusetts?"

The persistent thoroughness of Raimond's questions had brought Shaughnessey to the edge of annoyance, but then he said to himself, *Hell. It's probably his way of sizing me up. I can wait him out. He's going to do the paying . . . and we can use the work.* And so he answered patiently, "Yes, Mr. Raimond, you do. I've got one from the Boston Police Department."

"Good," Raimond said, and took a sip of his Perrier. He then asked, "What do you charge, Shaughnessey, for your services?" Raimond's unblinking eyes were on him behind his steel-rimmed glasses.

Shaughnessey considered the question and the circumstance by which he found himself in the garden of the Samoset Club. He knew nothing of Raimond yet assumed he was a member. They wouldn't be here otherwise. And Samoset membership, that took both bucks, big bucks—and blood, blue blood. The investigator did know Baxter, Blair and Burnham, and they didn't deal with the deadbeats of Boston. *So, what the hell,* he decided to himself, *I'll throw fifty bucks on the regular freight. If he's already checked with Baxter, Blair, I can always back down. If he hasn't, I've got a live one.* And so he answered, "That depends on the job, Mr. Raimond. Harry and me usually get three hundred for the day or any part of it. It's not like a dentist with the next job waiting outside. And three hundred fifty if we've got to go to court. That's for the aggravation of sittin', doing nothin'. Now, if what you need requires a surveillance, say a twenty-four-hour surveillance, then we need a team. I can get men, qualified men, twenty bucks an hour, but there's a minimum of a hundred bucks a man. And then there's other expenses, so, for them, whatever it costs plus ten percent."

"And just what's involved with expenses?" Raimond asked.

"That depends on the job, Mr. Raimond," Shaughnessey replied smoothly. "You put me out to tail a guy to California—there's airplane tickets, hotels, meals. There's cars. You want a surveillance in Chelsea, I go to Rent-a-Wreck, get something that fits with Chelsea. You want a job in Wellesley, the Chelsea car don't fit. I go to Hertz, get something good. And we change cars every day, to protect our cover. So, you tell me what you want, I'll give you a good guess what it's goin' to take."

"Very well," Raimond said, looking down at the quiver in his hands. "Although I thought Thornton Loring had told me your per diem was two-fifty."

Shaughnessey also noted Raimond's quivering hands. *This guy's up-tighter than a banjo and damned if he didn't check out the freight,* he thought. *A typical Yankee prick.* Shaughnessey answered blandly, "As I said, that depends on what you need done, Mr. Raimond. You tell me—I tell you."

"Yes, I suppose we have come to that." Raimond took a slow sip of Perrier, then cleared his throat. "But before we get on to it, I must have an understanding, an absolutely clear understanding that what I tell you, that what you may learn subsequently must be treated with discretion, the utmost discretion."

"That's understood. Part of the job. Harry and me are both clams when it comes to that."

"No, at the outset, I only want you involved. The fewer, the better."

"I can only put in so many hours of the day, Mr. Raimond."

"I understand that, Shaughnessey. If you need more people later, then we'll discuss it, but beforehand, not afterwards, and at two–

fifty. Understood?"

"O.K." Shaughnessey nodded.

Raimond reached into his breast pocket for a slim daily diary and a gold pencil. He scribbled a number on a business card and handed it to Shaughnessey. "You are only to call me at this number. That is my private line at the office. It bypasses the switchboard, even my secretary."

Shaughnessey glanced at the card, noting "Pedrick and Oliver— Private Trustees" and wondered what kind of a deal they had going. "Understood," he said, pocketing the card.

"On the phone, we will only discuss a time of meeting—nothing else. We will always meet here, at this club, until I say otherwise."

Shaughnessey nodded his agreement while Raimond paused. Finally, Raimond looked up and there was a mistiness in his eyes as he spoke, carefully, slowly, painfully. "I have reason to believe, Shaughnessey, that my wife is having an affair with another man."

So that's all there is, Shaughnessey thought, disappointed. With the sudden urgency of the afternoon call and the Samoset specified for their meeting, the investigator had climbed Beacon Hill full of speculative visions, dreams of a great stock swindle or some biggie deep in the till, something different, something new. And what comes up? The same old shit, another broad out fuckin' around. The investigator looked down at the table, trying to hide his disappointment.

In his thirty years of picking over human refuse, Shaughnessey had become a gumshoe philosopher. He had smelted human happiness to simplistic needs; three square meals a day, a reasonably regular relationship with a woman, and a fair amount to drink. You have those, you're as rich as the world can make you, in Kevin Shaughnessey's view. Another tenet the investigator had reached was that money had nothing to do with marital happiness, or any kind of lasting happiness, for that matter. This Raimond looked pretty well heeled, yet here he is, the world at the beck of a bell, a rich Yankee stick, just as ripped up by a broad as some poor working stiff. The poor shaky bastard still cares.

Despite his disappointment, Shaughnessey replied with the oiled sincerity of an undertaker. "That can be tough, Mr. Raimond—very tough." He took a gulp of his gin and then asked, "And you want me to get it together for an adultery rap?"

"Oh no, I'm not prepared to go that far." Raimond was again looking down at his shaking hands. "Not yet, at least." David Raimond well knew why his hands shook. He had spent the forenoon with the most reknowned divorce counsel in the Commonwealth. In that meeting, Raimond had his initial thoughts confirmed, namely that were he successful in a "faulted" divorce suit, while he might not be awarded any of the MacKay Trust principal, he had a reasonable chance of the Probate Court awarding him one-half of Ann's re-invested income over the term of their marriage. On return to his office, a hurried check of income from the MacKay trusts indicated to Raimond he stood to gain fifty-odd million were he to win such an award in an adultery suit. Curiously, for Raimond, it was not the money that mattered so much, for he was many times a millionaire in his own right when they had married; what did matter to Raimond was the prospect of finally beating Ann MacKay at something; even if it was only the internment of their marriage. A grim vengeance, but one to be played out with the utmost care.

"Then what do you want?" Shaughnessey asked.

"I want to know if my suspicions are right." Raimond looked up at Shaughnessey. There was a slight tremble of his chin as he spoke. "And the name and any details of the man involved."

"So you don't know the guy? And you're not so sure they're shackin' up?"

"No, and yes." Raimond said slowly. "I do know he drives a peculiar black sports car, a Lamborghini, and the registration plate reads SHARK."

"Well, that's certainly a start," Shaughnessey said.

Villa Barerra, Nahant, Massachusetts

Earlier in the day that David Raimond retained his detective, the black Lamborghini in which he had interest carved the turn of the Nahant traffic circle with a squeal of rubber and tore into the wide emptiness of the causeway with a throaty roar. Behind the small wheel, Michael Flaherty geared up smoothly, happily, for the long causeway that led out to the island village was one of the few stretches of road on the north shore where Flaherty could truly try his Lamborghini's legs. He hummed happily as he drove, his foot to the floor. Behind dark glasses, his gray eyes roved, first the causeway, next the green light on the radar scanner, and then, the soaring speedometer, 200 k.p.h. on clearing fourth. Not bad, he grinned.

Within a span of seconds, the Lamborghini had leapt the long causeway to outer Nahant, forcing Flaherty to gear down for a sedate climb by the police station that guarded the first rise of the small island village. Moments later, Flaherty arrived at the gates of Villa Barerra and the security ritual started. "Are you alone?" the gatepost speaker asked.

Realizing the impenetrable tint of the Lamborghini's windscreen, Flaherty answered patiently, "Yes, Guido, I'm alone." Later, as he slipped out of his sports car by the front steps, the beauty of his surroundings struck him. The summer sun made rainbows in the water sprinklers whirring all over the broad green lawns. Beyond the lawns, and below the cliff, the first of a sea breeze riffled the bottle green of the bay. Flaherty then heard the hopeful "skaw" of seagulls trailing a lobsterman as he tended a string of pots, while in the far distance, the towers of Boston shimmered in the heat haze.

As Flaherty went around to the luggage compartment of his car and took out his electronic gear, he asked himself, *Hey Mike, why in hell are you out here debugging this place on such a beautiful day? Christ, you've got all the bucks you'll ever need. Enjoy.* But then he answered his own question. Giovanni Barerra had his set ways of doing things, among them the regular sweeping of his residence, a chore to be done by a family member, Flaherty. So, as Flaherty entered the villa, nodding to the hovering housemen, he concluded that sure it was a pain in the ass, but he'd never had a deal that paid like this.

An hour later, after finishing his electronic chores, Flaherty joined the padrone on his patio. As the houseman came with luncheon trays, Barerra asked, "And you Michael, how are things going? What are you up to?"

"Well, your place is clean, and as you know, we've got nothing coming in till near the end of the month. So, I'm doing the Newport–Bermuda Race next weekend."

"Ah yes! I almost forgot." Barerra's nut-brown face broke into a great grin. "My congratulations. I read the *Globe* yesterday. You won the Lawton MacKay Cup."

"Why thank you, Gabbo," Flaherty replied modestly. "This new *Shillelagh* has really got it."

"That tickled me, really tickled me." Barrera chuckled.

"What's so special about the MacKay Cup?" Flaherty was curious. The old man had seldom shown any interest in his yacht racing. "That's how your grandfather and I got our start, as that old bastard's bootleggers." Barrera laughed. "With Lawton MacKay."

"What! Commodore MacKay's bootleggers! You're kidding me?"

"No, not at all, and if the truth be known, he was also our banker." Barerra laughed an even deeper laugh and went on. "When Prohibition first came in, there was a lot of competition—free enterprise if you will, rather like narcotics a few years back. It was only in the later years of the noble experiment that we really got that market organized. Your grandfather, Big Mike, he ran our boat. Being a Novie himself, he could talk to those mackerel snappers out on the mother ships. They were only a few miles offshore, just outside the territorial limits. Rum Row, they used to call it. With me, a young Italian, those Novies were hard and tough, very tough. You've heard the phrase 'Cash on the barrelhead.' That's the way it was."

"So how did MacKay fit in?"

"He lent us some of the cash for our first boat and cargo. We paid him back, mostly in booze, and in less than six months, as I recall, our cost plus fifteen percent for the risk of the run, a fair deal. MacKay had this great ark of a summer house on the ocean side of the Neck."

"The family still has it," Flaherty interjected.

"Well, you'll find there's a little cove in the rocks right out in front of that house, a tight little place. MacKay had steps carved into those rocks, swimming steps for any that asked. Your grandfather and I would run in on the top of the tide. We'd off-load with MacKay's butler for help and were out in no time. MacKay had the best cellar on the north shore all through Prohibition. And so now you've won his cup—that really tickles me."

"A small world, Gabbo," Flaherty mused, and then, knowing the old man's great zest for talk on things he knew well, Flaherty asked, "What kind of a man was Lawton MacKay?"

"Lawton MacKay." The old man seemed to savor the name as his mind riffed back through the dust of decades, and then he laughed.

"A psalm-singing thief if there ever was one, a great barrel of a man, imperious, pompous, shrewd, born with the silver spoon, old Salem money, shipping, rum, opium into China, clippers for awhile. As I remember, one of them was prosecuted for running blacks into the South just before the rebellion. I could look it up if you like." Barrera moved to rise.

"Hey, relax, Gabbo. Your memory is good enough for me," Flaherty said.

"Well, as I recall, the MacKays were key members of the cartel that bribed Congress for the western lands that became the Union Pacific Railroad."

"Jesus. Big bucks," Flaherty exclaimed.

"Michael," the old man spoke quietly, almost reverently, "Lawton MacKay inherited one of America's great fortunes, a quiet fortune built on the blood and buried bones of these United States. The MacKays had a piece of all the memorable swindles and monopolies. Credit Mobilier, Standard Oil, you name it. And I am certain, in his own time, he husbanded that fortune, doubled it again, maybe more."

The old man sipped his chablis. "Professor Morison once said of the Yankees, 'eternally torn between a passion for righteousness and a desire to get on in the world.' That fit Lawton MacKay to a T. When I knew him, he had an investment banking office on State Street. I was told he was heavy in steel and shipping when the First War broke out in Europe. He had a part of the Morgan consortium that sold supplies to Great Britain. But on the other side, he somehow got a source of the German textile dyes, they say by cargo submarine into New London. Even after we went in, MacKay brought the dyes into the States through Mexico. Later, he went into oil and real estate in New York. He was one of the early backers of the company that became IBM."

Flaherty let out a soft low whistle.

Barerra paused and then rattled on. "MacKay had a great mansion on Commonwealth, was on every Boston board that amounted to anything and some in New York. A vestryman of Trinity Church and kept a woman in the Parker House—a very handsome woman. MacKay was greedy as hell. Didn't miss a trick. Why, when he figured out how we were doing in booze, he wanted in for half—that's where we had our parting. By then, it was near the end of Hoover's term, we had organization in the market.

"MacKay died toward the end of the Second War. They found

him in a room in the Parker House. A sudden heart attack, the papers said, brought on by the pressures of all his war charity activities. I heard his pants were on backwards when the medical examiner got there. Died in the saddle, that would be my guess."

"Wife? Kids?" Flaherty asked.

"He was on his second marriage, the first wife died, childless. The second was a much younger wife. I don't think she turned out too well. Went alcoholic, I heard. There was a child, a daughter, as I recall, said to have inherited the largest trust in Boston."

"Yup, there sure is a daughter, Gabbo." Flaherty laughed. "She gave me the prize last night."

The MacKay Mansion, Marblehead Neck, Massachusetts

That same morning, farther down coast, in her home on Marblehead Neck, Lawton MacKay's daughter adjusted the shower to a needle setting. She stepped back into the torrent and went on with her scrubbing. Vigorous strokes with a prickly loofah soon brought the soft brown of her tan to flushed pink, and as she scrubbed, she hummed contentedly. From the uncertain start of a morning hangover, her day had gone well, very well. Ann Raimond had just returned from a long match on the tennis courts, leaving behind the morning's seediness in the sweat of three extended singles sets. Jean Howe, her opponent and many-times partner in winning the ladies' club doubles, had been at the top of her game, and that made for a good match, a long match. *But I got her in the end,* Ann thought. She put aside the prickly bush and smiled contentedly. She turned and cupped her breasts into the full force of the needling torrent, feeling the sensual swell of her taut nipples, delighting in the mesh of the rivulets to a warm stream of spent water trickling down her thighs.

Most of her morning, Ann had been trying to decide what to do with the rest of her day, volleying both sides of Michael Flaherty's casual invitation to come over in the afternoon for a sail on *Shillelagh*. He made the offer in his last hug before leaving, the polite thing to do. But was it only politeness? Was his invitation sincere? Ann's quandary centered on Flaherty's offhandedness. She had answered in kind, a casual "I will if I can, we'll see." All this offhandedness now caused her orderly mind a certain amount of annoyance. Ann Raimond was used to having her social engagements set forth on a far more formal basis.

Like the bronze weathercock wind vane over her garage, her thoughts on the night's events and Flaherty's invitation for the afternoon swung through all quadrants of consideration. Perhaps it was moon-madness, she would now like to believe, but then, she did get quite tight, and she did invite Flaherty back to her pool. *How was I ever that brazen, with David not that far away?* she thought. *Do I want to break it apart but don't know how? And the drinking, that's been happening more and more, lately. Drunkenness is no excuse. Well, that's what I should think, what I was taught to think, but do I?* Ann winced as she realized she had little or no remorse. As a matter of fact, while some of the night remained foggy, she had the clearest recollection of one mighty memorable orgasm—a long overdue experience.

She now thought, *Do I want this to go beyond the edge of the pool? It's up to me. Marblehead is a very large, very small town. I, of all people, can't move around unnoticed. Then again, maybe I can, maybe the town's much bigger than I ever thought, maybe it's only me and my circle of friends that's so small. How could I have missed Michael Flaherty, if it is such a small town? He sails, as we do and all our friends, apparently sails quite well, he's certainly attractive, and still we've never met. So maybe the town isn't so small.*

In her twenty-four years of married life, Ann had never fully dealt with the restlessness of her unfulfilled sexuality. She and David had done what one did and had two children thereby, but for Ann, sex had not been a source of pleasure. For years, she suspected a sybaritic world she had missed.

Like many of her friends, Ann's marriage was now little more than a habit, and perhaps out of habit, perhaps because of the smallness of her affluent circle where few secrets were sacred, Ann had never done anything about finding fulfillment, at least not with success. Not that she hadn't thought about it, wanted to, and even tried in a rather ill-conceived way. Last night, with Flaherty, was not her first stray from her marital vows. Ann's restlessness seemed to have blossomed with spring from long-dormant seeds. Earlier, in May, while closing their Hobe Sound winter home, David returned to Boston several days before her. Desirous of having her tennis in fine tune before returning to a colder clime, Ann took many lessons. One thing led to another, and she spent the night with a once world-class tennis professional, an irreverent Australian—so very handsome, so attentive on court, but so very selfish in bed. The night was a dismal failure, as she knew it would be. She subsequently realized she got what she deserved. She went to bed with someone for all the wrong reasons. No wonder she had been so tense and dry. An unpleasant memory to be put aside.

She snapped off her shower, put on a robe, picked up a towel, and went to her dressing room. "And why not?" she asked herself aloud. "Maybe there is more to it."

Last night with Michael, on the edge of her pool, things had indeed been different, deliciously different; warm memories of a moonlit night that seemed to hold the promise of a dawn for her long sexual darkness. For years, her life had been crammed and bustling, first in supervising the rearing of her children, and then, with their matriculation, she filled the space with tennis, golf, skiing, sailing, and sunning, and yet, it had not been an indolent life. She had more than met the expectations of her upbringing, as a mother and a hostess. She capably oversaw the staffing and operation of family homes on Marblehead Neck and Hobe Sound. As a matron to whom much had been given, she was diligent in attending her hospital trusteeships, museum boards, and several charitable organizations. She was always extremely generous to these charities.

In Boston society, it was well known that if Ann Raimond took on a task, she saw it through. To her circle of friends, she seemed to lead a full and worthwhile life, but then, many of her friends judged most everything by appearance. The possibility that Ann was a prisoner of her wealth and upbringing, with golden fetters of her own forging, that she had carefully filled her days with social obligations to ward off boredom—that possibility simply never occurred, not even to the most perceptive.

When she chose to think of it, Ann knew the deficiency in her upbringing was her lack of education to be a loving wife. A degree in English literature was slim preparation for the tempered judgment that leads to easy give and take, the luck, the love, the tendresse, that fosters an enduring marriage. From her debutante days, David Raimond had been her constant companion, a beau hand-picked by her mother, their relationship nurtured in a social environment controlled by Mrs. MacKay. Ann and David overlapped in Cambridge, she at Radcliffe, he at the law school after his naval service. With such a limited choice of men, Ann now had good reason to wonder if something wasn't omitted from her formative years.

As she dabbed away at her body with the towel, Ann realized none of these ruminations got her any closer to a decision about the afternoon and Michael Flaherty. It was not an easy choice. She knew, from his dress and speech, that Flaherty was from a different background, of a different class than she. That realization bothered her, for in a Jeffersonian way, Ann fancied herself democratic. She had never faced the reality of her snobbishness. She sometimes buried it under a facade of affected earthiness, but it came forth most often in her choice of language and comment when vexed. Ann Raimond knew she was not an outgoing person, and that knowledge made her night with Flaherty that much more of a wonderment. But an ongoing relationship with Michael Flaherty was a path to trouble. All her Yankee matron's instincts cried to let the invitation lie as it was left, casual, offhanded, unaccepted by means of nonattendance.

But then, the winds of her mind blew from the opposite quadrant, bringing memories of her sensual shower, where she seemed to have washed away any vestige of prudence. Finished with toweling, Ann announced to herself, "You're going." She walked to her closet and opened it. The backs of both doors bore full-length mirrors. She swung them in such a way that she had front and side views, then eyed herself critically.

Ann Raimond believed her eyes far more than her electronic scales with their digital memory. She considered her five-nine frame a bit of a disadvantage in a ballroom, but on a tennis court, it had its advantages. She now considered the facets of her body that were within her control. She was totally tanned, a soft golden tan, the reflection of many sunny mornings spent on her sun porch with all the right lotions. Her breasts were set high, still quite firm, she thought, as she held them up to the mirror for closer inspection. A highly competitive woman, Ann was well aware most of her friend's breasts had long gone to drooping pendulums or shriveled walnuts, and the awareness pleased her. She was content with her waist but a bit displeased with the swell of her belly. That she had drunk more vodka this spring was now apparent. Time to add more sit-ups to her fitness program and slack off on the vodka.

She turned for a quarter view, taking in her buttocks and thighs. They were still lean and flat, almost girllike, probably her best feature, quite good for forty-five, she decided. Ann Raimond paid a dear price for the fitness of her body. Three times a week, a strong Slavic woman came to the MacKay place to knead and pummel the mistress. Four times a week, a svelte young woman with a bobbing ponytail in bright leotards arrived with the latest and loudest cassettes. To the blare and bounce of hard rock, she led Ann through a tongue-dragging hour of aerobics. When those sessions drew to a close, Ann well knew the panting price she paid for her fitness.

For the most part, she had held her figure with a discipline of dining and soaking sweat. Unlike many of her friends, she avoided the vanity of remedial surgery, silicone implants, tummy-tucks, and buttocks-nips. She stepped closer to the mirror, touched the flesh about her high cheekbones, examining her eyes. *The crow's feet and wrinkles are there, my dear,* she said to herself. Maybe she'd better do something about that, soon, but not today. Time to get going.

Ann walked into her wardrobe with a wink for her mirrors and carefully selected her clothes, starting with the smallest of silken bras. *And why not?* she thought, grinning.

The Flaherty Condominium, Marblehead, Massachusetts

Later, driving over the causeway to the mainland side of the harbor, the Old Town section, Ann rationalized aside her last pangs of prudence. After all, Flaherty did win her father's cup, and going out for a sail on the winning boat was quite appropriate. Why, it was the logical, the acceptable, the polite thing to do, to visit the winner, wasn't it? Should anyone ever dare ask.

Ann wound down through the small streets of the old fishing town to the Glover's Landing condominiums and pulled into a visitor's slot beside Flaherty's black sports car. She got out of her station wagon, checked Flaherty's number, and on buzzing his bell saw that he had three floors to himself in a building that hung on a harbor-side cliff. *Pretty spectacular, the best,* she mused as the door clicked open.

"Hi. Good, you decided to come." His smile was wide, his greeting warm and friendly. He quickly followed up with a hard hug, smoothly hiding his surprise that Ann Raimond had really taken him up on his offer.

If he's surprised, he hides it well, Ann Raimond thought as she said, "And didn't you think I would?" She stepped into the middle-floor entry.

"I wasn't sure," he said openly, "but I'm damn glad you did." He put his arm about her, giving her a second hug, and guided her into his living room. "Hey, come on in. How about a glass of wine?"

"A glass of wine would be perfect." She smiled.

"You name it, we've got it." Flaherty went to a wall-alcove bar while Ann moved about the large living room. Over the stone fireplace, she noted a Fitz Hugh Lane oil, an exquisitely detailed dawn prospect of Gloucester Harbor, and on the other walls, quite a collection of modern marine paintings. Nor did the many blends of tan that made up the carpet and drapes and matched the soft Italian leather of the sofa cushions by the picture window escape her knowing eye. Very male and nicely done, professionally done. On that she would bet. His home more than made up for his inappropriate dress at the prize-giving. "So this is the den of the celebrated Captain Michael Flaherty, Marblehead's latest pirate." She laughed.

"Sure is." Flaherty grinned, handing her a glass. "And the treasure chest is over here, under this sofa," indicating a leather cluster of couches before the picture window.

Ann Raimond took a seat across from Flaherty, then a slow sip of wine, as she looked out on the sweep of moored yachts below them. "What a beautiful view you have," she exclaimed.

"I like it," he agreed. "Almost as good as yours."

"Oh, I don't know." She considered for a moment, then went on. "There's more activity here on the harbor side. You have all the goings and comings of boats. The launches at work. It's more active, more fun, I think."

"And you have the starting line for the races," he replied, "and the clear horizon and the surf when the wind's up . . . the open sea." His crinkled gray eyes were on the window, trailing the cotton blossom of a cumulus cloud, soaring on the summer heat.

Watching him, Ann spoke softly. "You make it sound like a Masefield poem, and you love it all—the sea and the sky, that is."

"You keep dragging in these Brits, first Churchill, now Masefield." He laughed, then his tone changed. His eyes came back to hers and held them as he spoke slowly, thoughtfully. "Yes, I do love the sea, it's both my love and my living. . . . I have the best of all worlds."

"Just what do you do?" she asked.

"Oh, I'm into a lot of things. I run some fishing trawlers, we have a fish-processing plant up in Gloucester, also a little ship repair. Then last year, we bought a small ship construction and repair yard up in Maine at Boothbay. Got a little marine electronics business over in Beverly. I do some importing and exporting, mostly into the Med. I keep busy."

"Sure sounds it to me," she agreed, feeling with each moment more at ease with Michael Flaherty. "But how do you find the time for all this business and your sailboat racing? All the drill you were talking about yesterday?"

"I get good people and delegate to them as much as I can. Try and treat 'em well, keep 'em happy. Some of it is having three generations of family in some of the businesses. Now, there's two sides to that. Too much family can be a pain. So, maybe I'm lucky to have the same people with me for a long time, people I trust."

"Yes, you are lucky. Holding good help is no easy thing, that I know," Ann said, putting down her glass, eyeing him levelly. "You seem to put a lot of store by your trust."

"That's the way I do business. I have to," Flaherty answered soberly. "Say! That reminds me." There came a mischevious glint to Flaherty's eyes. "Have you got a little cove out in front of that house of yours?"

"Why yes, yes, we do," Ann answered, somewhat surprised by

this abrupt conversational turn. "We used it for swimming before I put in the pool."

"Swimming, huh?" His tone was light.

"Yes, swimming. Father had the steps put in, bronze posts for the rails and all. When I was little, I remember it was a wonderful place for diving at high tide, when the water was warm. A lot of what Father put in is gone now—with the winter storms. And with the pool, I didn't think it made any sense to keep it up. But why? Why do you ask?"

"Swimming and diving, huh!" Flaherty exclaimed again. "No way! It was booze."

Ann was completely perplexed. "Booze?" she asked blankly.

"Yep," Flaherty replied. "My grandpop used to run booze right up those steps to your old man back in Prohibition."

"Your grandfather was a bootlegger?" she asked.

"That he was, and so was your father—in a way."

"He most certainly was not!" she exclaimed, ostensibly annoyed, inwardly uncertain. Ann was dimly aware her father had been a man of diverse enterprise.

"Oh, yes he was." Flaherty laughed, amused by her annoyance.

"You're saying my father was a bootlegger, a criminal," she protested.

"Well, I don't know about the criminal part," Flaherty temporized. "You like to drink, so do I. Probably your father did, too. Times change, laws change. For all we know, marijuana may be legal one day. Can I refill your glass?"

Ann Raimond declined the offer with a shrug of her brown bobbed hair as she asked, "But how do you know?"

"One of my grandpops's still going strong. When he saw we won your father's cup, he called me. Seems that your father lent him some of the bucks to get started. Some of them later went into Flaherty Fisheries. For that, my thanks to the MacKays. Anyway, it gave him a big boot, my winning that cup, and I thought you might be amused."

"So, the Flahertys and the MacKays may have met before," Ann allowed, deciding not to pursue the topic further, sensing a strong kernel of truth, yet wanting to remain uncertain. And she then asked, "Now where is this mighty *Shillelagh* of yours?"

"Which one?" he teased, curious to see if this now proper Mrs. Ann MacKay Raimond really did have a sense of humor.

"You have more than one?" she asked innocently.

"Why, of course," he answered blandly, "What good Irishman wouldn't? There's the boat," nodding toward the window, "and then over there in the closet, there's me blackthorn for dealin' with reluctant wimmin. And then," Flaherty jutted his thumbs into the bands of his slacks as he laughed, "there's always me own private all-purpose shillelagh for the less reluctant."

"Never mind," she said dryly. "The boat will do just fine . . . today. Thank you very much." Ann Raimond got to her feet and went to the picture window, but she was chuckling as she did so. "Which is the sailing *Shillelagh?*"

Flaherty came up beside her, put his arm about her, and pointed to a massive sloop moored halfway up the harbor. "There," he said. As *Shillelagh* lay to the southwest breeze, the western sun had caught the varnished gleam of her tawny topsides, turning her profile to a purposeful weapon of gold.

"Lord! She's beautiful!" Ann exclaimed.

"Yes," Flaherty agreed, grinning proudly.

"And she's wood?"

"Yes. What's so strange about that?"

"Oh, David's always saying you can't win anything anymore without something that's glass or aluminum or something exotic." Her words brought slight wrinkles across the bridge of her nose.

"Well, *Shillelagh* is wood all right, as you see it, but she's really a composite. She's made up with veneers of western cedar over a center of cellular plastic material, sort of like a club sandwich, many layers, all saturated and held together with epoxy glue. Sure, she's wood, but it's as light and strong a construction as there is that I could find. So this David, whoever he is, he's sort of right."

"David's my husband," she said, and immediately turned the conversation back to *Shillelagh*'s construction. "Sounds like you know quite a bit about it."

"I should." Flaherty laughed. "We built her up in our yard in Boothbay."

"Oh." Ann grew even more intrigued with the unfolding facets of Michael Flaherty. "I'm dying to see her," she added.

"Ready to go?" he asked.

"Ready. Which club's launch will we use?" She was the slightest bit anxious they might return to the Neck side of the harbor and use her own club's launch.

"None," Flaherty said flatly. "I don't belong to any of the clubs. I have my own launch right here." He went to a nearby bookshelf and picked up a portable VHF transceiver. "Base to the yacht *Shillelagh*. Come in *Shillelagh*," he called firmly.

The Yacht Shillelagh *off Marblehead, Massachusetts*

"Here comes your cook," Ann remarked with an edge of dryness as they waited on the launch landing below Flaherty's condominium.

"Yep," Flaherty agreed, watching the redheaded girl deftly thread the gray inflatable through the crowded anchorage to a soft landing by his feet "Nice job," he said to Jamie Quinn, then handed Ann Raimond down to a seat. Once underway for *Shillelagh*, he asked, "What's going on, Jamie?"

Never taking her green eyes from her high-speed steering, the girl replied, "Your electronics people have been with Fred most of the morning. They ran the check you wanted on the Sat-Nav. They were adjusting the sideband antenna when I left. Billy and Jim were buttoning down the winches, all regreased. I've got all the canned goods marked and stored. One of the sailmakers is already aboard, the other's due now. So, we're pretty much ready to sail when you are, Mr. Flaherty."

"Good, good, things are happening," Flaherty said. "Sounds like you shove off for Newport tonight, right on schedule. The tide's fair in the canal after eleven."

"As far as I can see, we're ready, Mr. Flaherty," the girl agreed, adding deferentially, "but you'd best check with Fred to be sure."

The deference did not escape Flaherty. As owner, he picked the races to be raced, the equipment to be used, and paid the bills. He purposely left the mundane operations of *Shillelagh*, the port-to-port, race-to-race movements, the bottom scrubbings, provisioning, fueling, sail and gear maintenance, all in the capable hands of young Fred Andresen, a brawny Marbleheader. In yachting days past, Andresen would have been deemed the boat captain. In racing days present, the position was less formally referred to as the head boat nigger, and where racing maxi-sloops was involved, the leader of a tribe of twenty. For nonracing operations and to accomplish his responsibilities, Andresen in turn chose and hired five assistants. While all six of the paid crew were for tax purposes carried on the payroll of Flaherty Fisheries as clerks or dock workers, the reality of their employment was the racing of *Shillelagh*.

The balance of fourteen crew were young men of other professions who loved to sail, enjoyed the comraderie of racing a great sloop on the leading technical edge of the sport. They raced *Shillelagh* with such regularity, they became quite proficient at their assigned tasks. Their reward: T-shirts, jackets, beer money, and transportation reimbursement.

The yacht *Shillelagh* was a male bastion with the exception of the cook. When, in fitting out *Shillelagh* at Marblehead before the season's start, Fred had mentioned he was thinking of giving a girl a shot at the cook's slot, Flaherty had deliberately held back his inherent skepticism of a girl racing at sea. His boat captain had to perform and best he did so with people of his own choosing, if it were to be a happy ship. Fred Andresen must have sensed the owner's skepticism. "I'm tellin' you, Mr. Flaherty, this broad's O.K.," he assured the owner. "She did the Halifax last year with a couple of our guys. They say she's all right, and these guys don't say that about broads on a racing boat."

Now, having watched Jamie Quinn in action, how the girl attended her duties with skill, alacrity, and unending cheerfulness, Flaherty put aside his skepticism. Freddy was right, Flaherty decided, and then, in wistful afterthought, asked himself, *I wonder if the son-of-a-bitch is tagging her, too? If so, well good luck to him.*

While the owner fantasized for a moment, Jamie wheeled the launch alongside *Shillelagh*. Ann Raimond nimbly scrambled up the boarding ladder onto the deck, closely followed by Flaherty. Jamie looked up and asked, "When do we shove off, Mr. Flaherty?"

"Oh, about a half hour, I'd guess."

"Then is it O.K. if I make a run in?" she asked. "There's a couple of things to fetch from the chandlers. Maybe the other sailmaker's waiting at the landing. And my father likes to hear from me kind of regular."

"Shove off." Flaherty laughed, and as his launch roared off toward the town landing, he turned back to his guest. "Welcome to *Shillelagh,*" he said.

"Oh, Michael, she really is beautiful. And teak decks, too!"

"Not really," he laughed. "They're a thin teak veneer over a light honeycomb. But they look like teak, don't they?"

"Yes, they do," she agreed.

"You want the ten-cent or the twenty-five-cent tour?

"The twenty-five-cent or upward. I really want to see her. You know, I do know a bit about boats. So, whatever you have time for."

"I would guess you do," he said and turned forward. "Let's start up at the bow."

As the pair moved on to the foredeck, Ann asked, "What's your plan for today?"

"Well, we've got four new jibs to check out. Two from two different sailmakers. They're duplicates. A little competition keeps those guys on their toes and we get a faster product. So, we'll power out to the bell. When we get hooked up, I'll hop in the inflatable with the sailmakers. You can see things better off boat. I take Polaroid pictures; keep a record of what needs alteration, that way. So, being a little shorthanded, you'll be doing the steering."

"Michael, you'd really trust me with this beautiful creature!" Ann exclaimed, wide-eyed.

"Don't sweat it," Flaherty ribbed. "Your pal Jamie'll be right there with you."

A yacht club launch passed close alongside, her wake throwing a small lurch into *Shillelagh.* "Corky, isn't she!" Ann shouted, catching her balance, and at the same time returning the smiling wave of a curious matron friend in the passing launch.

"Told you she was light, very light." Flaherty chuckled, and then putting his hand to a tapered extrusion of a double-slotted headstay, he said, "You've seen these before, they let us change headsails damn quick. Have the new sail set and drawing before we take off the old. Just about everybody's got 'em, but I've come up with a couple of wrinkles. We've got these little lubricating tubes that . . ." And so he took Ann on a tour of his deck, piece by piece of gear, explaining the uses, proudly pointing out Flaherty-conceived variations or modifications of standard equipment.

They were about to leave the deck for a tour of the accommodation when Jamie Quinn returned with the second sailmaker. "Ready whenever you are, Mr. Flaherty," the girl reported as she tied off the launch.

For her part, Ann Raimond was becoming intrigued with Michael Flaherty and the thoroughness, the obvious love he had put into his yacht. While listening to him demonstrate the controls on the cross linkage of the main winches, she shook her head and said, "You know, David just would not believe this."

"There are probably a lot of things your David would not believe." There was a touch of lechery in his laugh. "Come on, let me show you below."

Ann Raimond's first impression was that of a pigmy lost inside a giant aircraft's wing. The eighty-odd feet of yacht was virtually open from stem to stern, yet the openness was broken by aluminum struts and structural columns going off in all directions. The major portion of the space was given over to piped bins full of bagged sails. "Michael, there's almost nothing down here," she said.

"It's bird-cage construction," Flaherty explained. "She's got what she needs—no more."

"But what about bunks? And privacy?"

"Oh, there are bunks," he said, pointing to the sides. "They're sort of adjustable Pullman-like pull-downs. Not too bad sleeping. Stretched canvas on aluminum frames—light. And there's some privacy. We've got pull-around curtains here and there. The head for instance."

"How thoughtful of you, Michael," she said.

"Hey, look," he said emphatically, "you don't win races lugging around a lot of extra weight."

"I'm sure," she teased, "and not many other things." Then she went on more soberly, "You know, this whole sport has certainly changed since I used to race on *Gull*."

"I meant to ask you. What is *Gull?*"

"Oh, she's David's little yawl. She was in the race yesterday."

"Don't remember seeing her."

"With this, you wouldn't." She laughed. "At least not after the start. She's a Concordia thirty-nine, mahogany topsides."

"Then I must have seen her," Flaherty said. "That's a Ray Hunt design. Christ, they first came out before the Second War. Poor David. He's cruising the dark ages racing up against these new jets."

And then thinking better of his slight, he added, "They're good sea boats. I think they've won Bermuda once or twice, a while back."

"Right on all points," Ann Raimond said as they entered the navigation area where the blond young man who brought the champagne to the prize awards again caught her eye. He was now assisting some white-coveralled technicians in closing up their testing equipment.

"Where are we, Freddy?" Flaherty asked.

"It's all checked out, Mr. Flaherty," the young man replied. "We can sail whenever you want."

"Good boy. Crank her up. We'll hoist sail down harbor."

"O.K., Mr. Flaherty, I'll get Jamie to run these guys to the beach," the boat captain said, then led the technicians topside.

The owner turned his attention back to his guest. "And this is my part of *Shillelagh*. I like to navigate, and as I said, I'm in the electronics business."

"I would never have guessed," she teased. Ann had by now set astern any concern she once had about her visit to Michael Flaherty. She was at ease, excited with her day and more than ever attracted to Michael. She liked his exuberance, his complete involvement. It was such a contrast to her stodgy, predictable David. Looking about Flaherty's navigation cabin, she exclaimed, "Lord, Michael, you have more stuff in here than I've ever seen on an airliner. Just what don't you have?"

"Not much," he allowed, and then launched off on the capabilities and functions of his myriad electronic marvels while his boat captain started the diesel. The balance of Flaherty's lecture was given at a shout, barely overcoming the engine's whine as the big sloop moved down harbor. When finally the engine throttled back, Fred Andresen shouted down the hatch, "We're ready to hoist, Mr. Flaherty."

"Go ahead," he shouted, then asked Ann, "Ready to go up?"

"Certainly am. How much wind have we got?"

Flaherty glanced at the anemometer on his panel. "Fifteen knots out of the sou'west."

"Won't we need foul-weather gear?"

"Naw, not aft where you'll be. She's pretty dry. But maybe you better bring your bag up with you, in case I'm wrong."

On deck, they found Fred Andresen had *Shillelagh* head to wind, dead in the water, while the crew hoisted a gleaming buff-colored mainsail. "Which jib, Mr. Flaherty?" Andresen asked.

"Let's start with the reachers, Freddy. We'll fall off for Gloucester on starboard. Mrs. Raimond will relieve you." And then turning to her, "O.K., Annie babe, you're up. You got the wheel. When Jamie sets up on the runner, take her down towards Halfway Rock."

"Michael, are you sure? I've never sailed anything this big," Ann protested.

"Ya gotta start sometime. She works the same as your *Gull*. Maybe a little faster, but we got plenty of room out here. And Jamie'll be right there with you." Flaherty grinned at his cook, who waited by the mainsheet winch. "Jamie, keep her out of trouble." Flaherty picked up his gear bag and went to the port rail, to a painter that held the inflatable alongside. "Hey, Freddy, have those sailmakers come off with me," he shouted.

Moments later, Flaherty was a hundred yards off to leeward as Ann took *Shillelagh*'s huge steering wheel and put her off on a starboard tack reach. She shook her head in disbelief that Flaherty, this mad owner, could be so casual, so offhanded with his magnificent creation, but that thought was fleeting. *My God, what was she doing there?* she asked herself. The rim of the wheel came up to her nose, the boat was way beyond anything she'd ever handled. But then, when the great sloop's crew wound in on her sheets, the point of Ann's chin jutted briefly. *Give it a try, you can handle her,* she told herself.

With her sails trimmed, *Shillelagh* leaned into the sea and settled to her course. Ann had never felt so much power, such speed under sail. *Shillelagh* would gracefully lift with each quartering sea, then skitter off on a great long surge. To Ann, the motion seemed so effortless, so very beautiful. Her eye then caught a battery of instruments on the fore side of the cockpit bulkhead, blinking performance data in neonesque digits. The digits bounced up and down wildly. As best Ann could interpret, *Shillelagh* was doing better than thirteen knots in fifteen knots of wind. *Lordy, what a lovely boat.*

The wind indicator on the masthead then drew her attention, its black arrow pointing into a wind very close on the sloop's starboard bow. "I thought we'd have the wind abeam on this course for Gloucester," she said, surprised.

Close by Ann's elbow, Jamie heard the comment. "We do," she replied.

"Then take a look aloft, at the masthead. That arrow says we're just about beating."

"Oh, don't pay any attention to that." Jamie laughed. "We move so quickly, we pull the apparent wind way forward, sort of like ice boats."

Flaherty then nudged his inflatable up on the quarter wave of his sloop and picked up a loud-hailer. "Hey, Annie, you're doin' just fine. Now Freddy, let's have a look at the other jib." As his crew moved to make the sail change, his metallic voice boomed on. "How do you like her, Annie?"

"Michael, she's marvelous." Ann screamed her excitement.

"Yeah, I kind of thought you'd like her." Flaherty laughed.

For the balance of the afternoon, *Shillelagh* sailed back and forth between Marblehead and Gloucester, while off to her side, in his high-speed launch, her owner photographed sail flaws or shouted suggestions on trim. When finished, he came in close and ordered rapid fire, "Jamie, you relieve Ann. Annie, grab your bag, it's almost five. We got to get back to the beach. Freddy, I'll catch up with you in Newport. Jamie, put her head to wind. Freddy, give Mrs. Raimond a hand."

After Ann had gotten down into the rubber launch, a neat feat in the quartering seas, Flaherty spun the boat around, heading for Marblehead. He gave the craft full throttle, such power that she jumped off the waves at thirty knots, making conversation impossible on this bouncy ride. Ann held on tightly as a warm wind whipped by the speedy launch, streaming through her hair, drawing tears from her eyes. She was as happy as she had been in many a day.

A short while later, after climbing the ramp from the landing float to the parking space by his condominium, Flaherty put his arm about Ann's waist. "So now you've seen *Shillelagh*."

"Yes, and a marvel she is," Ann said. "What a lovely sail. I really enjoyed it."

"Good, I'm glad you did," he said as they walked over to her station wagon and he opened her door. "I'd ask you in for a drink, but I'm running late."

"I understand," she said, then added, "A pressing date?"

"Yes, sort of." His eyes were gay and good-hearted as they met hers. "The Celtics game with my sons."

"Oh, the Eastern Championships! That should be fun," she said. "Best you get going."

"Right," he said, a bit surprised Mrs. Raimond knew anything about basketball. His eyes had not left hers as he opened her door. "I'm glad you came."

"And I'm glad I was asked. It was great fun." She grinned. "And I thank you." She offered her hand through the window.

"I'd like to see you again," he said, taking her hand, then leaning in for a brief kiss. "I'm off for Newport in a couple of days. Doing the Bermuda Race next weekend. Be back in ten days, I'd guess."

"Oh, I meant to say good luck, I'm sure you and your *Shillelagh* will do it. I know you will." She had put in the key and started the engine as she said, "Why don't you give me a ring when you get back—tell me about the race."

"I'd like to do that." He smiled. "And I will."

She was about to drive off when she paused. "Michael Flaherty, I know you're in a hurry . . . I have one small question. Are you married?"

"Sort of." he answered, "but not very well."

"That I understand." Ann laughed. "See you after Bermuda, and again, good luck." She then drove off, her spirits soaring.

The Boston Garden, Boston, Massachusetts

The three Flahertys were amongst 14,899 Bostonians gone berserk in the Garden. From their first-tier box on mid-court, they screamed their Celtics support in this, the fifth pitched battle with Philadelphia's 76ers. The Eastern Championship of the National Basketball Association was at stake and this game had started with the series tied, two apiece. This first half was a dazzling display of fast-break offense and dogged defense by two of the world's great teams. The intensity of their play was such that they were never separated by more than two points.

With twenty-five seconds left to the half, the Celtics trailed by a pair. The crowd's din was awesome as the Green's D. J. Johnson brought the ball down court on their last foray. Beyond mid-court, Johnson made a move for what seemed an open seam from the top of the key. The Philadelphians instantly closed the gap, forcing Johnson to pass off to Danny Ainge, wide on the left side. Ainge started his own thrust, hastled by Mo Cheeks and almost got surrounded in a forest of Sixer sinew. Prudently, he passed back to D. J., who fed Larry Bird in the right corner. Bird darted for the net, square in the teeth of two Philadelphian towers, Barkley and Malone, in a stalwart double team, their long arms to the rafters. Bird leapt to float through them, a futile move, one the towers were expecting. They went up with him, wearing wide white grins, certain they made an insurmountable fence for even Larry Bird. In mid-air, at the last instant, the flying Bird passed to Kevin McHale at the top of the key, who, in one motion, let go a twisting two-handed fall-away. Sadly, the ball caught the steel rim and caromed upward. But "The Chief" was there, Robert Parish, all seven foot of him, in full flight for the rebound. With one second left, and one hand, he tapped McHale's carom down through the net and Boston Garden became bedlam as the buzzer sounded.

Mike Flaherty and his sons were participants in the standing ovation, their applause for both teams as they trailed off the famed parquet floor. Boston is a basketball town, the rabid repute of its fans legendary. Yet, as aficionados, the Boston fans appreciated the ferocity of play and thundered their approval. Over the years, the Celtics have given their fans an expectation and appreciation of excellence. Sixteen World Championship banners hang from the rafters of Boston Garden.

When the ovation finally died away, Flaherty slapped his youngest son, Patrick, on the back. "Wasn't that something?" he exclaimed.

"Wicked, awesome," the youngster agreed.

"I'll bet this goes to seven games." Flaherty now spoke to his elder son, Mick.

"No way, Dad. Old Larry Bird'll get hot, just you watch. Six games, maybe, but not seven. Betcha."

Before the father could reply, Patrick piped up. "I'm going to get some dogs. Everybody in?" Patrick was a gangly fourteen year old with a voracious appetite.

"Count me, with mustard and relish, and you better get three Cokes," Mike Flaherty added. "You got enough bucks?"

"I think so."

"Well, be sure." Flaherty drew out a thick roll and handed his son a fifty. The youngster climbed up the stairs toward the concession stands while Flaherty and his eldest settled back in their seats.

The father eyed his son for a time, deciding Mick was quite a curious mix in this, his seventeenth year. He had his mother's olive-dark skin and deep brown eyes, but they carried far more of their father's spark. In Flaherty's less-than-objective eyes, his son was quite good looking. Further, Mick had the promise of a multisport athlete, nearing six feet, with broad shoulders that sorely tested the fabric of the Celtics warm-up jacket he wore. Better get him a new one, Flaherty made mental note, but then that paternal thought triggered others and his mind ran back to that day, two years before, when he had moved away from his family. His move was precipitated by his dawn return from playing around Gloucester to a very angry wife. As Rosalie had lost all attraction for Michael, he soon lost his temper and concluded their argument with an announcement that he was leaving, for good. She said nothing, for Rosalie was still in love with Michael, despite his footloose ways. And so, Flaherty went and bought his condominium in Marblehead. With the accumulating affluence of his smuggling operations, maintaining a second home was no burden. Thereafter, Michael kept a cache of clothes on the farm, called when he would be there for a meal, and came and went as he wished, leaving parental discipline with Rosalie. Not long after, Mick and Patrick wanted to move to Marblehead to be with him. As Flaherty spent about as much time with his sons as he ever had, he saw their move as a potential inconvenience and vetoed the idea. And that memory brought him back to Boston Garden. Patrick would soon return, and so, Flaherty said, "Mick, your mom says we've gotta have a talk."

The young man looked down at his high-top sneakers, having no relish for what was to come.

His father went on. "Rosalie says you're not listening to her. You're not hittin' the books and you're out all hours. She right?"

"Hey, Dad," the young man protested. "School's almost over. I'm accepted at U Mass. Spring grades don't count, just so I graduate. I think I'm doing O.K. What Mom's pissed about is last Saturday night. I came home sort of late."

"Like six in the morning," Flaherty said dryly.

"Well, it was our prom."

"Mick, your mother says there's a lot more to it. That it wasn't the first time. That you're hooked up with some gal a couple of years older. That you're into the beer and playing with pot."

"Well, Mom's wrong." Mick looked out over the empty court. "She ought to mind her own business."

"You are her business. She's your mom, Mick." Flaherty eyed his son quite sharply. "And with me now living away, you've got to pay her some attention."

"I do, Dad. I do. But she sure gets on my case sometimes."

"Hey, Mick, I know what you mean. I've been there. She's good at it." Flaherty chuckled. "Now tell me about the girl."

"You'll like her. Her name's Linda Cantella, she's a waitress in the Beverly diner. Got her own wheels, a black Camaro."

"Oh yeah, and how old, Mick?"

"Linda's twenty."

"And you eighteen, next month," Flaherty said. "Don't you think you oughtta pick on kids your own age?"

"We have fun." Mick Flaherty grinned.

"I'll bet." The father laughed. "But maybe you ought to go a little slow for awhile, huh. There's a lot of bugs goin' around. I sure hope you're usin' rubbers."

"No sweat, Dad. Linda's on the pill."

"Bullshit on that. That's no protection for you," his father protested. "I don't want you taking any chances." He reached in his pocket, pulled out his roll, and peeled off another fifty. "Here, you go out and buy yourself a carton of snowshoes. You hear me, Mick?"

"Yes, Dad." Mick Flaherty pocketed the money.

"Now what's this about beer and pot?

"Gee, Dad, what's a few beers and a little weed?"

"Wait a minute, wait just a minute, Mick. You're seventeen. You want to be a jock. Right? Right. Smoking grass, that won't help any. Now your mother says . . ." Michael Flaherty was then interrupted by Patrick's return, his hands full with a carry-all of hot dogs and Cokes.

While Flaherty chewed on his dog, he eyed his son Mick, wondering when he might finish his talk. With Patrick there, tonight was out, he decided, and then rationalized, *Maybe I've said all I need to. The kid's not stupid. He got the message. And I'm the last guy to come down hard for a couple of beers, and just what in hell can I say about grass? Shit, I'm in the business. The kid's probably smoking my own stuff. What's the harm in a little grass? I'll just tell Rosalie*

I really gave the kid hell. That'll shut her up, for a minute or two.
At that moment, the two basketball teams returned to the court
and any further parental concerns went aglimmering in the roar of
the crowd.

The second half of the championship game was a mirror image
of the first, a saga of matching fast breaks, wheeling penetrations,
white-knuckle free throws, and continued ties.

On the Sixers' next trip down court, Andrew Toney swished a
twenty–five footer and Philadelphia trailed by two. With that, the
Celtics called time out. Their coach, K. C. Jones, would marshal his
troops. Strategy was called for.

After their time-out huddle, Bird inbounded to D. J., who brought
the ball up court with the assured aplomb of a field marshal. Thirty
seconds remained when D. J. passed off to Ainge. Between them,
they would run off as much time as they could. Ainge soon drew
the pressure of a double team and passed back to D. J. Dribbling
masterfully, D. J. glanced up at the clock as two Philadelphians sprang
at him. A disconcerted D. J. tried a hasty cross-court shovel pass to
Bird, when off the top of the key, Philadelphia's Julius Erving leapt
for the low pass and intercepted with one huge hand. The old master
flew off down court in long leaping strides with Green players in
dismayed pursuit. From the center of the Celts' key, "Doctor J" went
up on a graceful float for the net and drove the ball through with
a magnificent slam-dunk. The score was tied with nine seconds left,
the crowd stunned. The Boston players stood around slack-jawed.

K. C. Jones called another time out.

"I told you, it will go seven," Mike Flaherty said to his sons.

"There's still time, Dad," Mick replied.

On the Celts' mid-court inbound, Danny Ainge threw to a grim
D. J. Johnson, who drove toward the center to meet three resolute
men in red. D. J. tried another short pass, under the waiting giants,
to a now less-guarded Larry Bird. This time he connected, and in
one blinding microsecond, Bird had the ball in flight for the hoop
from twenty feet out. The ball was at the apogee of its arc as the
buzzer went. And then it fell through, catching nothing but net.

Patrick Flaherty jumped up and down on his seat, while Mick
pounded his father on the back. "See Dad, I told ya, I told ya Bird
would do it," he screamed.

Quite a while later, the Flahertys rolled down the ramps of the
Garden, their arms around each other, happily shouldering through

the milling crowd. When finally they got out into the warm summer night, a full moon hung over Boston. For the jubilant Flahertys, all was right and certain, the moon and the stars shone above, God was in His Heaven. The Celtics had won.

Part Three

U.S. Coast Guard Headquarters, Boston, Massachusetts

That afternoon, in an old building on the Boston waterfront, a heavy-set man ambled back to his air-conditioned office. As he opened the door, he wore a contented grin. The door was marked DISTRICT INTELLIGENCE OFFICE, and in an insert slot below; CAPT. OTIS N. OSBORNE, U.S.C.G.

The blue-uniformed Otie Osborne went around to his desk and flopped into his chair. On swiveling toward the window, he looked out over the harbor, across to Charlestown, at the stark rigging of the old frigate *Constitution*, heroine of the War of 1812. But Osborne's thoughts were not at all on the past feats of the Republic. They were very much on the present, specifically, the near-term operations of the U.S. Coast Guard in the First District, and tangentially, their impact upon his own career.

Osborne's eye fell on an admiral's pennant with its single star that lazily flapped high in the frigate's rigging, for *Constitution* was still in commission, and often served as flagship of the First Naval District. *You know Otie, you might get one of those stars yet,* he mused. *If this week comes off the way you think it will, there's a chance.* Knowing his weekly roundup of phone calls from his agents along the coast would not start for another hour, Osborne hunkered down comfortably in his chair, put his hands across his belly, and turned his musings to a review of recent events.

The night before, Old Pebble Voice had called him with the curt details of another drug deal. On getting to the office that morning, Osborne went down the hall for coffee with his admiral. He patiently learned of Haggerty's twilight tribulations on the golf course and then asked rather casually, "Harry, does that sailboat race go off to Bermuda this week?"

"Sure does—Friday noon at Brenton Reef Tower. Matter of fact, I've been asked down for a few of the parties. Why?"

"Oh, I wanted to see if it ties with something I heard last night."

"What's that, Otie?"

"Well, I've got reason to believe there's a red seventy-five footer, a sloop called *Renegade*. She's carrying Bermudian papers, but she's really out of the Carib. She's supposed to off-load two tons of grass at oh-two-hundred Thursday, in behind Nomans Land. The buyer's a sixty-foot dragger, the *Black Hawk* out of Barrington."

The admiral made his long fingers into a cat's cradle and swiveled to stare at the coastal chart on the wall. When he spoke, he spoke slowly, thoughtfully. "That's interesting, very interesting." He paused and then looked at Osborne grimly. "I hate to say this, Otie, but I think we've got a leak in this district. No, I don't think, I know," he added emphatically.

"Why so, Harry?"

"Well it was only a couple of days ago, Friday afternoon, as a matter of fact, that I decided to pull two of the patrol boats off the bottom of the Cape. They're ordered for Newport, twenty-four-hundred, Wednesday. I figure that spectator fleet at the start can get out of hand. I wanted to make sure we looked good. Also, my bird in Washington says the commandant's thinking of flying up for the start of the race. That's not firm yet. Apparently, our senior senator and a couple of congressmen and the governor of Delaware are all in the race. With the Administration cutting back on our funding, the commandant probably figures a little high-level flag-waving won't hurt. Anyway, I decided our Narragansett Bay boys could use a little help."

"The commandant, is he really coming up?"

"Yeah, that's what my birdie says," Haggerty said, "but what bugs me is you come up with a grass go-down under the Cape set for only two hours after I open the operational gap by pulling the patrols.

That's not a coincidence." Haggerty got to his feet and started to pace. "How good's your source, Otie?"

"One of my best," Osborne answered, somewhat evasively.

"Want to talk about it?" The admiral was eyeing him sharply.

"I'd rather not." Osborne returned the look squarely and went on. "Let's put it this way. My dope is as good as my batting average."

"O.K., that's good enough for me. We play it." Haggerty turned back to the chart. "Well, I guess we put those patrols back, south of the Cape. Another bust is more important than looking good at the Bermuda start."

"You might want to think about that," Osborne cautioned.

"Why so?"

"Well, if you're right, that we have a leak here in Headquarters, the trade might not go down."

"Hmm, good thought," the admiral agreed.

"What I'd suggest is we pull *Hamilton* in off the Banks to the east side of the Cape, say for eighteen-hundred Wednesday. We do it quiet-like. I'll come up with a cover story. And with your permission, I'd like to join her by chopper. Then, when I board her, not till then, I order her for Nomans Land. That way, even if there is a leak, he hasn't a clue where *Hamilton*'s heading." On duty, Osborne was both a knowledgeable seaman and a shrewd operations man.

"Otie my boy, I like it," the admiral mused. "Permission granted, and you know what—I think I'm going with you."

"Sir, it's about time you went to sea." Osborne laughed as he left.

Later that afternoon, when the admiral hauled Osborne back to his office for a second meeting, he was in an expansive mood. "O.K., Otie, it's go, a complete go."

"Good," Osborne said. "And you're coming, too?"

"Uh huh." Haggerty grinned. "And guess what?"

"Beats me. What?"

"The commandant's coming, too."

It was with this input that Captain Osborne had returned to his office and gazed on the harbor, contented to snooze and await his round of phone calls. *Old Gravel baby, just be right, just one more time,* he said to himself, still watching *Constitution*'s flapping pennant.

The U.S.C.G. Cutter Hamilton off Cape Cod, Massachusetts

Before starting down the steps, Captain Otis Osborne took one last look around the helicopter's main cabin. The spartan simplicity of the cavernous space again gave him pause, wondering how the commandant would react. On first boarding, he had tried one of the seats that pulled down off the side frames. It was tight, very tight. The designers had not envisioned the needs of the broad-bottomed Captain Osborne. *So it ain't trans-Atlantic first class,* Osborne rationalized, *but what the hell, it'll only be an hour's flight.*

On regaining the asphalt of Boston's General Aviation Terminal, Osborne walked to a nearby Coast Guard car. A young petty officer sprang from the front to snap the rear door open. Osborne eased into the air-conditioned comfort of the car and reported to the district commander, "Well, Harry, it's all go. Flight clearance—full fuel—engines warmed. Our gear's stowed. I went over the flight plan with the pilot. East out of here to a point eighteen miles nor'east of P-town. That gets us over the horizon from land. Then south for *Hamilton.* She'll be twenty miles sou'east of Chatham, over the horizon from Monomoy Point, about an hour's flight, the pilot reckons."

"O.K." Admiral Haggerty nodded. "But couldn't you have come up with something a little classier than that goddamn old Pelican?

It's not every day we have the commandant come out on an operation."

"Yeah, I suppose I could have, Harry. It would have meant a lot of jiggling around with the operations guys. If I started throwing weight around, there might have been a lot of questions. The way I figured it, this is the craft assigned to *Hamilton*. So I arranged that she comes in for some spares. It looked more routine to me, better cover."

"You're right, Otie," Haggerty agreed.

"Anyway, it'll give the big boss an idea just what kind of old crap we're still using in operations," Osborne added.

"Otie, he knows, but he doesn't control the bucks, not in this Administration."

"I also told our pilot to go low and slow on the chatter with the ship. Nothing said about who's on board. Not a word. You never can tell who's listening to what."

"Good idea, Otie." Admiral Haggerty laughed. "Boy, will they shit on the *Hamilton* when they see the brass step down. How'd you like to be her C.O.—have the commandant and the district commander drop out of the sky, unannounced?"

Their ability to converse was broken by the piercing whine of a small jet taxiing toward the waiting helicopter. As the white jet swung to a halt, she showed the red slash and the blue Coast Guard emblem across her tail.

"That's him. Time to go to work," Haggerty said, opening the car door. They strode to the jet and became a pair of saluting sideboys as the commandant stepped out into the humid heat. Lightly taking the steps, the commandant returned their salutes with a casual snap, then shook Admiral Haggerty's hand.

"Harry! How the hell are you?" he said heartily. The full brunt of the oppressive heat then hit, for he added, "Jesus, I thought I left this kind of weather in Washington."

As the two chatted on, Osborne remained at attention, all the while eyeing the commandant, curious about the man who had risen to the top of his trade. He first noted the affable ease and ready smile. That was a surprise. It did not fit with the man's intraservice repute as a no-nonsense, ball-busting administrator. Osborne was impressed by how slender and fit the commandant was for a man in his late fifties. Here he was in his tailored whites with his gold stars, the commandant in all his splendor, yet Osborne felt he had more the manner of a fit college kid just turned loose for the summer.

Haggerty turned to Osborne and said, "Admiral Sanders, I'd like to present our district intelligence officer, Captain Otis Osborne."

"Captain Osborne." The commandant's grip was firm while his eyes wrinkled to a friendly smile. "Bob Sanders. It's a pleasure. So you're the guy that's got 'em all talking back at Headquarters."

"Thank you, sir." Osborne acknowledged the compliment modestly. An aiguilletted young commander and the copilot came down the Lear's steps with the commandant's luggage and headed for the helicopter. The commandant eyed the luggage bearers and then the waiting aircraft. "Hey, an old Pelican!" he enthused. "I used to fly 'em back when Sikorsky first sold them to the Coast Guard. I was a contracting officer then." Then he turned back to Haggerty and Osborne. "I'm really looking forward to this. Let's get going." And he trotted off toward the helicopter.

As they trailed behind, Haggerty gave Osborne an "all's well" smile. Osborne's return look was a little less certain, as he held up crossed fingers.

The Pelican started to shudder and buck and whine as the three men strapped themselves into their seats. The whirling rotors soon revved to a smooth shrill, precluding all possibility of cabin conversation without headsets. The helicopter then lurched into the air, climbed out two hundred feet over Boston Harbor, and turned east toward Cape Cod. The aircraft had barely cleared the island chain of the harbor mouth when the commandant unbuckled his shoulder harness and headed for the cockpit. Through the open door, Osborne saw him introduce himself to the pilots. Not many minutes later, he replaced the copilot and took over the controls, while on the far side of the main cabin, Admiral Haggerty became engrossed in a report.

Within the predicted hour, they were well outside Monomoy Point, off the southeast side of the Cape. Below the chopper's port nose, the cutter *Hamilton* idled ahead into a slight onshore swell. Osborne took in the rakish white mass of the *Hamilton,* 378 feet of purposeful steel and aluminum, her jutting bow with its five-inch gun, the pods of twenty-millimeter machine guns, the wide helipad on the stern. Osborne thought ahead into the night. *Christ, how'd you like to have that come at you out of the fog? Maybe a bit of overkill.* He laughed to himself, watching *Hamilton*'s flight controller waggle and guide the helicopter to an approach with bright orange paddles. Osborne turned back to the cockpit and saw that the commandant was still at the controls.

After a smooth touchdown, Osborne was the first out and down on *Hamilton*'s deck. Crewmen were cinching the helicopter to flushed deck padeyes as Admiral Haggerty joined Osborne. They watched the flight controller go wide-eyed and chatter into his mouthpiece as he snapped to a rigid salute.

"Bet it's a bit busy on the bridge." Haggerty laughed.

By the time Commandant Sanders joined the pair, the entire flight-deck crew had come to attention. The officers returned the salutes, then started forward.

"Nice landing, sir," Osborne said.

"Gawd Ted, you weren't flying that thing?" Haggerty protested.

"Thank you, Captain," the commandant said to Osborne, and then broke into a collegiate grin as he slapped Haggerty on the back. "And the hell I wasn't. I haven't flown one of those in years. The kid rode it down with me, of course, just to be sure."

"Thank God I didn't know." Haggerty laughed.

Osborne spoke to the flight controller. "Chief, could you show us up to the captain's office?"

"Yes, sir," the young controller said, then spun on his heel, quickly guiding the trio up through the superstructure to the captain's quarters under the bridge.

The U.S.C.G. Cutter Hamilton *off Martha's Vineyard, Massachusetts*

The captain of *Hamilton* was hastily tucking a fresh shirt into his pants when Admiral Haggerty stepped into his office.

"Eddie—a bit of a surprise," the admiral said.

"Yes, sir," the captain agreed, looking over the district commander's shoulders at the gold epaulettes of the commandant. After proper introductions, the commandant, the district commander, the captain, and Osborne took seats around a small corner table. Upon acceptance of the ritual offer of coffee, Admiral Haggerty opened the meeting. "Sorry Ed, we couldn't have given you more notice," he said to *Hamilton*'s skipper. "This all came up rather quickly. Otie will explain."

Osborne spoke. "We've got pretty good reason to believe there'll be a grass sale in behind Nomans Land tomorrow morning at oh-two-hundred. The seller is supposed to be a red seventy-five-foot sloop, the *Renegade*. Her papers will say she's out of Bermuda for Newport, coming up for the race. I hear she's out of Grand Bahama. Now, there is a boat of her name and description entered for the race on Friday, that I learned from Castle Hill Coast Guard. The grass buyer is supposed to be a dragger out of Barrington, Rhode Island, the *Black Hawk*. There is a vessel of that name and hail in the *Registry*. So, we're planning to join their party."

"Hmm, Nomans Land by oh-two-hundred," *Hamilton*'s captain said, glancing at his watch. "It's now seventeen-fifteen; that should be no problem." He turned to his district commander. "Sir, if you'd like, we could head up to navigation, work it all out on the plot."

The district commander glanced at the commandant, who said, "Let's do it."

A few minutes later, after *Hamilton*'s skipper had cleared the navigation area of all but his visitors, he laid out a large-scale chart of Cape Cod and the islands and with dividers deftly walked off a safe loop from their present position off Chatham, south around Nantucket Shoals, then west to Nomans Land below Martha's Vineyard. "As I thought, sir," he said to Admiral Haggerty, "at twenty knots, we could be there a couple of hours early."

"And that's just what we don't want to do," Osborne interjected. The two admirals looked at Osborne as he went on. "When we make this grab, we want 'em both lashed up with grass on both boats. I'm told there's two tons on *Renegade*. Say at a hundred pounds a bale, they've got a hundred and twenty bales to shift. I think we should hit 'em at two-thirty earliest."

The commandant agreed. "Makes sense, illegal possession, conspiring to distribute, both vessels, a double seizure." And then he added thoughtfully, "Looking at this chart, these guys have got to be pretty ballsy, planning a transfer right under our nose here at Nomans."

"Oh, I don't know, sir," Osborne replied. "When you look at it, it's just off the trawler's track between George's Bank and New Bedford. And then, with all this heat, there's a good chance of fog. It could make a lot of sense."

"Sure was thick-a-fog out beyond George's last night," the skipper put in.

"But what about our patrols?" the commandant asked. "I thought we had a couple of the Point class vessels covering the south Cape?"

"We do," the district commander replied, "but I've ordered them into Newport as of twenty-four-hundred tonight. They're going to be the corners for the spectator patrol line on the Bermuda Race start."

"That's curious," the commandant said, then turned to Osborne. "Well, Captain, what are your thoughts?"

"Sir, I set up this Chatham rendezvous with two alternatives in mind. We could loop south of Nantucket, just like the cap here walked off—come in from the sea—have 'em pinned in territorial waters for sure. My problem with that is I've got to assume at least the dragger's got radar, maybe both vessels do. If we come in from the Nantucket side with any speed, and they spot us, we give 'em ten or fifteen miles warning."

The district commander's attention came up from the chart. "The Nantucket route seems the safest for navigation. You've got deep water outside the shoals. And on radar, they'd probably take our blip for an inbound trawler."

"Yes, sir, there's good water, I agree, and they might take our blip for a trawler," Osborne answered deferentially, "but if they're plugged in with the New Bedford Fish Auction, they just might have a handle on what's inbound for the morning sale. And I'd guess we paint a bigger blip on the radar than most trawlers. If I were they, I'd have a picket out, and then, their bales could be weighted."

"Captain Osborne, you mentioned two routes," the commandant reminded him.

"Yes, sir, I did. We could also steam west through Nantucket Sound." Osborne traced his second alternative on the chart with his finger. "We could hug the north and west side of the Vineyard. Keep the land mass between us and Nomans until we turn Gay Head. That would give us a screen from their radars."

"But what about the shallows here, here, and here," the *Hamilton*'s skipper protested, pointing out several warning-blue winnows on the chart, knowing full well, admirals on board be damned, any grounding of his vessel would be held as his responsibility at an inevitable inquiry.

"What are we drawing?" Haggerty asked.

"Well, we've burned off some bunkers, so we're a little lighter. We're drawing twenty-four feet," the *Hamilton*'s captain said.

"So where's the sweat?" Osborne said blithely, pointing to deeper shades of water on the chart. "The way I worked it out, you track south of Succonnesset Shoal, north of Hedge Fence. Where it gets tricky is getting on the east side of Middle Ground Shoal right here by West Chop. There's a slot for a couple of hundred yards here by at Alleghany Rock. It's tight, but we've got sonar."

"And two or three knots of current right up our pipe at that turn," the captain added. "That won't help if we hit. I'd like to study it, sir." He appealed to the district commander.

The commandant broke in. "You've obviously studied it, Captain Osborne, I have the feeling you like your second alternative."

"Sir, I can only make recommendations. Eddie here, he's the skipper," Osborne replied. He knew the rules of the game. "Of the two choices, the inside route's got this going for it. We enter Nantucket Sound with the dusk—there's a lot of ferry traffic between the Cape and the islands. We go low with the lights so even if these guys have a picket out over this way, they'll be hard-pressed to spot the difference between us and the big ferries on radar. Now, from Gay Head out to Nomans—it's only four or five miles. So if we wheel Gay Head at twenty-eight knots, then run without lights, they'll have less than ten minutes to spot us, break off their transfer, and sink the shit. No way they'll do it. So, we blindside 'em."

"That's my old running guard." Admiral Haggerty laughed.

"The John Wayne cavalry approach." The commandant grinned appreciatively, then suggested more sternly to *Hamilton*'s captain, "Skipper, why don't you and your navigator give both options a hard look. Get back to me with your decision. Come on Harry, Otie, let's take a look around."

Hamilton's skipper sensed the commandant's preference for the more perilous Vineyard Sound approach and in little time made that his recommendation. Later that night, by 1:45, he had his cutter clear of Hedge Fence Shoals and in a tight port turn under the bluffs of the Vineyard's West Chop. The skipper well knew the hazard of his choice and had personally taken the con on the battle-lit bridge. His exec was assigned to the navigational plotting. The dim red light of the battle lamps softened the hard set of the skipper's jaw and hid the dark patches of sweat beneath his arms. His career might well hang on this turn.

When the fog lifted under the West Chop headland, the visiting officers were out on the port bridge wing, watching the twinkling lights of the summer cottages, tactfully leaving the *Hamilton*'s skipper to the loneliness of his command.

When the brass had gone, the skipper muttered, *Why the Christ did I go along with this?*

Hamilton leaned to the turn, her Fairbanks Morse diesels purring away on "slow bell." The only sound on her bridge was a low litany of pelorus bearings from young officers out on the wings, radar and sonar bearings repeated in a steady chant by the talker.

"Recommend new course—left to two-four-zero, Skipper," the exec said from the navigation cubicle.

"Left to two–four–zero, helmsman," the skipper ordered sharply.

"Left to two–four–zero, sir," the helmsman repeated.

"Bow reports black can two hundred yards on port bow, sir," the talker said.

"Get a light on it, bo'sun," the skipper growled. In an instant, a silver shaft of light swung through the night to spear the buoy firmly. "Got it," the skipper acknowledged, eyeing the can, judging the set of the current.

"Sonar has shallows bearing three-three-zero relative, sir."

"Down to thirty feet, Skipper," the exec cautioned.

That leaves six feet under the keel, the skipper thought, then ordered, "O.K. Give 'em to me steady." His eyes never left the spotlit buoy as he said to the helmsman, "Left another five, make it two-three-fiver."

"Depth, twenty-nine feet," droned the exec.

"Sonar has shallows seven-zero yards at two-seven-zero and one-zero-zero yards at zero-four-zero, sir," the talker said, his voice rising.

"Twenty-seven feet."

This is it, the skipper thought. *It all hangs on the next fifty yards— I should have said no to that son of a bitch Osborne. Gone out around Nantucket. He must think Hamilton's some goddamn kind of harbor craft.*

"Twenty-six feet."

Well aware he had but two feet under his keel, the skipper glared at the black can that marked Alleghany Rock, wishing it, willing it, and, finally, watching it slide clear along the port side. His last course correction had countered the current set.

"Twenty-five-and-a-half."

"Sonar has shallows seven-zero yards—two-seven-zero and one-one-zero—zero-niner-zero relative." The talker's tone soared to a near scream.

"Twenty-five."

A foot left and nowhere to turn, the skipper muttered, bracing for the crunch, certain it would come. "Stand by, we may touch," he warned.

A long moment later, the exec exulted, "Twenty-five-and-a-half and dropping."

"Thank God." The skipper sighed.

"Twenty-six—and we're inside the middle ground, skipper," the exec advised. "Recommend new course, two-four-zero."

"Come right to two-four-zero, and half ahead, helmsman," the skipper ordered, and then to his exec, "Kill the lights and take the con. Hug the Vineyard shore as close as you can."

"Relieved, skipper," the exec said as the cutter surged ahead with the higher throb of her diesels.

The skipper stepped out on the port bridge wing, lighting a cigarette as he did so. The commandant came up beside him and clapped him on the back. "That was one hell of a piece of ship handling, Captain," he said.

"Sure was," the district commander agreed. "What's the e.t.a.—Gay Head, Eddie?"

"We're at half ahead, sir, and we've got two knots or more with us." The skipper paused, running the numbers out in his head. "Two-twenty at Gay Head," he replied.

"Right on the money, cap," Otie Osborne said.

"Could make it earlier, if you want," the skipper offered. "We're just out of the yard—clean bottom. Kick in the turbines, you've got twenty-nine knots plus the current."

"Let's stick with the plan," the commandant cautioned. "Give 'em some time for transfer. We go to the turbines at Gay Head."

Snug by the dark land mass of the Vineyard, the white cutter once again sliced through wraiths of sea fog. The second officer came out on the wing and reported to the skipper, "Boarding parties armed and ready, sir. I've briefed 'em and checked 'em all out. They go for the sea-cocks first."

"Very good," the skipper said.

The second officer continued. "Chief reports turbines ready. Bow guns and twenties manned. Pilot asks if you want the chopper warmed over, sir?"

The skipper turned to his district commander. "Think we'll want the chopper, sir?"

"Can't hurt—why not?" The district commander laughed. " 'Be prepared's' our motto."

"Tell 'em to warm her up and stand by," the skipper ordered, "and make sure their crew chief draws a weapon—one of the automatics."

At 2:20, the darkened cutter cut in her gas turbines. Under the combined urging of thirty-six thousand shaft horse, she cleaved the turn of Gay Head at twenty-nine knots to settle on course for Nomans Land. The visiting officers were out on her wing, anxiously trying to pierce the patches of fog with night glasses. *Hamilton*'s navigator had worked out the run—ten minutes flat.

Moments after the turn, the visitors heard the exec shout to the skipper, "Radar has a strong target just off the island, range three-point-seven-fiver, bearing zero-zero-zero."

The commandant let go an exhultant whoop while Admiral Haggerty grabbed Osborne in a bear hug. "Right again, you old bastard."

"We'll see," Osborne allowed, beaming.

Three minutes later, the exec again shouted, "Radar reports target separating, they now have two targets, Skipper."

At that moment, the cutter broke clear of the fog. "Recommend we give 'em a star shell," Osborne advised Haggerty.

"Hey, Skipper, the star shell," the commandant shouted excitedly, taking command by his tone.

A few seconds later, the bow gun thudded an ear-shattering thud, followed by two more in quick succession. On the burst of the shells, the black night broke into the brilliance of noon, an eerie stark silvery noon, a noon lit by three phosphorescent suns, dangling from parachutes.

"We got 'em!" the commandant shouted, his night glasses to his eyes. "The sloop's heading for sea."

Osborne had also picked them up. "Recommend we grab the

dragger first, sir," he said. The sixty-five-foot fisherman was low and black, a wallowing shadow on the sea, her presence dimly marked by the shape of dark nets hanging from hoisted outriggers.

"And let the sloop go? They've got the grass," the district commander objected.

"Hell, Harry," Osborne answered a bit testily, "if she can break eight knots, I'll eat her. When we come up on the dragger, we drop the launch. Send the chopper off after the sloop if you want."

"A lot of activity on the dragger," the commandant observed.

"No surprise," Osborne said. "Trying to dump the shit."

The first of the parachute flares now dangled close to the dragger. "Some more star shells, Skipper," the commandant ordered, all niceties of naval etiquette having gone with the first shell, leaving no doubt as to who was now in actual command of the cutter *Hamilton*. *Thud. Thud. Thud.* Three new silver suns. "And a light on each vessel," he added. Powerful searchlights added to the brilliance, pinning the diverging vessels in moons of white light.

"Bow lookout has objects in the water close ahead," warned the exec.

"Drop a light down," the commandant shouted. The cutter's searchlight beam soon swept the sea out ahead, catching the black glint of plastic bales floating in the water.

"Good! They weren't weighted," Osborne said. "We can grab 'em later. Only need a couple to make our case."

"Give me the siren," the commandant called. The night then filled with a piercing *Whoop. Whoop. Whoop.* "And now a shot across the dragger's bow," he ordered. With the sharp *crack* of the bow gun, a tall plume leapt from the sea not thirty yards ahead of the fleeing dragger. And with that first shell, the white moustache of the dragger's bow wave quickly fell away.

"That did it!" Admiral Haggerty exclaimed. "They've stopped!"

The cutter came up on the dragger at an awesome rate, while her siren screamed.

"Put us as close as you can along her starboard side, Skipper," the commandant ordered. "Have your port twenties cover the deck. They are not to fire without a direct command. Launch the boats when we lose way. Port launch after the sloop. Starboard goes for the dragger. Send the chopper after the sloop." *Whoop. Whoop. Whoop.* And cut that siren. Now. Hard astern, and may I have the mike?"

Not forty-five seconds later, the cutter came to a turbine-grinding stop not forty yards off the dragger. When the commandant spoke into the mike, his amplified voice boomed into the night. His calm tone carried a knife edge of total no-nonsense. "This is the United States Coast Guard. We are boarding you for a documentation check. You will have all hands on deck immediately. They will keep their hands on their heads until told otherwise." The warning was instantly followed by the grind of davit winches as the launches dropped into the sea. Next came the clatter and roar of rotors as the helicopter lifted off the stern.

"Boarding parties away—chopper launched," the exec reported.

A searchlight still speared the fleeing sloop as the launch and the chopper raced after her. Her flight was futile. She was speedily overhauled by the chopper. After a brief burst of automatic fire from the aircraft, the sloop went dead in the water, less than a half mile from the cutter.

Turning away from the sloop, Osborne looked down on the gap between *Hamilton* and the dragger and saw it strewn with jettisoned bales. On the dragger, four fisherman stood around the wheelhouse, squinting in the searchlight's glare. They wore the yellow skins and knee boots of their trade, their stance forlorn, their hands on their heads, awkwardly balanced for the small rolling sea. Osborne was studying the still-open hatch when the cutter's launch went alongside and ten sailors swarmed over the rail. Four of the boarders went aft and turned the fishermen face to the wheelhouse, hands high. Two covered the fishermen with submachine guns at the ready while the others went about a body search. Other boarders disappeared below through the wheelhouse while the last held flashlights down the open hatch. *Pretty professional for a bunch of youngsters,* Osborne thought.

Not many minutes later, a petty officer came to the dragger's bridge door, holding a small VHF radio to his face. His transmission came up on the *Hamilton*'s bridge radio, loud, calm, and booming clear. "Boarding party to *Hamilton*. Vessel's papers seem O.K. Fishing vessel *Black Hawk,* ninety-eight tons, documented at Providence. Sea-cocks secure. No fish on board. There are wrapped packages in the hold. Over."

"Investigate and report." The commandant spoke into the mike.

"Yes, sir." The VHF went silent. A few moments later, there came a second voice, a harried voice. "*Hamilton, Hamilton,* we're on this fuckin' sailboat. One of the bastards has smashed the head valves. Pumps ain't holding worth shit. Can't get at 'em. Cabin's crammed with grass."

"Have the chopper drop 'em a pump," the commandant ordered. "Let's get alongside her quick as we can."

The *Hamilton*'s skipper took command of his cutter and soon put her close alongside the sinking sloop. Thereafter, the Coast Guardsmen worked through the night securing their catch. By dawn, they had all three vessels underway for Newport.

Later that afternoon, at Newport, as the racing skippers congregated for their final prerace briefing, there came into the narrows of Narragansett Bay a small convoy. At the point was the cutter *Hamilton,* bedecked in bunting, siren wailing, her white-clad crewmen proudly manning the rail. The cutter was trailed by a rusty dragger and further astern, a red sloop under power. Herding the quarters of this odd convoy were two Coast Guard patrol craft, horns hooting, blue lights blinking.

The next day, the morning of the Bermuda Race start, the *Providence Journal* carried the following headline;

BIG DRUG BUST OFF BAY
C. G. COMMANDANT IN COMMAND
Bermuda Race Entry Seized

Going out on *Hamilton* to watch the start of the race, Captain Otis Osborne walked aft to the rail by the helipad. He had read the newspaper in the wardroom, and decided the commandant sure got what he came for. Now walking aft, the district intelligence officer wanted to get away from all the dignitaries celebrating on the forward bridge wings; he wanted some time to himself, some time to think. Otie Osborne was bothered. It had once again been so easy . . . so absurdly easy. But why?

The U.S.C.G. Cutter Hamilton *off Newport, Rhode Island*

Alone at the rail by the cutter's helipad, the *thud* of the Race Committee boat cannon drew Captain Osborne's attention to the milling fleet of yachts. A loudspeaker aboard *Hamilton* announced to the visiting dignitaries, "Five minutes to the start of Class A."

For all his years on and around the sea, Osborne was not much of a wind sailor. In his time at the Coast Guard Academy, he had sailed several cruises aboard the square-rigged *Eagle,* the massive training ship seized as a prize-of-war from Nazi Germany. Despite this time under canvas, Osborne preferred the reliability of diesel power to the vagaries of wind. To Osborne, the Bermuda-bound maxi-yachts now jockeying about for their start, with some a good eighty feet, seemed so many rich men's little toys. "So these are the maxis," Osborne said aloud. That morning, Admiral Haggerty had explained the phrase to Osborne; that there was a maximum-size boat allowed to race under the handicap formula; yachts built to that limit were called maxis. As a salaried government employee, Otie Osborne was less impressed by these boats' size and beauty than he was by their cost, a million or more apiece.

"Thirty seconds to the start of Class A," the loudspeaker said.

Hamilton was close in on the weather and westerly side of the Race Committee boat, affording Osborne a grandstand view of the long line down to the Brenton Reef Tower. About sixty yards below the Committee boat, a dark mahogany sloop was charging for the line on a close reach, when suddenly, her helmsman decided she would be early and spun head to wind, her massive sails thundering and slatting as she luffed to kill time. Osborne was certain the dark yacht would cleave a golden sloop reaching along just above her. *Boy! These guys really screw around,* the safety-minded Coast Guardsman thought. At the very last instant, the golden sloop luffed, a pirouette in parallel to the dark yacht, deftly avoiding a collision. A few seconds later, the dark yacht curtailed her luff and fell off toward the line. Quickly, the golden sloop fell off with her, neatly stealing for herself what might have been a coffin-corner, right under the Committee boat.

Thud! A white donut of cannon smoke spiraled upward from the Committee boat.

"The start of Class A was taken by the sloop *Shillelagh,*" the loud-speaker said.

So that's Shillelagh, Osborne mused, studying the white-slickered crew lining her rail, wondering where Lieutenant Quinn might be. Of all the agents in Osborne's nonproductive network, Jamie Quinn had become his favorite.

After the start of Class A, the thick herd of spectator craft clustered about the line soon thinned, opening a workable gap that the big cutter might maneuver. *Hamilton* then hauled anchor and took on speed, chasing the Bermuda-bound racers to watch for a part of the afternoon. Within a half hour, *Hamilton* had drawn abreast of the maxis. Still alone on the helipad aft, Captain Osborne saw *Shillelagh* held the slim lead she snatched off the starting line. Osborne boomed out loudly, "Go get 'em *Shillelagh.*" The captain's booming cheer indeed had some carry, for several of *Shillelagh's* crew raised their arms in clenched fist agreement.

The Yacht Shillelagh *on the Bermuda Race*

By the companionway ladder, Jamie Quinn took a last tug on the neck draw of her slicker, then climbed up into the sunlight. "Galley closed—you've got the scrub-up, Dickey boy," she announced cheerily to one of the crewmen perched on the weather rail.

"Oh shit," the crewman wailed and crawled down off the rail.

Jamie took the scrubman's place and happily looked about her. It was a sparkling morning, this first morning at sea. Aloft, high puffs of cumulus scudded with the fresh west wind. As the shadows of these flying clouds sped along, they cast fleeting dark patches on the bottle-green sea. While Jamie watched, *Shillelagh* bowled along, over and through the quartering sea, hard driven by a reaching jib and a reefed main, her lee rail most often awash.

From snatches of conversation she'd heard while cooking up breakfast, Jamie knew they would soon hit the gulf stream. Mr. Flaherty had warned Freddy about what to look for, lowering squalls to windward and sargasso weed on the sea. Jamie, who had sailed all her young days on the Pacific, looked forward to this, her first encounter with the Atlantic's famed gulf stream. She nudged Mick Flaherty lying beside her. "Hey Mick, where are they all?" she asked.

"Uh," he said, awakening. "Oh, that's *Kialoa* right below us. Then *Ondine*'s beyond her, you can see her sometimes under the boom.

129

She's a couple of miles off to leeward. I don't know where *Condor* went, way off to leeward, I guess."

Mick pointed out over the lee quarter, aft, where on the rising swells, three small triangles glinted white in the sunlight.

Appraised of the competition, Jamie turned her attention to *Shillelagh*. As she hungrily dove into the seas, the big sloop flung spray off her bow high into the sunlight, golden dust that glittered for its moment, then fell away with the wind. Much of this gold dust fell in pattering torrents on the started reacher, prisms of gold that came with each deep plunge of the bow. The big headsail was soaked by this spray and glistened blinding white under the continued cascade. For Jamie, with the tingle of salt on her face, the warm wind and the clean air, it was an afternoon to rejoice. *My God, what a day to be at sea, in a race . . . a good race.*

Jamie looked about the deck and spotted the shock-cord lashing that held the jib halyard coil over the leeward pedastal working its way loose. Jamie knew it was a detail that could go long unattended with little harm, yet, for her, there was one way on a boat, the right way. Quickly, she worked her way down the deck, and after prudently snapping her life-harness to the rigging, took up the loose lashing.

Meanwhile, from the weather rail, Mick Flaherty watched Jamie's every move. Of this young man's bloodlines, there could be no doubt. Mick was Michael at seventeen, the same easy smile, but darker of eye and skin. He was in his first major ocean race and had been assigned to assist Jamie in the galley. And like Jamie, he escaped to serve on deck as often as he could. Over the earlier races on Massachusetts Bay, Mick had come down with a mild case of puppy love for the exhuberant Jamie. His eyes seldom left her.

Just as Jamie started her climb back to the weather side, *Shillelagh* chose to take a great bite of the green sea and spew it along down the deck with tremendous force. The boarding sea swept Jamie's legs right out from under her, tossing her outboard of the lifelines into the sloop's hissing midwave. The instant Jamie went over the side, Mick was off the weather rail. "Dad! Dad! Jamie's gone," he screamed as he scrambled for the lee rail.

Luckily, Jamie's predicament was quickly resolved when her life-harness fetched up and her legs washed into the gap under the lifelines. With a flying open-field tackle, Mick Flaherty dove for Jamie's legs, nailed them in an iron grasp, then dragged her aboard.

With gasps and grins and spouts of salt water, Jamie got her harness untangled and free and followed Mick back up to the high side, getting there but a step ahead of another hungry wave.

Aft, at the wheel, Michael Flaherty had the best view of the incident. "You O.K.?" he shouted at Jamie.

"Yes, sir." She laughed.

"Nice one, Mick," he then said to his son.

Back on the weather rail, a winded Jamie was thoroughly soaked but didn't care. The water was warm and it was the kind of day at sea that made all of the grimy hours in the galley worthwhile. When Jamie got back her breath, she hugged young Flaherty and gave him a kiss on the cheek. "Thanks, Mick," she said. The teenager's cheeks flushed pink with embarrassment.

Aft at the wheel, Michael Flaherty thought, *The girl sure has guts,* and then he ordered, "Hey Jamie, come on back, sit by me." When Jamie had worked her way over the bodies of the rail-lining crewmen, aft into the cockpit, Flaherty said, "Here, sit beside me, get the feel of her. When you think you've got it, let me know. I could use some relief." For Jamie, the only woman aboard, this was highest honors indeed. Flaherty allowed but a select few, sailors of whose skill he was certain, to steer *Shillelagh* in a race.

Later, when relieved at the wheel, Flaherty climbed down into the navigation cabin. The drip off his slicker fell on an off-watch crewman, asleep in a lee bunk. "Close the goddamn hatch," the man growled, turning back to his sleep.

"You get your ass out of there," Flaherty retorted. "All weight to weather. We're in a race."

Grumbling, the sleeper shifted bunks as Flaherty settled at the navigation console to check his instruments and speed log. He then entered twelve and a quarter knots in the log book for his hour on the helm and noted the water temperature had risen to eighty-one degrees. After advancing the yacht's position on his chart, he drew from the drawer the gulf stream predicted plot furnished the contestants at the prerace briefing. On comparing the plot with his position, Flaherty saw he was right on the edge. He got up from the table and stuck his head out the companionway hatch. "Hey you guys, we're right on the edge of the stream," he warned. "Get a bearing on *Kialoa.* If she starts to move, we crack off and cover her."

With the owner's urging, the deck watch studied the waves and soon saw the change. Many were now strewn with yellow stringy tresses of sargasso weed, and their breaking crests, backlit in the sunlight, were no longer the bottle green of the North Atlantic, but far more the aquamarine and indigo of the Caribbean.

That forenoon, *Shillelagh* sliced through the greatest river of the world, the gulf stream, a river in the ocean. The water temperature soared to eighty-four degrees. The air grew heavy, moist, and tropical, as the morning's fluffy balls of cumulus clouds were replaced by charging ranks of gray squalls and the wind came on over thirty-five knots out of the southwest. Off to leeward, *Kialoa* started to march and now drew abeam of *Shillelagh* in a dead-even race for Bermuda.

Below, at the navigation desk, Flaherty was trying to locate a meander in the stream, an undulation away from the prevailing North Europe–bound flow of the great ocean river. He sought a friendly spin-off of the stream that might push his sloop toward Bermuda. Getting on the right side of such a favorable meander could add two or more knots to *Shillelagh*'s speed while she rode it.

For her next hour in the gulf stream, *Shillelagh* plowed eighty-four-degree water, her electronic positions giving no indication of a favorable meander, her bearings on *Kialoa* and *Ondine* never changed. In mid-afternoon, the water temperature dropped off two degrees, and that had Flaherty worried. Was he losing any chance of finding a ride in the stream already? The consistent compass bearings on *Kialoa* and *Ondine* were some consolation. Neither of them had found a favoring shove. And so they raced on, dead even.

For Mike Flaherty, that would not do. He was out to beat the fleet, not just the maxis. He decided to gamble and ordered the deck watch to harden up five degrees for an hour. Less than a half hour after the course change, *Shillelagh* found the warmest water of the day, eighty-six degrees. A few minutes later, the watch officer shouted down to Flaherty, "Hey Skipper, I make *Kialoa* at seventy-three. We've shoved her back a couple."

Flaherty smiled, but his joy was short lived. When the crews of *Kialoa* and *Ondine* saw *Shillelagh* starting to gain, they quickly altered course, caught their share of the favorable meander, and thereby held on to the fleet *Shillelagh*.

By late afternoon, the three maxis gained from their meander ten miles or more of free ride down the race course. Mike Flaherty rechecked his instruments and went forward for his supper. After telling Jamie how he wanted his steak, Flaherty started a discussion with the off-watch as they ate. He had brought with him to the dining settee the latest weather maps from his radio-activated electronic mapmaker. The twenty-four-hour North Atlantic prognosis was for the Bermuda high to drift to the southeast. The three maxis all had the same equipment, the same weather maps. With the gulf stream now astern, and the boats still even, the winner might well be he who read them best.

Flaherty presented the considerations to his crew. If the high-pressure pattern over Bermuda moved off as predicted, their wind would veer more westerly, giving the leeward-most *Ondine* the more favorable sailing angle, one that might well let her reach up into the lead. There followed a discussion on the whens of the wind change and the ifs of converting *Shillelagh*'s weather berth into speed made good down the course. The consensus of the below-deck gang was to drive off in the coming darkness, to plant *Shillelagh* squarely between her competition and Bermuda.

When finished with supper, Flaherty gave his son a wink. The youngster was at his scullery chores when the father plunked his empty tray into the salt-wash sink beside him. "Mick, you're doing all right," he encouraged.

When darkness settled over the ocean, Freddy Andresen drove off over *Kialoa* with Mike Flaherty on deck to watch the results of his decision to cash in his weather berth. Studying his rivals' lights as they porpoised along through the ink-black night, Michael estimated *Shillelagh* crossed *Kialoa* by little more than a hundred yards. When finally Flaherty had placed *Kialoa*'s red navigation light up on his own starboard quarter, he shouted, "Hey Freddy, we now cover in parallel. Split the distance, and stay ahead." All the while, out abeam to leward, *Ondine*'s green light winked on the crests of the waves as she sliced through the quartering seas.

In the hours before dawn, the wind lessened to twenty knots, then faired from sou'west around to the west. The Bermuda high had started to move. As the wind eased, *Shillelagh*'s crew cracked on sail, all the sail she could carry. Just before dawn, Flaherty ordered a small spinnaker set, and thereafter, *Shillelagh* gamboled along, steadily clocking thirteen knots.

With first light, *Shillelagh*'s deck watch reported *Kialoa* a half mile to windward and almost even on the Bermuda bearing, while *Ondine* was five hundred yards abeam to leeward. And so the spread of the racing trio held through the morning. At noon, *Shillelagh*'s forty-seventh hour at sea, Flaherty rechecked his instruments, took a sextant sight to be sure, then plotted his position on the chart. They were sixty miles north of Bermuda. As he went on deck to tell his crew, he checked his rivals; nothing had changed. He shook his head, wondering what might have happened had he held the lower course, *Ondine*'s course, right off the starting line. So maybe he'd have 'em by a few hundred yards, who knows, but none of them would ever have found the meander. No one knows what that will mean in the fleet race. Therewith, Flaherty dismissed all thoughts of what might have been. He was in one hell of a boat race on a beautiful day, and he loved it.

"Hey, you guys, we've got sixty miles to go," he informed his crew. "Now let's stay with it."

The wind held steady while *Shillelagh* tracked like a javelin in the settling seas. Up on the rail in the warm sunlight, Jamie and Mick and most of the off-watch were clustered near a portable radio. They listened to the clipped Oxbridgian tones of Radio Bermuda. "And the latest on the ocean race from Newport. Earlier this morning, our patrol plane reported the leaders one hundred miles north of the islands. They were beam reaching on starboard tack, most with spinnakers set. If the winds hold over the remaining course, the first yachts might be expected to finish off Saint David's Head Light late this afternoon. Our spotter plane reports the leaders are all new, all sloops, and all American. They are *Shillelagh* out of Gloucester, Massachusetts; *Kialoa,* hailing from Wilmington, Delaware, really a Californian entry. The third is the latest in a famous line of *Ondine*s, one of which set a course record back in seventy-four. *Ondine* is out of Larchmont, New York. Our spotters have these three great sloops dead even.

"We are told this is the first meeting of these maxi-yachts, the largest allowed to compete under the handicap formula. It could prove a remarkable race, indeed." Radio Bermuda continued, "The meteorological forecast from Kindley Field calls for fresh westerly winds up to twenty knots through the afternoon, diminishing towards evening . . ." This brought a cheer from some of *Shillelagh*'s crew, those who believed she, as the lightest of the trio, would fair best in lessening winds.

Jamie tried to hush them that they might hear out the broadcast. "If the winds hold, and if they keep to their present pace, they will

134

easily shatter the standing mark set by *Nirvana* in the eighty-two race."

Mike Flaherty was at *Shillelagh*'s wheel when Andresen came aft and congratulated him on what he saw as a slim lead that was about to grow. "Don't count your chickens, Freddy. It's too close," Flaherty cautioned. "Those guys over there are tough." He nodded at *Kialoa,* which had during the morning narrowed the beam distance to little more than two hundred yards and was less than a boat-length behind on the Bermuda bearing. "You remember Yogi Berra?" Flaherty asked with a grin. Andresen shook his head, so Flaherty added, "He's the guy that said 'The game ain't over till it's over.' "

Then, *Ondine* changed spinnakers, going to a far larger sail of red, white, and blue stripes with awesome shoulders. Her crew pulled off a slick 'peel change,' getting their new spinnaker up and drawing inside the old before dousing the latter. On *Shillelagh*'s starboard beam, *Kialoa* had closed to less than one hundred yards, making for a race so close, all three crews played every wave and every wind flaw. Therewith, *Shillelagh* found herself the ham in a steadily closing sandwich. With the slightest mistake in trim or the smallest veer of wind, *Kialoa* would pounce on her wind and drive over her. Meanwhile, off to leeward, with her new spinnaker drawing mightily, the blue-hulled *Ondine* started to march. Flaherty studied her gain, then barked, "O.K., you guys, we go to our big reacher, and we try a staysail under it."

But Flaherty was not looking over his shoulder, where the *Kialoa* crew were already changing spinnakers and had their new sail in place a minute or more ahead of *Shillelagh*. It was enough, for soon after Flaherty's gang got their new sail to draw, their huge swell of green nylon started to soften. They were in *Kialoa*'s wind shadow. In the next few minutes, the white sloop slid by them, their lead was gone.

Mike Flaherty got mad, very mad, mostly at himself. He knew he had been slow to call for the change. "Goddamn it, you guys, we should have watched *Kialoa,* too. Now let's get 'em back. I'm taking her up, so trim." Flaherty swung *Shillelagh* up across *Kialoa*'s wake, shaving her transom by inches, looking to grab his rival's wind. He was able to get up on *Kialoa*'s quarter, but not on her wind. The California crew skillfully countered Flaherty's every move, altering course in parallel, protecting their precious wind.

Anticipating the *Kialoa-Shillelagh* dog fight, the *Ondine* crew prudently ranged out to leeward, thereby keeping their wind clear. And so the trio went into the last thirty miles, *Kialoa* in the lead, *Shillelagh* on her weather quarter, and *Ondine* abeam to lee, all within a boat-length.

When *Kialoa* slid by, she dragged in her wake a pall of silence. There was nothing to be heard on *Shillelagh* but the swish of her hull on the slope of each wave. Her crew were grimly silent, their will to win so intense they set aside the watch-standing schedule and knuckled down to all-out racing. They had hands on every sheet, guy, and winch that could have any conceivable bearing on the outcome, all hands on deck in a gun battle to the finish.

To maintain this razor's edge of concentration through the afternoon, Freddy took to rotating his men at each station. When relieved of his stint on the pole guy winch, Mick Flaherty picked his way aft to squat by his father, who steered. "How do you like this one, Mick?" the father asked.

"They always like this, Dad?"

"Mick, I've never been in one like it. Can you believe it; three boats this goddamn close after six hundred miles. These guys are good."

"So are you, Dad. You'll get 'em," the son encouraged. "Get hot, like Larry Bird, at the end, when it counts."

"I hope you're right, Mick. I've made one mistake so far, should have watched *Kialoa*, too. That's the difference."

By mid-afternoon, a towering pile of cumulus cloud soared from the sea on *Shillelagh*'s southern horizon. Flaherty eyed the clouds and decided they must be rising thermals over the warmer Bermudian land mass. At 15:50, the purplish smudge of Bermuda eased from the sea. With each minute thereafter, the detail grew more clear; first the white flecks of the rooftops, then gray hillsides with white-washed gray catchments, pink houses on sun-bleached hills amidst scattered patches of green. Flaherty gave over the helm to Jamie and took a series of land bearings with a hand-held compass.

At 16:15, the three sloops slid by North Breakers Buoy and trimmed sheets for the leg to Kitchen Shoals Buoy. *Kialoa* still held the lead by less than a length. Just before reaching the second buoy, Jamie spotted the dark ridge of a squall coming off the land and warned Flaherty in hushed tones. He ordered Andresen to get a smaller jib up on deck as quickly, as unobtrusively as he could. Next came a game of "guts," while the ominous clouds came at them, for none of the racers wanted to shorten sail too soon. Be it luck or seaman's instinct, Flaherty timed his call perfectly. His crew had their spinnaker doused, the small jib drawing, and a reef in the main just as the squall struck, a warm blast of wind driving a blinding wall of torrential rain.

For Flaherty, in *Shillelagh's* cockpit, *Ondine* disappeared in the wall of rain. The more visible *Kialoa* was but a few seconds behind *Shillelagh* on her sail shift—a few fateful seconds. Under the brunt of the new wind, both boats went over on their sides to wallow in the rain-beaten, hissing sea. Flaherty was cat-quick in letting his mainsail run and flog. His quickness and his choice of the smaller headsail soon had *Shillelagh* back on her feet, charging ahead. As the two sloops approached Kitchen Shoals Buoy, *Shillelagh* had an overlap on *Kialoa,* just a few feet, but enough to claim room fairly under the racing rules. "Buoy room!" Flaherty bellowed.

Kialoa properly and promptly gave the room. And after rounding the buoy into the last leg, she found *Shillelagh* square on her wind. The new wind that filled behind the squall had drawn ahead, back into the south, making the remaining several miles a dead beat. Meanwhile, off to leeward on the outside of the last turn, *Ondine* had by no means dropped out of the race with the rain. To the contrary, her men had handled the squall with the same swift skill as Flaherty's Gloucestermen. *Ondine's* problem was to avoid *Kialoa,* which was knocked down in the blinding wind. Her helmsman threw over the wheel as hard as he could and drove off, barely missing *Kialoa's* near-horizontal mast. When Flaherty's visibility returned, there was *Ondine* bowling along on starboard, two lengths out ahead of *Shillelagh,* three lengths off to leeward. Dead even.

With coral reefs to starboard, *Kialoa* found herself boxed. She could not yet tack to the west because of the reefs, and were she to drive off, she would certainly fall into *Ondine's* backwind. On her windward beam, the Gloucesterman fully exploited his weather berth, camping on the Californian's wind. With two miles left, Michael Flaherty was not about to let this race slip through his fingers, and so he took the wheel back from Jamie. It would be his to win or to lose.

Kialoa shook the reef from her main; *Ondine* and *Shillelagh* matched her.

Ondine changed to a larger jib, smartly shifting one inside the other, not losing a foot on the exchange. Mike Flaherty was doubtful

Ondine could effectively carry more sail in the still blustery wind, but he was wrong. The blue sloop ranged forward another boat-length before Flaherty saw his error and ordered a jib change of his own.

The big sloops were joined by a hooting herd of powerboats and whirring helicopters with lunatic photographers leaning from gaping doors. After the relative peace of her ocean passage, the bedlam about *Shillelagh* made communication near impossible. Amidst the din, the golden sloop beat on toward the finish, a line between the tall red and white light tower on Saint David's Head Lighthouse and a rakish British frigate several hundred yards off-shore.

Lying as flat as they could to cut windage, *Shillelagh*'s crew hugged her weather rail, their portable radio turned up full. Radio Bermuda was covering the finish line. "Here we are, ladies and gentlemen, on top Saint David's Head Light. The afternoon squall has passed on, the rain has stopped. We now have brilliant sunlight. Below us, the great American sloops *Ondine, Shillelagh,* and *Kialoa* are locked in a remarkable race. This commentator has never seen anything like it. They have about a mile remaining, a mile directly to windward. After six hundred and thirty-four miles of racing, this is truly amaz-ing—this trio are less than three lengths apart. In the long history of this race, I don't think we've ever had a finish like this.

"All three boats are on starboard tack. The pale blue *Ondine* appears in the lead. She has perhaps four lengths on *Shillelagh*. One can't be certain of that, for she is a bit off to leeward; how far, it is difficult to judge through binoculars. Were *Ondine* to tack, I'm not certain she would cross *Shillelagh* without a foul, for *Shillelagh* on starboard tack would, of course, have right-of-way under the rules. *Kialoa,* the white hull, is about three lengths astern of *Shille-lagh.* She appears to be beaten, but now . . . as I speak, yes, *Kialoa* is tacking. She is now on port, heading in toward Kindley Field, probably looking for a favorable slant of wind. In any event, she had little to lose. *Shillelagh* was right on top of her."

Aboard *Shillelagh,* Freddy Andresen advised, "*Kialoa*'s going over, Mr. Flaherty."

"O.K., but I think we stay with *Ondine*," Flaherty said.

"*Ondine*'s about to tack," Jamie advised.

"Good," Flaherty said, "then we'll sit right on her. Cover both boats."

"I'm not so sure," Jamie cautioned, "it's going to be close. I think she might have us."

"No way," Flaherty said.

At that moment, *Ondine* spun head to wind and fell off on port tack. The two great sloops then converged for what seemed a certain collision. "Starboard tack," Flaherty screamed.

Ondine kept right on coming. *Christ, those guys are crazy,* Flaherty thought, then screamed again, "Starboard tack," and then to his crew, "Stand by for a collision."

But Flaherty was wrong. *Ondine* slid over *Shillelagh,* her blue transom clearing the golden bow by five feet or less.

"Boy, that took balls!" Flaherty exclaimed.

"They're coming back right on top of us," Jamie said.

"Two can play that game," Flaherty growled. "Ready about," he warned, then slammed *Shillelagh* over on to port. With that, the tacking duel started and went on for five tacks. *Kialoa,* left by herself under the island, found a slant of wind to her liking and came back at the duelists on starboard tack.

"Christ, *Kialoa's* got us, too," Flaherty groaned. "I'm going to go under her. Ease sheets." Flaherty slid *Shillelagh* under *Kialoa* as close as he dared. At the same moment, *Ondine* elected to tack under *Kialoa's* port bow while Freddy came racing aft to Flaherty. "They're fucked-up, Skipper," he jabbered. "They got an override on the starboard backstay winch. Look! Look! They can't tack on us."

"You're shitting me," Flaherty exclaimed in disbelief.

"No, no, he isn't," Jamie chimed in. "They do have a problem. And they're taking *Ondine* right along with them."

"So what do you guys advise?" Flaherty asked.

"Hold on till we're sure we can fetch," Jamie said calmly. "When we go back at them, we'll have the last starboard."

A minute or more later, *Kialoa* came over on port, trying to insure her lead on *Shillelagh. Ondine* came around with her. Aboard *Shillelagh,* Jamie was sighting over a compass, trying to calculate the shorter end of the finish line. "I think the destroyer end's a bit shorter, Mr. Flaherty. We can fetch in another fifty yards."

"Sure hope you're right, Jamie girl," Flaherty shouted. "Ready about you guys, make it a good one." To the rattle of winches and the thunder of sail, *Shillelagh* fell away on her last tack. With her jib sheeted home, her crew smartly sprang for the weather rail.

The race hung on the next crossing, but from the weather rail, they couldn't see their closing rivals; they were hidden under the sails. One of them took his portable from his pocket and turned it on.

The Oxbridgian voice on Radio Bermuda had climbed several decibels. "This tacking duel is unbelievable to watch! They are once again converging, ladies and gentlemen. This time, *Shillelagh* holds starboard, with all rights. The others are coming at her on port. They have but two hundred yards to *Prometheus. Kialoa* is now tacking on *Shillelagh*'s lee bow. *Ondine* is going around with her. Perhaps she just might get her nose across . . . My lord, what a finish this will be! Oh, oh, I think *Shillelagh*'s momentum will tell the tale. Yes, she is rolling over them, *Shillelagh* will have them.

"*Shillelagh* now has the lead. She is about to cross the line. She will most certainly shatter the standing record. *Shillelagh* is something beautiful to behold; a tall, very tall, high-aspect rig, gleaming varnished hull. She's slicing along under full main and a medium genoa jib. Here she comes, yes, there she is."

Thud.

"There you have it; the winner's salute from the frigate *Prometheus,* a white bright phosphorus flare. From here, it looks like a dead heat for second . . . Simply unbelievable!"

A grinning Flaherty stood by the wheel with a happy wave for the media in their milling launches and then shouted to his crew. "Hey! Good going, you guys. Now get the jib off her. Freddy, free up the prop lock, let's crank up the diesel."

Mick ran aft to his father for a high five and a great bear hug. "I told you, I told you, you could do it, Dad," pummeling his father's back. "And with a slam-dunk at the end. Wow!"

Powering into Hamilton, the three sloops drew abreast, while their crews lined their rails to exchange loud hearty cheers and lighthearted insults. Won or lost, theirs was a race to remember.

Part Four

The Princess Hotel, Hamilton, Bermuda

If spectacular storms with loss of lives are involved, the sport of yacht racing draws coverage by the television medium. Otherwise, there are too many difficulties to warrant industry interest. Yacht races are difficult to cover. They are not held in a stadium with prepositioned cameras and a predictable time of finish. The sport lacks advertiser support, the handicap rules are baffling to laymen, and only aficionados comprehend the finer points of tactics and seamanship. In simple terms of who won what and how, the sport is difficult to present on the great glass eye.

Shillelagh's Bermuda Race victory contradicted all this. For once, the television media had a comprehensible sailing event of international interest they could readily market, a transom-shaving tacking duel by the maxis in a record-shattering race, a three-way cliff-hanger with a bow-on-bow finish. That the finish took place on a picturesque island under a striped lighthouse with a Royal Navy frigate in the background lent that much more to the visuals. And so, for once, with sensible anticipation, the television medium was there with helicopters and cameras and all the requisite gear.

After finishing off Saint David's Head on the easterly end of the island, the three big sloops motored along the north side to arrive at Hamilton Harbor in the early twilight. There, they berthed as a three-boat raft, sterns to the quay of the Princess Hotel. With all the crews in a festive mood, they next broke out from their mastheads long bright strings of signal flags that crackled and snapped in the wind. All the while from the hotel's stone quay, TV reporters and their cameramen covered the arrival and pressed for interviews.

Before getting involved with the press, a jubilant Mike Flaherty called Jamie to his side and gave her a thick roll of money. Jamie and some of the winch gang were sent off down Front Street to buy cases of rum, gin, and champagne. This was Mike Flaherty's first international win, and he was going to give a party no one would forget.

Not long afterward, on *Shillelagh*'s stern with a rippling American ensign for a backdrop, Mike Flaherty stood being interviewed by a sports network blonde, a striking woman with a Southern drawl. Of all those who pressed for interviews from the quay, she was the first to catch Flaherty's eye and be invited aboard. The interview was moving along when Jamie and her brawny helpers came down the dock with a van full of booze, its horn honking. This caught the attention of all three racing crews, and a raucous cheer ensued. Willing hands noisily heaved cases of liquor up on *Shillelagh*'s stern, completely disrupting the owner's interview. A laughing Mike Flaherty had the presence to invite the pretty Southern woman and her cameraman to join his party in the making before he broke away. He then picked up a bottle of rum, and with that, the party was on.

The *Ondine* and *Kialoa* crews swarmed over *Shillelagh*'s lifelines, joining Flaherty and his gang. Within the hour, under the glare of television klieg lights and whirring cameras, Mike Flaherty was heaved by his rivals into Hamilton Harbor, last seen wearing a wide grin, holding his bottle of rum. There followed his entire crew, but when they got back on *Shillelagh*'s deck, the *Ondine* and *Kialoa* crews had not long to stay dry. With that, the night devolved into a rather drunken donnybrook.

The next morning, Flaherty groggily awoke in a Princess Hotel suite that overlooked the scene of his party. After a bit of adjusting, he went out on his balcony and noted with satisfaction that there were still sleeping bodies strewn about the three sloops' decks. "So I'm not the only one," he muttered aloud, holding his throbbing temples. "Boy, was that some party." He then went in to get out of the sunlight and waken his sleeping son. The younger Flaherty was due to return to his mother and a summer job as soon as the race was over. "Hey, Mick," the father shouted outside the son's door, "let's get it together. We've only got four hours to do some shopping, see the island, and get you on your plane."

After placing Mick on the afternoon plane to Boston, Flaherty again picked up on the party circuit, basking in the celebrity of *Shillelagh*'s record-setting race. For companionship, he asked his new Southern television friend to join him. Over the next several days that it took the tail-enders to complete the Bermuda course, it became certain Flaherty had swept the famed race, first-to-finish, first-in-class, first-in-fleet, and a new course record.

Four days of beach parties, flirting, mating, media interviews, and still more cocktail parties were enough to tax even Flaherty's iron constitution. He welcomed the finality of the prize-giving, boarded the next plane for Boston, and with a happy smile, slumped into exhausted sleep. *Shillelagh* was slated to sail for Gloucester the next morning crewed by only her paid hands.

At Boston airport, Flaherty was met by an attractive divorcee, who happened to be the real estate agent who had sold him his condominium. They drove out to Marblehead, had an early dinner, and went to bed. Early the next morning, he took his companion for a stout breakfast at the Driftwood, a waterfront eatery, where he spent most of his meal discussing the run-of-fish with the fishermen patrons. This was the final straw for his pretty realtor friend.

The night prior, on getting to bed, Flaherty had barely kissed her when he rolled over and fell asleep. Now, this morning, his major interest was the price of fish. Other Flaherty romances had ended for less cause. And so, after breakfast, Flaherty deposited the miffed young woman before her office and blithely set off up the coast for Gloucester. Along the way, while crossing the Beverly bridge, he was stopped by the swing barrier with its bells and blinking lights. The bridge section swung slowly, opening the channel for a small dragger outbound for sea. Flaherty, who was first in line at the draw barrier, started tracing out in his mind the detail of the dragger's rigging, and that led to other thoughts. Flaherty loved to tinker with technical problems, his restless mind ever seeking the better, the faster, the easier. This particular morning, he toyed with a different winch layout for *Shillelagh* and then another means, a faster, probably cheaper means of smuggling white narcotics for Giovanni Barerra.

The clang of the bells on the bridge broke in on Flaherty's thoughts, and as the barrier swung open, he slipped the powerful

Lamborghini into gear. At the next crossroads, he capriciously chose the twisting winding shore road through Prides Crossing to Gloucester. It was a longer route but a thorough test of the sleek car's cornering. Work would be work, Flaherty decided, but getting there might as well be fun on a warm morning in a world that went well. He flicked on his radar warning device and took off down the shore road with the whine of burnt rubber.

Later, when Flaherty came through his office doors, his secretary gave him warm greetings, "Good morning, Mr. Michael, we all saw you on television the other night. . . . Congratulations. They had you on at six and eleven . . . we stayed up to watch."

Flaherty nodded and grinned and went on to his inner office. Once behind his desk, he quickly realized neither his head nor his heart were with his work. He was restless, still on a Bermuda high. His night with his friendly realtor had been truly dull. He simply could not talk with the woman about things that now mattered to him. Mike Flaherty realized that few on his roster of available females could appreciate and share with him the meaning of *Shillelagh*'s victory to Bermuda. The realization led on to other thoughts.

Somehow, in the convolutions of his subconscious, Flaherty had linked in odd association his winning the Bermuda Race to his new friendship with Ann Raimond. He had filed it as her kind of event. Flaherty never considered the logic of the linkage; it was there, that was that. He next started to weigh the should-I, shouldn't-I conundrum of calling her. *I said I would, but what does that mean? I've said that before. She's married. Unhappily . . . So am I. Who isn't? She's pretty. I know prettier. She's older than I am. . . . Not by that much. Why not?* And with that, Mike Flaherty picked up a North Shore directory, looked up Ann's number, and placed a call. He learned that Mrs. Raimond was not at home, that she was not expected until late morning. Flaherty left his name and settled back to his paper work.

Within the hour, Flaherty's intercom buzzed. "Mr. Michael," his secretary said, "there's a Mrs. Ann Raimond returning your call."

The Flaherty Condominium, Marblehead, Massachusetts

Flaherty realized this was a special afternoon when he decided to shower for a second time. He also shaved again and completed his careful toilet with a generous slosh of a sandalwood lotion and a vigorous brush of his steely black hair. When finished, he dressed and returned to the full-length mirror on the bathroom door to inspect his efforts. His choice of a *Shillelagh* shirt, white jeans, and open sandals struck just the right note of casualness, he thought.

The nearby bells of Abbott Hall tolled two as he went in to check out his bedroom. He knew from the raised pile of the carpet that his cleaning lady had been through and vacuumed that morning. He walked over to the bed and lifted the cover to check that the linen was fresh when he heard the door buzzer. Assured that all was ship-shape in his bedroom, Flaherty went down through the living room and opened the front door.

Ann Raimond stood in the sunlight with a bright smile, a wicker hamper in her hand. "Well, the all-conquering hero," she greeted him cheerily, stepping into the hallway.

Before closing the door, Flaherty gave her a hug and a hard kiss. "Hi. I'm glad you came."

"How could I stay away? Decline an invitation from the Bermuda Race winner, the man with the new record?" There was a sparkle in her brown eyes as she stood back for a moment. "Well, we

147

certainly read a lot about you—and on the television, too. Why, I thought that only happened with the America's Cup winners." She drew close and gave him a big spontaneous hug. "Well done, champ. You did it. You really did it."

"Yep, that we did." Flaherty was beaming as he trailed his lithe visitor to the leather sofas by the picture window. He had been right in making the call, of that he was now certain. He sensed she no longer hid behind her invisible barbed wire of standoffish Yankee reserve. She was there for him, and they now met as equals, at least on this afternoon.

"And we must celebrate," Ann said while placing her hamper on the cocktail table. "I've never had such an invitation before." She opened her basket and drew from a cooler section a chilled bottle of Tattingers. She followed with a towel, two cut crystal goblets, and a plastic-wrapped plate of soft brie, neatly circled by an array of crackers.

"Wow, what a spread!" Flaherty exclaimed, eyeing the care that had gone into the hamper. "Can I help?"

"No, this is my party. I think I've got everything," she said, her face in a purposeful frown while she wrested the cork from the towel-swathed champagne. Upon the loud *pop,* she quelled the fizzing surge with her towel, carefully wiped the mouth of the bottle, then filled both goblets. "To *Shillelagh* and her skipper." Ann raised her goblet in toast, looking into Flaherty's eyes over the rim of her glass.

"And we thank you," he replied.

"Now, tell me how you did it," she said.

"Well, *Shillelagh* sure had her conditions," he launched off, "but *Kialoa* and *Ondine* were right there, too, they're so even, it's hard to believe. We had good air, all the way—not too much, but enough. Close reach, beam reach, broad reach—freed up on starboard all the way, except at the finish. We got the start on the weather end, *Condor* tried to squeeze us up off the line. I saw she was early, waited up on her hip till she had to bear away. When she did, we dove off, got inside her, and took the lead. The second day, we got one hell of a push from the stream. *Kialoa* and *Ondine* saw what was happening. They came up and hopped on the same meander. The next morning, they closed with us, one on each side. *Kialoa* got by us for a bit. One hell of a boat race! A tacking duel right to the finish!" Flaherty galloped along, nonstop, for twenty minutes of minute racing details.

Ann listened and watched and nodded, only turning aside to keep their glasses filled with the chilled champagne or to proffer a cracker with cheese. When Flaherty finally slowed to a winded trot, she asked, "And after the race?"

"Good fun," Flaherty allowed, but he smirked as he spoke.

"I'll bet," she laughed, "And with you going right to work on the waiting Class D and E wives. Michael, I've done that race twice, you know."

"I didn't know, and it wasn't wives, but I will admit I did a bit of hunting. Three days at sea is a long time," he added, putting his arm around her. They kissed.

When they drew apart, she purred, "And I'm sure successfully."

"So, so," he said guardedly. "Nothing like you."

"Why Michael, what a nice . . ." and she broke off to kiss him. Several kisses later, Ann wriggled away to refill their goblets. She then got to her feet and asked, "Michael, where's your loo?"

"Loo?" Flaherty was for an instant perplexed. "Oh, you mean the head. The one down here's on your right in the hall."

Not many moments later, Ann returned, sat down beside Flaherty, and after a deep sip of champagne, again nestled into his arms. He said, "You know something, Annie, ever since we've met, you've asked all the questions. Now, I've got a couple."

"Fair enough," she agreed.

"Marital status?"

"To use your own words, 'Sort of—not happily.' "

"One for your side." He laughed. "Doing anything about it?"

"Like talking to lawyers or actually filing for separation or a divorce, that kind of thing?"

"Yep."

"No." She paused. "Not yet, but thinking about it, more and more, lately."

"A jealous husband?"

"David! Jealous!" Ann laughed bitterly. "That would require emotion, an outward emotion. Simply not possible."

"I kind of wondered why you invited me back for a swim. He might have come home. What you're saying is that you have a deal, that it wouldn't have mattered?"

"No, there's no understanding like that, and I'm not sure about that night. I guess I must have thought about David. . . . I had done some drinking, you may remember. And there was no wind when we left the club. I do remember thinking about that. David will always finish a race, if it takes till Christmas. It's simply the right thing to do, and that's David. So, I must have thought he wasn't about to come home, or that even if he did, he seldom comes around to the pool side, that's sort of my place." Ann paused, then looked up at Flaherty with a certain sadness. "Oh, Michael, I think the truth of it is I just don't give a damn about David anymore, what he thinks, what he sees, what he does. All that's left is the when of it, the when we get it over with."

Flaherty looked at her. "Boy, you've got a heap of feelings all bottled up."

Ann looked into her wine glass. "Yes, I'm sure I have. I'm just beginning to realize how much. I'm not very fair to David, am I?"

"How the hell do I know, Annie? Is anyone fair on the back side of a marriage? The one thing I've sure learned is when the glue cracks, it cracks. It ain't easy, getting it back together, if you ever can. As for where you are, beats me. You tell me."

This was not a question Ann had expected, one she was not readily prepared to answer. Talk of her marriage made her uncomfortable; it was something she never did, and so she sipped more wine while she considered her answer. "I guess I'm maddest at the emptiness, the boredom, the absolute polite deadness of our relationship. I guess I'm as angry with myself as David. I know if you're bored, it's your own fault. So, I've got to do something. We share a house and two grown children. And damn little else. The children live away. David works in Boston, mostly managing my money, going to his clubs. He does that well. I run the houses. When the children were younger, whenever there were problems, they were for me to handle."

"Your kids a problem?"

"No, Michael, not now, I'm glad to say. The problem is David and me. He's so remote, so reserved, so very proper. I think many women looking in from the outside would think I'm crazy, that the man is most things one can expect in a husband after a lot of years. He's attentive to our affairs, sets a proper example for our children, he's as sober as a judge, a pillar of the church, all the right virtues. He's even faithful." Her look turned pensive. "That's more than I can say."

And then she paused while her mind ran ahead of her words. "If I were really honest about my marriage," she said, "I'm the one at fault. I've let it become a complete bore. David's a fine, upright person. It's rather like what you said about the cracked glue. I just don't seem to want to reach out and try to glue it together again. The attraction is gone. David's rather like having an iceberg living down the hall." As Ann spoke, she was surprised that she found it so easy to talk with a relative stranger, but then she thought how attractive Michael seemed, what an attentive listener. But then she told herself, *It must be the champagne.*

Michael never took his eyes from Ann's as she spoke. He listened to what she said, but was more fascinated by her manner of speech, so controlled, modulated, melifluous, monied. Flaherty had never met a woman like Ann Raimond.

Ann put down her wine glass, looked over at Michael, then asked, "What about your marriage? Are you heading for a divorce?"

"No, not yet at least. That would be difficult. Rosalie was brought up a Catholic. So was I, for that matter," Flaherty replied evasively. "The way we have it now, she's got the farm. I'm over here. We talk when we have to, not often. It seems to work."

"Good." Ann smiled. "So much for family, a topic for another day, not this afternoon. There are nicer things to talk about, to do." She moved into his lap and they kissed and then sipped more wine.

Ann slowly circled one of his nipples through the thin green cloth below the golden SHILLELAGH. "I see you're in uniform," she murmured.

"Uh huh, just for you. A special occasion. Want one?"

"You have extras?"

"I wouldn't call 'em extras." He laughed. "But I do have a supply. Keeps up the crew morale."

"Hmm, that rather lets me out," she said.

"Oh no, not so. Let's call it a souvenir for giving me that old bootlegger's cup," he said, getting to his feet, pulling her up with him. "Come on, let's get you one." Michael led Ann up the stairs to his bedroom.

"My father was not a bootlegger, Mike Flaherty," she protested.

"Have it your way, Annie-me-gal. We'll have a lunch one of these days. I'll have you meet the man who knows." He walked into his stand-up wardrobe and emerged with three cartons of *Shillelagh* shirts, setting them down on the dresser. "Let's start with a medium," he decided, handing her a shirt.

"You want me to try it on—right now? Here?" Her question was a mix of surprise and coyness.

"Where the hell else? I don't sail with a sloppy-looking crew."

With a why-not shrug, Ann Raimond peeled off her white shirt, revealing most of her breasts, the balance constrained by the thinnest of silken bras. She slipped on the green shirt and went to the mirror, "A bit big, I think, Michael. You should save this one as a spare for your cook."

"Well, that's an interesting idea, but I'm afraid Jamie has her own already," Flaherty said, reaching down into a second carton. "Let's try a men's small." When he looked up, Ann stood waiting, again shirtless, her look a smokey one that spoke for her.

Flaherty dropped the shirt and reached out for her. He kissed deeply, and reached down, and deftly unhooked the front of her bra. As the silk fell back from her shoulders, he bent down and kissed her nipples, coaxing them with his tongue.

Ann shuddered as wordlessly they moved to his bed and fell upon it, Flaherty on his back, Ann above him, about him, kissing him harder, deeper. For a time, he lightly scratched the small of her spine, but soon, his hands were strong on her buttocks as they started to writhe with a slow circular urgency of awakening need. When finally she broke aside for breath, Flaherty was pushing her snug slacks and panties down over her buttocks. "Here, let me," she said huskily. While Ann took off the last of her clothing, Flaherty wriggled free of his shirt and jeans and in a moment, they met naked in the middle of his big bed.

They kissed again, another long kiss as his hand moved over her tanned body, always coming back to her breasts, cupping them lightly. In time, his hand moved on down her body to her thighs, which were open and willing. His fingers spread her soft lips, searching, soon finding a small place of hardness.

Flaherty's patient fingers prodded further, gently, tentatively. When certain of her wetness, he came back to her hardness with his forefinger and circled the base slowly. She drew back for a moment from the teasing and then her whole body started into a paroxysm of wiggles and thrusts that quickly came harder, faster, and wilder, and suddenly the wildness became an urgency, and Ann lifted her pelvis in one great arching thrust, while uttering one long shuddering sigh. After a time, she fell back, spent.

Flaherty kept at his soft kisses and careful toying, and her tanned pelvis again began a slow circular writhing, a rhythm that soon mounted to a frenzy that could not long endure.

Four more times Ann Raimond came, and each time, she floated off to a world of brain beyond body, a short-lived voyage that soon ended in a reawareness of the maddening fingers of Michael Flaherty. More than any event in her long marriage, more than her brief bout with Flaherty by the edge of her pool, this afternoon in his bed was truly the site of Ann's sexual debut, her discovery of her own sexuality in a now liberated body.

Flaherty contentedly went on with his lovemaking, a bit bemused by their differing levels of lust. He knew that his time would come, that she would be there, and the thought that his reserved Yankee friend was about to get thoroughly fucked pleased Michael Flaherty, the son of a fisherman off the docks at Gloucester.

After her fifth orgasm, Ann became impatient. "I want you inside me *now,*" she said, moving under him, holding him, firmly guiding him into her waiting lips. Flaherty entered slowly, savoring the warmth of her wet, waiting sheath, holding her buttocks tightly, his mouth on hers, his tongue passing into her, hungrily searching, his detachment gone. Ann flung her slender legs around his buttocks, her arms about his back, capturing him in a long-limbed lock of total lust.

At that moment, the phone on his bedside table started to ring. With the fourth ring, Flaherty growled in anger.

With the sixth ring, Ann sighed, "Oh, Michael, answer the goddamn thing. It's probably important."

In exasperation, Flaherty reached for the receiver, propped it to his ear, all the while staying in Ann. "Yep . . . yeah, well anyway, Aunt Aggie, I was doin' somethin'. Oh Christ, he's not shit-faced again! Look, you tell that son of a bitch for me, I'm goin' to can his ass. He's supposed to make that goddamn voyage. Hey look, Aunt Aggie. I gotta get back to what I was doin'. Yeah, now do me a favor. Call Mrs. Grassie, tell her I'll skipper the trip. Have her tell Jake we shove off at seven. Yeah. Bye."

Flaherty reached across to slam down the receiver, and as he did, he slipped out of Ann. He rolled onto his back. "Shit," he screamed, his interest in Ann visibly waned.

"What's wrong?" Ann asked, getting up on her elbow.

"My goddamn Uncle Eddie, he's supposed to take the *Katherine M.* out tonight. He's gotten himself shit-faced."

"So?"

"So I gotta go."

"Why you, Michael? Don't you have other people?"

"Yeah, maybe, but not on such short notice."

"You're going out fishing? Tonight?"

"Got to," he said resignedly. "I've got a lot tied up in those vessels. They don't make bucks tied to the dock."

"Poor Michael." Ann turned to the bedside table to pour more champagne. She sat up better to take a sip, then offered her glass to Flaherty. "So now you fish. How long do you go for?"

"Depends what we catch." Flaherty laughed. "Three, maybe four or five days."

On a long-latent caprice, Ann twisted closer to Flaherty's thighs, gently taking the tip of his limp penis and dipping it in her wine glass. Over the past few days, Flaherty's "shillelagh" had been sorely tried in close combat. The cold champagne with its alcoholic twinge was indeed an assault from an unexpected quarter. "Hey!" its stunned master protested.

"Did I hurt you?" Ann cooed solicitously, making no effort to hide a mischievous smirk. "Here, let me make it better." And with that, she took his champagne-dripping organ into her mouth and gently circled it with her tongue. This was a war reparation Flaherty's "shillelagh" could more readily accept, and in little time, it valiantly rose to this new challenge. when Ann was fully assured of the durability of her reparations, she moved on top of Flaherty and slowly eased herself down upon him.

The Samoset Club, Boston, Massachusetts

The morning after the *Katherine M. Flaherty* went fishing, David Raimond sat alone in the reading room of the Samoset Club. He appeared calm and content with his world, the Boston club man engrossed in his *Wall Street Journal.* As the mantel clock tinkled ten, Kevin Shaughnessey was ushered into the room. When the pair was alone, Raimond asked, "Well, Shaughnessey, what have you got?"

The investigator drew a small notebook from his jacket pocket before he replied. "Yesterday afternoon, at one-fifty-five, your wife left Marblehead Neck in the green station wagon. By the way, Mr. Raimond, you were right. You can't hang around outside your gate. You stick out real bad, and most of it's 'No Parking.' The cops are comin' round all the time. So, I was waiting in the parking lot by the beach at the end of the causeway when she came off the Neck. I trailed her to the Glover Landing Apartments. I saw her enter the building owned by Michael J. Flaherty. She had a picnic basket in her hand. They kissed real good at the door. By the way, that condo set-up is kinda tight for good surveillance. I sort of stood out, so I went back to the main street. Picked her up again when she left just after six. She went back to your house. End of report."

"That's all?" Raimond asked, disappointed.

"Hey, Mr. Raimond, what else could there be?" Shaughnessey protested. "I can guess what went on, you can, too, but that ain't proof.

I wasn't about to peek in the windows or break down the door now, was I? Well, not in broad daylight."

"No, certainly not." Raimond paused. "Then what would you suggest we do now?"

"As I told you before, that depends where you want to get to, Mr. Raimond. You want to know where she's spending her time, that's one thing. You want to know for sure she's screwin' this guy, get enough to make an adultery rap stick in the courts, that's something else. I mentioned a wiretap. We could start from there, see what we come up with. If they keep usin' his place, that gets tough."

"Well," the trustee temporized, and then asked, "And what else have you learned about this fellow Flaherty?"

The investigator again referred to his notebook. "That guy's doin' all right. Forty-four years old. His grandfather and his mother were the big shareholders in Flaherty Fisheries. Flaherty bought 'em all out three years ago. Got that from his father's estate settlement over in Salem Probate. Incidentally, his old man was killed in a trawler accident seven years back."

"So the business is all his?"

"According to the court, Mr. Raimond," the investigator went on, "young Michael J. took over the business after that. Done O.K. Through a friend, I got hold of his file at the *Gloucester Times*. He's gotta have guts, this guy, a Navy Cross and a Purple Heart in Nam. He's got eight trawlers. I checked them out at the Customs House. They're hocked to some bank in Geneva. Has a fish-meal factory in Gloucester. Into ship repair, both Gloucester and Boothbay, up in Maine. Flaherty's got a marine electronics business over in Beverly. He's current on his bills. No debts that I could find recorded, besides the trawler mortgages. Has the reputation of paying cash for most things."

"Cash?"

"Yeah. That's pretty common with the fishermen. Let me keep goin'. No police record. Three sports, Gloucester High, big jock in his day. Captain of hockey. Married, two teenage boys. The kids live mostly with the wife, sometimes with him. She's got a farm over in Wenham. Place put in her name, a year ago. No mortgage. Taxes current. Flaherty's got the condo at Glover Landing. No mortgage. Taxes current. Incidentally, that's some shack he's got there, from the outside. One hell of a location. I ran the records while I was over at Probate. No separation or divorce pending that I could find. So he and the wife, they got some kind of a deal."

As Shaughnessey paused for breath, Raimond interrupted. "I find it difficult to believe that this man can live as he does from fishing and the ship-repair business. A condominium, a farm, and a large ocean racer. I know for a certainty one of those yachts costs close on two million, and that is not in any way taking into account the cost of operation. That could be close to another million a year."

"Yeah, well, there was a clipping about that in his file. The *Shillelagh*. Seems he built it himself in his own yard down Maine in Boothbay. And those new trawlers, they knock the hell out of a mill or more. So he's got to be doin' all right, Mr. Raimond."

"Perhaps," Raimond said, dubious, his doubt showing in his tone.

"So how far do you want to push it, Mr. Raimond?"

"I want you to find out everything you possibly can about that man," Raimond ordered testily. "Something tells me there's more to this man's way of living than the fish business."

"Well, maybe. That's not goin' to be so easy. I've done all the public diggin'. What's left is on the private side from here on out. He could wise up."

"I'll accept that risk, Shaughnessey. Try and stay discreet, but keep looking."

"O.K. But I'm goin' to need some help, if you want more diggin' and a tail on him and your wife at the same time. Can't be two places at once."

"All right. I understand. Take on what help you need. Do it right." The trustee made a cathedral spire with his forefingers. "I don't like it, but I think we should go ahead with the wiretap."

"I'll get my stuff together." The investigator grinned as he spoke. "Far as anyone else is concerned, you own it. Far as we're concerned, it rents for twenty-five bucks a day. The next day or so, you dream up a phone problem. One of my guys'll come out and take care of it."

"Very well, Shaughnessey."

157

Flaherty Fisheries, Gloucester, Massachusetts

The victorious *Shillelagh* had a fair-winds passage back from Bermuda to the latitude of Cape Cod. Before dawn on the fourth day of this reaching voyage, the fair sou'west wind veered into the nor'west, putting the sloop close on the wind for the last sixty miles to Gloucester. With only six hands on board for this return to the old fishing port, Freddy Andresen had divided his crew into three watches of two persons standing four hours on, eight hours off. Over the long reach, as constant sail change or trim was not a demand, the small watch system worked well.

As rank has its privilege, the boat captain had selected the pretty cook as his watch-mate. In their five months together on the yacht, Freddy and Jamie had grown close, very close. Jamie found Freddy attractive, a quiet brawny young man who shared her love of sailing—in summary, a "hunk." Jamie realized she was the swifter of thought, the better educated of the pair. She was also bright enough never to flaunt her realization.

For his part, Freddy Andresen was slow to acknowledge his red-headed friend from California knew as much about boats as he, maybe a bit more, where technical matters were involved. Even now, in late June, he would never put this realization in words. Of the pair, Freddy was the simpler soul, his pleasures centering on boats, booze, and babes. Freddy had come to accept Jamie's brightness and boat sense, but his major interest remained her body.

One way or another, they had worked out their relationship, both apparently pleased in their roles. This relationship was not of the kind that, in more conventional times, might mature from new love to marriage. The outlook of these young people in these days of now was far less fettered. The bronzed boat captain and the long-legged redhead had reached a relationship that in the language of their contemporaries was aptly described as "fucking friends." That, of itself, posed problems, for in the open yacht with privacy at a premium, and with a short-handed crew, their desires were not always so readily consummated. And so, as the big sloop loped along toward Gloucester, Freddy and Jamie looked forward to a night of their own.

They had the deck watch to themselves when the white tower of Eastern Point Light came up on their northern horizon. Under heavy genoa and single reef, *Shillelagh* was slicing along on port tack through a long even sea. When certain they would fetch Gloucester without another tack, Freddy gave over the wheel to Jamie and went below. In the navigation cabin, he placed a radio call through the Boston marine operator to the Bureau of Customs and made an appointment for an entry inspection at the Flaherty Fisheries docks.

Alone on deck at the wheel, Jamie held the big sloop hard on the wind, reveling in the loping beauty of her motion, the shuddering power in her hands. Taking a boat to weather was one of Jamie Quinn's great joys. She did it well. Jamie had sailed since childhood, when her father had taught her the subtle nuances of feathering and driving, taking the oncoming wave to best advantage in the wind of that moment. On such a clear sailing day, Jamie would usually be engrossed in the oneness that is a sailboat and a good sailor. But this afternoon, Jamie was not so enthralled. In fact, she was distracted, for she knew why Freddy had gone below.

As his blond curly head poked up out of the cabin, the boat captain spoke. "All set. They'll have a guy meet us between four and four-thirty."

"That's just nifty, Freddy, but what about the grass?" Jamie asked. "We both know Cotton and Jimmy have some in their gear."

"Don't worry about it," he laughed. Freddy had the offhanded attitude of the young people of the forepeak who sailed these maxi-yachts in their global quests. For them, smoking marijuana was as prosaic a part of their lives as smoking nicotine or drinking alcohol was for their elders. "Besides, those guys never look," he added.

"In California, they sure do," she cautioned.

"That's somethin' else. When the Customs know you're coming in from Mexico or Hawaii, they're on your ass. Bermuda, that's different, a nice clean little colony, no sweat."

"I hope you're right," she said. "We'll see."

By five that afternoon, *Shillelagh*'s crew had the big sloop secured with doubled-up lines to the Flaherty Fisheries dock, her decks snugged down, scrubbed down, and gleaming, when a jowly Customs officer with a great beer belly arrived on the dock. "Hey, where's the gangway?" he growled to the crew working on the deck far below him.

"Haven't got one. There's some rungs built into the dock by the stern," Freddy offered helpfully.

"Shit. They're all rusty and slimy," the federal officer grumbled. "Who's in charge here?" he demanded.

"Me, sir. Can I help?" Freddy said.

"Yeah. Bring up the ship's papers, the crew roster, any declarations you got."

With a polite "Yes, sir," Freddy hurried below for the papers while the Customs officer up on the dock lit a cigarette. The man was thoroughly annoyed by this assignment so late in his workday, well aware any overtime pay would be a long hassle at best; that his boss back in Boston, a Republican appointee, was a niggardly prick when it came to any sign-off on overtime. Nor had the heat and the late afternoon traffic helped the man's equanimity. After a time, the federal officer caught Jamie's eye. "Say, didn't I read about this boat somewhere?" he asked.

"You might have, sir," she replied. "We just won the Bermuda Race."

"Hmmph," he said while Freddy climbed up on the dock and presented the required papers. Within five minutes, the inspecting officer had stamped and signed the requisite papers, using the roof of the U.S. Customs car as his desk. Thereby, the American yacht *Shillelagh* was cleared for reentry into the customs zone of the United States and her crew cleared for debarcation. And with that for formalities, the man got in his car and drove off.

When the grinning Freddy Andresen regained the yacht's deck, he went over to Jamie and whacked her tight Levis. "Told you so, smarty," he teased.

"Incredible. That would never have happened in San Diego. I just can't believe that a Customs officer could be so lax. I just can't believe it." She laughed, relieved with the outcome.

"Welcome to Gloucester, Jamie babe."

When *Shillelagh* was secured to Freddy's satisfaction, he gave the keys of his old truck to his crewmates. They were more certain of a hero's welcome in the bars of Marblehead than in old Gloucester Town and stood on no ceremony in the haste of their departure. Minutes later, Freddy and Jamie padlocked the hatches of the yacht and climbed up on the dock. After identifying themselves to the night watchman, they strolled out through the gates of Flaherty Fisheries, up the hill, into the first fisherman's dive they came on.

After four days at sea, Freddy decided his thirst was the first priority of his several wants. Jamie thought that was a reasonable decision, and so they started drinking. Several hours later, Freddy's "a couple of quick cold ones" became a numberless march of mugs. For a time, Jamie tried to match her thirsty friend. It was an unfair contest, where tonnage told, one Jamie finally conceded by ordering several cheeseburgers. If they didn't eat something, the night would become a total disaster, of that she was certain. Near midnight, Jamie bought their way out of the bar and had to prop her sloshed boat captain firmly in his uncertain passage back to the yacht.

At the brow of the dock, the low state of tide posed Jamie's next major problem. With the tide out, *Shillelagh*'s deck was a good fifteen feet below the pair. With the long climb down, and the slimy state of the ladder rungs, getting Freddy aboard in one piece would not be easy. And so Jamie went over the dock edge first and with some persuasion, got Freddy to come along close in front of her so that she could hug him into the rungs whenever he slipped. Their descent was so slow and so clumsy, neither Jamie nor Freddy noted a newly arrived trawler now discharging her catch at the far end of the dock.

After another struggle at the yacht's rail, the cook got her boat captain aboard and below, propped in place at the dining settee in the cabin. Jamie then turned aft for a hasty trip to the head. For her part, Jamie was not exactly sober, nor was she drunk, and upon her return to the dining settee, she still had an interest in addressing their four-day state of celibacy. She nuzzled in beside her golden-haired companion to watch, in dismay, as he slowly toppled aside to slump in a heap on the cabin sole. Annoyed at Freddy's passing out, Jamie turned into her bunk, disgruntled and restless.

Sometime later, in the small hours before dawn, the clank of the cargo conveyor belts by the trawler came to a halt. Either the new stillness in the night or an uncomfortable pressure on her bladder bestirred Jamie to wakefulness. Her brain a blur, the girl decided to attend her bladder, crawled out of her bunk, and with a disdainful glance for the still-sprawled Freddy, went aft to the head. When finished, and finding herself uncomfortably awake, Jamie decided to have a look out the companionway to check that the docking lines were secure.

After a look at the yacht's lines, the operation on the floodlit deck of the trawler caught Jamie's eye. The conveyor belts on the dock had been wheeled aside, and a large truck with a closed box was backing into their place, stopping at the very edge. The driver got out of the cab and went around to open the back. Inside the opened doors, he fiddled with some controls, and then a steel I-beam with an electric cable hoist slid from the top of the truck, out over the hatch of the trawler. In her years along the California waterfront, Jamie had never seen a fish discharge operation like this, and she was now thoroughly curious.

A few moments later, a large square box, some sort of steel container, came up out of the trawler's hatch, dangling from the hook end of the cable hoist. In the stark glare of the deck lights, Jamie could make out most of the details of the container. What really caught her eye was the framework on top of the box, a steel pipe frame that protected a small reel winch and a submarine transponder. Jamie instantly knew what it was. She had seen similar gear used in positioning drill rigs off the California coast.

Quickly, the steel container was lifted clear of the trawler and shoved inside the truck. Two big men in fishermen's clothing clomped up the gangway, their gear in hand. Or was it gear? On closer look, Jamie saw they held machine pistols and banana clips of ammo. One of the fishermen got in the truck with the container, and the driver then closed the doors. Before entering the cab, the second gave a parting wave to a watching man at the rail, under the bright deck lights, in the shadows of the wheelhouse. As the truck drove off down the dock, the watching man returned the wave and stepped back into the wheelhouse. After a time, Jamie returned to her bunk but was unable to sleep, badly bothered by what she had seen.

Part Five

U.S. Coast Guard Headquarters, Boston, Massachusetts

Captain Osborne came down the hall to his office at a leisurely pace after a long liquid luncheon. That forenoon, he and the district commander had been the Navy's guests at the annual "sail" of the U.S.S. Constitution. The "sail" comprised deberthing the old frigate with several tugs, towing her out to mid-harbor, the firing of a measured round of salutes, and the reberthing in the opposite direction. The maneuver lacked any set of canvas that one might normally associate with wind sailing. Still, the old full-rigged ship afloat in mid-harbor, brightly decked out in a lofty pyramid of signal flags and flapping ensigns, was indeed a brave sight, a proud remnant of those days when Boston was still the seaport that "produced ships of a beauty and speed that swept the seven seas."

The intent of the forenoon "sail" was to expose uniformly the wooden sides and rig of "Old Ironsides" to the ravages of New England's wind and weather over the year. The side benefit of the sail was an opportunity for the maritime movers and shakers of the port to meet and swap yarns in a gala circumstance at an ongoing luncheon in a waterside restaurant where the Navy's abstemious regulations were in no way in force.

As the Coast Guard's seizure of *Renegade* and *Black Hawk* was still in the forefront of many minds, Captain Osborne had found

167

himself at the luncheon, the hub of a braided circle of Navy brass hovering to hear the details of the feat. One of the curious phenomena of military service is the quivering antenna that rapidly senses those whose careers are upwardly mobile. As with the more mundane world, military career mobility can hinge upon who you know and who you get on with. Otie Osborne now emitted all the right vibrations, so that his luncheon yarn-spinning was well attended, so well attended his glass was seldom empty but for a moment. As a result, Captain Osborne came back to his office with fond anticipation of an afternoon snooze.

While drawing out his keys, he became aware of the persistent ring of his private phone. A clumsy moment or two later, he was into his office and had picked it up. "It's about fuckin' time you got back to work," the caller greeted.

"What's up, Fitzy?" Osborne asked, recognizing the gruff voice of Eddie Fitzgerald, the Boston bureau chief of the Drug Enforcement Administration.

"A trucker just hit a bridge in Lynn, tipped over, box and all."

"So what," Osborne grunted, a bit befuddled. "Happens every day."

"Oh, no it don't, not this way. The box is a container and it's full of shoes and grass."

"That's a new wrinkle," Osborne agreed.

"Yeah. Now get off your fat ass. I'll pick you up out front, your place, five minutes."

"I'll be there," Osborne said.

Forty minutes later, Osborne, Fitzgerald, and their driver arrived at the accident scene, a steel-arched underpass beneath the Lynn railroad tracks. Sprawled across the road on its side was a green Mack tractor with a forty-foot container on its trailer. The once upper corner of the red container had been crunched open by the collision with the low bridge, spilling a jumble of shoe boxes and plastic-wrapped bales of marijuana onto the pavement. The area of the crash was cordoned off by a small army of whistle-blowing Lynn policemen diverting traffic from the road they had blocked with their blue-lit patrol cars.

A large crane was noisily backing over the tractor as Fitzgerald jumped from his car and strode toward the scene with the trot of a purposeful terrier. He headed toward a raffish young man with shoulder-length hair in a faded motorcycle jacket. Fitzgerald would later introduce this young man to Osborne as one of his best D.E.A. agents, but at this moment, the bureau chief was not standing on ceremony. "Where's the driver?" he demanded.

"Gonesville," the agent answered. "The Lynn cops say there was no one around when they got here."

"What about the trucking company?"

"Cops already called 'em. They got a guy comin' out."

"What do you think happened?" Osborne asked the agent.

"Far as I can figure, the guy musta really got rollin' good on this downgrade. The corner of the box musta caught the slope of the arch, just enough to tip him. The box is one of the eight-and-a-half footers. With an eight, he'd a made it, no sweat."

"Where was he heading?" Fitzgerald asked.

"Beats me, sir," the agent said. "The papers musta gone with the guy."

"That should be easy," Osborne offered. "You've got the numbers on the box right up there." He pointed to the large white numbers on the wine-red box. "Call up Customs, up at the container terminal. Give 'em the numbers, they'll have a record."

"Fuck callin' 'em!" Fitzgerald exploded. "I wanna see those guys. Have 'em tell me how a box of grass goes out on the street right under their nose." He then turned to his long-haired agent. "When they get that rig up, you ride it, right back to the container terminal. I'm goin' to stuff it right up Customs' ass. You have 'em put it in a bonded terminal. Take an inventory, make 'em sign off on it, have 'em put up a twenty-four-hour guard. Got it?"

"Yes, sir, Mr. Fitzgerald." The agent nodded. "But what about the Lynn Police?"

"Let 'em get their pictures for the papers, then tell 'em to blow. They give you any shit, tell 'em it's an international container on an international bill of lading—not delivered. Right? That makes it federal. An ongoing investigation, you tell 'em that for me. But get that box back up to Boston, under guard, quick."

"Yes, sir," the D.E.A. agent agreed as Fitzgerald and Osborne turned back to their car, which soon took off to the squeal of burnt rubber.

As he sat in the back of the speeding car, Osborne was lost in deep thought, his thoughts tied to the container and Fitzy's constant bitching about the plentiful "shit on the street." If Fitzy was right, and Osborne believed he was, it meant as much drug tonnage as ever was getting into America despite the efforts of Coast Guard and Customs. It had to be the containers.

Twenty-five minutes later, the D.E.A. car wheeled to a screeching halt by the door of the U.S. Customs Office at the Port Authority Container Terminal on Boston's Charlestown waterfront. Fitzgerald leapt from the car and stormed through the door, the uniformed Osborne a few paces astern. Inside the office, a young Customs officer was deep in a paperback novel, his feet on the desk, his back to the window on the dock. "Who the fuck's in charge here?" Fitzgerald demanded.

The Customs officer looked up, startled. "And who the fuck are you?" he asked defensively, very much used to the deference of truck drivers looking for expeditious clearance of their container papers.

"Fitzgerald, Bureau Chief, D.E.A." the firey little man said, flipping out a badge and credentials for a brief instant.

The Customs officer stared at Fitzgerald for an uncomprehending moment and then eyed the hulking Coast Guard captain behind him. Osborne was resplendent in gleaming whites with full decorations, the uniform for his forenoon "sail." The sight of the uniform brought a sinking pit to the Customs officer's stomach. "I guess I'm in charge right now, sir," he said to Fitzgerald. "The chief inspector's on vacation. My partner got called to the airport. They're workin' a big charter flight this afternoon."

"At the airport, huh," Fitzgerald repeated derisively.

Osborne then intervened. "I'm Captain Osborne, District Intelligence Officer. Perhaps you can help us, son. Take a look at your sheets, tell us what you've got on this box." He handed the young man a slip of paper with particulars of the crunched container in Lynn.

As the Customs officer turned to his clipboards, Fitzgerald picked up his phone and dialed. "Port Collector's office? Yes. Fitzgerald, D.E.A. Where's the boss? Washington? What's he doin' there? Budget review! How about the assistant? Giving a speech in Worcester! Naw, forget it." Fitzgerald slammed down the phone and exclaimed to Osborne, "Jesus H. Christ, would you believe it! Both gone."

The Customs officer then said to Osborne, "Yes, sir, that box came off *American Ace* this morning." He pointed out the window to a United States Line ship being discharged by the massive container crane. "The consignee was SteadFast Shoe Company, 307 LaFayette, Brockton. Women's shoes. One of three boxes. Duty prepaid."

"And who looked in the box?" Fitzgerald demanded.

"No one, sir. The papers were O.K. The duty was paid."

"Ya didn't even open it up!" Fitzgerald exclaimed.

"No, sir, we never do. Not unless the head office tells us."

"Why is that, son?" Osborne asked.

"Well, sir, I'm not exactly sure. I think it's politics, something to do with Port Authority handling charges and what the government is willing to pay."

"So you don't even look?" Fitzgerald asked derisively.

"No, sir," the young man answered.

Fitzgerald picked up the phone and dialed his office. "Terry. Get us a warrant. Yeah, importation of a controlled substance with intent. Yeah. SteadFast Shoe Company, 307 LaFayette, Brockton. Now, clean out the office. Yep, grab everybody. I want that place surrounded and searched a.s.a.p. Got it? Yeah, we're on our way."

While Fitzgerald was on the phone, the young Customs officer asked Osborne, "Sir, could you tell me what this is all about?"

"Yes. The container had an accident. It was loaded with marijuana," Osborne replied, as he and Fitzgerald hustled out the door.

"Marijuana," the young man repeated, watching the pair disappear into their car.

The D.E.A. car made slow progress from Charlestown through downtown Boston toward Brockton, for the Southeast Expressway was jammed with mid-afternoon traffic. As they plugged along, a thoughtful Captain Osborne finally spoke. "Hey, Fitzy, bet you a fiver this is a waste of time."

"Oh yeah, why?"

"Am I on for the fin?"

"Yeah, you're on. Now tell me why."

"Figure it out. The box tipped over in Lynn, on the north side of Boston. Now we're headin' south. The opposite direction—a spread of thirty miles or more."

"So?"

"So, the grass had to go first, before the shoes. I don't think we're going to find anything in Brockton."

"There's the other boxes," the Drug Enforcement bureau chief said.

171

"Yep. Well, we'll see," the Coast Guard intelligence officer allowed shrewdly.

Forty-five minutes later, six gray federal cars wheeled through the gates of the SteadFast Shoe Company. Seconds later, twenty D.E.A. agents surrounded the plant, and with guns drawn, had every employee on the shipping dock flat against the wall, their hands over head, thoroughly bewildered. Two red containers on trailers were backed against the receiving section. One had already been opened and was half discharged, the removed stacks of shoe boxes resting on pallets in a close-by storeroom. The shipper's seal on the other was still intact.

Within the hour, the containers had been opened by the raiding agents, every box of shoes checked. A glowering bureau chief came up to Osborne. "Nuthin'," he said disgustedly.

"Told you so." Osborne laughed, holding out his hand, watching Fitzgerald ill-gracedly reach into his pocket.

"So how do you see it?" Fitzgerald asked, while passing over a crumpled fiver.

"I see it that we're on to something big, Fitzy. Every time we made a grab, it didn't make a dent on the market. You've been bitchin' all along there's as much shit as ever on the street. So maybe we now know the way they've been getting around us." Osborne paused. "So we start with the driver and the trucking company." He then pointed to the sprawling, well-kept plant of the Stead-Fast Shoe Company, with its stolid brick smokestack that said "ESTABLISHED 1861. He added, "I don't think these people have a clue what's going on. That box wasn't heading here when it hit the bridge."

"Hummph," Fitzgerald grumped, dubious.

Osborne went over to the shipping clerk's cubicle on the dock and asked politely, "May I use your phone? It's a local call."

The clerk nodded, handing him the phone.

On dialing, Osborne was answered by, "District Intelligence Office, Chief Swett speaking."

"Hi, Chief. Captain Osborne. Yeah, I got called away sudden. What's up?"

"Not a hell of a lot, sir. Pretty quiet. There's been Lieutenant Quinn's trying to reach you, sir. That's about it."

"Oh yeah, wonder what she wants?"

"Didn't say, sir."

"Where's she at?"

"She's been callin' from a phone booth in Gloucester. Collect. Said she'd try again at five."

"That won't work. I won't be back by then. Take her next callback. Tell her to try me at the apartment after ten tonight. Give her that number. See you in the morning, Chief." As Captain Osborne put down the phone, he smiled. What had started as a frivolous day of festivity had indeed turned out eventful.

The Public Tennis Courts, Marblehead, Massachusetts

On the afternoon the federal agents eyed the tipped-over container in Lynn, two towns to the east, on the Marblehead public tennis courts, Flaherty glared at the lime-green ball in his hand and then across the net at Ann Raimond. There she stood, deep behind her baseline, white-skirted, pretty, poised, smiling as she slowly twirled her racket—prepared. If looks could kill, Ann would have long since been smithereens.

"Match point, Michael," she reminded him cheerily.

"Fuck you," he muttered, gasping for oxygen, stalling, hoping that somehow, some way, he might yet stave off defeat. Ann had run his ass right into the clay, that he knew. *You should know better by now, you dumb shit, you haven't guessed right about her yet, and remember pal, this match was your idea,* Flaherty berated himself. In the three days since Flaherty's return from fishing, Ann had mercilessly trounced him at badminton and backgammon. *That damn woman, was there anything she couldn't do?* Flaherty started to bounce the ball, still stalling, still starved for oxygen.

Chauvinism was not an often-used word in the vocabulary of Michael J. Flaherty. It was for him, however, a thoroughly attuned reflex, especially when it came to women. Behind his polite smile, there lurked the primal conviction that women had their place, best in bed, anywhere else, on trial.

173

In arranging this match, Flaherty had expected, as a fit male should, that he would win. He had simply assumed that Ann could play tennis well enough that he would get a workout and had planned to keep his margin of victory within bounds. Michael considered himself, and indeed was, an athlete. At Gloucester High and in his one year at the University of New Hampshire, before his service with the Navy's SEALs, Flaherty had been a three-sport letter man. He had since maintained a daily discipline of exercise, be it jogging, handball or swimming. Flaherty had taken up tennis three years back, went at it with his usual thoroughness, took many lessons, put in the practice, and built a solid game. In his opinion, the best part of his game was his serve, and he had come on the court certain his fireball serve would simply breeze by Ann.

And so, in his casual arrogant way, Michael had issued his challenge. Ann had accepted with an equally studied offhandedness, politely proposing they play on either the grass court at her place or a clay court at her club. Michael liked neither the idea of grass or Ann's club. He would reserve one of the municipal courts in the Old Town, a neutral court. And a day later, when he attempted to blow his first serve by her, war was declared on ground of his choosing.

Flaherty soon learned his assumptions had been in error. Ann returned his serves readily, steadily. Had he asked Ann of her game beforehand, he would have modestly been told what was now well apparent, that she loved the game, been given the best of instructors, had played all her life, and was singles champion of her several clubs. Alas, Flaherty had never asked.

Still waiting across the net, Ann had not a scintilla of compassion for the panting Flaherty. She hid her alertness behind a demure smile, a smile that masked a mirthful mind veritably abubble with vengeful glee. She was in no way fooled by the sometimes polite Michael Flaherty. Ann's lack of compassion could directly be traced to Flaherty's male arrogance. She knew a chauvinist bull when she saw one. She would play out their corrida to the last ritual move—paw as he might, Michael Flaherty would soon be a very dead bull, sprawled on the sun-baked clay.

Flaherty now discovered a loose lace in his sneaker, mumbled about it, and knelt to retie it—slowly. Finally back on his feet, he again started to bounce the ball, when suddenly he had a whimsical dream. He saw the ball as a weapon of war, a green grenade that somehow, some way, with a Merlin flick of wrist, with his graphite racket a rocket launcher, he would drive the grenade across the net, deep down the gullet of that goddamn woman. Flaherty liked this latest fantasy and again gave serious consideration to his serve. The stall had worked; he had his breath back. He was not about to get blown off the court in two straight sets by a woman.

Force having failed, Flaherty now tried stealth. He deftly dribbled the ball on the hard-packed clay, faster and faster, hoping to distract her somehow. Then, without warning, he threw the ball high over head, reared back, and served with all the powder left in his locker. *Thwack.* Flaherty smashed his grenade with two hundred pounds of coordinated force. The ball took off, a green streak that barely cleared the net to nick the baseline to Ann's offside.

To his complete chagrin, Flaherty watched Ann nail his pride with a firm backhand and return it with a sturdy *thunk*. Her return was as flat and fast as his serve. There followed a long, exhausting exchange from deep beyond their baselines. In frustration with this sustained duel, Flaherty hit out, harder and harder, flailing forehands that veritably hummed in their flat arc over the net. And yet, she kept sending them back with that same sturdy *thunk*.

That woman has got to go. Today's her last day, Flaherty vowed grimly as he watched Ann inexorably work forward inside her baseline, driving him back, deeper, foot by foot, shot by shot. Her returns took on a widening cross-court pattern, flat comets that forced Flaherty into a ragged run, first for a forehand and then to the back. *I break it off this afternoon, it's all over!*

Thunk. Ann's returns were a remorseless cross-court whipsaw of deep solid ground strokes. *Thunk.* Her latest shot took Flaherty to his left, far into the corner on his backhand.

With maximum effort, Flaherty caught up with her shot and returned a powerful blast, flat and low down the sideline. *Got her this time.* He grinned. But with a small swift shuffle, Ann was on to his backhand and returned to his right, as far as there was court. With his last reserve of strength, Flaherty sprinted cross-court. With a valiant dive by the back barrier, and a hay-making swing in mid-air, he caught up with her shot, returned a high weak lob, then sprawled on all fours, flat on his face. With tongue hanging out, the hapless Flaherty turned and watched Ann come to her forecourt, await the bounce of his lob, and with a soft flick of the wrist, drop his green grenade back on his side of the net. *Plop.*

Flaherty didn't move.

When finally, a few moments later, he regained his feet, Ann awaited him on the other side of the net, graciously offering her hand. "What a nice workout, Michael," she said, smiling.

With a churlish grunt, Flaherty barely touched her hand as he bent over to retrieve the last ball. As he did, he growled, "You cheated."

"Oh," she allowed. "How so?"

"On sportsmanship—you never told me you were that good."

"You never asked, Michael." She smiled.

"Hmm, six-two, six-one, twelve less three, Jesus Christ Annie, you mean to say I owe you nine bottles of Dom Perignon?"

"It would appear so, Michael. But if you recall, the bottle-a-game idea was yours."

"I suppose it was. Should have had a handicap."

"Want some more? Another set—double or nothing? I'll spot you three games," she offered.

"No, no. It's too goddamn hot. I just never expected to get wiped that bad."

"You do have a tendency to underestimate, Michael Flaherty, especially women. Now, if you'd like to cancel the bet, just speak up. We could negotiate."

"Screw you, Annie!" Flaherty exploded. "You think I'd let you have that to hold over my head! No way. We go to the liquor store right now. I pay prompt. There probably isn't that much Dom Perignon in all Marblehead, but we're going to find out. You drive."

Flaherty got in on the passenger side of Ann's wagon and thereby missed her grin as she walked around the back. When she got in and started to search her purse for her keys, Flaherty leaned over with a peck of a kiss. "Hey, good going," he said.

"Thanks," she replied as she returned his kiss and then started the engine. "Where to, me lord?"

"We'll start with the liquor store on Atlantic—then my place—a little ice, a long shower, a short screw, whatever."

Ann leaned over and patted him on his knee. "Hard to keep a good man down, isn't it, Michael?"

"You better believe it, Annie baby. Now just drive."

"Ah, bragging again, Michael."

"Annie, this one I win, or we both lose."

When Flaherty had purchased the champagne, they returned to

his place for a proper presentation. Getting out of the station wagon, he carried two of the bottles with him. On entering his home, Flaherty took a bucket and ice from his kitchen and started to chill the champagne. "This'll take a bit," he said. "Would you like a shower while we wait?"

"With you, Michael?" Ann asked.

"Whichever way you want." Flaherty grinned.

"Yes, I'd like that, with you," she said. And so they went to his bedroom, but didn't get to his shower. Ann had barely taken off her sneakers when she saw Flaherty sitting naked at the foot of his bed. She went to kiss him, and in moments, her tennis clothes were a heap on the floor by his, and with little foreplay, he was in her. Flaherty moved slowly at first, each jab drawing a moan of pleasure. As he increased his movements, entering her more deeply, Ann's gasps became more frequent and louder.

Flaherty was determined to hold back as long as he could, and he now consciously tried to relax the lower part of his body, but he was too fully aroused. With a quick wrap of her legs and a hard thrust of her pelvis, Ann pulled him in all the way. She felt him grow within her and arched to meet his rising. They met and clashed and parted again and again. Ann came first, meeting him with another wrenching thrust of her pelvis as he drove into her.

The full weight of Michael came down upon her, exhausted, panting, spent. Beneath him, Ann lay content, and for a long time, neither moved, lost in themselves, lost in each other. At last realizing the full press of his weight upon her, Flaherty rolled off to her side. "That was good," he said, sealing his withdrawal with a gentle kiss.

He soon fell into a light doze while Ann went down to the living room to fetch a bottle of champagne. She had just set the bottle down on the night table by the bed when a glass frame on the back side of the closet door caught her eye. She went over for a closer look and saw two framed military medals. One she immediately recognized from its ribbon as the Purple Heart, the second, a silver cross that she did not know. Neatly scripted near the base of the frame, it read; "Warrant Officer Michael J. Flaherty, U.S.N.—Mekong Delta—Viet Nam." *So, that explains the scars on his shoulder. He's been a hero before,* she mused, and that thought pleased her, for she was more than ever taken with this wild Irishman.

Ann returned to the bed and opened the bottle of Dom Perignon with a loud pop that woke Flaherty. When he had found full wakefulness, she handed him a glass and then lay down beside him, head to toe, sipping her champagne slowly. After a time, Ann spoke, huskily, dreamily. "Mmm, Michael, that was good. And now I wonder why."

"Why what?" he asked.

"The why is for me—the wonderings of an old married woman. Why me? You must have other, younger choices, of that I'm sure."

"Oh." He laughed. Over the past few weeks, what had started in the mind of Michael Flaherty as a one-nighter had moved along to that level of affection wherein he genuinely liked and enjoyed Ann's company. Beyond sex, and that was not to say he now gave sex a secondary role, Ann had become his pal. And so he said, "I think we have fun."

"Good, I'm glad you do. And I do, too." And then she added thoughtfully, "I guess my 'why' was wider than what I said. The 'why' of why I haven't ever felt like that before. You know, I never have . . . I suppose I shouldn't tell you that. You're bad enough as it is." She got up on her elbow to look at Flaherty squarely. "I feel like I've been suddenly released, sprung from some kind of trap, an emotional trap I didn't even know I was in. It feels so good."

Now sensing the drift of their pillow talk, Flaherty took a deep drink of champagne, set his glass down on the night table, and reached over to pat her brown pubic hair, now level with his chest. "And also because I knew you were a good fuck." His tone was a mix of teasing and encouragement.

"I'm not," she said, looking at him soberly. "Michael, I've never come like that in my entire life. I just haven't."

"It's good for you, now and then."

"Lord, Michael, I'm a totally wanton woman," she said, still disbelieving the depths of her release. "And I never really knew it. Maybe I sensed it sometimes, times when I had to play with myself, I got so uptight, but I never really knew it, not with a man."

"Annie, I don't know about the wanton. You sure are good goods when you get going."

"That just never happened to me." She twisted away from his toying fingers, reaching for the bottle of champagne. After filling both their glasses, she said, "It never happened with David, not in all those years."

"And now you feel bad about it?" he asked supportively.

"Hell no. I suppose I should, I can't do anything about yesterday, but I can about today, and I feel good."

"Then how did you both work it out?" he asked, puzzled.

"That's just it, we simply didn't. Maybe neither of us knew enough. I was quite young when we married, a bit of a wallflower then, shy. What Mother said, I pretty much did. David was my first, really my only beau. Our mothers were good friends. So I really didn't do much looking. I was a virgin when we married. Those were the days when a young lady did all the right things. I've been doing them ever since. But if I can feel like this, I know just how dead the relationship is. And I also know I sure helped kill it."

"Regrets?" he asked.

"No," she said. "I probably should have, but I don't. Certainly I did most of the killing—but I was not entirely alone." She looked away for a time. "David is a good person, if you take away love. Oh bullshit! Those are things I'm supposed to say. He's really a pompous ass. It would have been much easier if I liked him, respected him as a man. I don't. You see, since Mother went, I've pretty much run things—my way."

"Hey, Annie." Flaherty laughed, wanting to snap her back from the introspective drift of her thoughts. "I'm no shrink. You keep this up, I turn on the meter. A hundred bucks an hour. You got a Blue Cross number, or do I send you the bill?"

"A hundred an hour." She laughed. "I just might take you up on that. Full coverage?" And her train of introspection went away. When she spoke again, her tone was brighter. "Today is now and I feel good. No, Michael Flaherty, I feel better than good. I feel the best I have ever felt. And I don't seem to care about the rights and wrongs of it. The proprieties, the conventions—to hell with them." She looked across at Flaherty. "Shrink you ain't . . . shrunk you is." She giggled.

For a time, they played with each other, distantly. When she spoke again, her words were wistful, "Oh, Mike Flaherty, I wonder where we go from here."

"I don't know where we go, Annie. I surer than hell know where we've been." His tone was flippant, but his eyes twinkled. "And that was one hell of a fuck."

Villa Barerra, Nahant, Massachusetts

When the houseman led him down the stairs to the sauna, the grim import of his terse summons struck Mike Flaherty. He was of Barrera's family and had never been put through the full sauna security measures encountered by the less closely connected visitors to Villa Barerra. As Flaherty peeled off his clothes in the dressing room, he anticipated what was to come in this morning meeting. He had seen the tipped-over container on television the evening before and had immediately driven to his Gloucester office. Flaherty spent much of the night at the telex, cabling his Palermo agents encoded change-of-cargo orders. From the outset of his smuggling, Flaherty had realized that where humans were concerned, the probability of accidental discovery was ever present. As he worked alone in his office that night, what struck him was what he had not anticipated—the stupidity of this accident, the irony of Barerra's own people doing themselves the hurt rather than discovery by any of the agencies charged with drug interception. *How can one plan for stupidity?* he asked himself.

Over the past four years, Flaherty's mind-set came to match his link of responsibility within Barerra's organization. The machinery had run so smoothly, he gave little thought to what happened within the adjacent links, aware that the knowledge would do him no good. In Mike Flaherty's view, he was well paid to do a job, and he did it well. What happened when the product he transported hit the street,

Flaherty had chosen not to think about. And that was so until the last several days, when, playing about with Ann, Michael encountered the first twinges of conscience as to the business he was immersed in. He caught himself comparing his way of living with Ann's. Her money seemed so clean to him. Somehow, he had not fully comprehended what Barerra had told him of the roots of the MacKay fortune. Another source of Michael's emerging angst was the realization he was fallible, that his apprehension by the authorities could happen, be it by accident or otherwise.

As he hung his shirt, Flaherty considered the forthcoming meeting and was relieved that the container accident had not happened within his link of the chain. His sole assignment was the marine movement of shipments. Once a shipment was off the vessel and onto the docks, the subsequent truck transport and market distribution were out of Flaherty's hands.

Beyond Barerra and the people required to carry on the marine transportation of the production stream, Flaherty knew only two other people within the organization; the first, a man in Miami who phoned at random and told him in routine industry terms what cargos were to be lifted from which ports; the second, a truck company operator in East Boston whom Flaherty informed of cargo arrivals. Flaherty's communications with these two men were guarded and limited. That's the way Giovanni Barerra had set it up, and that's the way it operated.

As he went on with his stripping, the ever-attentive Guido took his clothing and frisked them for content. Flaherty almost got angry when the houseman next checked his armpits, then asked him to bend over and spread his buttocks. "You goin' Greek, Guido?" Flaherty joked rather lamely, realizing how deadly in earnest was Barerra's man.

On entering the sauna, Flaherty was surprised to meet the second man he knew in the Barerra chain, Phil Dimatio, the truck operator from East Boston. The small man squatted on a bench across from Barerra, looking withered and drained, far more drained than the usual sweating of sauna.

"Michael." Barerra acknowledged Flaherty's arrival, indicating the bench by his side. "You know of what happened yesterday in Lynn?" There was a growl in his voice.

"Yes, Mr. Barerra, I saw it on last night's TV and I've read the morning papers," Flaherty said as he thought, *And so today, we meet the other Giovanni Barerra.*

The old man's eyes were dark icicles that swiveled back on the wilting Dimatio. "Perhaps you might enlighten Michael on yesterday's events, Philip," he ordered.

"Plain and simple," the truck operator said, "our guy fucked up. He was runnin' late. Why, I'm not sure. There's talk he had a broad in Revere. Anyway, the dumb shit takes a shortcut off the regular route, he goes under the tracks in Lynn. The box was too big. End of story—what else can I say."

"What'll happen when they catch up with your driver?" Flaherty asked.

"They won't." Dimatio answered sullenly.

"But if they do?" Flaherty persisted.

"I said they won't, and they won't," Dimatio snapped angrily. "He's already over in Chelsea in the bottom of a ship loadin' scrap for Japan. They'll never find him. He'll come back as a Toyota."

Christ, Michael! What have you got yourself into? Flaherty asked himself. *Aren't you right there with him in this, an accessory to a murder?* He immediately dismissed the question from his conscious mind. The dumb driver was no part of his operation.

Barerra spoke calmly, matter of factly. "These things will happen. An example makes the point. Philip, the family is to be taken care of. Now Michael, what can we expect from our friends?"

"I'd guess, Mr. Barerra, the Feds will be all over that dock like ants. There were five boxes of grass on *American Ace*. They were split three and two, different consignees."

"And I got 'em all off the dock and out yesterday," the truck operator interjected. "The other boxes, no sweat. They were emptied, vacuumed, sprayed with that smelly shit. We had 'em all restuffed and delivered yesterday afternoon."

"O.K. Good." Flaherty went on. "So when they don't find anything, then I'd guess the Feds'll start checking all the cargo consignees off the *Ace*, real careful-like."

"Yeah, but that'll take 'em some time," Dimatio said. "And they won't find nothin." It all looks legit, now."

"Yeah, probably," Flaherty agreed.

"Look Mike, all the boxes are back in place. The Feds got their bucks and their papers. It's clean. The consignees got their goods, they don't know nothin'. And our guys got their grass. It's long gone by now . . . so fuck the Feds."

"What happens when they go lookin' for the truck owner?" Flaherty asked.

"The driver was it, an independent operator, far as they can look. He worked for a legit operation that don't know nothin'. So they hit a dead end."

"What about next week, Michael?" Barerra intervened. "Our business goes on."

"That could be a problem," Flaherty replied. "We've got two boxes coming over on a Zim ship out of the Med. She calls at Halifax where they transfer into a little feeder ship for Boston. We could leave the stuff up there in Halifax a week or two—see if the heat stays on."

"Do it, Michael," Barerra ordered. "And the next shipments, what about them?"

"Lucky I was watching the TV. We've got six boxes loading Palermo today. They're coming over U.S. Lines again. I got on the telex and changed the orders. They'll go into Newark. So it depends on the Feds. We can truck 'em out of Newark or bring 'em up to Providence by barge. That buys us almost a month."

"Good thinking, Michael." Barerra smiled for the first time, but it lasted only an instant as his attention again turned to the sweltering Dimatio. "Philip, I know this was not your fault, but only once will I say that."

"I understand, Mr. Barerra," the man said.

Flaherty spoke up. "You know, after I saw the TV I got to thinking. Phil, you better tell your guys to always check the box heights. They're used to the eight footers, but there's a lotta eight-and-a-halfs, even some nines, coming into the trade. It could screw 'em up. The boxes are marked, and that's why there's clearance signs on the bridges, huh?"

"I hear ya," Dimatio grunted.

"Philip, I think it's time you got back to your trucks." Barerra dismissed the man from his sauna. When the door had closed, he went on, "Well, Michael, what about our staying with Boston? Do you think we should switch ports?"

"Gabbo, I think we should watch for a week or two, see what the Feds do."

"What would you expect?"

"They'll start looking a lot harder."

"Then we might as well switch right away."

"Not necessarily, Gabbo. Depends what the Feds want to spend. They make things too tough, they'll slow things down, really screw up the port."

"What about our distribution?" the old man asked thoughtfully. "We have a market to maintain."

"So we can get tough, too, Gabbo. Screw up the port ourselves."

"How would you do that?"

"Maybe a truck strike for starters."

"Yes, that could be arranged."

"Say Gabbo, you going to take care of that guy's family?"

"You ask what you shouldn't, Michael. I consider the man a casualty, self-inflicted perhaps, but in our thing, we must expect stupidity. Loyalty is far more important." And as Flaherty watched, the shards of black ice that had been Barerra's eyes melted to pools of paternal encouragement. "Now Michael, I've been through these things before. We've lost shipments. That's part of the business. I think we'll be all right, that this will blow over. It takes something like this to make us carefully rethink what we are doing, recheck our methods. Now, I want you to think of other ways of doing business. In saying that, I don't want you to think I find any fault with what you have done. No, no, not at all. I am very proud of you, Michael." The old man reached over and patted Flaherty on the shoulder.

"Why, thank you, Gabbo," Flaherty said. "Yes, I have some ideas. Maybe the airlines out of Europe are the next play. I think we should study the aircraft service business at the airports, not the machinery maintenance. I mean the clean up, the wash down, the food and luggage, even the disposal of trash."

"Well, you do that, Michael." Barerra nodded. "And of course, any expenses you have, they will be for my account. Agreed?"

"Yes, Gabbo."

"Now to more pleasant things. I saw you on the television. I read of your victory. They made quite a thing of it. My congratulations."

"Thank you."

"It's wonderful that you can do such things while you are young."

"Hey, you're doing all right, Gabbo."

"Well yes . . ." Barerra was interrupted by a sharp knock on the sauna door. The old man got up and peered out through the small window. "Ah, Guido wants me. Excuse me, Michael," Barerra said as he left the small hot room.

The Samoset Club, Boston, Massachusetts

Later that day, Kevin Shaughnessey trailed the friendly maid into the Samoset Club garden and sat down heavily across a table from David Raimond.

"You look tired, Shaughnessey," Raimond greeted him.

"That I am, Mr. Raimond," he said wearily.

"Perhaps a drink would pick you up?"

"Worth a try. A double gin and tonic," the investigator said to the maid. He turned to Raimond, "I tried to get you earlier in your office. You weren't answering.

"Yes, well, I had a meeting away from the office. Things to attend . . . Well, how's it going?"

The investigator looked at his client for a long moment before answering. "I think we should drop the whole goddamn thing, right now."

"You what?" Raimond asked, startled. "Why? What's happened? Has Ann found out?"

"No, not that. Worse," Shaughnessey said, but then paused as the maid returned and served his drink. The investigator gulped down half the gin undiluted and emitted a tired sigh. "Now, here's what happened," he began. "Friend Flaherty called your wife this morning. I had the surveillance, so I picked up the call on the relay. He broke their lunch date, said something had come up real

187

sudden. So I decided to switch and tail Flaherty—see what he was up to. I hustled over to Glover Landing when he comes whistlin' out of the gate in that black Lamborghini. Lucky those Marblehead streets are small, with a lot of traffic. I was just able to hold my tail up through Swampscott, along the Shore Drive. At the circle, he turned off for Nahant and dusted me on that straightaway. So I figured Nahant's a small place—only one way out—not too many places to hide. I start up and down the streets. Finally, I spot his car on the drive by a big stone house behind some gates. I see I'm hittin' a dead end, so I turned back real quick. I pulled up down by the next beach."

Shaughnessey stopped to down the remaining gin. "So, I decide to walk back along the beach, maybe up on the rocks, maybe get a peek at what Flaherty's got going. Well, turns out the seaside is almost a goddamn cliff. I walk the beach till I'm sure I'm right under the big house, then I start the climb. Sweatin', huffin', I'm almost to the top when two guys jump me. They're up above me. One of them's got a .357 cannon pointed right at my head. The other says 'Who are you?' "

"I look at 'em—both in black pants, tan jackets, uniforms of some kind. So I said, 'Me, I'm a tourist, just out for a walk.' "

" 'Yeah, and you climb cliffs for exercise,' he says, and then he climbs down and starts the frisk. Meanwhile, I'm lookin' right square up the hole of his pal's cannon. So the first guy grabs my Smith and Wesson. The son of a bitch, he steps back, throws it right out in the ocean. Can you believe it? But I'm not about to move, not with the cannon still on me.

" 'A tourist, huh?' the guy grunts, and then he's into my pockets. Grabs the wallet. Comes out with my license, the private eye license. Looks at 'em. Looks at me. 'A private investigator, huh. You got some kind of warrant?' he says.

" 'Hey, not me. I'm just out for a walk,' I say.

" 'And you're on private property, trespassing, you can take a breather,' he says. 'Squat, right there. We'll see what the boss wants to do.' And he climbs back up over the top of the cliff with my wallet, disappears, leavin' me lookin' square at his pal with the cannon. I can't see where the first guy goes, I'm down too low. Besides, the guy with the gun never moves. Maybe ten minutes later, the first guy's back. 'Well, Shaughnessey,' he says, 'you got lucky, you're goin' out the way you came in. *Now.*'

" 'What about my rod?' I says.

" 'Sue us,' he says.

"I wasn't about to argue. He flips down my wallet. When I get down on the beach, the two of 'em are still up there watchin'. So, when I get back to my car, I start thinkin' those guys are pros. If they weren't, they'd have worked me over. Punk wiseguys would have. So I take a swing around by the gates of the big stone house. Flaherty's car is gone."

"What next?" Raimond asked.

"So I look at the gates, there's a plate. 'Villa Barerra' it says."

"So?"

"So, Mr. Raimond!" Shaughnessey exploded, "I'm fuckin' lucky to be alive!"

"What's it all mean?" the Boston trustee asked, baffled.

"You never heard of Giovanni Barerra—'Father Joe'?"

"No, I don't think so. Who is he?"

"Christ, Mr. R. He's the man, the head man—he's got a piece of every action in the whole Northeast."

"Action?"

"Yeah. Numbers, broads, rackets—some say drugs, nowadays. You name it, he's in it."

"A criminal?"

"That's one way of putting it." The investigator laughed. "Now, if friend Flaherty fits with Father Joe, we're in deep shit."

"Numbers, women, maybe even drugs," Raimond repeated thoughtfully. "I knew you couldn't run that kind of yacht on the fish business. Well good, we're getting somewhere."

"You're not thinkin' of goin' any further with this thing?" the investigator asked, disbelieving.

"Why certainly, Shaughnessey. My wife is involved. I'm not going to have her mixed up with this kind of person," Raimond replied righteously. "Would you?"

"Hey, Mr. Raimond. I don't think you're hearing what I'm saying. It's no longer chasing down an afternoon shack-up."

"Oh?" Raimond eyed the investigator glacially.

"Every agency in the East has been on Barerra for a lifetime. And I'm going this way once. I like life. I like sniffin' daisies. From up top. Sniffin' around Giovanni Barerra for two-fifty a day just ain't worth it."

"So." Raimond paused. "Then it's really a matter of money?"

"Mr. Raimond, we started out on a plain and simple shack-up. That's one thing. Barerra, that's somethin' else."

"Three–fifty?"

"Forget it."

"What then?"

The shrewd side of Kevin Shaughnessey was genuine in protesting no further interest in the assignment, but then, the old fire-horse instinct came to the fore. *What the hell, if the bread's good enough, it might be worth the shot. What a score this could be.* He considered asking reimbursement for the lost pistol, but then his professional pride intervened. It was his own fault he got jumped like an amateur. It was up to him to balance that account, when and if he could. And so he said, "Five for me, three for my help. And I'm goin' to need help, a lot of help."

"And for that, you'll look into the connections, the relationship between Flaherty and this man, Barerra?"

"I'll try. No one else has ever done it. I make no promises."

Joseph's Aquarium Restaurant, Boston, Massachusetts

Otis Osborne stepped out of the John Fitzgerald Kennedy Federal Building into the shimmering heat and blinding sunlight of City Hall Plaza. He quickly put on his sunglasses and walked down through the milling bazaars and outdoor bistros that made up Boston's Faneuil Hall Marketplace, headed for a restaurant down on the waterfront. Outward impressions and inward reality can indeed be deceiving, for as Captain Osborne ambled along through the crowd in a short-sleeved sports shirt, tan slacks, and a brightly banded straw hat, he was, to all appearances, the quintissential American tourist, visiting Boston, walking the Heritage Trail in the shadow of the historic halls that had spawned the Revolution that led on to the Republic.

Once down on the waterfront, Osborne entered Joseph's Aquarium Restaurant, a rendezvous he had selected with care as serving fine fish. As his arrival was just ahead of the noon-hour crowd, Osborne was shown to a table by the harbor-side window and was seated but a moment when an attentive waiter produced a welcome gin and tonic.

Osborne was taking a strong pull of his drink when the deep *toot* of a tug boat drew his attention to the window. Two tugs were churning down harbor to meet a massive container ship. In the strong summer sun, the brightly colored tugs and the many colored containers piled high on the ship's decks would have posed a challenge for the most vivid artist. Osborne had no artistic interest in the ship. He was far more interested in what was about to happen when that ship arrived at the Charlestown Terminal and her containers came onto the dock.

Captain Osborne had just come from an all-morning meeting in the Kennedy Building, a special meeting attended by the upper echelons of all the federal and state agencies involved with narcotics enforcement. The evening television and the morning press had given considerable coverage to the marijuana-laden container tipped over under the Lynn bridge, an intense media coverage that brought discomforting embarrassment to the attendees at Osborne's morning meeting.

Eddie Fitzgerald had called and chaired the morning meeting. As Osborne thought back on the proceedings, he decided it was a good thing a long oak table separated Fitzgerald from James Griffith, the collector of the Port and local chief of the Customs Service. Fitzgerald's opening comments on Customs' diligence were less than charitable and grew worse. Griffith retaliated with some unkind words about Fitzgerald's "cowboys" and then mounted a heated defense of his own service, citing budgetary constraints as the reason not all containers were opened on coming into the Port of Boston. In the end, cooler heads prevailed and it was agreed that a joint task force of Customs and Drug Enforcement agents would turn the container terminal upside down this very afternoon.

Osborne recalled with a certain mirth the heated exchange between Fitzgerald and Griffith when the latter protested, "And what are we going to do with the Port Authority and the Longshoremen's Union?"

"Fuck 'em both," Fitzgerald had snarled. "We represent the government of the United States. We got a job to do. They screw us up, we grab 'em—obstructin' a federal officer. They don't like it, tough shit."

"This I wanta see. You'll learn," Griffith had warned leadenly.

As the container ship entered her turn for the Charlestown channel, a throaty growl of her horn brought Osborne's attention back to the moment. *Well, we're about to find out who's right, Fitzy. Here comes your first ship,* he mused and then, after ordering a second gin, his thoughts ran on to his luncheon meeting.

Running a network of undercover agents was a new experience for Captain Otis Osborne. A year had passed since he had created his network and had placed five young Coast Guard officers in undercover roles along the New England coast. Ever since, his agents had come up empty-handed, not one lead to a narcotics bust. In light of the considerable expense to the federal government, Osborne could normally have expected carping criticism or at least some chiding for this lack of productivity. Such was not the case. The district commander, Admiral Haggerty, had left Osborne to his own devices. As a matter of fact, in the immediate wake of the *Black Hawk* and *Renegade* intercepts, Haggerty had forwarded to Washington a glowing efficiency report on Captain Osborne that read in part: "Outstanding performance—most highly recommended as fit for further command."

The district commander had chosen to believe the intelligence network created by Osborne was producing stellar results. In reality, Admiral Haggerty had asked few questions about the network, and those that he had asked, Osborne had somewhat deftly evaded. While not actually deceitful, Osborne had done nothing to disabuse the admiral of his misconception. Why should he? Over the past six months, Osborne's First District efforts had intercepted more narcotics tonnage than any other district of the United States Coast Guard. Why rock the boat? Everybody was lookin' good.

In letting things slide, Otis Osborne was neither derelict in his duties nor a fool. As a matter of record, at their most recent Monday morning review, the district commander had further expanded Osborne's duties, requesting him to discover who was leaking information out of Headquarters operations. Osborne was now mulling how to go about that request, but not sidetrack his major preoccupation—the big why of the phone calls and now, as the leak out of Headquarters became apparent, what was the connection between the leaker and the tipster?

As district intelligence officer, Osborne was well aware that these phone calls had a reason, but try as he would, he could not fathom it, or not until yesterday's container collision. That certainly changed things. The phone calls had to be tied to the containers. No one threw away tens of millions of dollars of narcotics, the street value of the First District intercepts, without good reason. *But why?* Osborne asked himself over a rapidly draining second glass of gin. Maybe the offshore busts were only a ruse, a trick to distract the federal agencies. Was there someone smart enough, big enough, he could afford to feed the federal agencies a string of small-craft cargos as bait—distracting, scent-throwing bait.

One strong reason Osborne now considered the container method the big play was Fitzgerald's comment at their morning meeting that the truck driver down in Lynn, a five-year man with his company, had not returned to his home in Chelsea over the night. *I wonder if he ever will?* Osborne mused. Well anyway, the afternoon shakedown of the container terminal may tell the tale. He glanced at his watch. 12:50. *She's late,* he thought.

And with that, Osborne's mind moved on to thoughts of his rendezvous with Lieutenant Quinn. Since she had first gone undercover, she had phoned Osborne regularly. She was always chipper but never had anything of substance to report. The girl seemed undaunted and to be having one hell of a good time, what with Bermuda and racing all the major regattas. That was all right with Osborne. In his head, he had relegated her to a role out of harm's way.

Thus, Captain Osborne was a bit taken aback when Quinn called him the night prior, urgently requesting a meeting. She was on to something she did not want to discuss on a phone, and so they set up this lunch. For his part, Osborne was now preoccupied with ramifications of the container tip-over and thus awaited his agent's arrival with a certain amount of indulgent skepticism. That is not to say his mind-set was completely negative. To the contrary, Osborne was hopefully curious, for this request by Lieutenant Quinn was the first positive nibble to come out of his net.

Osborne waggled his empty glass at the waiter when a tall girl in a white sundress came into the restaurant and went to the maître d', who led her to Osborne. The girl swept through the room with an easy grace, excitement in her green eyes, her long red hair trailing behind, her progress tracked by every male eye in the crowded restaurant. Lieutenant J.G. Jamie Quinn was indeed quite beautiful, Captain Osborne concluded as he watched her approach.

For Jamie, it was already a long day, a workday that had started with the dawn when *Shillelagh* was shifted across Gloucester harbor to the Flaherty boatyard's marine railway. The sloop was slated for a bottom scrub and polish over the day and then to sail for the Edgartown Regatta in the twilight. Jamie had agreed to lend Freddy a hand on getting the boat hauled out, and then she borrowed his truck to go in to the Graduate School of Naval Architecture at the Massachusetts Institute of Technology in Cambridge. After a lengthy and favorable interview with one of the screening professors, she got ensnarled in the noon traffic along the Boston waterfront and had difficulty in finding a parking space. As a result, she was twenty minutes late for her meeting with Captain Osborne.

To play out her role on arriving at his table, Lieutenant Quinn greeted her commanding officer with a breathless "Sorry, I'm late" and a filial peck on the cheek. To those that had tracked her entry, she was the ingenue daughter or niece in the city for luncheon. Osborne was well aware of the attention the girl's arrival had drawn and rather enjoyed it. The captain attended her seating and with a grin retook his own. "Well, that's a nice surprise," he said.

Jamie placed an MIT curriculum catalogue on the table as she spoke softly, "No offense, sir. Thought it would look better."

"None taken." Osborne laughed. "Never been kissed by a lieutenant before. Something to drink?" he offered hospitably.

"Thank you, sir, it is hot. A light beer would be great."

After placing their order for drinks, Osborne picked up the catalogue. "What's this?" he asked.

"It started out as part of my cover story, sir, but it looks like it might fit. I went over this morning and talked with one of their professors. They'll take me for the fall, that's if I'm still needed here in the East."

"Good for you," Osborne said admiringly, and went on, "Well, tell me what you've come up with."

"We got back from Bermuda to Gloucester two nights ago."

"And did O.K., I read," Osborne interjected. "Congratulations!"

"Yes, sir, thank you." Jamie laughed excitedly. "What a race. A great sail, a new course record, a really remarkable boat. She can reach like a witch."

"I saw your start. I was on *Hamilton* with the admirals. You almost got drilled by that mahogany boat."

"It sure was tight. Mr. Flaherty's got a lot of guts and a good eye. So anyway, sir," Jamie's voice dropped to a conspiratorial hush, "the night we got back, or more accurately, around four the next morning, I got up to check the docking lines. There was this trawler, the *Katherine M. Flaherty*, a little ways down the dock unloading fish. So I watched for awhile, and when they got to the end of the fish, this truck came up and lifted a small steel box out of the hold and then drove off."

"A steel box? You sure it wasn't some kind of fish gear?"

"No, sir." Her green eyes were level and certain. "I've been around a lot of fish boats. I never saw anything like that before. It was about four by four, had a protective cage on top. Inside that, there was a reel mechanism and a positioning transponder."

"What in hell's a positioning transponder?"

"They use them around the submersible drill rigs a lot—at least the ones I've seen off California. They send back a positioning signal. They allow a free-floating drill rig to stay over a hole in very deep water, without a whole bunch of moorings."

"So what do you think?"

"Well, sir, I think they're using the trawler to pull these boxes off the bottom, bring 'em right in with the fish."

"Come on, Jamie. How would the boxes get out there in the first place? And what about our inspections when they hit the dock?" Osborne was dubious.

"Well, sir, I don't know how the boxes get placed offshore. Maybe they're dropped by a mother ship. I do know what I saw, and it certainly looked strange to me. As to inspection on the docks, you wouldn't believe what a joke Customs was. Why, when we came in from Bermuda, that man didn't even come down on *Shillelagh*. As a matter of fact, sir, why would an American trawler ever have to go through Customs?"

"You're right, Jamie, a good point. They don't," Osborne agreed thoughtfully. "Incidentally, Lieutenant, I like your uniform." He laughed as he eyed her brief sundress. "So where do we go next?"

"Thank you." She smiled for a moment. "I'm not sure. I don't know that much about Mr. Flaherty or his business. Maybe he doesn't know what's going on. I'd like to believe that. From what I've seen, he's a nice man. Sails hard. Gives great parties. Been very good to those of us in his crew. But I do think that box was suspicious, very suspicious. Maybe we should run a check on Mr. Flaherty and Flaherty Fisheries."

"I think I remember Flaherty Fisheries from years past. It's an old-time operation." Osborne frowned. "Anyway, I'll do some checking."

The waiter came to take their order for luncheon. When finished ordering, Osborne picked up with Jamie. "Speaking of boxes, did you read what happened up in Lynn yesterday?"

"No, sir. We don't get the papers on *Shillelagh.*" She laughed.

With that, Osborne launched off on a detailed description of the prior day's events and the morning meeting of the enforcement agencies. As he wound down, he added, "Frankly Jamie, I'm going to guess that box you saw was some kind of specialized fishing gear. Maybe not. As I said, I'll do some checking. But I kind of think the big stuff is coming straight into this port in the regular shipping containers. It's pretty brazen, but that's my hunch."

Jamie was a bit crestfallen by her superior officer's discount of her discovery. She held back her disappointment and asked, "Well, sir, what would you like me to do next?"

"Just what you're doing," Osborne replied encouragingly. "Keep your eyes open—stay on the waterfront and keep me informed. And don't take any chances. I'll do a little asking about Flaherty. You keep right at your yachting. Never can tell what might come of it."

"I'm not sure how I can stay on top of the trawlers. We're leaving for Edgartown tonight. Racing the Regatta next week."

"Don't worry about it. The Vineyard, huh?" Osborne beamed and grew positively expansive. "Boy, we sure had some luck down there, a couple of weeks back. Busted two vessels off Nomans Land. You hear about that?"

"No, sir," Jamie replied politely. "What happened?"

The captain began a well-polished yarn of his latest coup while Jamie listened attentively, thinking her own thoughts, certain she was on to something herself, not certain of her next steps.

Villa Barerra, Nahant, Massachusetts

"Well, Guido, what did our people find out?" Barerra asked, putting aside his papers when his houseman came into the atrium.

"Shaughnessey's workin' private, best we can tell right now, Mr. Barerra. Used to be a state cop—ran the governor's detail. Been out on his own five years."

"Hmm, the governor's detail," Barerra wondered aloud. "Then he's not one of their dummies, by any means."

"Maybe not, Mr. Barerra, but comin' on us the way he did, that wasn't so smart." The houseman went on. "So when he left Nahant, he hit a phone booth on the Lynnway. Musta struck out, 'cause he hit another phone by the tunnel, then went straight to the Under-Common Garage. Parked, walked to a place called the Samoset Club on Beacon Street."

"Well, well. The Samoset Club no less. This does get intriguing."

"Shaughnessey stayed 'bout a half hour, then walked across the Common to his office on Tremont. We've got some guys on him, just like you ordered, Mr. Barerra."

"Any idea who he met, Guido?"

"One of our guys tried the bullshit approach, poked his head in the door, lookin' for a wrong address. An old bitch of a maid ran him off, but he did get a peek at the visitors' book. Shaughnessey was signed in as a guest by a Mr. David Raimond."

U.S. Coast Guard Headquarters, Boston, Massachusetts

Eddie Fitzgerald met Captain Osborne in the Headquarters ward-room for a drink after work. They fetched their drinks from the bar to an empty corner table.

"Well, Fitzy, what did you come up with on that guy Flaherty or his company?" Osborne asked.

"Not a damn thing. The guy's not on our computer. The company's been there for years, both clean."

"Kind of thought that would be the case. Goin' any further?"

"I will when I can, Otie. We're stretched right now. When I see a space, I'll get some guys down to Gloucester."

"You'll go for a warrant then?" Osborne asked, concerned for the cover of his Lieutenant Quinn.

"What's this warrant shit, Otie?" Fitzgerald replied testily. "If our guys find something, then we go for a warrant."

Osborne decided not to push the subject further. "So how's the container shakedown going, Fitzy?"

The normally feisty Fitzgerald was subdued as he spoke. "Zilch, as far as findin' any shit."

"How far have you got?"

"Who knows? Jeez, Otie, I never realized how many boxes were over in that terminal. Must be a couple of thousand."

"That shouldn't have been a surprise. You come to work over the Tobin bridge. You ever look down at those docks, Fitzy?"

"Yeah, well, it was new to me," Fitzgerald said leadenly. "We're maybe through five or six hundred by this afternoon, but now we got troubles."

"Oh?"

"Yeah—it started with the truckers at the lunch break. Have to admit we musta had 'em backed up a coupla miles waitin' for boxes. They started to bitch."

"Can't blame 'em. They probably get paid by the trip."

"Yeah, they do."

"So?"

"So now the longshoremen are with 'em. They're sayin' we can't open a box without their guys there. They want 'em on all shifts, whether they do a damn thing or nothin'. That means double time, triple time, you name it. Even Old Uncle can't lug that kind of shit."

"Yeah, well, Griffith warned you about that."

"Fuck Griffith."

"So what did you do?"

"I was just over at the dock, told their head clerk to go fuck himself. That I got two teams workin' tonight. We're goin' to keep right at it without those greedy bastards." The Drug Enforcement bureau chief glowered as he spoke.

"And?"

"I may have a strike on my hands in the morning."

Edgartown Regatta, Martha's Vineyard, Massachusetts

The southwest wind came on warm and strong in the afternoon. At the helm of *Shillelagh*, Mike Flaherty reveled on this last leg of the race, a blustery beat across Vineyard Sound, up the funneling channel, to a finish at the narrow mouth of Edgartown Harbor. In the afternoon's twenty-five knots of wind, the stability of the light sloop was sorely tested, so sorely her owner had prudently ordered a triple-reefed main, a small blade of a headsail, and the twenty-two of his crew as far out on the rail as they could get. As *Shillelagh* was the only maxi-yacht racing in the Regatta, when she passed under Cape Pogue on a long port board, the other yachts in her class were tiny white flecks on the Wianno side of the Sound. With her knot-meter hovering well over nine, it took only a few minutes for the golden sloop to slice across to the bell-buoyed side of the approaches.

"Eighteen feet, Mr. Flaherty," Jamie Quinn cautioned, her eye on the rising depth meter.

"O.K., we'll tack at sixteen," Flaherty acknowledged and then shouted to his boat captain, "Hey, Freddy, we're going about pretty quick. Everybody up. And let's make it a good one."

Ten brawny young men sprang off the rail to the winches while Freddy checked the coil of the jib sheet. "Ready forward," he advised.

"Sixteen and a half," Jamie said.

"Guess we shouldn't cut it too close," the helmsman muttered, then bellowed, "O.K., here we go. Hard-a-lee." When Flaherty spun up the wheel, his big sloop swung head to wind, while the headsail, freed for the tack, rattled and slatted. Its noisy freedom was brief, for as *Shillelagh* fell away on the new tack, her strong hands ground away at their winches, winding in on the new sheet.

"Backstay up, traveler down," Jamie informed Flaherty.

"Lee backstay off," Ann Raimond chimed in.

"Way up on the jib," Flaherty shouted. "Good job, ladies and gents." He grinned happily, squinting into the bright sun, eyeing the water ahead and the blue flag on the distant Committee boat, a rime of sea-salt etching the crinkles about his eyes. "Hey, I think we just might fetch the finish on this tack," he said.

Studying the same silver rifts of wind on the water up under the Vineyard, Ann said, "I doubt it."

"How the hell do you know?" Flaherty bristled, his seaman's judgment now in question.

"I used to race down here, when I was a girl—Adams Cup stuff," Ann explained. "It seems we always got headed on this last starboard. A lot of port lifts come off those Cape Pogue beaches. I think it's the heat of the sun on the sand. Of course, that was when I was a girl," she added.

"When you were a girl . . . Christ, that's ancient history. Things change." A few minutes later, he added cockily, "Betcha we fetch, Annie."

Ann watched *Shillelagh*'s slant for a time before taking up his challenge. "I don't think you'll make it, not without another tack."

"What do you want to bet?"

"You're on for a fifth of Mount Gay," she said, then added shrewdly, "but no pinching."

"No pinching," Flaherty agreed, and settled down to concentrate on the remaining mile of race course. For the next half mile, the wind held steady, allowing *Shillelagh* a course that would cleave the line between the white Committee boat and a bobbing orange flag. And with that, her helmsman started humming "The Wearin' of the Green."

But then, over the last half mile, the wind lightened, grew puffy, uncertain, and started to draw ahead ever so slightly. And with that, Flaherty's humming ceased, his jaw took on a granite grimness. Few boats could sail any closer to the wind than his, that he knew, but now, *Shillelagh*'s bow occasionally fell below the orange flag at the finish. He tried to sail her even closer, but several times the wind-starved headsail shuddered with the closeness of his course.

"Hey—you're pinching," Ann protested.

"Quiet! Hey, Freddy, shake out a reef," Flaherty growled. "Let's see if we can get her to lay up some." The crew dove for the cluster of winches by the mast, and in moments, shook out the lower reef and resheeted the main. Even with added sail aft, *Shillelagh* could point no higher. When, inexorably, she came up to the Cape Pogue beach, she had underfetched the finish line by a hundred yards or more.

"Ready about," Mike Flaherty ordered grudgingly.

Moments later, with the *thud* of the finishing cannon, Ann came up to Flaherty with a smirk and a light kiss for his cheek. "Well, nice race, Skipper," she said.

"Thanks," Flaherty grunted. "And it only cost me a bottle of Mount Gay."

"Why Michael—such a small price, and a lot cheaper than Dom Perignon," she teased. "And look at the horizon. You can't see another boat."

"Yeah, maybe, but we owe some of 'em one helluva lot of handicap.

I suppose we could hang around out here for awhile. See how we do on time. It is pretty early."

"I have another thought. Why don't we go up by the Beach Club?" Ann pointed to the harbor entrance, to a cluster of tents on the shimmering sands of Chappaquiddick Island. "We could anchor right there, have a swim while we wait."

"That's one hell of an idea, Annie," he agreed. He called forward, "Hey, Freddy, when you get 'em furled, we're headin' up under that beach—then anchor. We'll need the swim ladder out and the sun-shade rigged over the cockpit. Maybe a little party, huh."

The last drew a roar of approval from the crew, and with the prospect of a party, it took but a few minutes for the parched young hands to have the sloop snugged down and anchored off the Beach Club. As the swim ladder was rigged overside, Ann came up the companionway, tucking the last of her chestnut strands within a swim cap.

Through the good offices of Jamie Quinn, Flaherty already had a glass of iced rum in his hand as Ann came on deck. The coral bikini on the ambered gold of her lithe body was indeed a sight to draw a sailor's eye. With a wink for Flaherty, she neatly dove into the warm water and swam for the beach with a smooth graceful stroke. Flaherty watched her, and was about to follow her when Jamie again came up and asked, "Mr. Flaherty, O.K. if we do some spinnaker flying?"

"Yeah, sure Jamie, you'll have to anchor off by the stern to keep your halyards clear. With this breeze, the storm chute might be the best for it."

"Thank you." She smiled. "I've done it before—I'll make sure it's all rigged right."

Flaherty watched his beautiful redheaded cook with her tight shorts and tighter T-shirt as she went away forward. She moved with the sure stride, the prowling certainty of a Siamese cat. *Boy, if I were fifteen years younger,* he mused, *would I take a shot at that.*

Ann now stood in the shallows of the Chappaquiddick shore, beckoning Michael. After a long sip of rum, Flaherty pulled off his shirt and dove. Minutes later and slightly winded, he pulled up beside Ann, who happily wallowed and splashed in the warm wavelets. Regaining his wind, Flaherty put his arms around her and drew her to him for a deep salty kiss, one that she met and returned with depth and interest.

"Mmm—good," he mumbled when finally they drew apart. "What about a little P.R.M.?"

"P.R.M.?" she asked quizzically.

"Yeah—post race matinee." He laughed.

"Right here, Michael?" She protested. "'Tis a bit public."

"No, no. *Shillelagh* or back to the inn, your choice."

"Not *Shillelagh*, that's for sure. There's more privacy on Boston Common. Now the inn, that makes more sense," she said as she rolled over on top of him that they might kiss, and as she did, she slowly ground her bikinied pelvis into him.

Flaherty could feel his want come upon him, but he was in no hurry, he wanted it to be slow, to be good for them both. Flaherty had driven any and all worries from his head for the day. Ann was beautiful and golden, the beach sand white and clean, the sky the bluest of summer blues, Edgartown the right time and the right place—but there was no hurry, none at all.

When Flaherty grew introspective, an infrequent event, he had to admit his life was indeed fuller and happier than it had been before meeting Ann. He found the woman to be as bright or brighter than he, and for once, the possibility of female superiority did not bother him. He loved Ann's ability to anticipate his thoughts and wants and needs, to do so without words. While he would never admit so openly, he truly admired her ability to challenge him four-square, and often trounce him in games he thought his, her dry Yankee sense of humor, her ability to cut through to the absurd in very few words. Mike Flaherty had come to like Ann Raimond in a few brief weeks, and in consequence, had narrowed his dating pattern to the very border of monogamy. This in turn probably helped him in his newfound happiness, for it certainly cut down the tensions of dealing with a plethora of sexual partners, his past pattern of operation.

A rattle of activity on the deck of *Shillelagh* drew Flaherty's attention. Her crew had taken her anchor to the stern, so that she now lay bow downwind. With her spinnaker gear all rigged, Jamie Quinn had been deeded the dubious honor of the test flight. With a cheer from her crewmates, Jamie dove off the bow and paddled over to a bo'sun's chair that floated in the water. When later she had the spinnaker flying above her, she would control her altitude and position by guiding sheets to the clews of the great sail.

With another loud roar from the crew, they hoisted the spinnaker in restraining stops, and then, with a snap and a crack, broke it out into the full brunt of the wind. Like a leaping porpoise, Jamie was snatched clear of the sea, and in seconds was soaring sixty-five feet or more over the harbor waters, the billowing sail firmly in her control.

Ann and Michael still wallowed in the shallows of the Chappaquiddick shore. "Hey, that looks like fun," she exclaimed.

"Want to try it?"

"No, I don't think so," she said thoughtfully. "I like your other idea better."

"What's that?" he teased.

"P.R.M., you idiot." She elbowed him sharply.

Aboard *Shillelagh*, the lustier puffs lifted Jamie eighty-odd feet clear of the surface. From that height, she had the finest view in Edgartown, the full sweep of the harbor approaches, their competitors still slugging uphill to the finish, off to the north, the green crook of Cape Cod, and far to the east, out beyond the Chappaquiddick bluffs, a golden streak on the dark green sea, Nantucket Island.

But then, a strange thing caught Jamie's eye. Abeam of *Shillelagh*, a fiberglass runabout slowly idled in toward the beach club. In its bow, partially concealed by a large beach towel, she saw a man furtively working a camera with a huge telephoto lens. Thoroughly curious, Jamie twisted around in her bo'sun's chair to see what he was photographing. The only thing there worthwhile was Mr. Flaherty and Mrs. Raimond necking in the shallows. Jamie then wondered if Captain Osborne had already initiated a second surveillance of Mr. Flaherty.

Edgartown Regatta, Martha's Vineyard, Massachusetts

Never had he seen a wiretap pay off so handsomely—that was the professional opinion of Kevin Shaughnessey as he worked the controls of the small boat off the Chappaquiddick beach. With information gained from the tap, the investigator had known for several days of Mrs. Raimond's plans to fly with Flaherty to the Vineyard that morning, race in the forenoon, and attend the yacht club dance that night. Shaughnessey also knew Flaherty had booked the best suite at the Whaler's Inn. All this allowed Shaughnessey to make plans of his own.

"How's it going, Jack?" the investigator asked his photographer as the younger man worked his telephoto lens under a towel in the bow.

"Just fine, Mr. Shaughnessey. Got half a reel of this kissin' crap. Want any more?"

"Naw, that should do just fine, Jack. My guess, they'll soon be headin' for the inn. We'll get that on tape tonight, then it's back to old Boston tomorrow." There was a wistful trail to the investigator's voice. "You know, Jack, I kind of like this case. Good pay, nice places—and that Annie, she's not so hard to look at."

"A little old for me," the young photographer said.

"I bet she looks a lot better later." The investigator laughed a deep ribald laugh. "Speakin' of that, you must have done quite a job on that clerk."

"Hope so . . . Yeah, I'm takin' her out again tonight—later, after we get the job done. She's all right." The photographer chuckled. "All I needed was a couple of days lead time, a little cash to splash, you get a lot of things done." The photographer was a handsome young man with an olive-oil tan and a wide irreverent smile. His night with the desk clerk at the Whaler's Inn led on to his successful booking of the suite adjacent to that reserved for Michael Flaherty.

"So, we're all set?" Shaughnessey asked.

"Sure are, Mr. Shaughnessey. Their side, it's just another mirror over the bureau. Our side, we get full coverage of that pad, just so long as they leave on some lights."

"And the sound?"

"Three mikes, all tied to the video take-up."

Yes, as he reviewed this stake-out, Shaughnessey was indeed pleased. He even knew the story Ann would feed David, were he to ask about her activities and whereabouts on the Vineyard. The private investigator had heard her tell Flaherty of phoning an old friend, one Natalie Farley, to arrange a cover story that she was staying in the Farley's guest cottage, should David call. *Clever girl, this Annie,* Shaughnessey thought. Subsequently checking the Vineyard's telephone directory, the investigator deduced and noted Natalie must reside with one Frederic Farley on the Shore Road at Edgartown. Yep, tonight should button it up. He would miss her, but not as much as David's five hundred clams a day. Still, there was a matter of ethics. You can't string a client out too bad. Tonight, they would get what they needed for the adultery rap, then it was back to Bean Town and on to the Barerra part of the job. That'll take sometime, to pin down the tie with Flaherty. That won't be so simple.

Flaherty glanced at his gold wristwatch and then eyed two sloops slogging along under Cape Pogue. Knowing the distance, he quickly calculated they were not within a half hour of finishing, and adding that to the time elapsed since *Shillelagh*'s finish, he said to Ann, "Hey, I think we have a shot at the corrected prize on this one. Let's swim back to *Shillelagh*. I want to check it out."

After they had swum out to the sloop, Flaherty went below to the navigation cabin for the handicap sheet and to calculate more carefully the times owed. His rough guess on the beach proved quite close, for not long thereafter, the time allowed by *Shillelagh* to her competitors for the distance raced that day ran out before any had finished. With that, a pleased Flaherty called his boat captain away from the spinnaker flying party on the bow. "Hey, Freddy, see if you can whistle us up a launch—our luggage is at the club. We're staying at the Whaler's Inn. And for tomorrow's race, it's ten o'clock, all hands on board."

At that moment, high overhead, Jamie decided others deserved a turn riding the spinnaker. With a leg-flailing jump and a happy squeal, she dropped a strong forty feet into the water and swam aft for the ladder. As she came over the rail, an exhuberant Flaherty met her, grabbed her in a hug, and pounded her on the back. "Hey, Jamie, we blew 'em away today."

"I thought we might, Mr. Flaherty." The girl beamed. "You had her flying on that second reach."

A few steps away, Ann Raimond eyed the exchange. In the warm sunlight, the pair seemed so healthy, so animated, so attractive, freckled Jamie with her long red hair, black bikini bottom, soaked T-shirt, and twenty-four years, hugging bronzed lusty Michael with his curly chest hair, raffish smile, and roving eye. Ann then wondered if there was more between them than she knew of, and the thought instantly brought a painful pang of jealousy, followed by visions of competing with a girl young enough to be her daughter. But then, Ann took hold of her bubbling thoughts, and ever the composed lady, she masked her worries behind a wide, even smile.

Meanwhile, Freddy whistled and waved at all passing power craft and finally conned two young boys, cruising about in their low little launch, to come alongside the high-sided *Shillelagh*. He asked if they'd like to make a buck taking two people into the yacht club. One of the wide-eyed boys, buried beneath a floppy sun hat, his face a swath of zinc oxide and melded freckles, looked up at the big sloop and politely mumbled they would be glad to do it for nothing. "No—no way," Flaherty insisted laughingly. "Five bucks to the club. You've got to pay for your gas."

Ashore, on the outside of the yacht club fence, Kevin Shaughnessey and his photographer nonchalantly watched the boys' launch approach the float, and after paying off the youngsters, Flaherty and Ann go into the club office, pick up their luggage, and come out into the street. When Flaherty next whistled up a cab, the investigator's jaw dropped. In the scenario Shaughnessey had envisioned for the late afternoon, Flaherty and Mrs. Raimond were expected to stroll arm in arm the two hundred yards from the yacht club to their reservation at the inn and happily fornicate through the twilight for the benefit of Shaughnessey's videotape camera. But with only a couple of bags, who needs a cab for a two-hundred-yard walk? They were not following Shaughnessey's scenario, and if not, what the hell were they up to?

Had Shaughnessey been privy to the conversation of the pair in their launch, he would have heard Flaherty ask with feigned lechery, "Your place or mine?" then seen him lightly slap Ann on her scantily clad rump.

"Remember on the phone, Michael, I told you of Natalie Farley's home on the harbor? Why don't we at least take a look at it? They're over in Newport for the weekend. We could have the place all to ourselves, and as we need, it's fully staffed."

"And supposedly, we have the best suite reserved at the inn," he countered.

"Michael, when I say a home is exquisite, I don't say it lightly. I'd simply like you to see it. Nats has done a wonderful job of restoring this old whaler's home. It was in her husband's family a century or more—badly neglected. With her means, I assure you, it has been done right. I'd like you to see it."

"O.K., let's take a look," he agreed. "Say, who is this Nats pal of yours?"

"She was born Natalie Boardman. Her family had a large farm in Wenham. She was my roommate at Saint Tim's and one of my brides-maids."

Flaherty chuckled softly. "A small world we live in."

"How so?"

"Rosalie and I bought the Boardman Farm—that's where my kids live."

"My lord. Yes, it can be a small world," Ann agreed, "and for that very reason, I also think we should stop by the Farleys . . . just in case."

"Just in case what, Annie?"

"Discretion, my dear, discretion. David and your Rosalie do exist, you know. I'm sure we both have many friends here in Edgartown. There are proprieties to be observed. There could be an emergency. One never knows. By the way, how are you and Rosalie getting along?"

"Not very well. She thinks Mick's gotten mixed up with the wrong kind of girl, that he's playing around with pot, and I'm not helping any."

"I know how she feels. I've been in that boat."

"Oh, what happened?"

"Young David almost got himself expelled from St. Pauls. Cocaine was involved."

"So, how did you handle it?"

"He took a term off. I sent him to a center for that kind of thing in New Hampshire."

"And it worked out O.K.?"

"Yes, it worked, best I can tell. You never know with drugs." Their conversation broke off, for at that moment, the freckled youngster brought his launch alongside the yacht club float. Later, in the cab, Ann said, "Now, Michael, if we like the Farleys' place, then you can check in and pay for your suite at the inn later. That's not too much trouble."

"Sounds like you've pulled this caper before," Flaherty teased.

"No, I haven't," she denied firmly, "but we are married, and there is such a thing as common sense, Michael, just in case there were ever a question." *Not that I really give a tinker's damn,* she thought to herself.

Watching the taxi drive off, Kevin Shaughnessey's stomach sank. *Oh shit, something tells me they're going to that Farley dame's place,* he said to himself. Quickly, he consulted his notebook, whistled up the next cab in line, gave the driver the Farleys' address, and piled in behind his photographer.

Sure enough, half a mile later, they saw Flaherty's cab driving away from an old sea captain's home, a magnificently maintained Greek revivalist home snug by the lower harbor, a handsome home that shimmered blue-white in the shade of rustling elms.

Shaughnessey quickly mumbled something about the wrong address, ordered his cabbie to drive several homes further along the waterfront, and there, paid him off. When the investigator and his photographer walked back by the Farley place, they grew discouraged for the outcome of their mission. The long narrow lot that led down to the harbor was dominated by the big house. On each side of the house, there were tall wind-break fences that made the harbor-side yard into a tightly enclosed compound, with fences so stout and tall the prospects of successful surveillance were indeed dim.

The private investigator noted at the far end of the enclosure what seemed a two-story boat shed close by the dock. Shaughnessey decided he would try a water approach if this is where his quarry nested for the night.

On the harbor side of the boat shed, Ann pirouetted to Flaherty's waiting arms for a long salty kiss. "Well, what do you think?" she asked.

"Your place wins in a walk. Gawd, what a set-up."

The boat shed had been converted into a small and very private guest house, the lower floor an open awninged cabana facing on the dock and harbor. The room was fitted with canvas furniture done in soft pastels. To get to this guest house, the Farleys' butler had led the pair through the great home and down through a seaside garden of hollyhocks and humming bees.

For Flaherty, the Farley place was the perfect ending to a magnificent sailing day. His competitors now beat through the harbor narrows, tacking close by the boat-shed dock where Flaherty relaxed on a sofa. He watched and listened and grinned contentedly, the air about him redolent with bellowed commands, whining winches, slatting headsails, and the heady bouquet of the garden.

As the incoming racing boats thinned, Ann asked, "Can I mix you a drink?"

"Uh-unh," Flaherty declined.

"What then?"

"You," he said, drawing her toward him.

"Well, what an interesting thought," she said, flirting. "Right here?"

"Anywhere you want."

"Then why don't we start with a shower. At least, Michael, we can get the salt off."

"All right with me. What comes with it?"

"Me—if you behave yourself."

"And if I don't?"

"Me." Ann smiled and led Flaherty up to the second floor to a spacious bedroom that charmingly combined the hewn-beamed saltiness of an old boat shed with the carpeted sumptuousness of extreme affluence and excellent decorative taste. The bath was appointed with all the oils, emolients, and lotions one could ever ask for. Still in her coral bikini, Ann went into the shower, setting it to a warm needling sting. Flaherty trailed after her and promptly undid her bra. He took up a sponged mitten and gently scrubbed her back. "There—no, just a little bit higher up. Ah—there—just right, hmm." She writhed in the sensuality of Flaherty's scrub, guiding him by her squirming to the tension points where neck joined shoulder.

After a time, Ann turned to him and they kissed a long salacious kiss while Flaherty peeled off her bikini bottom as she rolled down his swim trunks. He moved his mittened hand down between her legs, and ever so gently, slowly rubbed her.

On first touch, Ann shuddered a small shudder that soon was a long deep shudder. Not long after, she impatiently pulled Michael back to her. "Come on," she said, snapping off the shower, stepping out into the carpeted bedroom, and spreading a great plush bath towel over the thick carpet. Wet and dripping, she lay down upon the towel, drawing Michael down upon her and into her.

There was neither gentleness nor consideration to their mating—sheer lust on a champagne-colored towel. Flaherty's initial entry was so insistent, it drew from Ann a startled grunt. Thereafter, he became a slippery insistent jackhammer of need—one she was hard-pressed to match.

Later, they went down to the cabana, where Ann poured them each a stout rum. She then took a lounge beside Flaherty as they lapsed into companionable silence. The bluster of the day-wind drew down with the setting sun, leaving as sounds of the twilight the distant mutter of launches and the soft lap of the running tide on the thick posts of the dock, a lull that left each to wander within their own thoughts.

The afternoon Ann had hammered him into the tennis court, Flaherty had his first inkling he was falling in love with the woman. In near times past, Flaherty's sensing the slightest scintilla of a commitment to a female would have sent him skittering for the horizon. Now, he found himself for several weeks going out with the same woman, surprisingly happy with his lot, indeed a marked change in the mind-set of Michael Flaherty. As he lay back in the warm night, listening to the lapping waters, Flaherty now dealt with the reality of his feelings for Ann, that what had been a strong attraction had that very afternoon raced far beyond, into the wider world of love.

This was not the only change in the thoughts of Michael Flaherty. The execution of the unfortunate truck driver and Michael's resultant awareness of his own involvement was indeed a turning point, and with increasing frequency, he found himself wondering how he could ever get clear of his Mephistophelean ensnarement by Giovanni Barerra. The more he thought about his involvement, the more Flaherty came to realize the prosperity of Barerra's slick money-making entailed an awesome price for the addicted, that there was far more involved than beating the Feds in a fun game for easy money. And now there was Ann, and when he was with her, he had this growing feeling of shame and filth in what he did. As he lay beside her, the feeling came again, and Flaherty found himself bothered more than ever. His ever-facile mind now groped for an opening in the maze. But after a time, the rum, the sex, and the setting took effect and Flaherty fell off into a light doze.

Ann's search for where she was, was equally complex. This brash younger man beside her could make her body sing, that she knew better with each passing day, sing like a violin to soaring heights, sing a song so high, so beautiful, she worried that it would endure. And with that bittersweet thought, she went on to others, for as the daughter of Lawton MacKay and the descendant of a long line of cold-eyed Yankee merchant princes, she knew nothing was constant but change. Ann didn't like the thought, but it was with her for a time, and followed by other, more somber considerations.

Ann MacKay Raimond knew she could never, would never be owned by a man. In matters fiscal, she had long since established her independence. In matters physical, that she might find a man to share time with, share space with—openly share—without any devouring dominance or obsessive possessiveness on either side— that was indeed a hope, perhaps an unrealistic hope the extremely independent, offhanded Michael Flaherty just might meet. But of that wish, she was wary; they had known each other but a meteoric moment. Would what was now between them stand the test of time?

No matter the outcome, she would ever be grateful to Michael Flaherty for furnishing the key to a long-rusted padlock on an unrealized chastity belt. Ann had years before known of her wants and the inhibitions that encrusted them. That, until now, she had done little about them was part circumstance, part upbringing, and part inertia. But now, those inhibitions were gone, it was never too late.

One new resolve she made in the tranquil twilight was that she would finally do something about her marriage. There was little sense prolonging the farce any longer. On her return, she would call her attorney, Thornton Loring, and get on with the first steps of that long journey. David would huff, puff, and posture, and most certainly would drag his heels. Could it be done quickly, surgically, with the quick finality of a guillotine? Probably not, not with all the familial and financial strings that bound them. So it will take a machete, and the time for the machete is now, on returning from Edgartown.

Ann gave virtually no consideration to the effect of a divorce on their son and daughter. They were off on their own, independent, her daughter in college with a year in France, her son at law school. The children knew how dead their parents' marriage truly was. Young David, his addiction problems behind him and now a bright spot in his mother's life, often kidded about his father's stodgy ways. So, duty done, it's time for me, she now decided.

And on that thought, Ann's mood abruptly swung. With a last sip of rum, she started to chuckle, a soft contented chuckle. No matter what, be it mid-life madness, middle-aged infatuation, whatever, she would enjoy Michael, happily, zestfully, one day at a time, each joyous in its time. With that decided, Ann got to her feet and quietly went into the boat-shed bar to refill her glass.

The clink of the ice cubes woke Flaherty. He got up with a deep stretch. "Must have fallen asleep," he allowed.

"That you did," she agreed.

"Too much sailin', swimmin', and screwin'." He laughed.

"Too much?"

"Well, maybe not." Flaherty walked into the boat house and gave Ann a great hug from behind. "We still going to the yacht club dance?" he asked.

"That's up to you, Skipper," she said while making him a fresh rum.

"It's more your thing than mine," he temporized. "Still, we've got to get some supper sometime—your choice."

"No, not at all," she said. "We can stay right here. I looked in the fridge. There are hors d'ouvres, wrapped steak sandwiches, a romaine salad, even champagne."

"Hey, I've got to meet your friend Natalie. She thinks of everything."

"Well, we'll see about that. She is quite attractive, and yes, thoughtful, too."

"O.K., that settles it. No dance—back upstairs, in bed this time."

"In a bit," she agreed.

Out on the dark harbor in his runabout, a discouraged Shaughnessey surveyed the well-lit dock and the dim boat shed. Any approach to the Farley boat shed over that dock would most certainly be spotted, he decided.

Pointing to a similarly walled garden that abutted the Farleys', a garden far less lit, the young photographer suggested, "Hey, Mr. Shaughnessey, I could try the middle of that fence."

"Yeah, and what do you do when you get out in the light here on this side?" Shaughnessey asked acidly.

"That would be a problem," the photographer agreed. "Say, what about a hit-and-run raid approach? I'm sure they're up on that second floor—no lights. They gotta be fucking. So, I go over the wall, bust up the stairs, get my shots, run like hell for the dock. We're off."

"No way, my boy." The elder investigator shook his head. "We're not to blow our cover under any circumstance—client's orders." And with that, Shaughnessey put the runabout in gear, turned, and as he puttered up harbor, he muttered to himself, *Well Annie, you beat us tonight—there's always tomorrow.*

Crane's Beach, Ipswich, Massachusetts

After their return from Edgartown, Ann and Michael did not meet for several days. While they did talk a few times, each was caught in a schedule that precluded a meeting. This separation weighed heavily upon Ann, finally prompting her to call Michael before dawn and arrange a noon rendezvous at Crane's Beach.

They were to meet on a mid-summer morning, a day of lowering grays and slender promise. The early forecast gave a high probability of rain by mid-day, discouraging the usual throng of summer swimmers, leaving most of the five-mile stretch of white sand to Ann. She had suggested a beautiful site for their meeting, a gold-white ribbon of beach bordered to the east by the open Atlantic, backed to the west by the tawny sway of wind-stirred salt marsh. As she slowly waded the water's edge, carefully turned out in a blue windbreaker and rolled-up white ducks, Ann was engrossed by her surroundings, listening to the hushed break and spend of the wavelets, feeling the tingle of the swept sands about her ankles, wondering where it all went. Occasionally, she glanced off to the south'ard, to the bold granite headland of Cape Ann and the far-distant spires of Gloucester, willing their clock hands to move more swiftly.

Ann had spent a worrisome night spinning webs, webs that all seemed to center on Michael and her affair with him, an affair that grew more ensnaring with each day. Her recognition that this off-handed rogue now seemed to own her mind, as well as her body, had made Ann angry with herself and worried.

Their differences in background and makeup mattered less with each new day. Ann came to accept Flaherty's off-the-docks, today-is-where-it's-at, I-am-now outlook and liked him the more for it. Yet her acceptance brought its own worries. Through her long night, before she finally called Michael, she had walked the circuitous paths of her mind, from one worry to another, making new ones as she moved along. The progression of her worries were badly lacking in logic but impossible to ignore.

Now, seeking time with herself, Ann had come to the beach an hour before her rendezvous with Michael. While she sloshed along, she realized that in many ways her affair with Flaherty was both new love and first love, her adolescence having been so insulated, her marriage so early, so preordained. Be it new love or first love, she found the new wine that was Michael indeed heady, her spirits soaring high when with him, her joy so total, she worried.

One quandary of her new relationship was the how of playing a new game whose rules she did not understand on a quagmire of a playing field. Ann could neither comprehend nor accept the reality of a physical relationship uncomplicated by the possibility of enduring commitment. For her, there had to be more behind these happy matings than the mating itself, and in her monogamous mind, there was. Perhaps the genetic traces of Puritan ancestors in a purposeful world, the proprieties, entanglements, and manifestations of marriage were still very much ingrained in Ann MacKay Raimond. Yet, she desperately wanted her present marriage behind her.

Not all Ann's thoughts while wading Crane's Beach were of gloom, disaster and despair. To the contrary, each glance at her wrist watch told her Michael would again be with her, and soon, and with that knowledge, there came a slight catch to her throat and her heart warmed with joy.

On the middleground of her mind, she recognized her thoughts were a confusion of differing wants. She wanted to be with, to have Michael, to own Michael, yet she could anticipate her own reactions and resentment, were anyone to cross uninvited into her own preserve of privacy. Coldly, she told herself, *You want to own, yet not be owned, to have what you want, on your terms. And how will that work?* A practical woman, Ann realized she wanted the unattainable. Early in her relationship with Michael, she had ascertained his high esteem of his own freedom. She knew the very first scent of the quicksands of commitment would send Flaherty skittering for sea-room.

But the acceptance of such a loose alliance by such an organized woman of orderly bent and possessive mind-set was difficult. Ann Raimond was a born pigeon-holer, and in groping about for good order in her thinking, had made a mental balance sheet of Michael Flaherty and her David. In all reality, her comparisons were devoid of fair-mindedness. Poor David, unknowingly caught on the wire in a field of fire unleashed by the full fury of a disenchanted woman— a woman in want of a change.

Ann's comparisons did, however, serve one useful purpose, bringing to focus for her those attributes of Flaherty that drew her to him beyond her initial preoccupation with his sex. Ann perceived Michael Flaherty as a gentle, warm, and patient man. She was comfortable and trusting in his arms. Theirs was a free and easy interchange, one that she had never had with David.

Her most discouraging conclusion in her assessment of her relationship with Flaherty was her awareness, upon her resolve to break out, that the chances of success were sadly slim. Michael was her first venture of any consequence on the outside of a long yet deeply flawed marriage, one that, the day before, she had taken steps to dissolve with her first visit to divorce lawyers, and the probable cause of her restless night, a topic for this day's discussion with Michael.

Ann did not hear the Lamborghini rumble into the parking lot behind the dunes or see the eagerness with which Michael tore off his shoes and trotted up onto the sand. When once he spotted her, he set out after her at a fair jog. So lost was she in her wandering thoughts, Ann was not aware of Michael until he splashed up behind her and spun her around for a startled hug and a kiss.

Flaherty kissed Ann hard and long and eagerly, but soon, sensing some distance in her manner, he pulled back and saw the shadows beneath her brown eyes. *Oh, oh, one of those days,* he said to himself and immediately elected a teasing approach to see if he could dispel her gloom. "Hey, did you ever check up on that Blue Cross policy of yours?" he asked laughingly.

"You mean when we were talking about my coverage for your hundred-an-hour analyst consultation deal?"

"You better believe it Annie—and what a bargain!"

"Well, yes, I did." She laughed. Michael was here, her gloom was gone, her heart full of happiness. "I did some checking, and I found, Michael Flaherty, that you are a complete fraud, a quack. You have no license to practice in this Commonwealth."

"The hell I haven't," he asserted. "But I'll have to admit my practice is restricted, it's undercover research—very hush-hush medical stuff."

"Now that I will believe," she agreed gleefully, "but then, the hundred might be no great bargain. There could be better practitioners about."

"Bullshit," he protested. "The best bargain you'll ever make. I might get a Nobel for my work."

"We'll see, Michael." She giggled at his silliness, and then, for a time, they walked through the wavelets, hand in hand, silent, each with their thoughts. After a while, Michael asked softly, "Hey, where are you, Annie?"

"Oh, I'm not sure, as I said when I called. I just wanted to see you, be with you, to talk to you, when I could. I was bothered by a lot of things. But you're here. Things are better now."

Flaherty leaned over, nuzzled her ear, and squeezed her hand. "Good, I'm glad you did. You know Annie, I have nights like that, too. I call 'em the twisty-turnies. They started in Nam. I still get 'em now and then. Anyway, I'm here. I took off as soon as we got the trucks on the road to market."

Ann looked at him, concerned. "Oh, Michael, I've probably taken you away from something important."

"Hey, the catch is on the way to auction, almost all the trawlers are at sea. I'm here because I want to be. Don't sweat it. Now, where are you? What's bothering you? That's more important to me."

"Thank you, Michael. As to where I'm at, I'm not sure. Yesterday was a bad day. I went to my lawyer about divorcing David. It's not all that easy. This no-fault process can take eighteen months, that is if everybody agrees, and there's a property settlement. Did you know that?"

"No, can't say that I did," Flaherty said, then joshed, "But while we're waiting, maybe we ought to think about lunch. Otherwise, we won't be around to see how it all comes out."

"One of your better ideas." Ann laughed, and they turned back toward the parking area, and their cars, and as they did, there came the first sprinkle of a summer rain. For Ann, the silence of their walk was companionable, comfortable, but for Flaherty, by her side, holding her hand, other worries came flooding back.

With each new day, the container tip-over seared deeper the psyche of Michael Flaherty, leaving him badly shaken. He had gone into smuggling for reasons of need and greed and the challenge. Since the game had gone entirely his way, he had prospered beyond his wildest dreams. Barerra's words, "If we succeed, you will be an extremely wealthy young man," had been good, good in gold. Mike Flaherty was now rich, his gold and currency on numbered deposit in Zurich, Nassau, and Grand Cayman. *But does it matter that much anymore? Who wants to be the richest guy in the graveyard?* he now asked himself. And so, despite his financial security, he felt uncertain and unsure where he was going, and neither his wade with Ann nor the summer rain would wash away his uneasiness.

Part of Flaherty's uneasiness could be directly traced to his feelings for Ann, his perception that her way of living was so proper, secure, and straightforward, that her grass seemed far greener, her world more solid, than his. With that as an emerging perception and his worry about the fallout from the container, Michael Flaherty sensed a sudden wind shift in his life, a major shift that held the foreboding of an ice storm at sea, and then he said to himself, *It's a shitty business you've got yourself in, Mike Flaherty. Now do something about it.*

The MacKay Mansion, Marblehead Neck, Massachusetts

For the Raimonds and many of their friends, their major effort in life was their first breath. That accomplished, their lives simply unfolded, first on lamb's wool blankets in nurseries with cuddling nannies and visiting parents, later on, a carpeted progression of the right schools, the right places, the right parties, planned rites of passage that led on to the right friends. This carpeted path led to a narrow intermingling of the wealthy, with predictable results. They bred with their own kind, as was the intent of their rearing. Intent was one thing, results quite another matter.

The enduring-happiness part of her plan was somehow omitted, Ann Raimond felt as she sat alone on her patio. It was a beautiful place on the inner side of the pool, where a chill wind off the sea rustled the tall beeches and tinkled the crystal chimes that hung by the dining wing doors. With David delayed in the city, Ann was left to a gathering twilight, listening to the pitter of rain on the canopy, feeling the chill of an icy vodka in her hand.

Ann knew this was to be a bittersweet day, that sadly, the sweet part was behind her, the bitter lay ahead. She and Michael had spent a good part of their afternoon in an Essex clam bar close by the rain-swept salt marsh. It was a grungy place, sawdust strewn with many smells and a jukebox that assaulted the eardrums, but that didn't matter. All their senses were for each other, none for their surroundings. And so, they ate too many clams, drank too many beers, and were intermittently gay, serious, or silly as their conversational winds blew about. Eventually, Michael had to return to Flaherty Fisheries. On her return to Marblehead, Ann went to her bedroom and curled up for a nap. Her unusual sleep could be directly traced to too many pitchers of beer, but was also, perhaps, a subconscious retreat in apprehension of what lay ahead. In any event, she slept well into the cocktail hour.

Near seven, when Ann came downstairs, she learned from the butler that David had been detained in the city and could be expected by eight. Ann had been braced for the bitter part of her day, the confrontation with David that could no longer be put aside, but now it was delayed, and so to her patio and vodka.

Before meeting Michael, when Ann asked herself the whys of her unhappiness, her immediate answers were boredom and purposelessness. What else could it be? She had no other worries. Over the last few years, the predictability of David and his friends, their bigotry, their narrowness, the monotony of their conversations, had for Ann grown beyond wearisome to the point of total vexation. In analyzing her unhappiness, Ann faulted their friends, their whole way of living, as much as David. The Raimond friends, for the most part, were middle-aged money managers, brokers, and bankers, long-established people with vested roots around Boston. Ann saw this circle of friends and her marriage as but a part of a larger tapestry, one to be rewoven.

Little commonality remained for her with the small social world of Marblehead Neck. Until Michael, Ann accepted these dull relationships as she accepted the inevitability of the New England seasons; they came, they went, they were. A whimsical thought then struck her. Ann and David regularly attended St. Michael's Church in Marblehead's Old Town. She wondered, a bit wryly, what the ladies thereof might think, were her relationship with a less saintly Michael to become better known. If it didn't matter to Ann, then logically, with a new life to live, there now seemed little sense in maintaining the crust of propriety that formed the facade of her marriage. Who was she fooling but herself? And why?

For most marriages, there comes a point of unhappiness where the unspoken speaks for itself. This was not so for the Raimonds. They lived as strangers in opposite wings of a large mansion, meeting for meals and amusements, their meetings preplanned and polite.

Had Ann not met Michael, this pattern would most probably have continued, as both Raimonds were capable of letting their marriage go free and, adrift for a numberless span of years. But the unspoken would be spoken this night, the die cast, the Rubicon crossed.

Ann now had mixed feelings about the crossing, knowing what she was about would deeply wound her husband of twenty-four years. In fairness, it was she who had done the drifting, she who had wanted her freedom. David had simply stayed David, not a major crime. Was there a way to minimize the hurt? Probably not, and prolonging matters would not be a kindness. It was best done quickly.

Behind Ann, the patio door opened. "Isn't it a bit chilly out here?" David Raimond asked.

"Oh, I don't know. It gets warmer with a drink. Best pour one now, dinner's at eight," Ann replied.

David went to the bar wagon, started to make a drink, and as he did, he said, "Oh, Ann, I've been meaning to talk with you about the club cruise next month. I'll be racing *Gull* of course, but as commodore, I'll be expected to do quite a bit of entertaining. I think we should charter a large powerboat, maybe something around a hundred feet, perhaps a bit larger. What do you think?"

"I have no opinion," she said. "I'm not going."

"Oh." David finished pouring his Scotch and carefully put the stopper back in the decanter before he went on. "I am the commodore this year. Your not coming would look rather strange." He took a seat across from her.

"David, I don't give a damn how it looks. I'm not going on your club cruise."

"I hope you'll reconsider," he said softly, having met this mood before.

There was a steely edge to her tone as she answered, "Well, I won't. I haven't read the cruise announcement, but I can guess . . . We will rendezvous at Padanarum, then Newport, Cuttyhunk, Edgartown, a lay day at Edgartown, Nantucket, then disband at Woods Hole. Now, would you like me to tell you who we will meet at each port? Who we will dine with? What they will say?"

"All right, all right," David temporized. "I just hope you will reconsider."

"Damn it David! I won't. I'm planning to divorce you."

"Divorce me!" he sputtered, "Why, Ann . . ."

"Divorce you, as soon as I possibly can. I talked to Thornton yesterday. He obviously is caught in the middle and won't take the case. He sent me to others." Ann got up and poured another vodka, her fourth of the twilight.

David waited for her to finish, the while staring at her back through his button glasses, blinking. When finally Ann returned to her lounge, he said, "Well I knew something was bothering you. Has it really come this far, Ann?"

"Yes."

"Is there someone else?"

"No, that's got nothing to do with it," Ann lied as she shook her head. "It's just you and me I'm speaking of, and we're through."

"It's not that simple, Ann. There are so many things to consider."

"David, I'm afraid I don't care what you want to consider. I simply want you out of here, out of my life, as soon as possible."

"I don't see why I should move. This place is quite large. We never see each other as it is."

Ann was about to reply when the dining room door opened, the butler came on to the patio, and said, "Mrs. Raimond, your dinner is served."

Part Six

Drug Enforcement Administration Offices,
Boston, Massachusetts

The agent-in-charge had his hand over his office phone as he waved Shaughnessey into a seat across from him. "Hi, Kev," he said, and then spoke into the phone, "Will, I don't see why we can't get an injunction against the whole goddamn Longshoremen's Union. They're tryin' to stick it to us right in the middle of an ongoing investigation. They think they got us by the balls. You know it, I know it. Hey, Will, they're a national union. We hit 'em with obstructing an investigation with narcotics involved, how will that read in the *Herald?* Washington my ass . . . those longshoremen are paid plenty already. Look, Will, you don't get that injunction, my guys go nowhere in seein' what's in those containers . . . then not one of those boxes goes out that gate, not till I'm goddamn sure what's in it. I don't give a shit if I tie up this whole port forever. You tell 'em that for me. Yeah, right Will, and you lean, lean as hard as you can."

Edmund Fitzgerald put down his phone and calmly turned to Shaughnessey. "And so much for the United States attorney, the spineless prick. Now, Kev, sorry I had to stand you up for lunch. I got troubles."

"So I heard." Shaughnessey eyed his old friend. They had served together twenty years on the State Police. "I heard they won't open your boxes for anything under four hundred a pop. That right?"

"You heard right, and I've got almost two thousand boxes to look at. What'll that do for the boss man's deficit? Now, anyway, what's with you offering to buy a federal officer lunch? You win the lottery or somethin'?"

"I need information, Fitzy, what else. I won't waste your time. Giovanni Barerra—how does he fit in all of this?"

"You open strong, Kev, and I wish I knew. For sure, he has a piece of it. His guys show up all the way down to the street corner on the distribution side. We know he's there, but we can't prove it. The blacks and Hispanics, they've been moved. They've only got street retail left. Barerra's guys have the clout. How? Why? I don't know."

"In everything?"

"Everything—grass, hash, coke, they've got it. Now Barerra into drugs, that is something new, in the last couple of years. But he has to have a piece of it. There are just too many of his guys involved for him not to be in it. Anyway, Kev, why did you bring up Barerra?"

"I've been out on this shack-up job, Fitzy, more than a month now. Tailin' a guy named Michael Flaherty. He's out screwin' this rich broad up in Marblehead—her old man knows about it, he's pissed, but no balls. Or not yet. You ever hear of this guy Flaherty, Fitzy?"

"Nope, can't say that I have," Fitzgerald lied with professional aplomb. "Go on."

"So anyway, I tail Flaherty out to this place in Nahant. I got jumped by two pros with cannons. That cost me my Smith and Wesson. Fuckers had me on trespassin'. Turns out to be Barerra's place. Wasn't a hell of a lot I could do."

"So where's the fit between Barerra and Flaherty?" Fitzgerald asked casually.

"That's why I came to you. Don't know, but Barerra's not the kind you just drop in on for a beer out of the blue. There's always a reason with him."

"No, you probably don't. So, tell you what Kev, I gotta get back on the phone with my guys on the dock. We got a shitload of boxes to open. See that computer over there?" Fitzgerald pointed to a large computer console in the far corner of his office. "It's up already.

You got direct access to our Washington files. All you need's a name, an address, that'll get you started. You worked one of these?"

"Yes."

"Well, scan away, Kev. Bring up Barerra—then try Flaherty—see what you come up with. As far as having access to the D.E.A. files, you never saw 'em, don't know a thing about it. Right?"

"Right," Shaughnessey agreed as he went across to the console.

Half an hour later, Fitzgerald put down his phone and came over behind Shaughnessey, who was still reading the monitor. "You almost through, I'll buy you a drink. Come up with anything?"

"Nothing on Flaherty direct—clean—but Fitzy, your cross-indexing sucks. Under Barerra's relatives, the old bastard's got a granddaughter, Rosalie. She married Michael J. Flaherty of Gloucester eighteen years ago. So Barerra's got two great-grandchildren named Flaherty."

"Well, maybe you're on to something," Fitzgerald said noncommitaly. "Now, what about that drink?"

"Fitzy, I'm bushed," Shaughnessey said wearily. "Two days ago, I get jumped by Barerra's guys. Yesterday, I had a helluva go-around with my client. It's been a shitty day for me. How about a rain check?"

The instant the private investigator left his office, Fitzgerald went to his Roladex, looked up a number, and punched it out on his phone. "Otie, Fitzy. Yeah . . . naw, they're still playin' hardball and Washington's shittin' the bed . . . couple of congressmen on their ass. That's not why I called. That broad of yours, the one that came up with this guy Flaherty, how do we get hold of her? She's racin' a sailboat! Jesus, Otie, what kind of ship you runnin'? Your people out yachtin' . . . Oh. She's with Flaherty? Edgartown. No, good, leave her on it. Yeah, she just may have somethin'. Don't know yet, but I'm on it. On your request, I'll have some guys down there tonight. Keep me plugged in when I can talk with the broad. No, no way, we don't talk on the phone. See ya."

Villa Barerra, Nahant, Massachusetts

Within the breakfast alcove, the houseman served tea laced with honey as Giovanni Barerra put aside his newspapers and asked, "Well, Guido, what's the report on that investigator, Shaughnessey?"

"His guys are still on the tail of Mr. Michael, Mr. Barerra. We've been tailin' 'em since he came here. They went down on the Vineyard, still on Mr. Michael. Then Shaughnessey visited Fitzgerald, the agent-in-Charge, D.E.A."

"But what could he want with D.E.A.?" Barerra interrupted.

"Well, I had our guy talk with our friend at D.E.A. Seems Shaughnessey and Fitzgerald are close, old buddies, both state cops. Fitzgerald mentioned the visit the next morning meeting. It looks like Shaughnessey has Mr. Michael tied in with you. So now they're going to take a look at Mr. Michael."

"Oh, oh. He has, has he? Well that won't get them very far." Barerra was thoughtful. "What else?"

"Well, Mr. Barerra, Shaughnessey's also got his guys on Mr. Michael's lady friend, Mrs. Ann Raimond. They got her house out on the Neck staked out round the clock."

"Ah ha! So now it comes together. So that's why he was so curious about the old commodore. And he said it was tennis."

"Don't know about that, Mr. B. They say she's some good-lookin' head though."

228

"Her mother certainly was. Now, does Michael know about Shaughnessey on his tail, or his visit to us?"

"I don't think so, Mr. Barerra."

"Just how many people does Shaughnessey have on this operation, Guido?"

"Six, and himself, Mr. Barerra."

"Then someone's going for a lot of money on this."

"Sure is, Mr. Barerra. So, anyway, we got to a guy in the bank that Shaughnessey and his partner McDonough use. Lately, all their deposits are cash. So, there's nothing for sure who they work for. But remember when we tailed Shaughnessey up to that Samoset Club, up on Beacon Hill. He met Mrs. Raimond's husband, David. So Raimond's gotta be the bucks behind Shaughnessey."

"Yes, I've thought so since you first mentioned him. It all makes good sense. The jealous husband with the rich wife, he'll never let go, willingly."

"What would you like now, Mr. Barerra?"

"I don't want this investigation to go any further. Somehow, we have to stop it. If the federal agents tie Michael in with us, that could lead to problems, very big problems. If Shaughnessey does their work for them, and remember, he ran the governor's detail, he's got to be quite capable, it's still the same result. Not that I approve what Michael is up to with this Raimond woman. He is married . . . yet he is family, and he has served us well." Barerra made a church steeple of his bony fingers as he rambled along, then paused to reflect. "If we move on Shaughnessey, if we take him out, we must remember he is an ex–State Trooper. They will always stick together, they take care of their own. And in any event, if something happened to Shaughnessey, Raimond would simply hire a replacement. There are plenty of ex-cops in need of a dollar. And Raimond can afford to hire an army, so nothing would be gained by tapping Shaughnessey." After a reflective pause, Barerra spoke swiftly, harshly, gutterally. "No, Guido, we strike at the source. Without cash, Shaughnessey withers. We go for the money. David Raimond, Guido—that's your man. Have it done quickly."

Marblehead Harbor, Massachusetts

The dog days of August, the tensions brought on by Ann's infidelity, and now their separation, had drained the never-robust David Raimond to a reed. Realizing the tautness within him, he took to leaving work quite early that he might knock about on his beloved *Gull* in the late afternoon. Like most people under stress, Raimond found solace in the happy places of times past. Puttering around Marblehead on the meticulously maintained *Gull* was such a place for him.

His investigator had come to the Samoset Club that morning and offered Raimond what he considered strong circumstantial evidence of Ann's infidelity. Raimond could not steel himself to look at the photographs. The entire matter now made him sick to his stomach. He told Shaughnessey to keep his photographs in a safe place until he, Raimond, made up his mind on a final course. Raimond paid Shaughnessey in full, in cash, to go on with the investigation discreetly, most specifically the Flaherty-Barerra tie, and there let the matter rest. What Raimond did not tell his investigator was that his initial resolve to pursue retribution in the courts was waning, that Ann's ordering him from their home to a room at the yacht club was taking its toll, that he needed time to think through all the ramifications of a law suit.

At 3:30 of this August afternoon, Raimond left his Boston office and drove out to Marblehead well ahead of the rush hour traffic. There, he took the club launch out to *Gull* and changed into chinos and sneakers. It was the day off for *Gull*'s paid crew, so Raimond had his yawl to himself, and he preferred it that way.

Much like antique-car buffs, Raimond was a purist who prided himself on maintaining the prewar equipment on *Gull*. One particular piece of gear, a small thirty-five-horsepower gasoline engine, was a consistent source of irritation, with replacement parts most difficult to obtain. Raimond knew that for both safety and smooth operation, this gasoline engine should have long ago been replaced with a compact modern diesel. With any other owner but "Deep Water" David, it would have been.

When Raimond came on deck in his sailing togs, the windless harbor was a mirror of a myriad of jostling yachts. Raimond decided he would putter around the harbor under power and possibly poke about around the south side of the Neck, for from there he would have a view of the MacKay mansion. With his usual thoroughness, Raimond went into the lazarette, took out a notched stick, and checked his tanks for available gasoline. He found them better than half full, far more fuel than he could conceivably need for several hours of slow-speed puttering, but not enough for David Raimond. He decided to take *Gull* over to the Transportation Company fuel dock and top off.

By the mouth of Marblehead Harbor on Lighthouse Point, there is a public park donated in perpetuity to the town by Chandler Hovey, a generous yachtsmen. Hovey Park is dominated by a tall spider-legged light tower. The park itself is a headland that affords a sweeping view of the harbor and the adjacent coastal waters as far east as Gloucester.

In the shadow of the light tower, close by a large picnic basket, a shirt-sleeved man sprawled on a blanket, sipping a bottle of beer. Standing by the blanket, also in casual nondescript dress, a small man studied the harbor through powerful binoculars.

The beer sipper quietly asked, "Hey, Guido, where is he?"

"He's just left the fuel dock—he's headin' this way."

Guido sat down and took a beer from the basket. After a long sip, he asked, "You sure of this set-up, Jack?"

"Relax, Guido," Jack assured, laughing. "When I rig a job, it's rigged right. It's pretty much the same remote control radio set-up the I.R.A. used on Mountbatten. The circuitry is new, smaller, less to trace. It's French stuff, the latest. You see on TV any of those car

231

bombs in Paris? It's the same stuff."

"What about tracing it later?"

"Not a chance. Won't be much left after the fire. There's two small charges that go on the first button. One's nothin' but a smoke bomb, the other's to crack the gas tanks—they make less noise than a car backfire, but enough to pull him down out of the cockpit into the cabin to see what the problem is. When we see him go down into the cabin, we give it the second button. With the sloshed gas in the bilge, that's it—good-bye *Gull*."

"Here he comes," Guido said as the yawl rounded Lighthouse Point, not fifty yards off the rocks. Jack sat up for a closer look at David Raimond, who in loose white shirt, tan chino pants, and a floppy white sun hat, looked every inch the proper yachtsman.

"See ya, pal." Jack laughed as he reached into the picnic basket for another beer. "Let me know, Guido, when you want it," he said, flopping down on a blanket. "And remember, the farther out he gets, the less chance anybody else gets to the fire. Our signal range is no sweat."

Through the binoculars, Guido trailed the puttering *Gull* as she headed south between Marblehead Rock and the bell buoy. Beyond the Rock, Raimond put his *Gull* on a course paralleling the Neck. About twenty minutes later, with *Gull* two miles south of Hovey Park, Guido said. "He seems to be turnin' back."

Jack sat up, opened the picnic basket, took out what appeared a medium-sized portable radio, and extended its antenna. "Now?" he asked.

"Now," Guido said.

"Fire one."

A few moments later, Guido said, "There's the smoke." There was no discernable sound. "And there, he's up, goin' below."

"Now?"

"Now."

"Fire two."

Ten seconds later, there came over the mirrored sea a sharp crack of thunder. The varnished *Gull* burst into an orange ball, capped by a soaring mushroom of black smoke.

"Holy mother!" Guido exclaimed.

"Told ya so." Jack smirked.

Two skin divers who had been lobstering off Hovey Park were trudging back with their gear to their truck when the crack of thunder came. "Holy shit," one shouted, "look at that fire!"

"Better call the Coast Guard," the other said. "That house there," he added, pointing to an adjacent home. "I'm sure they'll let us use the phone." And the divers ran for the house.

As matters turned out, the Coast Guard had no vessel or aircraft in suitable position and relayed the call to the Marblehead Police. The police boat and two yacht club launches were dispatched but were almost a half hour in getting on the scene where *Gull* had burned. They found little but flotsam and charred life rings. The wreckage had gone down in seventy feet of water.

The next morning, at the family's request, police divers recovered the remains of David Raimond. With the cause of the accident obvious to the knowledgeable along the Marblehead waterfront, there was no official urgency to raise the wreckage of *Gull*.

Marblehead Harbor, Massachusetts

Shillelagh lay at her Marblehead mooring when the crack of the explosion rolled across the harbor. She was taking on supplies for the weekend's race, the Monhegan Island Race along the coast of Maine. As supply purchase and stowage were now Jamie Quinn's responsibilities, the young woman was shuttling cartons out to the sloop in the fast inflatable when the crack came.

Michael Flaherty had just returned to Glover Landing from a day in his office when he thought he heard a clap of thunder. Curious, he went to his picture window and scanned a cloudless sky. Confused, he went to a shelf and turned on a radio scanner. A few minutes later, he heard the Marblehead Police Station relay a Coast Guard request to their harbor patrol boat. They reported an explosion and fire on an unknown boat offshore, to the south of Tinker's Island.

Flaherty switched to his own channel and reached Freddy Andresen on *Shillelagh*. He ordered his boat captain to grab several fire extinguishers, throw them in the inflatable, then fetch him off his dock. The *Shillelagh* people were not the first to reach the scene of the fire, but they were not far behind, and once there, they saw the charred debris on the ocean. While milling about, Flaherty learned from officers in the police launch the boat was David Raimond's *Gull.*

On reaching shore, Michael phoned Ann. Her phone was busy. He was tempted to drive over to the Neck, to hold her, just to be there, but decided his uninvited appearance could prove awkward. It was not the place for a lover, and so Flaherty kept trying to phone, but without success. From the television news, he learned David Raimond had been aboard his yacht. Michael wanted so much to reach out, to help Ann, knowing she must be buried by the depressing details attendant a sudden death.

That evening, as Flaherty futilely kept at his phoning, he paced his place with a string of strong rums in hand. The demise of David brought new considerations to his relationship with Ann. While Ann was five years his senior, their age difference had no bearing on their sexual attraction for each other. As Michael thought about it, he decided Ann was more sexually voracious than he. That conclusion Flaherty did not reach lightly, having previously prided himself on a well-above-norm level of libido. In bed, Ann and Michael were becoming a well-matched pair. *So where did it go now?* Flaherty asked himself.

They could now be far more open about their affair—or reasonably so, for Michael did, on occasion, if not often, remember his marriage to Rosalie. *Perhaps now is the time to do something about ending it,* he thought. But that would take a talk with Barerra, and that, Michael knew, was not an easy undertaking.

As to Ann, and beyond sexual attraction, Michael had grown fascinated by her style. She had a certain grace and was always polite, but her way was an unpredictable mix of the casual and the attentive, a style that intrigued him. Of late, Flaherty found himself feeling far less competitive and defensive. He became open in his praise of the things she did well, even if it involved his losing at something. In all events, over the summer, Michael dated no other woman, a definite sign of involvement.

Ann's ways amused Michael. She was given to occasional outbursts of arrogant affluence. The most recent started at Edgartown, when she imperially announced she would take Michael's summer wardrobe in hand at her expense. Thereafter, like a returning schoolboy,

Flaherty was dragged through all the swank shops on the Vineyard, then later, on the North Shore. Initially amused by the largesse, Flaherty was soon irritated, for when Ann's shopping spree was over, there were few surviving remnants in a wardrobe that had once been his pride. Even his green SHILLELAGH shirts came under scrutiny. Ann had thoughts of a dark blue shirt with silver lettering, "something less showy" were her words. Wisely, she backed off on Michael's first growl.

Michael kept trying to call the Raimond place until eleven, never getting through. The next morning, he was able to reach the Raimond butler, and moments later, Ann returned his call. Their conversation was tender, on how the other was, without hypocrisies on the un-timely death of David. Ann said she very much wanted to see him, but the police diver was about to go down on *Gull,* her children were arriving, and it was best she stay at home. She would try to meet him the next afternoon and would call when it was possible.

Thus, that forenoon, Flaherty stood by the window of his condo-minium with time on his hands, when the flashing red hair of Jamie Quinn streaking across the harbor in his launch caught his eye. She was still at work, shuttling supplies out to *Shillelagh.* The big sloop was slated to sail for Portland, Maine, later that night.

Possibly Flaherty had not quenched his Edgartown memory of Jamie in her soaked T-shirt spiritedly riding the spinnaker off *Shille-lagh.* Be it subconscious lechery, boredom, or restlessness, in any event, with little to do, Flaherty decided to help. He went down to the float, whistled, then shouted, "Hey, Jamie, need a hand?" Two trips later, they had all the supplies aboard the sloop and stowed. Flaherty then proposed to take his cook up into the Old Town for lunch. "If we hustle, we can beat the crowd. . . . Buy you a lunch at Maddie's?"

Surprised by all this sudden help and attention from her normally quite-distant owner, Jamie readily agreed. "Town Landing next stop, Mr. Flaherty, sir," she laughed.

As the Abbott Hall bell tolled noon, Flaherty and Jamie strolled up State Street and turned into the air-conditioned din of Maddie's Sail Loft, the Old Town's most renowned bar. Quickly grabbing the last available table, Flaherty asked, "Your pleasure, ma'am. A beer, a bloody mary, you name it."

"How about a light Bacardi and tonic, Mr. Flaherty?"

"Now there's a drink, and as soon done. Hey, Billy," he shouted to the bartender, "two light Bacardis and tonic with lime."

When their drinks were served, Jamie clinked their glasses with a "Cheers," took a long sip, then said. "Gee, that sure was too bad about Mr. Raimond."

"Yeah," Flaherty agreed. "One thing, it had to be quick."

"How's Mrs. Raimond?"

"Talked with her this morning. She's doing O.K." Flaherty looked into his drink for a time, then abruptly switched the conversation. "Say, Jamie, you still thinking about that MIT course this winter?"

"Yes, yes I am, Mr. Flaherty. Why?"

"I had a thought we might be able to help you out and do Flaherty Fisheries a favor while at it."

"Oh, how's that?"

"We've got this seventy-five footer, the old *Florence T.,* she's in darn good shape for her years, structurally that is. I was looking at new construction costs—wow, they're out of sight. Then the thought came to me, maybe we jumboize her fifteen feet, repower with some new Cats while we're at it. Got one hell of a proposal and price from a yard in East Boston. They sure want the work. You familiar with that kind of job?"

"Yes."

"Good." He smiled. "Well, my thought was to have you as owner's rep for the job, sit on that yard while they're doin' it, get over there several times a week, make sure they're delivering what I think I'm buying—sort of a construction superintendent. Any interest?"

"Sure have, Mr. Flaherty," she said eagerly.

"O.K. Know much about specs? That kind of stuff?"

"I've written some for my dad. He does some commercial work—some big tuna boats. We use American Bureau of Shipping specs mostly. I've worked with Norske Veritas."

"Good, good, so, say we pay you what you're getting now, and you get over from Cambridge to East Boston a couple of times a week . . . Hey, maybe you might want to fly down, do a couple of races down Florida this winter? *Shillelagh's* doing the southern circuit."

"Sure. Why not!" She laughed.

"Good." One thing led to another, and they drank rum for several hours. Flaherty soon out-distanced Jamie on the reorders.

"Mr. Flaherty, I probably should get back to *Shillelagh,* Jamie suggested tactfully. "Freddy might need a hand."

"Relax, I'll take care of Freddy. How about a hamburger and one more round, then we take the dinghy up to my place. I've got the specs up there. Like you to take a look at 'em while you're headin' up coast. Tell me what you think when I get up to Portland."

When they got back to his condominium, Flaherty was totally relaxed. As Jamie excused herself to go to the bathroom, Flaherty went to the telephone answering machine, turned up the volume, and started the playback. The third message was from Flaherty's cousin, Jake O'Brien. "Hey Mike, Jake. My old man's back in the hospital—bleedin' inside again. Bad. Gotta stick with him. Look's like you got tonight's trip, if we're goin' to go. Call me at the shop. See ya."

In turning up the volume, Flaherty did not hear Jamie come back into the room, but Jamie certainly overheard some of what Jake had to say.

Michael went to his window to think for a time. It was a trip he didn't want to make. The timing was all wrong. He wanted to be with Ann. Flaherty knew he had to face his feelings some time, yet once again, he put aside what he knew was his real resolve, to get out of his deal with Giovanni Barerra. *Just one more trip, the last trip,* he said to himself, *then I talk to the old man.*

Flaherty went to his telephone, and after returning Jake's call, put down the phone and turned to Jamie. "We've got a change of plans. Something's come up. It could get tight on time, my getting up to Portland this weekend for the race. I don't want to disappoint our gang. So, if I don't make it, you start *Shillelagh.* Tell Freddy he's coskipper—but use that beautiful head of yours. Now, if you'll excuse me, I've got to get some things together." When Jamie left, Flaherty hastily packed, left a brief message with a Raimond maid, then drove to Gloucester.

The Offices of Shaughnessey and
McDonough, Boston, Massachusetts

Shaughnessey had barely entered the office when his partner, Harry McDonough, growled, "You see the mornin' papers?"

"No."

"Your pal David Raimond. He's gonzo."

"Shit! When? What happened?"

"I tried to call you last night—no answer—your place."

"Christ, Harry. How many times do I tell you. That's Mabel's night, remember."

"Yeah, Kev baby, you shaggin' ass at your age, ya oughtta be ashamed. And yeah, I remembered—but ya never gave me her last name or her number. Remember that, too."

"Never mind." Shaughnessey sighed his exasperation. "Tell me about Raimond."

"An accident on his boat. An engine explosion and gasoline fire. Burned and sank in pretty deep water. He was alone."

"The missus? Where was she?"

"She's O.K. She was at home. Your friend Flaherty, he was at his pad."

"An accident?" Shaughnessey eyed his partner skeptically.

"Hey, Kev, how the hell do I know? That's what my pals on the Marblehead Police say. That's what the papers got. Guess the boat had some engine problems before. So, there's no heat from nobody, so, the Marblehead cops, they're sort of leavin' it up to Marine Safety at Coast Guard. There's a hearing next month. What do you think, Kev?"

"Harry, that's no accident—look at the timing."

"Flaherty?"

"Naw, I doubt that. He's had the training though, quite a record in Nam. But you know, the more I watch that guy, I kinda think he's O.K. Sure he's into somethin' besides Annie baby, no question about that. Naw, not Flaherty, not his style."

"Barerra?"

"His friends—my guess."

"You gonna do anything about it?"

"No way."

"Why not?" McDonough needled.

"Look, you dumb asshole!" Shaughnessey exploded. "So, we're out a couple of pay days. Who do we go to, to collect? Annie? Come on, Harry. We did all right with David. Now, we got a couple of grand of equipment in Raimond's cellar, right? Right. Things cool off, we know the alarm system, we get it back some night. Things get hot, forget it. The gear'll be gonzo, too."

"Yeah, I forgot about the bug."

"And takin' on Barerra—Barerra without pay—forget it. Life's too short."

U.S. Navy Headquarters, Boston, Massachusetts

Captain Osborne was in his Charlestown apartment when Lieutenant Quinn called and informed him Michael Flaherty was suddenly taking a trawler to sea that night. She thought the vessel would be the *Kathleen M. Flaherty,* but of that she was not certain. She expected Flaherty would be offshore three or four days, as he was doubtful of making *Shillelagh*'s Saturday noon start of the Monhegan Island

Race off Portland, Maine. She thought the trawler voyage must be very important for Mr. Flaherty to miss a major race. Lieutenant Quinn was about to shove off on *Shillelagh* from Gloucester for Portland.

After the call, Osborne considered the information for two rum and tonics. He decided that for security reasons, on this play, he would go it alone, bypass all within Coast Guard, all but his district commander, Admiral Haggerty, for Osborne had met no success in accomplishing his admiral's latest orders, to find the leak within First District. And so, with only Osborne and his admiral on the inside of this next move, there was little likelihood of a leak.

A month before, on the annual "sail" of the frigate *Constitution,* Osborne had found a kindred spirit and established a working relationship with Chuck Fisher, his opposite number in the First Naval District Intelligence slot. They both liked to drink and soon found they had other areas of common interest. Operational areas. To follow up on Jamie's lead, Osborne phoned Fisher at his home and arranged an appointment at Naval Headquarters for the next morning.

At their morning meeting, Captain Osborne requested a continuous flow of prints of all naval, air and NASA satellite photographs of the western North Atlantic, commencing the night prior, be relayed up from Washington. As befit two friendly intelligence officers, Captain Fisher was far too professional to inquire of Osborne what he was up to. He furnished Osborne with a secure room, a plotting desk, and all the aerial photographic and photogrametric equipment he would ever need. Fisher instructed Osborne on how he could, on his own, after identifying a target, request detailed amplification of a specific portion of a satellite photograph. He said that while these pictures were taken from an altitude of several hundred miles, they could be amplified and enhanced by electronic means to a minute magnification of detail. Therewith, in little time, Osborne could assemble a complete record in color for daylight or infrared for night of all marine activities off his district.

Early that afternoon, Osborne received and scanned over fifty satellite photographs, and using a process of elimination by vessel tracks, he was soon convinced he had identified the Flaherty vessel. Later, upon receipt and study of amplified photographs, he saw that he was on to a dark green trawler with cream-colored trim. A phone call to his Gloucester base verified these were the Flaherty fleet colors. Thereupon, Osborne requested and received a rerun of all infrared photos of the previous night. In little time, he was able to establish the green-and-cream trawler had indeed sailed out of Gloucester the night before and held an arrow-straight course due east. Osborne became curious about the course. He knew the most frequented Gloucester fishery, George's Bank, lay more to the southeast. So why was Flaherty sailing east?

His second morning in the Boston Naval Headquarters, Osborne ran a check of the past night's satellite shots and found the Flaherty trawler fishing on the southern end of Brown's Bank. The third morning of his satellite spying, he was surprised to find the Flaherty trawler heading west, clearly returning to Gloucester. As Osborne had hourly satellite over-flights to work with, he could only establish the vessel had changed course sometime between midnight and one. Not much of a fishing trip, Osborne concluded as he rolled up his photos and charts and went out to find Captain Fisher. With profuse thanks, Osborne invited Fisher over to Coast Guard Headquarters for a luncheon with his admiral that next week, took a cab back to his offices, and phoned Admiral Haggerty at his home.

That afternoon, a Saturday, Admiral Haggerty convened and chaired a special meeting at his home in Swampscott. The other attendees were Captain Osborne, Edmund Fitzgerald, and Milton Schwarz, a youthful assistant U.S. attorney who oversaw the legal needs of the several federal agencies involved with narcotics interceptions.

Osborne recited Lieutenant Quinn's observations of the month prior, of a mysterious box coming off a Flaherty trawler in the small hours of the morning, and her most recent tip of Flaherty suddenly sailing his own vessel on a fishing voyage.

"But what does that establish?" the young attorney asked. "We don't know what the box was about. It could well have been fishing equipment. Certainly this man Flaherty has a right to take his own trawler fishing."

"Maybe so, but this son of a bitch is related to Barerra," Fitzgerald threw in.

"Mr. Fitzgerald," the young man explained patiently, "we're dealing with 'probable cause.' You're asking me to get a search warrant from a United States magistrate on a Saturday night. That's not going to be easy. Spectacular arrests are one thing, solid convictions are another. I need something that will stand up. The magistrate is going to ask me questions. They're very sensitive to Fourth Amendment issues. He will be looking for, and I quote the Supreme Court, 'specific articulable facts.' "

"And it's that kind of bullshit that's fucked up the country," Fitzgerald broke in testily.

"Go on, Mr. Schwarz," Admiral Haggerty encouraged.

"Thank you, sir. . . . Let's see if I understand this case. A month ago, your Lieutenant Quinn is serving undercover on Flaherty's sailboat up in Gloucester. She sees a small box come off a trawler and go into a truck, but she's some distance away, and it is dark—so, she's not really sure what the box is all about. Could have been fish gear, trawl boards, whatever. Right?"

"Right," Osborne agreed.

"So now, three days ago, Lieutenant Quinn overhears Flaherty get a phone message. He's supposed to take his trawler out in a hurry. Now, what have we got on this guy? And remember, I can't bullshit a magistrate. I'm an officer of the court. So, we have Flaherty, no prior record, a war hero, respected in his community—so he's married to Barerra's granddaughter. Can't hang him for that. Matter of fact, when you think about it, we've never hung Barerra with anything. So, what have we got? Your lieutenant, our witness to the prior event, she's presently out on a sailboat race. The captain's got a bunch of satellite photos. They show this trawler leaving Gloucester, going out to Brown's Bank, fishing some, and now she's coming in tonight. A short voyage. I'll admit that looks strange. Incidentally, we may have a problem with those pictures. Getting them into evidence could be a new precedent. I can see the defense demanding we bring down the satellite. I'm not here to be negative, but frankly, I don't think we have such a strong case."

Fitzgerald exploded. "Look kid, who the hell do you work for?"

The admiral calmed matters immediately. "That's all right, Fitzy. The young man is only pointing out what we should know about the law."

"Frankly, Admiral," the young man responded, "rather than going for a search warrant, I recommend you have one of your cutters pull a safety check."

"What do you think, Otie?" the admiral asked.

"Well, sir, we have *Cape Fairweather* sitting right there in Gloucester. She's had a generator problem. That shouldn't . . ."

"Hey, Otie, I want my guys in on this," Fitzgerald interrupted.

Osborne understood what he meant. He was calling in a marker. A few days back, Fitzy had his agents go through Flaherty Fisheries at Osborne's request. That they didn't find anything didn't matter. What did matter was the interagency I.O.U. that Fitzy was now collecting. And so, Osborne looked at his admiral, the shrug of his shoulders and his nod unmistakeable—let's do it, sir.

The admiral understood. "O.K., Fitzy, you're in. Now, Mr. Schwarz. I'd like you to go for the search warrant. If we get it, then it's a combined operation, Coast Guard and D.E.A. We'll nail 'em at the dock in Gloucester. Any problems with the search warrant, then we intercept offshore with *Cape Fairweather*. That fair, Fitzy?"

"Fair," the D.E.A. agent-in-charge agreed.

"Well, if you're going to intercept on the beach, don't you think Customs should be brought in?" Schwarz asked.

"Young man, you go get the search warrant," Fitzgerald ordered heatedly. "Customs. Why those assholes, they can't smell a container of shit right under their nose." And so the meeting broke up.

Osborne drove Schwarz back into Boston to Coast Guard Headquarters so they could make out a search warrant. Osborne had phoned ahead and arranged that his trusted chief clerk was on hand to minimize any possible leak. After Schwarz had dictated most of the warrant verbiage, the chief asked Osborne, "How do I describe the vessel, sir?"

"Take it right out of the *Coast Guard Register,* Chief," Osborne replied. "It's all there, the trawler *Kathleen M. Flaherty*—Gloucester registry—the official number, the works, you got it all right there. And Mr. Schwarz needs it a.s.a.p.—it's gettin' into a Sunday night. He's got to get a magistrate to sign it."

"Yes, sir, I know about the Sunday night, sir," the chief agreed leadenly.

Gloucester Harbor, Massachusetts

While Captain Osborne worked on a search warrant in Boston, Mike Flaherty brought his trawler by the Gloucester breakwater in the gathering twilight. The container recovery on Brown's Bank had been routine, but thereafter, the fishing had gone poorly, so poorly there were barely two feet of fish in the lower hold of his trawler. The paucity of fish mattered little to Flaherty. What he did care about was getting this trip over, with getting back to Marblehead, getting back to Ann. Over the voyage, he had been possessed by the woman, thoughts of how she was, concern with how she was taking her husband's death, just wanting to be with her, to touch, to hold.

To create plausibility for the return of the trawler after such a short trip with a thin catch, Flaherty had written into the vessel's log the fiction of a continuously overheating shaft bearing. Were they to be boarded by Coast Guard, and were they asked, that would be the reason for the premature return. On the return voyage, Flaherty was not expecting a boarding, for all of his radio bearings on the district cutters that were at sea plotted out down on George's Bank, well away from Flaherty's return course.

That afternoon, as the gray smudge of Cape Ann slowly grew from the western horizon, Mike Flaherty had the wheelhouse to himself with time to think. In tracking the Coast Guard cutters' positions, Flaherty had been amused to find his last and only boarder, the *Cape Fairweather,* was securely lashed to the state pier in Gloucester and keeping Boston Headquarters informed in detail of their generator problems by radio. *The skipper and chief probably have broads in the town,* Flaherty mused.

Flaherty was annoyed that he had missed the Monhegan Race on *Shillelagh.* He recognized his business commitments came first, that with Jamie's brain and Freddy's brawn, *Shillelagh* would do very well. Still, sailboat racing was Flaherty's love.

A new sound came into the wheelhouse. "Boston Marine Operator to the trawler *Katherine M. Flaherty,* come in please." Flaherty flicked the radio over to transmit, "Boston Marine, this is the *Katherine M. Flaherty.* Over."

"Yes, on your call to Marblehead, I now have your party, over."

Ann was finally returning his call, and this greatly pleased Michael. Within the constraints of such a public venue as a marine radio-call, he learned that she and her children were still stunned, that David Raimond's Saturday morning memorial service at St. Michael's had been well attended. Michael, in a gentle way, expressed sympathy. Their conversation concluded with agreement upon a noon meeting at his condominium the next day. It was a sterile conversation, for both parties were conscious of the countless ears that listened—the vibrations of their true feelings lost in the megaphonic hollowness of a radio call.

The headlands of Cape Ann had grown from the sea and were well defined as Flaherty put down his microphone. His taciturn cousin, Jake O'Brien, came into the wheelhouse, and with a low whistle exclaimed, "Holy-be-Jesus, Mike, take a look at that." He pointed to the west, to a purple hedgerow of soaring thunderheads sheared to silver anvils by the stratospheric winds.

"Yeah, we've got a front coming through tonight," Flaherty said.

"Going to be a piss-whistler. Glad we'll be at the dock for this one."

"Yeah, maybe that's good." Flaherty laughed.

Within the hour, and just ahead of the squalls, Flaherty breathed easier as he eased back on the throttle, conning the trawler through the inner harbor to the Flaherty Fisheries dock. When the *Katherine M. Flaherty* was berthed alongside, Jake O'Brien went up through the plant and checked with the night watchman. All was well. A short time later, after the truck had arrived, the trawler crew had opened the hatch, positioned and started the cargo-discharge conveyor, the first of the squalls struck with sullen sheets of cold rain driven by kettledrums of thunder. It was a tar-black night indeed, the blackness broken by the crack of lightning, blinding spider legs in the night.

As he watched the fish catch go ashore, Mike Flaherty toyed with the idea of packing it in, heading for Marblehead, leaving the balance of cargo discharge to Jake and the crew. Deciding that would be irresponsible, he continued to watch them from the shelter of the wheelhouse, thinking, *This is the week I go talk with Barerra.*

Just after midnight, with the fish ashore, the container aloft and almost into the truck, the blackness was broken by the blinding incandescence of brilliant searchlights. There suddenly boomed the loudest of loud-hailers down along the Gloucester docks. "Federal agents. *Freeze!* No one moves or we shoot—*now*, get your hands over your heads, *slowly.*"

Despite the blinding brilliance, Flaherty was just able to see the source of the sound was a Coast Guard launch on the harbor side of the trawler. Then, through the tightest of squints, he saw machine-gun-toting shadows swarming down off the dock. Slowly, Michael Flaherty raised his hands over his head.

Drug Enforcement Administration Offices, Boston, Massachusetts

If ever a cocky man came a-cropper with a crash, it was Michael Flaherty that lightning-lit night. Stunned by the terrible swiftness of the discovery, Flaherty stood impotent, helpless, the cocaine-laden container dangling over his head in mid-air between vessel and truck.

The armed Drug Enforcement agents came down onto the deck of the trawler and put the crew through a thorough body search. The agents were cold and silent and went about their work with a professionalism that sent a shiver through Flaherty. By their efficiency and silence, the agents made it clear they were working with scum, and this coldness cut Flaherty to the quick.

The agents read the trawler men their constitutional rights to remain silent and then, under handcuffs, led them off to separate cars waiting outside the gates of Flaherty Fisheries. Over the hour's drive from Gloucester to Boston, not one of the three agents in the car with Flaherty said a word. Near four that morning, Flaherty was led into the elevator of the Federal Center, taken up to the D.E.A. offices, put through another body search, then left alone, still in handcuffs.

Curiously, in all his detailed planning of the smuggling operation, Michael Flaherty had never thought of, or set up, any contingency for the event of his personal apprehension. He simply never expected to be caught and had wasted no thought on that which was not to be.

So what comes next? he asked himself in the lonely room. He assumed he would be allowed to call a lawyer, but when, and who would he call? The only lawyer he knew and trusted was old John Joseph Tobin in Gloucester. Old J. J. had been of counsel to Flaherty Fisheries from the founding of the firm, was his mother's widower boyfriend and beano partner. But, did the old man know anything of the criminal side of the law? *Well, I've got to start somewhere,* Flaherty thought, *so, I'll start with old J. J. But before I'm through, I'm going to need one slick son of a bitch of a fighting lawyer to beat this one.*

As Flaherty paced the office, contemplating the consequence of his circumstance, three faces came to the fore. They were those of his mother, Kathleen; his partner, Giovanni Barerra; and his lover, Ann Raimond. Kathleen would be totally uncomprehending, ever-present, and completely supportive. Barerra would be totally comprehending, never-present, and untraceably supportive. Of Ann, Flaherty was uncertain, desperately afraid he'd seen the last of her. With David's death, and now, his bust on a drug rap, Ann would probably disappear into a castle of Brahmin propriety with the clang of the portcullis. That thought was Flaherty's saddest of a sad night.

Two men came into the office, closing the door behind them. The first was a bald wiry little man. He came up to the far-larger Flaherty and deftly removed the handcuffs. "I'm Fitzgerald, agent-in-charge, D.E.A.," he said. "This is Captain Osborne—district intelligence officer, Coast Guard. Here, take a seat." Fitzgerald indicated the remaining seat across the desk from his. "Want a cigarette?" he offered solicitously.

Flaherty shook his head.

"Look, Flaherty, you've been warned of your rights—you want, I'll read 'em again."

Flaherty shook his head again.

"You've got a clean record—no priors, war decorations. How you ever got mixed up in this shit, I'll never understand. Anyway, we've never had a tighter case, even the transfer to the truck on infrared TV. So you want to cooperate, maybe we can work a deal. With your record, and if we put in a word, I'm sure the judge will go light. You want to go tough, that's up to you—your choice."

Flaherty said nothing, haunted by the warning words of Giovanni Barerra. "No matter what, Michael. Your life will depend on your silence." Flaherty knew if there were any certainties in this uncertain world, one was the far-reaching force behind his grandfather-in-law's warning of silence. Flaherty stonily stared at the floor.

Fitzgerald went on. "Look, Mike, we've got you by the balls. You know it, we know it. No one's shittin' nobody. You play ball, we play. You don't, we don't. I want to know two things—only two things. I want to know who dropped that coke on Brown's Bank and where it was headed, who gets it when it leaves your place. If we can talk about that, if you get cooperative, then you could come out of this a lot better."

Flaherty shook his head, maintaining his blank fixed stare at the floor, while his brain raced around wildly. *So they know where we've been. But how? The radar was clear for forty miles. A tip? A leak? . . . No, who but the container ship skipper up in St. Johns and I knew the drop bearings? Have they broken into my hidden office? No sign of that, and it wouldn't tell 'em anything, anyway. I took the plot sheets with me to sea.* Then, the technical gears in Flaherty's brain started to mesh. On the overall play, there could be a leak, but on locating the drop site on Brown's Bank, there were only one or two ways the Feds could have done it—tracking the trawler by submarine or satellite. *Not bad,* Flaherty thought, a bit pleased with the challenge he must have posed for the Feds. But who or why or what had triggered it all?

Fitzgerald saw he was getting nowhere with his plea-trading and grew impatient. "It's your ass, Flaherty. Maybe fifteen hard ones in the slammer. You think I'm kiddin', take a look at some of the new drug statutes." He paused, then blustered on angrily. "Not even

Barerra's goin' to save your ass on this one, Mike. You goin' to play?"

Flaherty never took his eyes from the floor.

In exasperation, Fitzgerald stood up. "Come on, Otie. This dumb bastard doesn't know enough to save his own ass. Mike, you get one phone call. You tell your lawyer, arraignment and bail hearing before the magistrate, the McCormick Building at ten. Tell him on the bail business, I'm askin' the U.S. attorney to go for twenty mill surety or two mill cash.

"Yeah, you heard right Mike, twenty big ones. And why not? You're the biggest coke catch in the country. That ought to impress the judge. And on the bail, that oughtta catch even old Father Joe's attention. Two million might dent his petty cash. Yeah, Mike, maybe you're goin' to be with us a while . . . Now, you can use this phone right here, one call." And with that, Fitzgerald and Osborne left the office.

So, it looks like they nailed me with a leak, and it's somewhere close to Barerra, Flaherty concluded as the door clicked shut.

U.S. Magistrate's Court, McCormick Building, Boston, Massachusetts

On Post Office Square, in downtown Boston, there stands a gray granite government building, the federal presence marked by enfrescoed eagles and fasces, ancient symbols of Roman justice. The granite building was a part of Roosevelt's W.P.A. attempt to wrest the Republic from the deep Depression, and was once a giant of the city. It is now a twenty-story pygmy dwarfed on most flanks by soaring glass towers. This federal edifice was initially called the New Post Office Building, and a half a century later, in a city slow of change, it is still called that by many. But, in so doing, they are wrong. The building is now officially the John W. McCormick Post Office and

Courthouse, renamed to honor a lately departed patron saint of the Boston Irish.

Tipped by phone calls from Fitzgerald's people, the television media had the McCormick Building encircled when Flaherty and his trawlermen were brought in for their arraignment. Using a street-market value near one hundred million, the capture of the *Katherine M. Flaherty* was ranked the biggest in the history of the federal narcotics enforcement program. The federal authorities were not about to let such a publicity opportunity pass them by, and as a result, a hoard of journalists stalked the corridors of the courthouse, their microphones and notebooks at the ready for anyone with anything cogent to say on the capture.

At five of ten that morning, a handcuffed Michael Flaherty was brought off the elevator by two husky D.E.A. agents into a jostling pack of journalists. On the instant, television lights came on, cameras whirred, while Flaherty tried to hide his head under his arms. He was not successful, his handcuffs preventing any real coverage. And so, a clearly recognizable Mike Flaherty was escorted down the corridor to the magistrate's courtroom, unshaven, unwashed, still in the fishing clothes of his capture. He was a very different man from the jaunty yachtsman last seen on the screen accepting his Bermuda Race trophies. Needless to say, on this morning, Flaherty was not giving interviews.

Such could not be said of the two men who trailed Flaherty down the corridor. Edmund Fitzgerald was at his feisty best, posing for the cameras, answering the reporter's questions, a big cigar in the side of his mouth. At his elbow, Captain Otis Osborne stood, impassive and impressive, in his Coast Guard blues.

"Mr. Fitzgerald," a glitzy blonde with a TV mike in her hand asked, "how did the federal authorities know to seize this particular fishing boat?"

"We have our ways." Fitzgerald grinned. "We can't always talk about everything. On this raid, we had the full cooperation of Coast Guard . . . Captain Osborne, here, and his men, and we expect this is just the beginning, that we'll have several more seizures soon. We're going to break the back of this filthy business." Fitzgerald rolled on expansively, and, thereby, earned top billing on the TV evening news.

Meanwhile, in the courtroom, Flaherty's old family attorney, John J. Tobin, asked the magistrate for a one-day continuance. A dignified silver-haired man, Tobin told the magistrate he had not learned of the proceedings until seven that morning, that while he had been of counsel to the Flaherty family for near on thirty years, he had no experience at the criminal bar and would retain appropriate counsel for the defense later that day. Tobin had told Flaherty this is what he would do. They needed time to get the very best, start the record out right from the beginning, even if it meant a night in jail for Flaherty. Tobin's continuance request was granted and Flaherty taken out into the lights of the corridor and down to a U.S. marshal's van to spend a bleak day in the Charles Street Jail.

The next morning, the U.S. attorney for Eastern Massachusetts made a rare courtroom appearance, as he usually relied on his skilled prosecutorial staff for that. The arraignment and bail hearing for Michael J. Flaherty, owner and master of the trawler *Katherine M. Flaherty,* was an exception, a well-publicized exception. The seizure of a container of pure cocaine with a street value near $100 million was not an everyday occurrence. It was national news, the largest narcotics seizure in the history of the Republic, according to Boston's agent-in-charge, D.E.A. When this was announced, William Wetmore, the U.S. attorney, decided he would go to court himself. Publicity was one reason for his attendance. He had another.

Wetmore had come to his decision the evening before, when, on returning to his home in South Hamilton, he settled down with his son, Ned, to watch the evening news on TV. Once again, he learned what a small world was that of the affluent on the north shore, a very small world indeed. The capture of the trawler in Gloucester Harbor with photos of Michael Flaherty being led into the initial arraignment proceedings was the lead story and had young Ned wide-eyed. "Hey, Dad, Dad, look—there's Patrick's Dad."

"Patrick who?" the U.S. attorney asked, baffled.

"You know Patrick. Patrick Flaherty. He's been here. Lives over in Wenham. We play lacrosse, remember?"

A discreet phone call to the headmaster of the boy's country day school soon tied the whole picture together for Wetmore, and with that, the U.S. attorney took a very personal and angry interest in the prosecution of Michael J. Flaherty.

At this second arraignment hearing, as Wetmore spoke to the U.S. magistrate in the district court, he did so with care and precision. "And with due respect for the report of the probation people, your honor, the government does not argue the fact the accused Michael

J. Flaherty is a war hero, nor that he is a responsible citizen of the Gloucester community, that he is a successful businessman, that he is a caring parent, that he is a well-known sportsman. To the contrary, your honor, the government points out these very attributes are the despicable means, the camouflage, the way that enabled Flaherty to conduct an insidious criminal activity, a conspiracy for the illicit importation of a controlled substance at a monetary magnitude this country has never seen.

"The tragedy of this case, your honor, is that Michael Flaherty has used all his assets, all his attributes, all his skills, his position in the community, all these things to the detriment of his fellow citizens. It is for these very reasons, your honor," the prosecutor's tone took on the hellfire and brimstone of the Puritan pulpits, "yes, for these very reasons, the government asks that bail be set at twenty million dollars of surety bond or two million dollars of cash."

"I object, your honor." Munroe Lee, Boston's most celebrated criminal attorney sprang to his feet. "Eighth Amendment. It's excessive, your honor. Why, for a man of Mr. Flaherty's background . . ."

"You'll have your say, Mr. Lee, and I have read the Constitution, thank you," the U.S. magistrate observed dryly. "There has been nothing said that warrants an objection in my view. Please be seated."

Munroe Lee smiled and resignedly retook his seat. For him, objection on the record was a reflex, a part of his craft, the constant building of a handy set of hand-holds in the event an appeal became necessary, an unlikely event, for the criminal defense career of Munroe Lee was a long streak of victories. As an aside, in no way apparent to the casual courtroom "back-bencher," Lee and the U.S. magistrate had been firm friends for thirty-odd years, going back to the days when both worked on the Law Review at Harvard Law School. Once a week, as members of the Union Club, they met at the club's open luncheon table to share their old friendship, their relationship totally above board.

Lee's client, Michael Flaherty, sat in the dock with U.S. marshals at each elbow. Now dressed in a somber cotton business suit, Flaherty looked every inch the prosperous Gloucester businessman that he was, uncomfortably misplaced for the morning by some absurd mistake of the federal justice system.

"Thank you, your honor." the U.S. attorney smiled, enjoying this temporary setback of his famed rival. "As I was about to say, there is every indication this conspiracy, this smuggling operation before you, is of worldwide significance. There is irrefutable open-and-shut, firsthand evidence of the accused's involvement. It may well have struck home with the accused that he is about to lose his freedom for fifteen, perhaps twenty years in a federal penitentiary. With that kind of very real prospect, your honor, this man might well consider an alternative course and flee bail, leave the United States. We have reason to believe he has considerable assets offshore, in foreign bank accounts. While not of direct consequence to this hearing, your honor should know we intend to proceed against all his assets by way of an organized crime conspiracy complaint. That will take time.

"When you think on it, your honor, two million of cash against twenty years incarceration, why that's peanuts for a man like Flaherty, your honor, just peanuts; a loss of one hundred thousand a year, a loss the accused can well afford when you consider the monies he has made in his smuggling. Bluntly put, the government expects the accused will take off, your honor."

Bickering on the bail went back and forth for another hour. For Michael Flaherty, the words washed around him, mostly unheard—the principle charges, conspiracy to commit a felony, illicit importation and possession of a controlled substance—cocaine, conspiracy to possess with intent to distribute. Despite the leaden weight of words laid upon him, Flaherty's heart was light and large with joy.

That morning, when a now-scrubbed Michael J. Flaherty was again brought to the court in handcuffs, his eye first caught the care-wrinkled face of his white-haired mother. Then, two rows back of Kathleen Flaherty, he saw Ann Raimond, and his heartstrings soared. But then he almost became sick with worry. What could she be thinking?

With Ann in the room, Michael had only half an ear for his defense counsel, the renowned Munroe Lee. Curiously, Munroe Lee was retained at the recommendation of two distinctly different sources. Tobin had called several lawyer friends, corporate types about Boston. The consensus of their recommendations was Munroe Lee. At the same time, on Flaherty's request, his mother called Giovanni Barerra's unlisted phone number in Nahant, seeking an appointment. Barerra immediately sent a car for Mrs. Flaherty, and at their meeting, she asked his recommendation for counsel. She came back later that afternoon with Barerra's opinion, that Michael should retain Munroe Lee. She also had a message for Michael: Break off any contact with Barerra until contacted.

The hearing dragged on until finally the magistrate called for a luncheon recess. Munroe Lee was closing his briefcase when he felt a light tap on his shoulder and turned to meet Thornton Loring, a senior partner at Baxter, Blair and Burnham. "Hey, Thorny." He laughed. "What are you doing here? You lost? This is a criminal session."

"No, Munroe, I'm not lost. As a matter of fact, I'm here to see you on business. What about a quick bite? Take you up to my club. It's right down the street, on top of the bank."

Toward the end of that luncheon, a stunned Munroe Lee reviewed what had been said to him. "Thorny, I find this hard to believe. Baxter, Blair and Burnham are willing to put up the two million cash bail for Flaherty this afternoon. Is that right?"

"Right." Thornton Loring nodded emphatically. "And as you choose, not that we think you'll need it, you also have the full use of our staff for any research, any reviews, to prepare any briefs that you might require, without charge to you or your client."

"Wow! The whole team! That could run a pretty penny." Lee let off a low whistle. "And as far as Flaherty's concerned, he is not to know anything about this?"

"That's right."

"What about me? You going to tell me why? Who?"

"No. It has to be anonymous, Munroe, totally, completely anonymous," Loring said with finality, carefully folding his napkin, rising from the table.

Five minutes later, as Munroe Lee returned to the arraignment hearing, he was halfway up the granite steps of the Federal Building when he was again tapped on the shoulder, this time by a black-liveried chauffeur. "With respect, Mr. Lee. Mr. Solito asks a word with you." The man indicated a gleaming stretch limousine with opaque windows that straddled a nearby hydrant.

"You'd best tell Sal . . ." Lee started to decline but then thought better of it. Salvatore Solito was the acknowledged consigleri of the northeastern organization and controlled the distribution of its criminal legal business. His invitations were never sent lightly, and those in the criminal practice did not decline them. Like the U.S. attorney, he seldom went to court, but when he did, he was also one of the more successful, if not circumspect, practitioners of the criminal defense trade in the nation. With this in mind, Munroe Lee turned back down the steps and got into the air-conditioned comfort of the limousine. "Good afternoon, Sal," he said, offering his hand.

"Munroe, I thank you." the swarthy small man in the tailored blue suit said. "I know you've got to get back. Matter of fact, I'll be up there with you, watching. I'm appearing later, for the two crew they lifted off that trawler. Now, on Michael Flaherty's, bail, if you can haggle them down some, good. Two or twenty, Jesus, that's pretty strong, even for that Puritan prick Wetmore. Anyway, you settle for what you have to. Whatever it takes, we want Flaherty out tonight. Those are the orders, so, soon as you've got a deal, come to me. I'll be in the court. We'll post the surety."

"We?" Munroe Lee inquired.

"We," Salvatore Solito said flatly.

Going back up the Federal Building steps, Munroe Lee was very annoyed with himself. He had been retained by an unknown Gloucester lawyer, an old gentleman, on very short notice. Albeit, the old gentleman had told Lee all the details of the seizure and the client, somehow Lee had gotten the idea the client was a run-of-the-mill fisherman with his tit in a ringer. Lee had probably listened without full attention, for he was ever in a hurry, in a trade where the clock-tick meant money, and the rates he quoted were his impression of what the traffic would bear, a business that was cash in advance, credit nonexistent. Lee had asked and received of the old gentleman a retainer of $25,000 and settled on an hourly rate of $250. Now, going back to court, Munroe Lee was far from happy with himself. He realized he might have received more, far more. As the veteran lawyer reentered the courtroom, he was both annoyed with himself and perplexed. How did this fisherman, this Flaherty, have the unlimited support of one of Boston's most august law firms and, at the same time, the full backing of Giovanni Barerra? What in hell was going on?

U.S. Attorney's Office, McCormick Building, Boston, Massachusetts

Early that afternoon, the magistrate concluded the arraignment proceedings, setting bail as the U.S. attorney had requested, $2 million of cash or $20 million of surety. This was of some satisfaction to the U.S. attorney. He got what he asked for. It would read well in the newspapers, even if it was but a temporary inconvenience to Flaherty and his friends. Wetmore had no doubt the people about Flaherty would soon post the surety freeing Flaherty until trial, with that event five or six months away. The U.S. attorney realized that once Flaherty was free on bail, there would never be another opportunity to deal with him on a man-to-man, humankind basis. This afternoon was it, and with this realization, Wetmore decided to use Flaherty's remaining hours in federal custody in a unique way.

First, he asked his bail bond specialist to his office and instructed the woman that she was to examine minutely any collateral proposed. In short, she was to stall Flaherty's release as long as she could.

Wetmore next called Flaherty and Lee into his office to see if there was any possibility of a trade. Wetmore realized Flaherty was but one link in a massive chain and after Fitzgerald's briefing earlier that day, he now believed the chain was a fine forging of Giovanni Barerra. At their trading session, Wetmore spelled out his suspicions of Barerra's involvement. If Flaherty would assist toward such a conviction, Wetmore would really ease up. Flaherty showed no inclination to trade, and with that, Wetmore called back the marshals.

An hour later, Wetmore called Flaherty and Lee back for a second meeting. When a handcuffed Flaherty was brought into his office, Wetmore told the marshals to free him and leave. He then nodded to Lee and spoke. "Mr. Flaherty, I'm not sure you are aware of this, we have something in common. Our sons play on the same lacrosse team at Shore."

With mention of his son, some of Flaherty's stoniness fell away to a thin smile. The U.S. attorney went on. "I thought my Ned was pretty good until I saw your Patrick play. You should be very proud of him."

"Yeah, Pat's all right." Flaherty brightened.

"Where is all this taking us?" Munroe Lee asked.

"Well, I'll tell you," Wetmore replied. "When I talked to you and your client earlier, I had a fair idea of what he's in and who he knows. Who is his backing. He hasn't told me anything that in any way disinclines me from throwing the entire federal code at him, Mr. Lee. So, in answer to your question, I'm going after every asset he has, his company, his boats, the last penny. I'm going to go for twenty years on every count, that I promise you, Mr. Lee, and I'll get a judge and jury to listen."

"Yeah, well, we haven't asked any favors," Lee said.

"No, not yet. But you will. You know damn well, we've got an open-and-shutter. Satellite photos, infrared television tapes, and a container full of cocaine."

Lee nodded noncommittally.

"Frankly, Mr. Lee," Wetmore went on, "I don't think your client really understands the nature of the business he's in. With your permission, I want to show him a bit of what goes on downstream from him. What I propose is completely off-record, on that, you have my word, but will also require the U.S. marshal's agreement. Now, it will be a couple of hours before you get all the bonding buttoned up. I propose your client and I take a drive out to one of the state hospitals. I want him to see where kids and drugs can get to. I don't think he has the guts for that." The U.S. attorney then paused for effect. "By the time we're back, you'll have the bonding done and he's released. Incidentally, Mr. Lee, I'm going to push for trial just as fast as I can. There'll be no stalling this one. Now, what do you say about our trip to the hospital, Mr. Flaherty?"

"Completely off-record? No matter what gets said?" Lee asked suspiciously.

"Agreed."

Munroe Lee looked to Flaherty, who said in a subdued tone, "I'll go with him."

During their afternoon visit to the State Mental Health Hospital for the Criminally Insane, Flaherty was not lulled by the off-record assurances of the U.S. attorney. To the contrary, he was totally attuned, alert, and wary. His pride and interest were piqued by what the man had said earlier, that he, Flaherty, had little realization of what happened downstream of his delivery of narcotics along the Barerra chain or the guts to see the hospitalized ending thereof. Flaherty had agreed to the visit because he knew what Wetmore had said was true.

His capture had taken its toll on Flaherty. He was now wrung out, his nerves raw. Making big bucks while beating the U.S. government had once been a zestful, challenging game. But with his capture, his perception of smuggling as a game rapidly changed, replaced by the grim realization the other side had very sharp teeth and carried big sticks.

A few minutes later, in the garage under the Federal Building, when Wetmore indicated the right front seat of a bright red Ferrari 350 G.T., Flaherty was amused. He recalled Munroe Lee's comment that Wetmore was from an old Yankee woolen-mill fortune, utterly unreachable. There was even talk in the city of his making a Republican run for a Senate seat soon. In all events, for that moment, the car indicated a common interest in speed. "When I get out, we ought to try a drag some time," Flaherty said.

"That might be a long time." Wetmore smiled bleakly.

"I've got a Lamborghini—the Countach." Flaherty ignored the barb in the prosecutor's comment. Further conversation was then precluded by the roar of the Ferarri's warming wild horses. Not until they reached the expressway and high speed did Wetmore again speak. "I saw in the probation report your decorations in Nam," he said.

Flaherty nodded.

The U.S. attorney's gaze was far down the highway as he continued. "I was there, too—and saw how we lost it. Mike, when a nation loses the will to stand up and fight, fight for what it believes— what I'm about to say will probably sound like some kind of right-wing nut, still, I believe it. Marx, Lenin, Stalin, Khrushchev, they all

258

believed they would bury the American system. Now, they could be right, but for reasons they never foresaw; that we in the West would do them the favor, bury ourselves. We're sure doing it fast, with narcotics addiction.

"It's not just the importation and sale—that's bad enough. You've got to add in the criminal careers people get into to support the habit, throw in the overall cost to the country, shattered families, productivity loss, accidents, medical and criminal activity. Add it all up, the cost to this country, it's incredible.

"Have you any idea, Mike, what would happen to you if you'd been nailed with that coke in China, Russia? Don't answer on advice of counsel—me." He laughed. "I'll tell you. Your head would be in a basket by now in some town square—no appeal. The Communists know about drugs. The Cubans are in the trade. They're already using drugs as a weapon against us. They get hard currency, while screwing us.

"Sometimes Old Uncle's a little slow to get going, but once he does, he gets there. You'll find out . . . you're about to see this government really come down on the drug trade. The sad part, it'll be the little guys like you that take the weight. The big guys, Barerra, the organization capos, the foreign governments, the big wholesalers, they'll only feel it financially. The street people, the pushers, the amateur smugglers, they're the ones that'll really get hurt."

For a few moments, Wetmore fell silent as he deftly sliced through a slower-moving snarl of tractor-trailers. The silence gave Flaherty time to wonder where in hell Wetmore was going with his monologue, what was expected of him.

"You know, Mike, when you dig into this drug business, I have a theory that my employer, the United States government, and your people, Barerra and his scum, are partners in the strangest marriage there ever was, one that might well lead to the death of this nation.

"When we get to the State Hospital," Wetmore went on, "You'll meet Terry Williams, who runs the detoxification program. He'll show you what you're involved with. But while we've got a minute, let me first finish my unholy marriage theory. It's really pretty simple. Your people have the things that grow in nature. Our government has the narcotics people dream up in the labs. So when we stomp the hell out of your business, then, what will we do? We grab your market. We serve it with artificial drugs, sedatives. You name it. On

259

our side, it's politely called the pharmaceutical and mental health industries, doctors, lawyers, medical insurance, all neatly sponsored, controlled, and taxed by the U.S. government. And that's what you're going to learn, Mike. If there's anything our government always insists on, it's revenue and control, that they get their slice. That Old Uncle, when he makes up his mind, he's just too big. You don't believe me? Well, look at a bottle of liquor, a pack of cigarettes, who's there for his share? Your Old Uncle. Get in his way, you go to the slammer."

A short while later, the U.S. attorney wheeled off the expressway onto small rural roads, then turned into a long leaf-laden nave of tall oaks. The far end of the drive was blocked by steel gates and armed guards. On admission through the gates, Wetmore led Flaherty at a vigorous trot through a blur of ivied buildings, steel-meshed windows, and more gates with guards, down long corridors with shiny brick walls and dirty floors and the astringent smells of strong disinfectants. Professional people in white hospital suits were talking in hushed tones to professional people in green hospital suits and each sterile corridor was segregated by wire-mesh gates and guarded by a smoking dragon of a hard-nosed male nurse. Finally, Wetmore knocked, then entered a varnished door marked DIRECTOR—DETOX.

A slender man got up from behind his desk and came across the waxed floor of his spartan room. He was a light black man, casually dressed in a buff jogging suit. "Well, Bill, you certainly made good time." He laughed.

"No cops on the road," the federal prosecutor kidded, and then, "Terry, this is Michael Flaherty. Terry Williams, director of the detox program. Terry, Mike's the new national record holder, the guy they nailed with one hundred million dollars of coke down in Gloucester the other night."

"Mr. Flaherty," Williams said, coming over and firmly shaking his hand, looking squarely at him, without a hint of judgment in his eyes. "Nice to see you. Have a seat."

"Terry, we can stay an hour at most," Wetmore said. "Mike gets out on bail this afternoon. As I said on the phone, Mike and I have sons at school on the same lacrosse team. What I'd appreciate is you showing Mike just where it's at with these kids—where they can get to."

"Well, Mike, this detox step is only a small part of a much bigger package." Terry Williams's voice was soft and sure as he spoke.

"Frankly, there's not too much to show out here anymore. A few years back, you'd come out here, it was a different scene. Guys screaming, strung out on the floor, twisting, turning, cold turkey withdrawal. Man, that was something you just didn't want to see. Now we cure 'em—boy do we cure 'em." Williams laughed sardonically. "These guys, these kids, they get all fucked-up on the drugs— so, when they cross the law, get caught, they wind up here, we cure 'em. Know anything about methadone?"

"I know the name, never tried it."

"Well, I'd guess it's about as powerful a narcotic there is. Hitler's people, Nazi doctors, when they got blockaded during the War, they ran out of natural narcotics like heroin, so they invented methadone. And that's where we start out detoxifying these kids. We get 'em off the natural shit. We upgrade their habit, put 'em on the best, the purest shit any laboratory can build. Makes a lot of sense, doesn't it?"

Flaherty said nothing, looking at the blank wall behind Williams.

The detox director went on. "You know who knows this business better than anybody else, better than all the doctors, nurses, psychologists, psychiatrists, all of 'em rolled together? I'll tell you—the victims, the addicts—they're the experts, man, they're involved. They spend all their time thinkin', thinkin' 'bout their own body, what the shit can do, how they're goin' to get at it." Williams then asked, "So anyway, your kids, Mike. How old?"

"Fourteen and eighteen—boys."

"Well, the oldest is just the right age—transition time. Young adults to adulthood. All the confusions, all the fuck-ups, all the uncertainties. Hour-to-hour thinkers, no long plans, not yet. You know, Mike," Williams caught and held Flaherty's eye, "none of these druggies ever aimed to be addicts. *No way.* But drugs, booze, they do offer a beautiful escape, a run from the real issues. And with that, they get caught up on the shit. They start to experiment. Some idiots try and mix 'em. That's when they can blow themselves away. Where do you live, Mike?"

"Me? I live in Marblehead. My kids live over in Wenham most of the time."

"Upper-class white suburbia, huh?" Williams smiled. "You know, in a way, the black street kids, the inner-city kids, they have a better deal. When the cops grab 'em, they kick their ass, and I mean kick. Sittin' back in the cell, achin', those street kids, they ask themselves,

'How'd I get here?' Now, the white kids in the suburbs, hell, their daddies, they've got lawyers, they have 'em out in no time. Those kids, they never see what they're walkin' into, not till they're hooked, then it's too late. Anyway, when they get fucked-up far enough, cross the law, we get 'em down here. Then they become a piece of a very big industry. America's great new growth industry—treatment of chemical dependency for profit. Sounds good, don't it?" He chuckled, but his tone was leaden.

"You know, you look 'round here, all the wire, the guards, the goon squads with their sedatives, it's all bullshit. These people, they got hooked with street shit that costs 'em. You think they want out of here? *No way*. With the detox programs, why man, they got it made, their addiction is now sponsored and supported by the United States government. How can you beat that! Sure, later, back on the street, so they gotta show up at some agency some time every day to get their shit, so they get the purest shit our guv can buy. So they lose a little control of their lives. So what—big loss."

"Hey, Terry," Wetmore interrupted. "I promised Mike's lawyer, I'd have him back in Boston by five."

"O.K., O.K." Terry laughed. "Never saw a U.S. attorney so anxious to turn a guy loose . . . Mike, you put this all together, the illegit drugs, the legit drugs, you're talkin' the biggest numbers in the world. Where does it go? It could blow away the big part of a generation—bad as any war. Now, as I told you, out here, there's not a hell of a lot to see any more. Anybody gets out of line, we got goon squads, they hit 'em fast with enough tranquilizers, they're sleepin' puppies on the floor.

"Come on." Williams got to his feet and led Wetmore and Flaherty out into a corridor. "I'll show you two kids, a little older than yours, Mike, not by much. Both here forever."

At the end of a long corridor, a guard-nurse admitted the three into a subsection marked off into smaller rooms or pens by extra-heavy wire mesh. Terry Williams led on into one of the pens where an emaciated black youth in a white hospital johnnie lay strapped to a bed, electronic sensors taped to his chest and forehead, intravenous tubes in his arms, the space filled with the amplified chirp of his vital signs. The guard-nurse took a seat by the foot of the bed, glanced at the several monitors for a moment, picked up a paperback, and went back to his reading.

"What happened to him?" Flaherty asked in hushed tones.

"Don't worry 'bout wakin' Josh, Mike," Williams replied. "Only God's goin' to do that. This kid's been in coma six months or more."

"Yeah, but what happened?"

"He was in Walpole, doin' fifteen for armed robbery. Got hold of some angel dust—overdosed—shut down his whole body. No breathing. At room temperature, the brain can go six, maybe seven minutes without oxygen. This kid was gone a lot longer. Doesn't have much of a brain anymore. Come on, I'll show you another."

In the next section, a tall young man in a green johnnie stood staring at the rain on the window panes. "Hey, Teddy, you've got visitors," Terry William shouted cheerily, and then said to Flaherty, "Teddy was once a basketball player, Mike, a good one, they say. Now we got to hand-feed him, change his diapers, standing's about his only move left."

Flaherty walked to the window side of the youth and saw a tall young man in his late teens, downy cheeked, gaunt with a trimmed halo of golden hair that caught the outside light. The boy had the deepest blue eyes Mike Flaherty had ever seen, the blue of a winter sky, but the eyes were empty, unblinking, dead.

"What happened?" Flaherty asked.

"Pretty much the same story, a bad batch of cut coke, some Mexican shit. They revived him a little earlier this time, than Josh. He's a little less brain damaged. Lucky, huh?"

"Sometimes you wonder if they should have," the U.S. attorney said.

"Hey, Bill," the detox officer protested, "you takin' to playin' God? Doctors, nurses, they have oaths, just like you. They've got to try, give it their best shot, play it out."

Later, Wetmore and Flaherty drove back to Boston in silence. When Wetmore had wheeled the Ferrari into his reserved space under the Federal Building, he turned off the engine, and in the new silence said, "Michael, I can guess what's involved with Barerra, I understand why you can't talk. O.K. You hadn't thought much about the tail end of the track. That doesn't change things. I'm still going to hang your ass, if you don't come over, so . . . what happens now is up to you. Here." The U.S. attorney reached into a breast pocket, drew a calling card from his wallet, and scribbled two numbers on the back. "They're home and the office. They're secure . . . and direct to me, Michael. Some day, you and I are going to talk. When? Who knows. It's up to you. I can only guess what you're thinking. We do have the federal witness protection program. It's that or we play it out until the door closes. Your choice. Mike, you're better than the team you're on. It may take us a while, but Old Uncle's going to take your team apart."

The MacKay Mansion, Marblehead Neck, Massachusetts

As he turned on to the gravel drive of the MacKay mansion, Michael Flaherty and his powerful Lamborghini were both in low gear. His brief stint in jail and his afternoon in the mental hospital hung heavily upon him. While free on bail, his mood remained grim. Flaherty now saw himself, and what he had been doing, and he saw it all mirrored in the brain-injured blankness of the boy's blue eyes, the boy in the state hospital, the drug-destroyed zombie.

Sitting for a time in his sports car, the gathering darkness matched his mood, the second night of a summer storm, a wild night of slashing squalls, driving rain, and Atlantic combers that crashed to salt-tanged spume on the granite beyond the great house. Watching, smelling, listening to this awesome interplay of the irresistible and the unyielding, Flaherty did not hear the great door open to back-light Ann.

"Michael, I thought I heard a car." She came out into the raw rain and opened his door. "Come inside." She tugged him along.

Michael got out of his car hesitantly. "I wasn't sure you'd want to see me."

"We'll talk about that," she said, then hugged him warmly in the doorway. She led him through the great hall to a small panelled sitting room with a cheerful log fire, a snug room on the sea-side of the house. "We have the place to ourselves. Servant's night off, by arrangement," she said. "An early or light supper, whichever you'd like." She came into his arms, kissed him, and instantly sensed

264

Michael's gloom. *Well, we'll have to do something about this first,* she thought. "I'd hoped you would come." She sighed, then said, "And so, just as I suspected, you really are a pirate."

The absurdity of her words and the incongruity of his day struck Michael, a day that started in a grimy cell in Charles Street Jail, a morning spent in a bickering courtroom, an afternoon behind the wire of an asylum, and now, an evening by a warming fire in a handsome room of a magnificent mansion with the woman he knew he loved. It was absurd, it was incongruous, and it was just what Michael needed, an instant and total transport from the filth of where he had been, an emotional bath, warm, welcome, cleansing, and so he laughed. "On advice of counsel, I have no comment."

"Sound advice," she agreed. "Now, first, what would you like for a drink?" Ann turned to a neatly arrayed, fully stocked alcove bar.

"A good stiff rum on the rocks."

"How stiff?"

"Stiff."

Ann poured a hefty slug of brown rum on ice into a glass and handed it to Flaherty. "I hope this will do," she said.

Flaherty took a great gulp and instantly coughed, spluttered, and wheezed. "Holy be Jesus, what in hell is that?" he gasped when finally he regained his breath. She handed him the bottle of a very dark rum and smiled as he read the label aloud, "Demerara—product of Guyana—bottled in Miquelon? 1929? How's that? Where did you come up with this stuff, Annie?"

"Oh, after David's service, I had some time to myself. I started rummaging around this old place. You know, Father kept a very well-organized cellar. I had never paid it any attention. I always left liquor and wines to David. Well, Father's people kept a steward's book. Their entry for that case of Demerara was September of twenty-nine. I knew you liked rum, so, I thought we'd give it a try, you first, of course."

"Holy shit! You mean this stuff's over fifty years old?"

"Yes, you said stiff, my dear, didn't you?" She laughed gaily as she returned to the alcove bar to replenish her own drink. "And did you notice something else?"

"No, what's that?"

Ann replaced the cork as she spoke. "No revenue stamps, no seals—bottled in Miquelon? Now what does that say, Michael?"

"Beats me. What?"

"It's apparent from our cellars, my father did do a fair bit of bootlegging." She came over to him and nuzzled his nose. "So, my dear, maybe there's a little larceny in both our veins."

"A little!" And with that, the once-feisty Flaherty again flickered bright. "From what the old man told me about the MacKays, what they pulled, Christ, we're small time."

"Perhaps," Ann allowed with aplomb as she took the seat beside him. "I wouldn't know what they did, nor do I care." Concern came into her eyes. "What I do care about is you, Michael Flaherty."

Flaherty reached over and gently put a grateful arm about her, but his eyes remained dark, dark as the depths of the Demerara in his other hand.

"Where are you, Michael?"

Flaherty took a long pull of his rum and sighed as he slowly swallowed the brown fire. "I really don't know . . . but I'll tell you one thing I do know."

"What's that?"

"That I love you." For Flaherty, the words came easier than he would ever have expected.

"And I love you, Michael."

"And something else."

"What's that?"

"That surer than hell, I'm through with what I was in."

"Good. I thought you'd come to that. Drugs are a bad business, Michael, I know. I've been through it, but let's not beat on that, not tonight. You must be exhausted."

"You better believe it. Anyway, I'm pretty beat up inside, Annie. They've got me."

"For sure?"

"That's what my lawyer thinks."

"Do you know how they got you?"

"No, not yet. I have some ideas."

"Can you trade anything?"

"Not and live."

"Want to talk about it?"

"Best I don't—for both of us."

"That bad? I was afraid it might be." And a mist welled in her eyes. With the death of David and the arrest of Michael, she had indeed had a wracking week. Alone these past few days, she had made a discovery that surprised her—her ability to appreciate Michael for what he was as a man, her man. Certainly his capture as a smuggler of narcotics was a grievous wound. On reading the paper that morning, her first instinct had been to drop the relationship that instant. But then, she took time to think her feelings through, and found she loved Mike Flaherty, the good and the bad. With that decided, Ann discovered within herself a new strain of tendresse, a stout strain sinuously intertwined with her resolve to stand by Michael, help him, perhaps even guide him, as he might let her.

Her discovery of her ability to accept Michael as is, as apprehended, an accused criminal, was indeed a surprise. Not many weeks past, Ann MacKay Raimond had correctly considered herself constrained, proper, and prim. But all that was now changed. Here she was, a widow less than a week, sitting in her home, her lover in her arms, and he an apprehended smuggler. She understood how far, in so little time, her Brahmin world had turned, that despite their now-flawed friendship, how her heart now brimmed with happiness.

Once, in one of her blacker moods, Ann had wondered if Michael could be bought. She now knew he could be, had been, was now hers, but not bought with money. Ann had bought Michael with intermingled currencies of support, encouragement, and love—the eternal coin of enduring relationships. This realization was now her delight, for Ann also needed Michael, his strong arms were now her safe harbor. Ann took the drink from Michael's hand, set it aside with deliberation, moved back into his lap, and kissed him even harder, while outside the MacKay mansion, the angry Atlantic crashed on the granite.

Part Seven

Villa Barerra, Nahant, Massachusetts

The consigleri returned to the sauna dripping from a cold shower. When the door closed, he asked, "And the first shipment arrives tomorrow night, Mr. Barerra?"

"That's right, Sal. The Air Italia flight, tomorrow night at Logan. I want you to coordinate the distribution with Phil. Tell him I am sorry that it is only fifty kilos, a lot less than he used to get from Michael. It's only a stop-gap, something to hold his market. There will be another, later this week, on Air France at J.F.K."

"Mr. B., I've got to hand it to you. When you had me buy those cleaning and catering companies at the airport, frankly, I had my doubts. I couldn't see it. Then, to let 'em lie there doing a legit business for four years, that was brilliant."

The old man smiled. "I'd like to take the credit, Salvatore, but I can't. It came from a market study I had Michael do, a long time ago."

"You mean Flaherty's in on this one, too?"

"No, no, when he first came up with the idea, I told him I didn't like it. He's mentioned it again in more recent work. He never knew I made the move the first time. It was once said, 'We shall provide in peace, what we shall need in war.' "

"Oh, who said that, Mr. B.?" the consigleri asked.

"One of our own, Salvatore." Barerra laughed. "A noble Roman, Publicus Syrus, in the first century, B.C. Now, as for what we will need in war, I have Michael out of everything as of this moment. Even the grass containers. He'll continue to get his share, but for now, I've changed the control. They're coming in through Detroit and Chicago, as long as the Lakes remain ice-free."

"Well, the Feds certainly won't be looking for grass from that direction."

"That's what I thought," Barerra agreed. "Now, how do you see Michael's case, my consigleri?"

"I hate to say this, Mr. B. I think they've got him nailed."

"Nothing we can do, Sal?"

"Maybe a little, once they get to trial. Maybe we can get to a juror. It only takes one." the consigleri laughed.

"Nothing before?"

"Mr. B., if he were up on a state rap, there's a lot we could do. But the federal bench, they're straight, far as I know. Of course there are some liberals, judges that come down for the defense more often than others."

"Salvatore, I think we should see if we can nudge the docket before Michael's case gets before the wrong man."

"That'll cost, Mr. B. Maybe twenty big ones. Is it worth it just to get before a liberal judge? I just don't see the edge, not at that price."

"You can never tell, Salvatore. The smallest details often come back to help or hurt. It's a small amount for the service Michael has given us."

"I'll do my best, Mr. B. Now, anything else you want to talk about here in the hot box?" The consigleri was once again sweltering, very much wanting to move their conversation to more hospitable surroundings. Salvatore had observed, ever since Michael's capture, that the old man was more cautious than ever, now meeting even his most trusted consigleri in his sauna.

"One more thing," Barerra went on, in no way bothered by the heat. "What about our lady friend in D.E.A.? Are we still taking care of her? Has she anything new to say for herself?"

"Oh yeah, she got hers last week, the regular amount. It seems our friend Flaherty just had shitty luck. There were no mistakes, no leaks on our side. The Coasties had some plants working the coast. One of 'em got lucky with Flaherty."

"Oh, tell me about it."

"Well, from what our friend has put together, they had somebody on Flaherty's sailboat. That's how they spotted the box."

"But what has his sailboat got to do with his trawlers?"

"That, I didn't ask, but somehow, that's the way they learned about the trawlers."

"Did she have the name, Salvatore?" Barerra's dark eyes regained the glint of glass.

"Yeah, Mr. B., a broad named Jamie Quinn, a Coast Guard lieutenant." Solito stood up, wondering if the old man would ever give up this business in the sauna bit. It's got to be bad for the heart, the consigleri was certain.

"Hmm." Barerra paused for thought. *So, it was a Coastie. I wonder if she'll testify.* He then said aloud, "Speaking of Coast Guard, Sal, have we closed that account?"

"Yes, sir, our man was transferred to the Canal Zone. We had twenty-five big ones waiting for him down there." The consigleri's heart was really starting to race. "Mr. B., I can't keep up with you. I've got to have another shower." And with that, he went out the small wooden door.

The Flaherty Farm, Wenham, Massachusetts

The Flaherty clan gathered on the Wenham farm in the forenoon of Thanksgiving. Within the snug farmhouse, it was a day of festivity; without, a day of uncertainty, with intermittent shafts of sunlight and blue shadows of prancing scud racing across the cropped hayfields driven by a raw wind. For the most part, it was a drab threatening day, with a nor'east wind carrying winter's first spit of snow.

In the old stone house, Michael Flaherty stood with his back to a crackling fire, looking about the low-beamed living room, a frosted bloody mary in hand. Despite his pending troubles in the courts, the man was content with what he saw on this holiday with his family. He knew, in another year, the next Thanksgiving, his surroundings might indeed be different. But today was today, a day to enjoy.

Snug by the fire in a deep leather chair, with one stout rum under hatch, Michael's eighty-eight-year-old grandfather, "Big Mike" Flaherty, snored away as he awaited his holiday dinner. On the far side of the room, his mother, Kathleen, and his two sons were locked in a loudly contested game of chinese checkers, while beyond them, outside the small lead-paned windows, the autumn leaves and the cropped farm fields with their fleeting shadows were a kaleidoscope of the shades of fall.

On the opposite side of the massive chimney from where Flaherty stood, a double-flued chimney that also served as the central column of the farmhouse, his mother-in-law, Ginny, and his wife, Rosalie, bustled about the kitchen. Ginny had arrived an hour earlier in the chauffeured Barerra limousine. She brought along a basket of wines, the old man's best wishes to his family for the holiday, and a private message for Michael, his regrets at not attending the family gathering. Barerra believed it was not prudent to meet, not until Michael's trial had been dealt with. Flaherty knew this had not been an easy decision for the old man, that he looked forward to and thoroughly enjoyed these family gatherings.

The old farmhouse kitchen was a three-century combination of culinary convenience, ranging from wrought-iron pot arms with ancient iron kettles of Puritan fabrication to a small microwave oven. The women hovered over a big black iron stove, wherein a swaddled turkey sweltered and sputtered to a brown turn. When finally they had their repast in readiness, the Barerra chauffeur came out through the butler's pantry and set down a steaming silver tureen of oyster stew amidst the gleaming array of china and crystal on the dining room table. He went on to the living room and announced, "Miss Rosalie says your dinner is ready."

A few minutes later, with his family standing around the splendid table, Flaherty said Grace, then raised his glass of wine. "A happy Thanksgiving to us all," he toasted, touching glasses first with his mother to his right and then with his son Mick on his left. Flaherty caught his wife's appraising look from the far end of the long table, and again, he lifted his glass in toast to her. As he sipped, he looked across the rim at her, in his eyes, a happy mix of appreciation and contentment, a day of peace and thanks. *Why not?* he asked himself.

Rosalie returned Michael's toast, then turned to serving the stew. Michael fell into conversation with his son, Mick, for along with Patrick, their Sunday plans called for a trip to Foxboro to watch the Patriots play against the Dallas Cowboys. Could Grogan play, that was the opening question, and thereafter, the sumptuous repast moved apace, accompanied by the inconsequential babble of family chatter.

Twilight was on the Wenham hills as the Flaherty family saw the last of their flaming plum pudding. Mick was the first to finish and the first to rise from the table, but only after dutifully asking his mother if he might be excused. The young man had spent his fall on the freshman football team at the University of Massachusetts. Thanksgiving was his first visit home after the season. And with training over, it was to be a weekend crammed with reunions and parties, the next of which started in Manchester at six. After a hasty kiss or handshake for each of his relatives, Mick left the farm in his Jeep to the roar of a muffler, badly in need of replacement, in a swirling cloud of snow-dust.

Patrick soon followed his brother off the farm, bicycling for the close-by home of a classmate. Michael politely stayed on for another hour, a time primarily spent in a cribbage battle with his grandfather, a battle the old man won with loud glee. When finally his mother drove off with his grandfather to their Gloucester home, Michael Flaherty took his leave with a formal handshake for his mother-in-law, a distant peck on the cheek for his wife, and hearty high praise for their cooking. His wife's brown eyes never left him as he pulled on his coat and went out the door. Michael drove over to Marblehead, to Ann's place, and with her, watched a televised movie tape until just after eleven. As both had busy mornings planned, plans that would take them off in different directions, Flaherty decided he would spend the night at his place. After a long kiss and a good night hug, Flaherty headed for Glover Landing.

On entering, one of the first things Flaherty noted was the red glow of the message light on his telephone answering machine. He immediately went to it, flicked on the rewind, and in moments was surprised to hear Rosalie's tremulous voice. "Mike—there's been a horrible accident. It's Mick . . . The Pride's Crossing Police called. They took him to Beverly. They didn't say much . . . I think it's pretty bad. I'm going to the hospital."

Flaherty's hands shook as he dialed the Wenham farm. His mother-in-law answered. "And where have you been?" she demanded querulously.

"That's not important," he said, holding his temper. "What's this about Mick?"

"Rosalie just called from the hospital. He's alive. They've taken him up to surgery. It don't sound good. Something about compression on his spine."

"Jesus," Flaherty exclaimed in a low moan.

"And well you might pray to Him," Ginny added venomously.

Flaherty's temper was on the edge as he asked, "What happened?"

"The police, they said he was going like hell on Hale Street—hit some ice. The Jeep, it went off the road into a wall. His girlfriend, a girl named Cantella, she was killed."

"Oh, God." Flaherty sat, certain he was about to be sick. After several gasps, he asked, "Do her parents know yet?"

"Rosalie didn't say."

"Does my mother know?"

"Yes, I called her. She's on her way to Beverly. I'm staying here with Patrick."

"And your father?"

"Yes—I've told him."

"Please call the hospital, tell Rosalie I'm on my way, quick as I can." Flaherty broke off the call and punched out a second number. When Ann answered, he told her what he knew. She volunteered to take him to the hospital. He declined, said he could make it, that he would call her when he knew something, and then tore out his door.

With his Lamborghini at full bore, Flaherty fled the small winding streets of Marblehead. Had another car come through the tight turns of the Old Town the other way, death would have been instantaneous for all involved. In but minutes, Flaherty drew to a screeching stop across from the emergency room entrance of the Beverly Hospital. He raced into the waiting room, instantly spotted Rosalie, sitting beside an attentive young police officer, and ran to her. She jumped up into his arms and they both started to sob, long, wracking sobs, convulsed with grief, certain of the worst.

When the pair were spent for the moment, Rosalie groped in her purse for another cigarette and her lighter. When finally she found what she sought, Michael took the lighter from her shaking hand and, fumbling badly, gave her a light. "When did they take Mick up?" he asked.

"More than an hour ago," the young police officer replied, then added, "Mr. Flaherty?"

"Yes," Flaherty said, offering his hand.

"I'm Officer Biddle, Pride's Crossing Police. We found your son. Sure am sorry what happened."

"What did happen?"

"You know Hale Street?"

"The shore road with the big bends? Yeah, I take it to work sometimes."

"That's the one." The officer nodded gravely.

"Oh shit," Flaherty groaned as the officer started off into a grisly description of what they had found. It was apparent Mick had really been flying when he hit the ice patch, that neither Mick nor the girl had been wearing seat belts. When the Jeep went over, the Cantella girl's neck was snapped. She must have died instantly. Mick's door had opened when the Jeep flipped, he was tossed clear and later was found in the snow, bent backward around a small tree, his head smashed against a stump. Five empties and one full beer can were also found in the wreckage.

Flaherty then asked, "Do Linda's parents know yet?"

"Yes, yes they do," a shaken Rosalie intervened.

Officer Biddle picked up, "Our night sargeant talked with Mr. Cantella. He's given his permission for an autopsy. They'll do it in the morning."

"An autopsy?" Flaherty repeated, disbelieving.

"I'm afraid we have to, Mr. Flaherty," the earnest young officer said, "where there's a moving vehicle fatality, and beer cans and packets are found, when we're not sure of everything."

"But what good is that!?" Flaherty exploded.

"It's not up to me," the police officer said.

At that moment, Kathleen Flaherty entered the emergency waiting room, went to Rosalie, took her in her arms, and they talked in hushed tones. Flaherty joined them for a time, and then his mother led his wife off to a chapel as Flaherty went back to Officer Biddle. "Well, you're putting in a long day. It's really nice of you to stick around."

"No, no, I'm not." The young officer looked down at his shoes, obviously embarassed. "I'm still on duty."

"Why?" Flaherty asked, surprised.

"Because I'm here to arrest your son—if he ever wakes up."

"Oh," Flaherty said leadenly, then walked away to pace by himself.

Within the next hour, the physician in charge of the emergency room came over to the Flahertys. "Dr. Bright has finished the surgery," he said. "He'd like to talk with you. He'll meet you in the waiting room by his office. This young lady will show you." The doctor indicated a nurse-trainee by his side.

Flaherty noted how professional were the man's words and manners, the compassion in his eyes, and again he felt sick. He had seen eyes like that before—a lot of them—the medics along the Delta in Nam, zipping up body-bags.

The doctor then spoke to Rosalie. "Mrs. Flaherty, I'd like to give you something. I know what you're going through . . . It will only calm you down."

Rosalie blinked back her tears and shook her head, quietly, bravely refusing the doctor's offer of a sedative, clutching Michael's hand. The three Flahertys trailed the young nurse, their footsteps and Kathleen's recitation of the Rosary the only sounds in the corridor. The attending surgeon, Dr. Bright, paced his waiting room as the Flaherty's entered. He looked up at each one in turn, then said, "Your son is alive."

"Thank God," Rosalie sighed, turning to Michael, burying her sobs on his chest.

"Blessed be the Lord," Kathleen Flaherty said.

"I'm afraid it's not that simple," the doctor went on. "He's a tough youngster, but . . ."

Flaherty looked into the doctor's eyes and waited, certain he knew what was coming, not wanting to hear, not wanting to accept, not yet. Rosalie started to fumble for another cigarette when Dr. Bright asked, "May I have one with you, Mrs. Flaherty . . . I don't usually smoke."

With that, Flaherty saw how shaken the doctor was. *Oh God, poor Mick,* he thought. *A green doctor on a holiday night in a suburban hospital, the second team on duty, this guy's thirty at best.*

After a clumsy draw on his cigarette and a wracking cough, the young doctor went on. "Your son is severely hurt. I am in no way certain he'll live." The doctor tried a second puff of nicotine, went into a bout of coughing, then snubbed the butt on the polished floor. "To begin with the worst of it . . ."

Over the next twenty minutes, Dr. Bright launched into a clinical description of Mick's multiple injuries. Upon his arrival at the emergency room, the first X-rays had indicated a misallignment of the lower spinal column, most probably the result of hyperextension. Dr. Bright had operated almost immediately on the hope the misalignment might be straightened, any possible compression relieved. He described what he found on operating in terms of a snapped telephone cable made up of many sub-cables of equal complexity, none color-coded, none spliceable. The young doctor held no hope that were Mick to live, he would ever walk again. "If we get lucky, and if he ever regains consciousness, I'm afraid he'll be a paraplegic."

But the spinal injury was not the only reason the young surgeon was so uncertain of Mick Flaherty's chance of survival. The youngster's skull was badly smashed, the internal bleeding severe and diffuse, the resultant pressures within the cranium intense and extensive, quite probably fatal.

As Flaherty listened, he was trying to assess the thought process of this shaken young surgeon. In Nam, Flaherty had seen gore, gore all over, his best buddy's brains on his own fatigues. Flaherty had seen the best of the medics in action at close hand. He now rethought his initial assessment of Dr. Bright as a second-team greenhorn, hacking his way along in a small suburban hospital. The man knew what he was talking about, that was for certain. He'd given Mick the best of his skills. He cared.

Dr. Bright went on describing what he had done to address Mick's many brain injuries and ticked his way down a long list of trauma; a ruptured spleen, two broken legs, one broken arm, and a smashed pelvis.

The surgeon now looked up and looked square into Michael Flaherty's eyes. "Your son is now in coma," he said. "How long, who knows. It could be a few days, it could go on for several weeks. I don't know. It is all so complicated—so interrelated. Until he regains consciousness, we won't really know how badly hurt his brain is. Sadly, Mr. Flaherty, that's not all of it. . . . When your son came into the hospital, they drew blood, a standard tox-screen. I have the results back from our lab. Your son had done some drinking, point nine-oh by their count—just below the legally drunk level in this state. Now, Mr. Flaherty, all these records will become available to the police. And sadly, there's more. Our people found a considerable amount of a chemical substance in your son's blood—cocaine."

Later, at dawn, after looking in on Mick, a swaddled mummy that chirped with instrumentation in the intensive care ward of the hospital, Michael Flaherty put his mother in her car and then took his wife away from the Beverly Hospital, back to their home on the Wenham farm.

That afternoon, Mick Flaherty developed major complications and was transferred to the neurological division of Boston's Massachusetts General Hospital.

The Massachusetts General Hospital, Boston, Massachusetts

Michael Flaherty was profoundly sad as he stood by the window, looking down on the river. He could only watch his son for a time, and then he had to turn away. Mick's face was hidden by an oxygen mask, his body encased in casts, swathed in bandages, speared by tubes, wired to electronic monitors. By the foot of the bed, a doctor and nurse watched the electronic screens, listening to the chirp of the heart monitor, the thunk of the respirator, adjusting the oxygen input or the several intravenous bottles that dangled from above. On the far side of Mick's bed, his grandmother softly recited the Rosary.

Far below Flaherty, across the drive, on the banks of the Charles, a raucous noon-break game of touch football was in progress, a game so loud he could hear the happy shouts. Out on the river, down by the Museum of Science, two Harvard eights lined up for a practice race. Soon, these golden shells swept by in a sprinting start, their young oarsmen swinging along in smooth cadence, their crimson blades flashing in the sunlight, their catch leaving white puddles on the dark water. And if it were possible, watching these young people at their play made Flaherty even sadder, for he knew his son could never play again.

A stir behind him drew Flaherty away from the window. He turned and was stunned to see Jamie Quinn standing in the doorway. Despite her natty Coast Guard uniform, Jamie looked tentative, uncertain. Their eyes locked, then he ran to her, and they hugged. Flaherty broke into wracking sobs.

"Oh, Mr. Flaherty, I just heard about Mick from Freddy last night. I flew up this morning." She hesitated, then asked, "How is he?"

Flaherty wiped back his tears with his fists, then took Jamie's hand. "Come on. Let's find a place we can talk. God, I'm glad you came."

Flaherty led Jamie down the corridor to an empty visitor's room and corner seats, never letting go of her hand. He looked at Jamie, and the tears came again. Between sobs, he said, "He's not, Jamie . . . he's dead."

"Oh, no." Then Jamie burst into tears. After a time, she asked, "But those people, the doctor, the nurse . . . I could hear him."

"Jamie," Flaherty sighed, "you heard the Boston Edison Company. Only electricity is keeping it going. Mick's brain is gone."

"When?"

"A couple of hours ago. They thought they had a handle on him, his subdurnal hematomas, there was just too much damage, some clots got loose—they nailed him. His EEG went flat—that was that. I haven't told his mother or my Mom yet. I was trying to get up the guts when you came."

"Oh, Mr. Flaherty, I'm so sorry," Jamie sobbed, "and not just about Mick, about everything."

Flaherty looked her square in the eye as best he could through his tears and squeezed her hands hard as he spoke. "Hey, Jamie, I would have called if I knew where you were at. You did what you had to do. I've got no bitch. I'm proud of you."

"I wish it were summer again. *Shillelagh* was so much fun," she said.

"Yeah, so do I, and it was. We did all right," Flaherty agreed, trying hard to get hold of himself, clearing his throat, dabbing at his eyes. He reached up and touched the gold-braided loop of an aiguillette on her shoulder, trying to smile as he asked, "I see you're a full lieutenant. Now what's all this about?"

"Oh, I'm Admiral Osborne's aide. He was promoted when he went to Washington, head of Coast Guard Intelligence."

"That's great, good for you, Jamie!"

"Thanks, but Mr. Flaherty, I wish there was something I could do for you. Can I help in any way?"

"No, it's pretty much done, or will be soon enough." Flaherty shook his head wearily. "They're waiting on a couple of doctors, for outside opinions, so, the next hour or so, it's over. They're lining up recipients right now. I gave the O.K."

"Recipients?" Jamie was wide-eyed, unsure of what she heard.

"Yeah, his heart, his eyes, most of his organs, they're all right." Then Flaherty broke off in an unconsolable spasm of sobs.

Jamie held him as best she could, groping for something she could say, and then she said softly, "Micky would have liked that," she said softly. "In a way, he'll live some more."

Part Eight

The U.S. District Court, McCormick Building, Boston, Massachusetts

On a bleak December morning, with the first stroke of nine, a slight white-haired lady climbed the granite steps and entered the near-empty lobby of the McCormick Building. The woman was sensibly dressed for the day in a thick lamb's wool coat, a black wool watch cap, black wool mittens, and overshoes, the morning forecast having warned of snow. She crossed the lobby to the elevator banks and pushed the call-button.

As she waited, the woman looked overhead, where, on the wall, she eyed a stern portrait of the late John W. McCormick, forty-three years the representative of South Boston, eight years the Speaker of the House of Representatives. When the elevator door clanged open, the woman gave a wink for luck to the portrait, entered, and pushed the twelveth floor button, the level of the Federal courtrooms, then nodded and smiled at those who crammed in around her. By her manner, she seemed a friendly, garulous woman, given to chatting with those who would chat with her. As the elevator rose, the white-haired woman thought for a time of the portrait and the man behind it. She had met the speaker in his day. He was her kind of man, and had he been about this morning, as she sensed he was, when he asked of her welfare as he always did, she would tell the Speaker of her troubles, her story seasoned with sea-salt, her manner pithy, pointed.

My name is Kathleen Margaret Flaherty. I am the daughter, widow, and mother of fishermen. I have lived my sixty-seven years in the fishing town of Gloucester, Massachusetts. My home on the hill overlooking the harbor was my mother's before me. The men of my family have lived from the sea—they fished for the most part—not always. My father and my late husband and his father, Big Mike, they made most of theirs in Prohibition. They were seamen, fishermen, did a bit of the runnin', we have lived comfortably. I have no complaint, the Lord has treated us well, till now.

I am widowed these seven years and have come to accept the Lord's will. Sometimes, I wonder at His ways, for now, once again, I have another great sadness. My only child, Michael, will soon be on trial here in Boston. They charged him with smuggling cocaine into Gloucester last August. Of course, they are wrong.

It is now December—another bitter winter. I should know. This morning, I walked down to the station and took the Boston train. Michael offered to have me driven. I didn't want the bother for him. He has enough on his mind, and the walking does me good, though I wonder what good I do here. I sit in the court and I listen and I watch and I knit and I pray. The truth of it is I just want to be near my Michael.

There is another woman who came to the court last week. She listens and needlepoints, very well from what I could see. Her name is Mrs. Raimond, a widow from Marblehead, a friend of Michael. He introduced us, and now we smile. I should talk with her more, I know, but I don't know what we would talk about. She has tried several times to be friendly. Frankly, I find these new relationships very uncomfortable. I don't understand them. My Michael is a married man. Now, I know his wife has not come to this court, that they don't get on. I don't understand that either, her mother's fine hand, my guess. Still, they are married. There are times a woman should be with her husband, no matter what.

Jury selection for Michael's trial may start today. It all depends on the judge. The whole mess was put off three weeks, first for poor Mick's funeral, God rest his soul, and then for something I had a hand in. You see, last week, they were arguing before the judge. Michael's lawyer, Mr. Lee, had all kinds of motions and things. Mr. Wetmore, the United States attorney, fought every one of them. He's a very argumentative man. As I understood it from Michael, the hearing last week was going to be arguments about details before the trial, pretrial motions, he called them. Now this Lee is a Yankee. That would have been enough for me. I don't trust them, plain and simple. Michael should have had one of his own—that's my opinion—but who am I to argue when John Joseph Tobin and Giovanni Barerra both say Lee's all right—we'll see.

So last week, up before the bench, they had this long meeting, Mr.

Lee, Mr. Wetmore, and the judge, the Honorable Charles A. Weinstein, if you will—a Truman appointment and a Jew. I watched it all. Michael says it was good luck that he drew Judge Weinstein—he's known as a defendant's judge, a liberal. Well, we'll see. He was a Jew first. Now I'll grant you this Judge Charles A. Weinstein looked bright and interested. He nodded all the time, a man in his early seventies, my guess. Very intelligent, an intellectual, they say. Maybe, we'll see. Frankly, I think the whole thing is unfair—a Yankee prosecutor before a Jewish judge, and my Michael with a Yankee lawyer, very unfair. As if he hasn't enough troubles.

Sitting up in the second row, I could see the judge clearly. He was bald, shiny bald, with a silver wisp of a halo of hair. At first, he reminded me of a Trappist, the black robes and all—but then, the way the ceiling lights of the courtroom hit his head, his thick glasses, he reminded me more of a bobbing lightbulb.

I found that funny, but I still listened carefully, very carefully, and needless to say, I was quite shocked to hear my own name mentioned. Mr. Wetmore was reading from the search warrant they had used when they took Michael. Now, I know for a fact my own name and I know for a fact the trawler they seized was named for my sister, Katherine Mary Flaherty. She's gone now—a bit of a wild one, she was, and well I should know, she was my twin and like us, those trawlers are twins, too. We christened them.

So, when the court broke at mid-morning, I went up to Michael and his smart Yankee lawyer as fast as I could, and I said to them, "Mr. Lee, Michael, I believe Mr. Wetmore mentioned the wrong trawler this morning. I would like you to straighten that out, if you please."

"What's that, Mrs. Flaherty?" Mr. Lee asked me. He was polite enough, he was, for a Yankee.

So I said to him, and I said it slowly, "That was my sister Kate's boat they grabbed, not mine. Now I want that record corrected."

They both looked at me like I was balmy, but then went back to their desk and looked at their papers. Sure enough, I was right. My name was on that search warrant of theirs, but it was Kate's boat they grabbed, it was Kate's boat Michael took to sea when and if he ever brought anything in, which he didn't, of course.

So, when the judge came back into court, Mr. Lee asked to approach the bench with Mr. Wetmore. They had a long meeting up there, very hushed. I could not hear them, and I still hear well, very well, when I want to. Next, the judge took Mr. Lee and Mr. Wetmore off to his chambers. All the newspaper people and all the television people sat around. All the spectators, the back-benchers, they call them, they all left. They knew nothing would happen. They were right. Nothing did until after six that night, when Judge Weinstein came back and told everybody the defense would be filing several new motions, motions to suppress, he called them. They would be filed the next morning, the court would reconvene in a week, on a Monday—today.

And so we wait. It is just ten. The press people are back. The room is full, that's why I came early. We will not have to wait much longer. The court officer shouts "Court," so we stand while the judge comes in and takes his seat. He puts on his big glasses—not half-rims like mine—he seems a very careful man, a priss, if ever there was one. Then he looks at us all with a funny little smile. I don't trust him. My fingers are white, they tremble. My beads are wound too tight.

Judge Weinstein starts to read. "Ladies and gentlemen, last week, several issues were brought before the court on pretrial motions. Indeed, this court has found them extremely interesting issues of a far-reaching import—a national import—so much so, this court expressly encourages the interested parties that this decision should be appealed." Judge Weinstein put his papers aside and smiled his little smile, first toward Mr. Lee and then at the prosecutor. Now I don't think anymore. I know he's a priss, and that means trouble for Michael.

The judge went on. "First, we will try and state our findings in simple terms. For all interested parties, the clerk will have copies of the full text of my decision. Simply stated, the defense has raised a Fourth Amendment issue, the citizen's right to protection against unreasonable search and seizure. This court has found this Fourth Amendment argument most fascinating—indeed brilliantly presented." The Judge again put his papers aside and smiled at Mr. Lee. "Yes, it is most appropriate this issue first comes to ruling in a Boston court—figuratively in the shadow of Faneuil Hall, Bunker Hill, Dorchester Heights." I am getting very angry with Weinstein. The man will be the death of me, he's so full of words. I wish he would get on with it, this wordy Jew.

"Most appropriate indeed, for the opening scenes of America's War for Independence were right here about us. The founding fathers of the ongoing Republic, Washington, the Adamses, Jefferson, Madison, they were all particularly sensitive to the issues raised by the defense— their sensitivity, of course, for different reasons in different form for a different day—those gentlemen had firsthand experience with George III, his red-coats, and his hired Hessians in their lamentable attempt to force his will upon the colonists. Yet, the issue is always the same—the citizen's inalienable right to protection from unreasonable search and seizure." This little Jew should be teaching Civics, I said to myself.

Yet, he kept droning on, "Briefly, the defense has moved that the court suppress any photographic evidence obtained by radio signal from certain satellites placed in orbit about this planet by the United

States Navy. The defense has cited the defendant's Fourth Amendment rights. The government has agreed by stipulation of the United States attorney these satellites were placed in orbit for military reconnaisance purposes. Further, the defense has asked, were these photographs to be allowed in evidence, that the government produce the satellites that the authenticity of the equipment and the photographs be put to proof. Subsequently, the court has received a telegram of protest from the Secretary of Defense which states the retrieval of these satellites is an undue burden upon the government and would do irretrievable harm to the security and defense of the nation. The United States attorney has informed the court the government will also be filing appropriate briefs under the Classified Information Procedures Act." Judge Weinstein put aside his paper and smiled at Mr. Wetmore.

"Now, for this court to order the retrieval of a so-called spy satellite does indeed pose a dilemma. Setting that issue aside for the moment and moving on, the defense has also contended the defendant's constitutional rights may be offended by admission of military-furnished satellite photographs. They mention the now-amended Public Law 86.70, the so-called 'posse comitatus' act. As those of you who are students of history will recall, this nation has always been sensitive to the use of the military for police purposes, except of course, in time of tumult. Now, to paraphrase this act, 'The Armed Forces are generally precluded from assisting local law enforcement in their duties.' " Could you believe it, this wordy Jew had again lost his way. He put aside his paper and said to Michael's lawyer, "A brilliant piece of research, Mr. Lee. The court's compliments to you and your staff. Good solid work. I hope it is appropriately published. Now, as to the 'posse comitatus' issue, this act came about in the wake of the War of Rebellion, the Civil War, when the Southerners retook their seats in the Congress, they passed this act to assure federal troops were prohibited from policing former Confederate states where a civil government had been restored.

"While this Court recognizes the long-accepted tenet of law, namely, 'The eye of the constable can not trespass,' it is also our opinion, were the government to persist in an attempt to introduce into evidence satellite photographs for purposes of this prosecution, photographs taken by a U.S. Navy satellite, a military satellite, as stipulated by the government, this court hereby rules such evidence would indeed offend the defendant's constitutional protections despite all amendments of the 'posse comitatus' act."

With that, I watched Mr. Wetmore slump forward at his desk, slowly shaking his head. I didn't feel sorry for him, not at all.

Judge Weinstein went on. "In the best interests of ongoing law, for this matter might indeed come before the courts again, we again express our desire for an appeal of these findings." And he again smiled his funny little smile, and then went further, this Judge Weinstein, and with that, I liked him.

"Several days ago, it was also brought to the attention of this court that there are two identical trawlers in the Flaherty Fisheries fleet. They are the *Kathleen M. Flaherty* and the *Katherine M. Flaherty*. Why this matter was not mentioned earlier, this court will never understand. Now, on the basis of a motion to suppress as filed by the defense last week, the government has agreed and stipulated that it was the trawler *Katherine M. Flaherty* that was boarded by federal agents of the Drug Enforcement Agency on the night of August fourteenth last. Further, that while in close proximity, United States Coast Guard personnel did not participate in the initial boarding, nor were they among the discovering agents of any alleged controlled substance. Now, there is no doubt, since 1790, Customs officers of the United States could and can board any vessel at any time and at any place in the waters of the United States to examine a vessel's manifest and other documents, that Customs officers can do so without suspicion of wrongdoing in waters that provide access to the open sea. Most recent reference, *United States* v. *Villamonte-Marquez et. al.,* Number 81–1350. Now, that Coast Guard personnel can also, in certain circumstance, be Customs officers is not at issue, not yet, at least.

"Briefly, this court finds the vessel *Katherine M. Flaherty* was improperly boarded in Gloucester Harbor—waters providing ready access to the open sea, by agents of the Drug Enforcement Administration, that they are not Customs officers, that unfortunately for the government's case, the search warrant authorizing said boarding was for the vessel *Kathleen M. Flaherty*. An honest error, a human error, an error made in haste—but an error.

"And so, as it relates to the defense motion to suppress, any and all evidence obtained under said warrant is inadmissible. This court finds the warrant lacked probable cause for issuance and was indeed defective. The defense motion to suppress is herewith granted." With that, my old heart almost stopped. God love us all. He is back in His heaven and He did listen.

The courtroom went wild. The press people ran for the doors. Wetmore was ashen with anger as he got to his feet. "Your honor, you've simply ignored the Sheppard case, amongst others. The government asks for a month's continuance that the rulings of this court might be studied, no, appealed. We all know full well, your honor, without the satellite photographs and the evidence seized aboard the *Katherine M. Flaherty,* the government does not have much of a case."

Michael's lawyer was also on his feet, shouting, "And the defense, your honor, asks for a directed verdict of not guilty. The United States attorney has just admitted he has no case. My client has a constitutional right to a speedy trial."

With a vigorous rap of his gavel, Judge Weinstein brought order back to his court, and then replied most courteously, "I understand your position, Mr. Wetmore, and you have a good point, Mr. Lee." The judge beamed at both men. "However, I don't think justice will be that badly served if Mr. Wetmore is granted his continuance. So be patient, Mr. Lee. This is, after all, a most interesting case—a landmark." With that, the Honorable Charles A. Weinstein got to his feet, slammed his gavel, and said, "Continuance so granted." He then left the bench, a tiny little man with a funny little smile in black robes that were far too big and I loved him.

Michael came out from behind the barrier, over to me. He was laughing and he was almost crying, he was so happy and he looked very handsome and we hugged and I cried, I was so happy for him.

Michael next went to his friend, Mrs. Raimond, and he hugged her and they kissed. It was a very long kiss—too long, I thought.

Later, on leaving the courthouse lobby, I again smiled at the Speaker and thanked him. There are those who say I am a bit superstitious.

Villa Barerra, Nahant, Massachusetts

Flaherty stomped from foot to foot to fight the December cold. It was a black night, thickly overcast, so thick darkness had come quite early. Standing out in the raw wind, Flaherty's cheeks were stung by the first of a wind-lashed snow. He stood uninvited on the floodlit steps of Villa Barerra, more than surprised he had been allowed through the gates, knowing the houseman would be several minutes obtaining his clearance into the villa, if it were to be granted, by the padrone. Flaherty was not looking forward to this meeting, his stomach was knotted, yet he knew it had to be, no matter the consequence. It could no longer be avoided, the vow he had made at his son's funeral.

That morning, fortune had indeed smiled on Flaherty in the Federal Court. That afternoon, in a postcourt briefing at Baxter, Blair and Burnham, Flaherty was apprised that his present good fortune might well be brief, that at the appeals level, there were several justices of a cerebral firepower that matched Judge Weinstein's, that these gentlemen took delight in overturning Weinstein in finely drafted decisions. In short, Flaherty had best be prepared his case was heading for the Supreme Court of the United States before it ever came to trial, and with so much at stake, the Justice Department would wheel up all their artillery. Sitting quietly, listening to his lawyers, Flaherty was again reminded of Yogi Berra's indelible "The game ain't over till it's over."

Despite these cautions of his lawyers, as he drove away from Boston, apparently relieved from threat of twenty years in a federal penetentiary, Flaherty might well have been joyous and jubilant. But he wasn't at all, quite the opposite, as he stomped on Barerra's steps. He was somber and anxious, even scared, knowing this Barerra meeting would not be easy, knowing there was the possibility he might never walk down these steps, knowing what he had to do, he had to do.

The great door softly clicked, then swung open on oiled hinges. A houseman stood aside for Flaherty as he said, "Mr. Michael, Mr. Barerra said he would be pleased to see you. May I take your coat, and please be sure to empty your pockets." He indicated a silver tray on the hall table.

Moments later, Flaherty was ushered into the great library, where Giovanni Barerra stood, his back to a crackling fire. "Ah, Michael, what a nice surprise! And my congratulations! Salvatore called from the court. I am delighted with the news."

"So am I, Gabbo, but it's not quite over," Flaherty said as the old man crossed the room to embrace Flaherty heartily, vigorously thumping his back. "My lawyers say Weinstein sometimes gets overturned on appeal."

"What will be, will be. I don't believe they overturn Weinstein, not that often. Your lawyers are probably looking for more work. Now, go over by the fire, Michael. I'll pour us some brandy. This calls for a celebration." The old man moved toward a crystal decanter on a sideboard as he went on. "Incidentally, your move in diverting the containers through New York and barging them up to Providence has worked out brilliantly. Perhaps we should stay with Providence. I hope, after, shall we call it, a little rest, when things quiet down, you'll be ready to take over again."

"That's part of why I came. I'm glad it worked out for you, Gabbo. I'm not sure you'll be pleased with what I have to say." Flaherty's lips were a thin line, his face gray as he spoke. "I want out."

Barerra put the stopper back in the decanter, and slowly swirling a snifter in each hand, walked over to Flaherty. "Oh, Michael, there's always a big let-down after something as trying as you have been through. It's perfectly understandable."

"It's more than a let-down . . . I want out," Flaherty repeated.

"Don't be silly, Michael. Why, in a few years, you have become a very wealthy man."

"Yeah, and what has that got me!" Flaherty exploded. "I've got the government of the United States with a blowtorch up my ass and a dead kid."

The old man looked into the amber swirl of his snifter before he replied. "I know, Michael, I know. I think of the boy often. He and his young brother are all that will come behind me. These things happen, Michael."

"This didn't have to happen, Mr. B. It was probably our shit the kid got his hands on, our shit sent him off into those trees. And the dead girl."

"Yes, Michael, it probably was our material. We control the market now." The old man sighed leadenly, but then added, "If it hadn't been ours, it would have been someone else's. It would have happened."

"That doesn't make it any better. That doesn't let Mick live again."

"No, it doesn't." The old man put a compassionate arm around Flaherty. "You'll learn to handle it, Michael. I know you will."

Flaherty shrugged off the friendly arm, took a deep gulp of brandy, put the snifter on the marble mantel, and turned to glare at Barerra dead level. "I'm getting out."

The warm compassion of Barerra's dark brown eyes switched to a steely glint on the instant. "That's not so easy, Michael. Need I remind you of your commitment?"

"I don't need any reminding, Gabbo. I know what I promised. I didn't realize what I was getting into. That's my fault, not yours. I've paid my dues, my oldest kid. You can have back all the money, every goddamn cent of it. Take it! That doesn't buy me back my son."

"Oh, Michael." Barerra again swirled his brandy and then paused for a long sniff. "Michael, it was not your fault, it was an accident. Life can be a series of accidents. There is no way we can control all the events around us. To many things, we can only react." Barerra again put a soft hand to Flaherty's shoulder. "I grieve as you do—

perhaps more. There is nothing I can do about it . . . I cannot restore him."

"And we made the bucks off the shit that fucked-up my kid forever!" Flaherty exploded. "You know it, I know it. How do we live with that, Mr. B.? I'll tell you how. We can see that it doesn't happen to other kids."

"You're right about the cocaine, Michael, I cannot deny it." Barerra sighed a very deep sigh. "And I have also thought about what you suggest. Michael, you will learn, as I have, and it is a hard lesson, where money and greed are concerned, no one, no thing, is irreplaceable. The business has gotten too big."

"That's bullshit! Look, maybe I can't take on you, your organization, your whole shitty world of dope peddling. I'd like to, but I can't. You say it's too big. Maybe. But when something's wrong, it's wrong, so I'll do what I can, and that's me. I can do something about me. And I'm taking me out of the deal."

"Michael." There was an edge of steel in the old man's voice. "There are things we cannot walk away from."

"Look, Gabbo, your people want the money back, they've got it. I'll sign 'em over my foreign accounts, give 'em the access code. They're in it for the bucks, they're gettin' the bucks back. They want me? I'll be waiting . . . if that's what they want.

"Michael, how do I explain? You can be so hotheaded—so very Irish." Barerra's tone was now one of total sadness. "It's not just the money, Michael. People don't walk away. It's a matter of discipline. We can't have these conversions. Think, think, think your way through it. I can't have my people come to me and say I did not hold my kin to the code. That would lead to anarchy. That I can not tolerate."

"Look, Gabbo, far as I'm concerned, I just don't give a shit what you think, what others think."

"But I must hold to the code, Michael. That is my responsibility."

"If it comes to hardball, Gabbo, I've made some provisions. There's an envelope in a place no one's going to get to. Something happens to me, that's something else. I'll take the whole deal down with me."

"Michael, there can be no threats. That is not done."

"I'm not threatening, Mr. B. All I'm saying is I have taken precautions. I'm through with narcotics. I'm out as of now."

Barerra put down his snifter, put both of his hands on Flaherty's shoulders, and looked at him through soft brown eyes of infinite sadness. "I want you to think about this. I want you to sleep on this. We will talk tomorrow."

"There is no tomorrow," Flaherty vowed grimly. "Not for Mick, not for us."

Barerra hugged his grandson-in-law and kissed him on each cheek. "Please, Michael, we will talk tomorrow."

"Never." Flaherty shook his head, shrugged from the embrace, and strode from the room.

Giovanni Barerra went to the leaded casement windows, his eyes on the lit towers of Boston as they shivered in the winter wind. Above the snow-blurred towers, silver spears floated down through the overcast, the landing lights of aircraft inbound for the runways of Logan. Barerra watched for a time, then suddenly smashed one fisted hand into the cup of the other. He knew he would never move Michael Flaherty, what the word "never" meant to the man. Barerra turned away from the window and strode for the phone, the pupils of his eyes picks of steel. Half across the empty room, a small aneurysm ruptured in Barerra's cerebral artery, then quickly widened, flooding the brain tissue with arterial blood. The pain lasted but an instant as the old man slumped to the floor.

The Flaherty Condominium, Marblehead, Massachusetts

Near dusk on the day Giovanni Barerra was buried, a long limousine with black windows drew up by Flaherty's home. A chauffeur quickly got out and opened the rear door for a small swarthy man in a dark blue overcoat. The chauffeur nodded to the passenger, indicating Flaherty's door.

After several rings, Michael Flaherty opened his door. "Mr. Solito, we meet twice in one day. What a surprise. Would you like to come in?"

295

"No, Mr. Michael, thank you very much," the consigleri declined deferentially. "I have a package for you. I was told by you-know-who to deliver it personally." The man handed Flaherty a well-wrapped package, bid him good afternoon, returned to the limousine, and drove off.

The address of "Mr. Michael" by the consigleri of the Barerra organization did not escape Flaherty. He then wondered about the contents of the package, for Flaherty would never underestimate Giovanni Barerra. The man was fully capable of reaching out from the grave. Flaherty considered the package for a time, held it to his ear, shook it gently, and had just started to carefully unwrap it when Ann arrived. After a hug and a kiss, she walked through the living room to lay her shearling coat on the picture-window settee. "Well, Michael, the departure of your Mr. Barerra was certainly well covered."

"Yeah, they sure gave him a play," Flaherty allowed.

"And by the way, Michael, no more comments about any of my late relatives."

"You mean about bootlegging?" Flaherty laughed. "You probably guessed, it was Barerra who told me the deal with your old man. You see, he was partners with my grandfather."

"I might have known," Ann said dryly, but then added, "Was his service well attended?"

"Well attended! You got to be kidding. Standing room only, and as many outside the church as in. What a service! What a strange man! Somehow, with all this ecumenical stuff, he pulled off the old Latin Mass. Knowing him, he's got a plea bargain going with God, hedging his last bet with a High Mass. I haven't heard a Mass like that since I was a kid, the full Gregorian Mass for the Dead—in Latin—and sung by the auxiliary bishop with the seminary choir. Must have been ten priests on the altar. It was unbelievable."

"It must have been very beautiful."

"Annie, it was beyond beautiful. It was awesome." A slight mist came over Flaherty's eyes. "I don't know how he pulled it off, but he did."

Most probably money, Ann thought to herself, but then, pointing to the partially opened package on the cocktail table, she asked "Oh, what have you there?"

"I'm not sure. It just arrived. The old man's consigleri dropped it off, in person, no less. For all I know, it could be a bomb. Maybe you'd better go outside while I open it."

"Oh, come on, Michael. Finish opening it. I'm always curious about mysterious packages."

"Tell you what. You do it. If it's a bomb, then I won't feel so bad. I'll pour us some drinks. Wine? Scotch?"

"Gee, thanks pal," Ann said, yet she went to the package. "A glass of white would suit fine." A few minutes later, she carefully drew away the last of the excelsior, revealing some kind of multiringed navigating instrument of finely chased silver. "My lord, Michael. Whatever it is, it's exquisite!"

Michael took the instrument from her and examined it closely. "I'll be damned, an old astrolabe—an early sort of a sextant."

"There's a card." Ann had continued probing the straw. "And a typed envelope."

"Read me the card," Michael said as he put down the astrolabe and took up the envelope.

Ann read:

Villa Barerra

Dear Michael,

If there was another way, I would never write. Please accept this token of my esteem. The instrument requires a strong steady hand. Learn to use it well.

With my love and respect,

Giovanni Barerra

"Oh, Michael, what a thoughtful gift," she added.

"It's beautiful," Flaherty agreed. "And this sheet in the envelope says the astrolabe has been in the same English-Irish noble family since the Spanish Armada of 1588. That it was the personal instrument of the Spanish vice admiral, second-in-command. Seems his vessel survived Drake and his friends in the Channel—got wrecked on the west coast of Ireland. An all-hands job. Those that got through the surf got nailed by Brit soldiers on the beach. The instrument came up for auction at Southeby's, last August." Michael shook his head in wonderment. "Only Giovanni Barerra would have sent it."

Ann put aside the card, went to Michael, and hugged him. "Michael, all this gives me the shivers. What kind of man was he?"

Flaherty took a long pull of bourbon before answering. "Annie, I hated and loved that son of a bitch. He was the damnedest mix of a man I'll ever know. You know from the TV who and what he was, far as his business was concerned. According to them, he was the biggest crook in New England, maybe the country. Maybe . . . I sort of think of him like some kind of medieval baron or prince. He sure ran his turf his way. The iron fist never far. No one crossed him. Far as I could see, tough but fair. Got along O.K. with his neighbors in Nahant. Friendly, but never close."

After Flaherty took another sip, he went on. "He must have been a genius. No matter what you read or heard people thought he was, or thought he did, just remember, the Feds never nailed him— and boy, did they try."

"Small wonder," Ann said, "with people like you around him, Michael, how could they get at him? But also remember, Michael, he left you out there on your own, that you got lucky."

"Annie, that's not completely right, I wasn't all alone. You were there for me, and he was, in his way. Barerra didn't walk away on me. Sure, after I got nailed in Gloucester. After that, I couldn't talk with him direct—no way—but I heard from him. He helped. Anyway, you asked about him. Take his funeral today. That didn't just happen. I'll bet he planned every last detail, years ago. No one around him with that kind of smarts. He had class, a style all his own. That was him, that Latin Mass, he was there. You know, the rafters of that old church just rattled with that 'Gloria.' And he sure had the power; every top crook in the country was there, all under one roof, all standing, singing their fat guts out in a Catholic church. Can you believe it? It wasn't because they loved him. The limousines must have stretched two miles down the causeway, down beyond Little Nahant, probably as many Feds with cameras as friends at the funeral. That would have amused him. You know the little cemetery as you come up on Nahant? Tonight, it's a mountain of flowers in the snow. Yup, they all came to say good-bye to Giovanni Barerra, farewell to a prince."

Flaherty stopped for more bourbon. "Annie, I really don't know what kind of man he was. He could be ruthless, I saw some of that. The night I told him I was getting out, I never thought I'd get out of his house. And he could con a bird out of a tree. He put the smuggling thing in front of me, and I bit. Sure I made a pot full of money." Flaherty's voice dropped away. "And lost my Mick. Barerra loved Mick, too, but he was a strange man. When I said it was our shit that nailed his great-grandson, Barerra sort of said, it would have happened anyway, that it was part of the business. And this same man grew rare orchids. Sometime, I'll take you over to his place, see it for yourself. It might tell you something. You'll find it hard to believe—a perfectly appointed seventeenth-century Italian palazzo perched on a granite cliff. Every piece of furniture an Italian antique. Best we do it after Ginny moves over to Wenham. She's moving in with Rosalie."

"That reminds me, Michael," Ann interjected, "a thought I had watching the television today. You know, they carried some of it live." There was an appraising look in Ann's brown eyes. "It seemed strange to watch Rosalie on your arm. Oh, I understood. She is your wife and he was her grandfather, but then, it occurred to me, Barerra was why you never did anything about your marriage. Am I close?"

"Yes," Michael allowed. "But now, I'm going for a divorce. I was going to talk to Barerra about that—never got to it. He had a big thing about family. He would not have taken the divorce of his only granddaughter lightly, not with our sons the last of his blood, no way."

And then an edge of irony came into Flaherty's voice. "Hey, Annie, I'm not kidding myself. I know some, no, most of the bucks behind Barerra had blood on 'em, one way or another. Can you imagine booze, broads, numbers, all controlled by a genius who could reel off Dante or Homer . . . I'll never know what kind of man he was."

"And you loved him."

"The hell I loved him. Maybe, you know, respected him, maybe. He scared the piss out of me sometimes. He had the goddamnedest eyes, made me feel I'd dealt with the devil. No, I guess I hated the son of a bitch. If it weren't for him, Mick would be here."

"What do you think he meant by this card?" Ann again picked up Barerra's card. "This 'Learn to use it well.' He didn't think this would be useful on *Shillelagh,* did he?"

"No, I doubt that." Michael laughed. "I'll have to think about it. I don't know. Maybe it was for my marine collection, something to mount on the wall. Considering the way I left him—as I said to you the other night, when I told him I was getting out, he was pissed, some pissed. I wasn't sure which way he'd go. Then, when you think who brought it here, the consigleri himself, maybe Barerra didn't have time to give any orders, change anything after I left him, I don't know. But I do know I wasn't completely kidding when I said it could have been a bomb. He could have gone that way, too, you know Annie. Far as I'm concerned, Giovanni Barerra is dead. I saw him buried today. And that's that.

"Oh, Michael." Ann looked vulnerable as she spoke. "I'm not so sure. I look at this card, and something tells me that man is in this room. I don't think he ever wasted a word, Michael. I don't think you are free of Giovanni Barerra."

"To hell with him. I've had enough of Barerra for one day, for one lifetime!" Flaherty shouted angrily, but then, he went over to Ann and held her. "I'm sorry. Let's talk about something else. Now, what did that poet pal of yours say, 'To begin to live the rest of my life.' I want to get at that. So let's do something. Let's go out for dinner—Jacob Marley's, the Barnacle, have a few pops, maybe more than a few, grab a lobster, some swordfish—you name it."

"Fine by me, Michael," Ann agreed. "I'd like to go home for a quick change, freshen up. Be about a half hour. That O.K. with you?"

"You got a date," Flaherty agreed, then he helped Ann into her coat, escorted her to the door, and gave her a big hug. He turned back to the astrolabe, took it over to his desk, and examined it closely under a bright reading lamp. With Flaherty's eye for minute technical detail, he soon saw the center pintle of the recording arm could be twisted in a certain way and thereafter removed. Once he had backed out the pintle, the arm came free, and it took Flaherty but moments to disassemble the instrument totally. He saw the main body was made of two thin plates of silver, a fabrication in no way apparent to the casual eye. Michael Flaherty parted these two plates, and between them found a small parchment with writing and a waxen thumbprint. Flaherty noted the date of the document, the day after his capture on the *Katherine M. Flaherty*. The parchment read;

Dear Michael,

All that is mine is now yours, as you will. You are free to take what you want, if you want, as you want, all, or selectively—that choice is yours. Treat our people well and they will treat you well. Take your time to decide.

Consult with the bearer. He can be trusted. Tell him of your decision. He will see that my wishes and yours are carried out. If you decide to remain doing only what you have been doing, that is acceptable. Just return this letter to the bearer.

See to my greatgrandsons—see that they are reared as educated men of culture. The bearer will tell you of provisions I have made for them.

Being of sound mind and given of my free will,

s/s Giovanni Barerra

"Holy be Jesus H. Christ," Flaherty exclaimed, realizing the full import of the astrolabe. "Annie was right. He was here . . . And he trusted me, even after I got grabbed. The whole kit and caboodle can be mine. Christ."

The Barnacle Restaurant, Marblehead, Massachusetts

They walked the waterfront through a windless winter night, a star-strewn night, the scrunch of their boots loud on the crusty snow. Michael and Ann had decided to walk to their dinner, down to the Barnacle, a seaside restaurant at the east end of the Old Town. They walked on in silence, each with their own thoughts. Michael was aware of all things about him, the diamonds of the night sky, the silver clouds of his breath in the streetlight's glow, the small warmth of Ann's gloved hand in his mitten. For the first time in many a night, Michael Flaherty breathed deep of the salt air, felt clean, at peace with himself, and alive.

In some ways, Michael deluded himself as to his cleanliness and peace. He was far from clear of the courts. Monroe Lee and the

Baxter, Blair people had said as much, warning him there was a good chance Judge Weinstein's rulings would be reversed on appeal, that in any event, an Internal Revenue audit would most certainly follow close on the criminal proceedings—that win or lose, the U.S. government was a poor loser, with not a scintilla of sportsmanship, that when the Internal Revenue Service was told to lean, they seldom lost. That didn't worry Michael. Years before, Barerra's accountants set up Flaherty's financial affairs so that most of his prosperity could be defended against Internal Revenue Service audit as either cash from fish auctions, or loans by offshore banks on his trawlers, his container-trading venture, or his fish plant. The loans were made by banks in nations where the United States had no reciprocity arrangements for the exchange of financial information. With this ruse long in place, should he wish, Flaherty could mount a very stout defense against an I.R.S. audit. But now, a far larger question than money was on Michael Flaherty's mind.

With Ann by his side, Judge Weinstein's decision in effect, and Barerra's will in his safe, Flaherty's mind might well have been soaring for the stars. It wasn't. Flaherty's feelings were at dead low ebb. The irony of how his karma had evolved had not passed by him. On this night that should have been a jubilation, his very being was a pit of leaden slag. He had everything, he had nothing, his Mick was dead, the ultimate Promethean punishment.

As Flaherty looked up at the stars, the irony of it all fell upon him. Were he to take command of the Barerra organization, he would have in hand all that money and power could buy. That had once mattered more than anything to Michael Flaherty. No more. What mattered was what to do next, and for that question, he had no immediate answer.

As the pair walked down off the slight rise before the restaurant, Michael's eye was drawn to the constellation Orion now lifting clear of the ink-black sea. No matter where his spirits, Flaherty's eyes were ever those of a seaman, and this constellation held bright navigational stars, old friends from Flaherty's boyhood, when the sextant was the instrument that brought sailors home.

Michael, as a boy, had been taught the two ancient legends of Orion, the first tale, that of the mighty hunter accidentally slain by his beautiful lover, Diana, goddess of the hunt; the second, that of the arrogant hunter who could best any animal that lived, until he mistakenly stepped on the lowly scorpion. Be it fate or hubris, either legend fit Flaherty's views of the twists that were his life, and as he entered the restaurant, he wondered where now his stars led.

Michael and Ann were pleased to find the patrons few on this cold night. They took a table to themselves by the window, and for a time quietly watched the moon silver dance on the sea. Later, when a waitress produced their drinks, Ann lifted her glass of wine and looked across it, deep into Michael. "Here's to your freedom, Michael," she toasted.

"'Tain't over yet, but I'll drink to it anyway, Annie," he said, clinking her glass with his.

"Oh, I think it is, Michael."

"Then why did Weinstein give 'em that goddamn continuance, that I'll never understand."

"Face, Michael, face. He found for you twice—the search warrant and the 'posse comitatus' issues. He had to give Wetmore time. There are politics, even in the courts. And your little peccadillo wasn't unnoticed in the media. I think Weinstein played it pretty well."

"Say, you really were listening."

"Yes, yes, of course I was. Your freedom was at stake." Ann reached over and took Michael's hand. "And as I was saying, I think the continuance was a matter of face-saving. After all, Judge Weinstein has to work with the U.S. attorney's office over the years. You'll be all right, I think."

"I sure hope so. You know, life is a lot of luck."

"How so?"

"Well, take what happened, you know, the *Kathleen M.* and the *Katherine M.* business. The obvious had slipped by the best legal brains in Boston—yet my old lady spotted it in a second."

"Not necessarily luck, Michael. Don't underestimate your mother, she's a pretty sharp old gal, from what I've seen."

"Damn right. I haven't, and tough as a boot, too." He grinned.

"Hardly a nice way to describe your mother, Michael."

"Hell, I meant it O.K., that she's all right."

"And that Mr. Lee of yours, don't underestimate him. He's very good."

"Oh, I don't. Not at all. He's smart. He knows what he's good at—trial work. Smart enough to know his limitations, he went out and got help where he needed it, he made some kind of a research deal with this big firm, Baxter, Blair and Burnham. Anyway, they've got an army of whiz kids that just won't quit. They wrote briefs on briefs. They buried the U.S. attorney, and boy, did old Weinstein eat it up. I hate to think what that bill's going to be."

"Not to worry, Michael. That's the nice part of having money. Your freedom is far more important. It will all be over soon, and we'll all be constitutional experts." She laughed.

"I sure hope you're right, Annie."

"Oh, I am," she said confidently, then suddenly, deliberately, she changed conversational course. "Michael, I think we need a change of scene. Let's get out of town. Do you ski?"

"Yes, some. I like to sail better. I was thinking, the way it went in the court, they have to give me *Shillelagh* back, I could send her south. A winter passage can be tough, but if we hustled, we could still make the Southern Ocean Racing Circuit."

The waitress came along, pad and pencil poised. The pair quickly settled on bowls of fish chowder, shrimp scampi, and a carafe of chablis. That settled, Ann picked up. "I think that's a marvelous idea, Michael. Am I included?"

"Yes, of course," Flaherty reached across and patted her hand. "But one thing, none of your goddamn bets."

"Not always, but agreed, no bets. Now, if we're going to do it, let's do it right. I'd like to make a contribution."

"What's that?"

"I'll charter a motor yacht, something big and comfortable, with stabilizers for offshore passages, two or three large staterooms, one big suite for us."

"What the hell do we need all that for?"

"For between races, Michael—a tender—so you and I can stay in bed while she's underway, something of a decent size to live on."

"What's wrong with *Shillelagh*?" Flaherty growled.

"I'm not about to live in a men's gym, not any more than I have to while racing. Why, you've barely got curtains around the head, Michael. No thank you."

"Why not hotels on the beach between races? Save a few bucks?"

"Michael, let's do it with style. Besides, it's my contribution to the campaign."

"You understand, a rig like you're talking—that's going to run twelve thou or more a week?"

"It doesn't matter that much, Michael. It's my contribution, my gift, my way."

The waitress came by with their chowder as Ann bubbled on. "Now, what about a crew?"

"We'll use the same gang we had on last summer. They got god-damn good by August." Flaherty beamed, his thoughts running back to happier times.

"You said they would, when we first met, I recall." Ann eyed him carefully. "So, we'll only need a cook."

"How about you? Naw, maybe I'll send Jamie some plane tickets. She's working for that Admiral Osborne now."

"I don't think that's such a good idea," Ann said icily.

"Why not? That gal did her job, damn well. I respect her for it. I told you she was there the day Mick died?"

"Yes, you did, Michael, and that was very nice of her. Now, for a cook for the races, count me out. You wouldn't catch me dead in that galley at sea, Michael. As for Jamie, she did turn you in. Remember?"

"Hell, she was only doing her job. I don't hold that against her. She's all right."

"Michael, you're incurable, an incurable romantic. I'll hire a professional cook."

"O.K." Flaherty shrugged resignedly, sniffing the first stirrings of a storm, not wanting to argue about it—not tonight. "But I pay for him, not you. A deal?"

"Agreed and thank you." Ann smiled. "Now, when are those races over?"

"Probably the end of February. The Governor's Cup off Nassau."

"Good. Then we'll take the motor boat down into the Caribbean for March. I've always wanted to do the Grenadines."

"Hey, Annie, I can't play all winter. I've got a business to run. Got to make a legit buck now."

"Not to worry, you'll be my guest. You can fly up to Gloucester between races, or while the boat's on passage."

"Yes, I suppose I could," Flaherty said noncommittally. His own words had sent his mind down a different path. There were so many things to think about. *What business am I going to run? Back to Flaherty Fisheries? Take over the Barerra organization? No way, not after Mick. What about the groundwork for a tax audit? I've had my warning, and think I have a defensible paper stream in place, untraceable offshore loans. Better check that out pronto. Should I tell her about the Barerra will? Best not.* And then he thought further, *Hey wake up, buddy, your trial isn't really over and here you are, dreaming. Annie's got you cruising the Grenadines on a motor boat. Now, a little racing on Shillelagh, that could be different. Come on, Mike, stop kidding yourself, stop putting it off. What are you going to do?*

Across the table, Ann prattled along happily as Flaherty's attention returned. "And after that, I think we should go over and ski. Do Gstaad for two weeks. I have a friend with this marvelous little chalet. She has been after me for years to use it. I'm sure you'll love Gstaad."

"Hey, Annie, you and your friends! What have you been smoking? I've got things to do, I'll probably be broke, and I'm still on the hook with the court."

"As I said, not to worry, Michael. The court's behind you. Let's look ahead. I can take care of most things. I have all the money we could ever need. I want you to take time and think things through. I know what this has done to you. You have got to get away, decide things for yourself."

"You're right about time." He laughed. "But what's this we stuff, we use my money, long as I have some, and by the way, you're also a piece of work, one of a kind—and I love you."

The pair laughed and touched and happily went on with their dinner.

The MacKay Mansion, Marblehead Neck, Massachusetts

Michael Flaherty's brain had several extraordinary capabilities. One was an uncannily accurate diurnal clock that now told him, in total darkness, it was time to get up and get going if he wanted to get in a jog, have breakfast, and still be in his office by 8:30. Another was an ability to awaken fully on the instant, and in so doing this morning, he found his happiness of the prior night had carried over. Eager to get on with his day, put their plans in motion, Flaherty gently eased himself from the bed where Ann still slept. In his endeavor not to disturb her he was unsuccessful. "What time is it?" she asked sleepily.

Glancing at the red numbers of the alarm clock on the night table, Michael said softly. "Just after six-thirty. I'm going out for a run. Want to come?"

"Un-unh, too cold, you go. I'm playing badminton later."

"How about some breakfast—the Driftwood?"

"Maybe. Ask me when you get back."

Flaherty went off to the dressing room, quietly closed the door, and turned on a light. In a few moments, he had on his sweat-streaked woolies under running tights and a thick warm-up suit. He went over to the dresser to change the tape in his Walkman, selecting a tape of Men at Work. That's me, he chuckled to himself as he turned off the light, picked up his gear, and quietly went out into the bitter cold blackness to start.

The man had his habits. One was to start his jog as slowly as he could, letting his wind and muscle warm to their task, easily, steadily raising the pace, nothing forced, knowing he must cross the plateau of pain before he could finally settle into the float of a full-stride run. Later, when his chest had shrunk, his breath grown small, and his muscles screamed, then, Flaherty would seek the support of his music.

The first faint gray streaked the eastern sky as the runner turned off the Neck toward the Old Town. Engrossed in his running, Flaherty took no note of a sedan, parked in the shadows of a side street, nor did he see, as he started up the main street, that moments later, so did the sedan.

The runner had his routine, a convoluted loop through the alleys, byways, backwaters, boatyards, and cemeteries of the former fishing village. In not many minutes, his tailers learned, what with one-way streets and the predawn darkness, they had no chance of stalking Flaherty through old Marblehead. Soon lost, they elected a slow patrol of the major streets.

Unaware of the tail, Flaherty ran on through the gathering gray with a careful eye for the treacherous ice. He took the waterfront at full stride and arrived on the parapet of Fort Sewall as the rim of an orange sun rose from a carpet of sea-steam into a cloudless sky. The beauty of this dawn stopped Flaherty dead in his tracks— the wonderous birth of a day—a new day in a cold winter, a day of promise, a day to get things done.

When he saw the sun safely afloat in the china-blue sky, a happy Michael Flaherty went on his way, back along the waterfront, where he watched a lonely lobsterman, huddled against the biting wind, sculling a dinghy out to his boat. Flaherty gave the man a friendly wave and a comradely grin. He had gone fishing like that into far worse dawns.

The fisherman reminded Flaherty of his music, and as he ran through the boatyard up toward Old Burial Hill, he flicked on his headset. Anticipating the rollicking rhythms of the Aussies at their work, Flaherty was startled by a swelling crescendo of violins. *What in hell is this?* he asked himself, then realized he must have picked up Ann's Walkman in the darkness of the dressing room. Classical music being not for his ear, Flaherty was about to switch to radio when the soaring song of the strings caught his fancy. Unbeknownst to Flaherty, he listened to Vivaldi's "The Four Seasons" and jogged along as the violins sang the song of "Spring," a song that seemed to match the joy within him.

Flaherty had a fixed turning point to his run, the crest of Old Burial Hill, a 1638 cemetery on one of the higher hills in the town. He liked this hill for several reasons; the view was magnificent, the steepness challenged his cardiovascular capacity, and six hundred fisherman-veterans of the War for Independence lay there beneath slate headstones. The idea of fishermen rescuing the great George Washington always amused Mike Flaherty, so much so that on warmer days, he often slowed to read the epitaphs. But this day was bitter cold and so he happily turned back, down the path, halfway home to a hot shower and a stout breakfast, a very welcome thought.

The sedan was parked at the foot of the path, its engine running. As Flaherty ran toward the car, the right front window went down, the nose of an Uzi automatic came out. The muzzle of the weapon must have caught the sun, for the glint triggered a Nam-honed reflex in Flaherty's brain. He instantly dove for a sheltering gravestone, an instant too slow. The first burst shattered his left forearm before he heard the soft burp of the automatic. Huddled behind the headstone, bleeding in the snow, his brain raced on, while in his unhearing ears, the Vivaldi piece pounded on into the stomping rhythms of "Winter."

The bastard's got a silencer, he realized, but who? Why? What does that matter, you dumb jerk? This guy's a pro with a contract. So that means Solito, who else? He's read Barerra's will, he knows it's all his, if he plants you. A man of trust—balls. Flaherty laughed sardonically. *So, Mr. B., you can't run your troops from a bronze box. Your greedy lawyer wouldn't even wait to hear what I was going to do.*

O.K. if that's the way you want it, Mr. Consigleri, that's the way you'll get it . . . Bullshit, Mike, cut the heroics, you're up here on a hill, down sun of a gunner, without a weapon. What about that?

Flaherty heard the car door quietly open, then close. *Shit! The son of a bitch is coming up after me. Got to get some space somehow. But how?* Flaherty looked around, picking out a pattern of the larger headstones and taller memorials. As soon as he spotted his next landing place, Flaherty unplugged the headset with his serviceable right hand, took off the Walkman, then lobbed it high down the path like a grenade. On the instant, he was off on a ten yard dash for a tall memorial. He won, beating the bullets by a microsecond as they pitted the stone beside him.

What now? Flaherty looked down at his feet, picked up some snow, and clumsily patted together a snowball. He tried the lob and run game again and won. The third time, halfway up the hill, Mike Flaherty's luck ran out. A burst of the automatic stitched his body, hammering him into the snow.

As the gunman closed for the coup de grace, a spry old lady came along, briskly walking her dogs down a side street near the foot of the path. At the same time, a Marblehead Police cruiser came up the main street and stopped by the dog walker.

Up on the flank of Old Burial Hill, the gunman had closed within ten yards of the sprawled Flaherty when he heard two quick beeps of his sedan's horn. He looked over his shoulder, saw the police car, and hastily put his automatic inside his coat. The gunman walked down out of the cemetery, got in the sedan, and drove off.

Neither the dogwalker nor the policeman noticed the gunman or his departing sedan. They were busily chatting away as they had for twenty-odd years. Her name was Penelope Peach, a spinster schoolteacher, now retired from the grammar school. She had taught

309

the officer English, thirty years back. They met almost every morning, at about the same place, and every morning, the policeman laughingly reminded Miss Penny about the town's leash laws. Meanwhile, her two yipping balls of fur were foraging about when one of them spotted Flaherty, a carmine blot on the snowy hill, and took off at full yap.

The policeman noticed the dog. "What's he after, Miss Penny?" he asked. And so, within thirty minutes, Michael Flaherty was in the adjacent town, in the emergency room of Salem Hospital. Within the hour, he was in the operating room and remained there most of the morning. The last burst of the automatic had cut a swath across Flaherty from his right breast to his left pelvis, smashing his rib cage, puncturing his right lung, stitching his stomach, and chipping his pelvis. Had the cold and the shock not slowed the bleeding, and medical aid been so prompt, Michael Flaherty would most certainly have bled to death in little time. As it was, with the luckiest timing and the best medical attention, he hovered on the brink of death, a badly shattered man.

Meanwhile, back out on Marblehead Neck, in the MacKay mansion, when Ann's alarm went off at eight, she bestirred herself, then wondered where Michael was. She drew on a robe and went down to the main floor, where the maid was already at her chores. "Kate, has Mr. Flaherty come by?" Ann asked.

"No ma'am, I haven't seen him," the maid said.

Slightly bothered, Ann returned upstairs, thinking Michael would never have left, not without saying good-bye. She then saw his clothes were still in the dressing room. *Lord, he's been hit by a car or he's slipped on the ice.* Ann rushed into her clothes then took off in her wagon. From several conversations, she had a good idea of Michael's running route. In not many minutes, when she had driven the route with no sign of Michael, she went to his condominium. He was not there. And with that, Ann became totally alarmed, went to the police station, and learned of an unidentified man found shot on Burial Hill.

Flaherty lay unconscious on Salem Hospital's critical list for three days. Outside, in the hospital parking lot, the several television channels had set up a death watch, their camera people waiting in their vans for the next bulletin, their roof antennae focused on the Boston relay towers. Having won the Bermuda Race, set a record for the

nation's biggest drug bust, with blood ties to the Barerra organization, and now gunned down in sedate Marblehead, Michael Flaherty
was a celebrity. His passing would be news.

Inside the hospital, by the side of Flaherty's bed, Ann waited and
quietly wept. She had been thoroughly briefed by the attending
surgeon, with the president of the hospital and the chief of staff in
hovering attendance. The man held little hope. As the MacKays had
been very generous to the hospital for many years, there were no
objections when the appropriate chiefs of service at Massachusetts
General and professor-specialists at Harvard Medical were whisked
in Raimond-rented limousines to Salem for consultation. The consensus of these opinions was that Flaherty had at best an even chance
of surviving the shooting. And so, Ann wept.

On the third afternoon, Flaherty regained consciousness. Ann was
there with him when he came around. When at last his eyes focused,
he had a weak smile for her, while she did her brave best to hold
back her tears. She leaned over and kissed him gently on the forehead, avoiding the oxygen mask and tracheal tubes in his throat.

"Good, you're here," he gasped.

"I'm here, Michael," she said with the brightest smile she could
muster, "and you be quiet."

He shook his head, then spoke, his speech badly belabored, "Love
you."

"And I love you, Michael," she replied, touching his hand. "Now,
you're to take it easy."

"Can't . . . things to do."

"Michael, I want you to rest," she chided him softly. "You need
all your strength."

"Envelope?" he persisted.

"I have it in a very safe place, and with a cover letter, in case
anything ever happened to me. So not to worry. Michael, please
take it easy."

"Wetmore here, quiet, quick," he insisted.

"I will, Michael. I will. I'll call his office right now." Ann gave
him a kiss, and was about to leave the room, when Flaherty found
further reserves.

His grin was weak, nonetheless a grin, as he spoke very slowly.
"Teach bastards lesson, don't fuck with a Flaherty."